...es
bestselling author Nora Roberts

"Characters that touch the heart, stories that intrigue, romance that sizzles—Nora Roberts has mastered it all."
—*Rendezvous*

"Roberts' bestselling novels are some of the best in the romance genre. They are thoughtfully plotted, well-written stories featuring fascinating characters."
—*USA TODAY*

"A superb author...Ms. Roberts is an enormously gifted writer whose incredible range and intensity guarantee the very best of reading."
—*Rave Reviews*

Praise for *USA TODAY* bestselling author Sarah Morgan

"Morgan's brilliant talent never ceases to amaze."
—*RT Book Reviews*

"This touching tale will draw tears of sorrow and joy, remaining a reader favorite for years to come."
—*Publishers Weekly* on *Sleigh Bells in the Snow*, starred review

NORA ROBERTS

#1 *New York Times* bestselling author Nora Roberts is "a storyteller of immeasurable diversity and talent," according to *Publishers Weekly*. She has published over 160 novels, her work has been optioned and made into films, and her books have been translated into over twenty-five different languages and published all over the world. In addition to her amazing success in mainstream, Nora has a large and loyal category-romance audience, which took her to their hearts in 1981 with her very first book, *Irish Thoroughbred,* a Silhouette Romance novel. The last decade has seen more than 100 of Nora's books become *New York Times* bestsellers—many of them reaching #1. Nora is truly a publishing phenomenon.

SARAH MORGAN

USA TODAY bestselling author Sarah Morgan writes hot, happy contemporary romance. Her trademark humor and sensuality have gained her fans across the globe and two RITA® Awards from the Romance Writers of America. Sarah lives near London with her family. Visit her at sarahmorgan.com.

NORA ROBERTS

COURTING CATHERINE

Silhouette® BESTSELLING AUTHOR COLLECTION

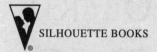

SILHOUETTE BOOKS

ISBN-13: 978-0-373-01017-2

Courting Catherine
Copyright © 2015 by Harlequin Books S.A.

The publisher acknowledges the copyright holders
of the individual works as follows:

Courting Catherine
Copyright © 1991 by Nora Roberts

French Kiss
Copyright © 2015 by Sarah Morgan

Originally published as Doukakis's Apprentice

First North American Publication 2011

Copyright © 2011 by Sarah Morgan

Recycling programs
for this product may
not exist in your area.

This edition published by arrangement with Harlequin Books S.A.

For questions and comments about the quality of this book,
please contact us at CustomerService@Harlequin.com.

® and TM are trademarks of Harlequin Enterprises Limited or its corporate affiliates. Trademarks indicated with ® are registered in the United States Patent and Trademark Office, the Canadian Intellectual Property Office and in other countries.

Visit Silhouette Books at www.Harlequin.com

Printed in U.S.A.

CONTENTS

COURTING CATHERINE

Nora Roberts

To Maxine
For being my friend as well as my sister

Prologue

Bar Harbor, Maine
June 12, 1912—

*I saw him on the cliffs overlooking Frenchman Bay.
He was tall and dark and young. Even from a distance,
as I walked with little Ethan's hand in mine, I could see
the defiant set of his shoulders. He held the brush as
though it were a saber, his palette like a shield. Indeed
it seemed to me that he was dueling with his canvas
rather than painting on it. So deep was his concentration, so fast and fierce the flicks of his wrist, one
would have thought his life depended on what he created there.*

Perhaps it did.

*I thought it odd, even amusing. My image of artists
had always been one of gentle souls who see things*

we mortals cannot, and suffer in their quest to create them for us.

Yet I knew, before he turned and looked at me, that I would not see a gentle face.

It seemed that he was the product of an artist himself. A rough sculptor who had shorn away at an oak slab, carving out a high brow, dark hooded eyes, a long straight nose and full sensual mouth. Even the sweep of his hair might have been hewn from some ebony wood.

How he stared at me! Even now I can feel the heat rise to my face and the dampness spring to my palms. The wind was in his hair, sweet and moist from the sea, and ruffled the loose shirt he wore that was splattered and streaked from his paint. With the rocks and sky at his back, he looked very proud, very angry, as if he owned this jut of land—or the entire island—and I was the intruder.

He stood in silence for what seemed like forever, his eyes so intense, so fierce somehow that my tongue cleaved to the roof of my mouth. Then little Ethan began to babble and tug at my hand. The angry glare in his eyes softened. He smiled. I know a heart does not stop at such moments. And yet...

I found myself stammering, apologizing for the intrusion, lifting Ethan into my arms before my bright and curious little boy could rush forward toward the rocks.

He said, "Wait."

And taking up pad and pencil began to sketch as I stood immobile and trembling for reasons I cannot fathom. Ethan stilled and smiled, somehow as mesmerized by the man as I. I could feel the sun on my back and the wind on my face, could smell the water and the wild roses.

"Your hair should be loose," he said, and, putting the pencil aside, walked toward me. "I've painted sunsets that were less dramatic." He reached out and touched Ethan's bright red hair. "You share the color with your young brother."

"My son." Why was my voice so breathless? "He is my son. I'm Mrs. Fergus Calhoun," I said while his eyes seemed to devour my face.

"Ah, The Towers." He looked beyond me then to where the peaks and turrets of our summer home could be seen on the higher cliff above. "I've admired your house, Mrs. Calhoun."

Before I could reply, Ethan was reaching out, laughing, and the man scooped him up. I could only stare as he stood with his back to the wind, holding my child, jiggling him easily on his hip.

"A fine boy."

"And an energetic one. I thought to take him for a walk to give his nanny a bit of a rest. She has less trouble with my two other children combined than with young Ethan."

"You have other children?"

"Yes, a girl, a year older than Ethan, and a baby, not quite one. We only arrived for the season yesterday. Do you live on the island?"

"For now. Will you pose for me, Mrs. Calhoun?"

I blushed. But beneath the embarrassment was a deep and dreamy pleasure. Still, I knew the impropriety and Fergus's temper. So I refused, politely, I hoped. He did not persist, and I am ashamed to say that I felt a keen disappointment. When he gave Ethan back to me, his eyes were on mine—a deep slate gray that seemed to see more than my face. Perhaps more than anyone had seen before. He bid me good day, so I turned to walk with my child back to The Towers, my home and my duties.

I knew as surely as if I had turned to look that he watched me until I was hidden by the cliff. My heart thundered.

Chapter 1

Trenton St. James III was in a foul mood. He was the kind of man who expected doors to open when he knocked, phones to be answered when he dialed. What he did not expect, and hated to tolerate, was having his car break down on a narrow two-lane road ten miles from his destination. At least the car phone had allowed him to track down the closest mechanic. He hadn't been overly thrilled about riding into Bar Harbor in the cab of the tow truck while strident rock had bellowed from the speakers and his rescuer had sung along, off-key, in between bites of an enormous ham sandwich.

"Hank, you just call me Hank, ayah," the driver had

told him then took a long pull from a bottle of soda. "C.C.'ll fix you up all right and tight. Best damn mechanic in Maine, you ask anybody."

Trent decided, under the circumstances, he'd have to take just-call-me-Hank's word for it. To save time and trouble, he'd had the driver drop him off in the village with directions to the garage and a grimy business card Trent studied while holding it gingerly at the corners.

But as with any situation Trent found himself in, he decided to make it work for him. While his car was being dealt with, he made half a dozen calls to his office back in Boston—putting the fear of God into a flurry of secretaries, assistants and junior vice-presidents. It put him in a slightly better frame of mind.

He lunched on the terrace of a small restaurant, paying more attention to the paperwork he took from his briefcase than the excellent lobster salad or balmy spring breeze. He checked his watch often, drank too much coffee and, with impatient brown eyes, studied the traffic that streamed up and down the street.

Two of the waitresses on lunch shift discussed him at some length. It was early April, several weeks before the height of the season, so the restaurant wasn't exactly hopping with customers.

They agreed that this one was a beaut, from the top of his dark blond head to the tips of his highly polished Italian shoes. They agreed that he was a businessman, and an *important* one, because of the leather briefcase and spiffy gray suit and tie. Plus, he wore cuff links. Gold ones.

They decided, as they rolled flatware into napkins for the next shift, that he was young for it, no more than thirty. Outrageously handsome was their unanimous vote while they took turns refilling his coffee cup and getting closer looks. Nice clean features, they agreed, with a kind of polished air that would have been just a tad slick if it hadn't been for the eyes.

They were dark and broody and impatient, making the waitresses speculate as to whether he'd been stood up by a woman. Though they couldn't imagine any female in her right mind doing so.

Trent paid no more attention to them than he would have to anyone who performed a paid service. That disappointed them. The whopping tip he left made up for it nicely. It would have surprised him that the tip would have meant more to the waitresses if he had offered a smile with it.

He relocked his briefcase and prepared to take the brisk walk to the mechanic at the end of town. He wasn't a cold man and wouldn't have considered himself aloof. As a St. James he had grown up with servants who had quietly and efficiently gone about the business of making his life simpler. He paid well, even generously. If he didn't show any overt appreciation or personal interest, it was simply because it never occurred to him.

At the moment, his mind was on the deal he hoped to close by the end of the week. Hotels were his business, with the emphasis on luxury and resorts. The summer before, Trent's father had located a particular property while he and his fourth wife had been yachting in Frenchman Bay. While Trenton St. James II's instincts as to women were notoriously skewed, his business instincts were always on target.

He'd begun negotiations almost immediately for the buy of the enormous stone house overlooking French-

man Bay. His appetite had been whetted by the reluctance of the owners to sell what had to be a white
elephant as a private home. As expected, the senior
Trenton had been turning things his way, and the deal
was on the way to being set.

Then Trent had found the whole business dumped
into his lap as his father was once again tangled in a
complicated divorce.

Wife number four had lasted almost eighteen
months, Trent mused. Which was two months longer
than wife number three. Trent accepted, fatalistically,
that there was bound to be a number five around the
corner. The old man was as addicted to marriage as
he was to real estate.

Trent was determined to close the deal on The Towers before the ink had dried on this last divorce decree.
As soon as he got his car out of the garage, he would
drive up and take a firsthand look at the place.

Because of the time of year, many of the shops were
closed as he walked through town, but he could see the
possibilities. He knew that during the season the streets
of Bar Harbor were crammed with tourists with credit
cards and travelers' checks at the ready. And tourists
needed hotels. He had the statistics in his briefcase.
With solid planning, he figured The Towers would cull
a hefty percentage of that tourist trade within fifteen
months.

All he had to do was convince four sentimental
women and their aunt to take the money and run.

He checked his watch again as he turned the corner
toward the mechanic's. Trent had given him precisely
two hours to deal with whatever malfunction the BMW
had suffered. That, he was convinced, was enough.

Of course he could have taken the company plane up from Boston. It would have been more practical, and Trent was nothing if not a practical man. But he'd wanted to drive. Needed to, he admitted. He'd needed those few hours of quiet and solitude.

Business was booming, but his personal life was going to hell.

Who would have thought that Marla would suddenly shove an ultimatum down his throat? Marriage or nothing. It still baffled him. She had known since the beginning of their relationship that marriage had never been an option. He had no intention of taking a ride on the roller coaster his father seemed to thrive on.

Not that he wasn't—hadn't been—fond of her. She was lovely and well-bred, intelligent and successful in her field of fashion design. With Marla, there was never a hair out of place, and Trent appreciated that kind of meticulousness in a woman. Just as he had appreciated her practical attitude toward their relationship.

She had claimed not to want marriage or children or pledges of undying love. Trent considered it a personal betrayal that she suddenly changed her tune and demanded it all.

He hadn't been able to give it to her.

They had parted, stiff as strangers, only two weeks before. She was already engaged to a golf pro.

It stung. But even as it stung, it convinced him he had been right all along. Women were unstable, fickle creatures, and marriage was a bloodless kind of suicide.

She hadn't even loved him. Thank God. She had simply wanted "commitment and stability," as she had put it. Trent felt, smugly, that she would soon find out marriage was the last place to find either.

Because he knew it was unproductive to dwell on mistakes, he allowed thoughts of Marla to pass out of his mind. He would take a vacation from females, he decided.

Trent paused outside the white cinder-block building with its scatter of cars in the lot. The sign over the open garage doors read C.C.'s Automovation. Just beneath the title, which Trent found ostentatious, was an offer of twenty-four-hour towing, complete auto repairs and refinishing—foreign and domestic—and free estimates.

Through the doors, he could hear rock music. Trent let out a sigh as he went in.

The hood was up on his BMW, and a pair of dirty boots peeked out from beneath the car. The mechanic was tapping the toes of the boots together in time to the din of music. Frowning, Trent glanced around the garage area. It smelled of grease and honeysuckle—a ridiculous combination. The place itself was a disorganized and grimy mess of tools and auto parts, something that looked as though it might have been a fender, and a coffee maker that was boiling whatever was inside it down to black sludge.

There was a sign on the wall that stated No Checks Cashed, Not Even For You.

Several others listed services provided by the shop and their rates. Trent supposed they were reasonable, but he had no yardstick. There were two vending machines against a wall, one offering soft drinks, the other junk food. A coffee can held change that customers were free to contribute to or take from. An interesting concept, Trent thought.

"Excuse me," he said. The boots kept right on tapping. "Excuse me," he repeated, louder. The music upped its tempo and so did the boots. Trent nudged one with his shoe.

"What?" The answer from under the car was muffled and annoyed.

"I'd like to ask you about my car."

"Get in line." There was the clatter of a tool and a muttered curse.

Trent's eyebrows lifted then drew together in a manner that made his subordinates quake. "Apparently I'm the first in line already."

"Right now you're behind this idiot's oil pan. Save me from rich yuppies who buy a car like this then don't bother to find out the difference between a carburetor and a tire iron. Hold on a minute, buddy, or talk to Hank. He's around somewhere."

Trent was still several sentences back at "idiot." "Where's the proprietor?"

"Busy. Hank!" The mechanic's voice lifted to a roar. "Damn it. Hank! Where the devil did he take off to?"

"I couldn't say." Trent marched over to the radio and flicked off the music. "Would it be too much to ask you to come out from under there and tell me the status of my car?"

"Yeah." From the vantage point under the BMW, C.C. studied the Italian loafers and took an immediate dislike to them. "I got my hands full at the moment. You can come down here and lend one of yours if you're in such a hurry, or drive over to McDermit's in Northeast Harbor."

"I can hardly drive when you're under my car."
Though the idea held a certain appeal.

"This yours?" C.C. sniffed and tightened bolts. The
guy had a fancy Boston accent to go with the fancy
shoes. "When's the last time you had this thing tuned?
Changed the points and plugs, the oil?"

"I don't—"

"I'm sure you don't." There was a clipped satisfaction in the husky voice that had Trent's jaw tightening.
"You know, you don't just buy a car, but a responsibility. A lot of people don't pull down an annual salary as
rich as the sticker price on a machine like this. With
reasonable care and maintenance, this baby would run
for your grandchildren. Cars aren't disposable com-
modities, you know. People make them that way because they're too lazy or too stupid to take care of the
basics. You needed a lube job six months ago."

Trent's fingers drummed on the side of his briefcase.
"Young man, you're being paid to service my car, not
to lecture me on my responsibilities to it." In a habit as
ingrained as breathing, he checked his watch. "Now,
I'd like to know when my car will be ready, as I have
a number of appointments."

"Lecture's free." C.C. gave a push and sent the
creeper scooting out from under the car. "And I'm not
your young man."

That much was quite obvious. Though the face was
grimy and the dark hair cropped boyishly short, the
body clad in greasy coveralls was decidely feminine.
Every curvy inch of it. Trent wasn't often thrown for a
loss, but now he simply stood, staring as C.C. rose from
the creeper and faced him, tapping a wrench against
her palm.

Looking beyond the smears of black on her face, Trent could see she had very white skin in contrast with her ebony hair. Beneath the fringe of bangs, her forest-green eyes were narrowed. Her full, unpainted lips were pursed in what, under different circumstances, would have been a very sexy pout. She was tall for a woman and built like a goddess. It was she, Trent realized, who smelled of motor oil and honeysuckle.

"Got a problem?" she asked him. C.C. was well aware that his gaze had drifted down from the neck of her coveralls to the cuffs and back again. She was used to it. But she didn't have to like it.

The voice had an entirely different effect when a man realized those dark, husky tones belonged to a woman. "You're the mechanic!"

"No, I'm the interior decorator."

Trent glanced around the garage with its oil-splattered floor and cluttered worktables. He couldn't resist. "You do very interesting work."

Letting the breath out between her teeth, she tossed the wrench onto a workbench. "Your oil and air filter needed to be changed. The timing was off and the carburetor needed some adjusting. You still need a lube job and your radiator should be flushed."

"Will it run?"

"Yeah, it'll run." C.C. took a rag out of her pocket and began to wipe her hands. She judged him as the kind of man who took better care of his ties than he did of his car. With a shrug, she stuck the rag back into her pocket. It was no concern of hers. "Come through to the office and we can settle up."

She led the way through the door at the rear of the garage, into a narrow hallway that angled into a glass-walled office. It was cramped with a cluttered desk, thick parts catalogues, a half-full gum-ball machine and two wide swivel chairs. C.C. sat and, in the uncanny way of people who heap papers on their desk, put her hand unerringly on her invoices.

"Cash or charge?" she asked him.

"Charge." Absently he pulled out his wallet. He wasn't sexist. Trent assured himself he was not. He had meticulously made certain that women were given the same pay and opportunity for promotion in his company as any male on his staff. It never occurred to him to be concerned whether employees were males or females, as long as they were efficient, loyal and dependable. But the longer he looked at the woman who sat busily filling out the invoice, the more he was certain she didn't fit his or anyone's image of an auto mechanic.

"How long have you worked here?" It surprised him to hear himself ask. Personal questions weren't his style.

"On and off since I was twelve." Those dark green eyes flicked up to his. "Don't worry. I know what I'm doing. Any work that's done in my shop is guaranteed."

"Your shop?"

"My shop."

She unearthed a calculator and began to figure the total with long, elegantly shaped fingers that were still grimy.

He was putting her back up. Maybe it was the shoes, she thought. Or the tie. There was something arrogant about a maroon tie. "That's the damage." C.C. turned the invoice around and started down the list point by point.

He wasn't paying any attention, which was totally out of character. This was a man who read every word of every paper that crossed his desk. But he was looking at her, frankly fascinated.

"Any questions?" She glanced up and found her gaze locked with his. She could almost hear the *click*.

"You're C.C.?"

"That's right." She was forced to clear her throat. Ridiculous, she told herself. He had ordinary eyes. Maybe a little darker, a bit more intense than she had noted at first, but still ordinary. There was no earthly reason why she couldn't look away from them. But she continued to stare. If she had been of a fanciful state of mind—which she assured herself she was not—she would have said the air thickened.

"You have grease on your cheek," he said quietly, and smiled at her.

The change was astonishing. He went from being an aloof, annoying man to a warm and approachable one. His mouth softened as it curved, the impatience in his eyes vanished. There was humor there now, an easy, inviting humor that was irresistible. C.C. found herself smiling back.

"It goes with the territory." Maybe she'd been a tad abrupt, she thought, and made an effort to correct it. "You're from Boston, right?"

"Yes. How did you know?"

Her lips remained curved as she shrugged. "Between the Massachusetts plates and your speech pattern, it wasn't hard. We get a lot of trade from Boston on the island. Are you here on vacation?"

"Business." Trent tried to remember the last time

he'd taken a vacation, and couldn't quite pin it down. Two years? he wondered. Three?

C.C. pulled a clipboard from under a pile of catalogues and scanned the next day's schedule. "If you're going to be around for a while, we could fit that lube job in tomorrow."

"I'll keep it in mind. You live on the island?"

"Yes. All my life." The chair creaked as she brought her long legs up to sit Indian-style. "Have you been to Bar Harbor before?"

"When I was a boy, I spent a couple of weekends here with my mother." Lifetimes ago, he thought. "Maybe you could recommend some restaurants or points of interest. I might squeeze in some free time."

"You shouldn't miss the park." After unearthing a sheet of memo paper, she began to write. "You really can't go wrong anywhere as far as seafood, and it's early enough in the season that you shouldn't have any problem with crowds and lines." She offered the paper, which he folded and slipped into his breast pocket.

"Thanks. If you're free tonight maybe you could help me sample some of the local seafood. We could discuss my carburetor."

Flustered and flattered, she reached out to accept the credit card he offered. She was on the point of agreeing when she read the name imprinted there. "Trenton St. James III."

"Trent," he said easily, and smiled again.

It figured, C.C. thought. Oh, it absolutely figured. Fancy car, fancy suit, fancy manners. She should have spotted it right off. She should have *smelled* it. Seething, she imprinted the card on the credit card form. "Sign here."

Trent took out a slim gold pen and signed while she rose and stalked over to a pegboard to retrieve his keys. He glanced over just as she tossed them to him. *At* him was more accurate. He managed to snag them before they hit his face. He jingled them lightly in his hand as she stood, hands on hips, face dark with fury.

"A simple no would have done the job."

"Men like you don't understand 'a simple no.'" C.C. turned to the glass wall, then whirled back. "If I'd known who you were, I'd have drilled holes in your muffler."

Slowly Trent slipped the keys into his pocket. His temper was renowned. It wasn't hot—that would have been easier to dodge. It was ice. As he stood it slid through him, frosting his eyes, tightening his mouth, coating his voice. "Would you like to explain?"

She strode toward him until they were toe-to-toe and eye-to-eye. "I'm Catherine Colleen Calhoun. And I want you to keep your greedy hands off my house."

Trent said nothing for a moment as he adjusted his thoughts. Catherine Calhoun, one of the four sisters who owned The Towers—and one who apparently had strong feelings regarding the sale. Since he was going to have to maneuver around all four of them, he might as well start here. And now.

"A pleasure, Miss Calhoun."

"Not mine." She reached down and ripped off his copy of the credit card receipt. "Get your butt back in your big, bad BMW and head back to Boston."

"A fascinating alliteration." Still watching her, Trent folded the paper and put it into his pocket. "You, however, are not the only party involved."

"You're not going to turn my house into one of your

glossy hotels for bored debutantes and phony Italian counts."

He nearly smiled at that. "You've stayed in one of the St. James hotels?"

"I don't have to, I know what they're like. Marble lobbies, glass elevators, twenty-foot chandeliers and fountains spurting everywhere."

"You have something against fountains?"

"I don't want one in my living room. Why don't you go foreclose on some widows and orphans and leave us alone?"

"Unfortunately, I don't have any foreclosures scheduled this week." He held up a hand when she snarled. "Miss Calhoun, I've come here at the request of your liaison. Whatever your personal feelings, there are three other owners of The Towers. I don't intend to leave until I've spoken with them."

"You can talk until your lungs collapse, but... What liaison?"

"Mrs. Cordelia Calhoun McPike."

C.C.'s color fluctuated a bit, but she didn't back down. "I don't believe you."

Without a word, Trent set his briefcase down onto the piles of paper on her desk and flipped the combination. From one of his neatly ordered files he withdrew a letter written on heavy ivory paper. C.C.'s heart dropped a little. She snatched it from him and read.

Dear Mr. St. James,
The Calhoun women have taken your offer to The Towers under consideration. As this is a complex situation, we feel it would be in everyone's best

interest to discuss the terms in person, rather than communicating by letter.

As their representative, I would like to invite you to The Towers—*(C.C. gave a strangled groan)*—for a few days. I believe this more personal approach will be of mutual benefit. I'm sure you'll agree that having a closer, more informal look at the property that interests you will be an advantage.

Please feel free to contact me, at The Towers, if you are amenable to the arrangement.
Very truly yours,
Cordelia Calhoun McPike

C.C. read it through twice, grinding her teeth. She would have crumpled the letter into a ball if Trent hadn't rescued it and slipped it back into its file.

"I take it you weren't apprised of the arrangement?"

"Apprised? Damn straight I wasn't apprised. That meddlesome old… Oh, Aunt Coco, I'm going to murder you."

"I assume Mrs. McPike and Aunt Coco are one and the same person."

"Some days it's hard to tell." She turned back. "But either way, both of them are dead."

"I'll sidestep the family violence, if you don't mind."

C.C. stuck her hands into her coverall pockets and glared at him. "If you still intend to stay at The Towers, you're going to be neck deep in it."

He nodded, accepting. "Then I'll take my chances."

Chapter 2

Aunt Coco was busily arranging hothouse roses in two of the Dresden vases that had yet to be sold. She hummed a current rock hit as she worked, occasionally adding a quick *bum-bum-bum* or *ta-te-da*. Like the other Calhoun women, she was tall, and liked to think that her figure, which had thickened only a little in the past decade, was regal.

She had dressed and groomed carefully for the occasion. Her short, fluffy hair was tinted red this week and pleased her enormously. Vanity was not a sin or character flaw in Coco's estimation, but a woman's sacred duty. Her face, which was holding up nicely, thank you, from the lift she'd had six years before, was scrupulously made up. Her best pearls swung at her ears and encircled her neck. Coco decided, with a quick glance in the hall mirror, that the black jumpsuit was both dramatic and sleek. The backless heels she wore slapped satisfactorily against the chestnut floor and had her teetering at six foot.

An imposing and, yes, regal figure, she bustled from room to room, checking and rechecking every detail. Her girls might be just a tiny bit upset with her for inviting company without mentioning it. But she could always claim absentmindedness. Which she did whenever it suited her.

Coco was the younger sister of Judson Calhoun, who had married Deliah Brady and sired four girls. Judson and Deliah, whom Coco had loved dearly, had been killed fifteen years before when their private plane had gone down over the Atlantic.

Since then, she had done her best to be father and mother and friend to her beautiful little orphans. A widow for nearly twenty years, Coco was a striking woman with a devious mind and a heart the consistency of marshmallow cream. She wanted, was determined to have, the best for her girls. Whether they liked it or not. With Trenton St. James's interest in The Towers, she saw an opportunity.

She didn't care a bit whether he bought the rambling fortress of a house. Though God knows how much longer they could hold on to it in any case, what with taxes and repairs and heating bills. As far as she was concerned, Trenton St. James III could take it or leave it. But she had a plan.

Whether he took or left it, he was going to fall head over bank account with one of the girls. She didn't know which one. She'd tried her crystal ball but hadn't come up with a name.

But she knew. She had known the moment the first

letter had come. The boy was going to sweep one of her darlings away into a life of love and luxury.

She'd be damned if any one of them would have one without the other.

With a sigh, she adjusted the taper in its Lalique holder. She had been able to give them love, but the luxury... If Judson and Deliah had lived, things would have been different. Surely Judson would have pulled himself out of the financial difficulty he'd been suffering. With his cleverness, and Deliah's drive, it would have been a very temporary thing.

But they hadn't lived, and money had become an increasing problem. How she hated to have to sell off the girls' inheritance piece by piece just to keep the sagging roof they all loved over their heads.

Trenton St. James III was going to change all that by falling madly in love with one of her darling babies.

Maybe it would be Suzanna, she thought, plumping the pillows on the parlor sofa. Poor little dear with her heart broken by the worthless cur she had married. Coco's lips tightened. To think he had fooled all of them. Even her! He had made her baby's life a misery, then had divorced her to marry that busty bimbo.

Coco let out a disgusted breath then cast a beady eye on the cracked plaster in the ceiling. She would have to make sure that Trenton would suit as a father to Suzanna's two children. And if he didn't...

There was Lilah, her own lovely free spirit. Her Lilah needed someone who would appreciate her lively mind and eccentric ways. Someone who would nurture and settle. Just a bit. Coco wouldn't tolerate anyone who would try to smother her darling girl's mystical bent.

Perhaps it would be Amanda. Coco twitched a drapery so that it covered a mouse hole. Hardheaded, practical-minded Amanda. Now that would be a match! The successful businessman and woman, wheeling and dealing. But he would have to have a softer side, one that recognized that Mandy needed to be cherished, as well as respected. Even if she didn't recognize it herself.

With a satisfied sigh, Coco moved from parlor to sitting room, from sitting room to library, library to study.

Then there was C.C. Shaking her head, Coco adjusted a picture so that it hid—almost—the watermarks on the aging silk wallpaper. That child had inherited the Calhoun stubbornness in spades. Imagine, a lovely girl wasting her life diddling with engines and fuel pumps. A grease monkey. Lord save us.

It was doubtful that a man like Trenton St. James III would be interested in a woman who spent all of her time under a car. Then again, C.C. was the baby of the family at twenty-three. Coco felt that she had more than enough time to find her little girl the perfect husband.

The stage was set, she decided. And soon, Mr. St. James would be walking into Act One.

The front door slammed. Coco winced, knowing that the vibration would have pictures jittering on the walls and crockery dancing on tables. She worked her way through the winding maze of rooms, tidying as she went.

"Aunt Coco!"

Coco's hand lifted automatically to pat her breast. She recognized C.C.'s voice, and the fury in it. Now what could have happened to fire the girl up? she wondered, and put on her best sympathetic smile.

"Just coming, dear. I didn't expect you home for hours yet. It's such a pleasant…" She trailed off as she saw her niece, stripped down to fighting weight in torn jeans and a T-shirt, traces of grease still on her face and the hands she had fisted and jammed at her hips. And the man behind her—the man Coco recognized as her prospective nephew-in-law. "Surprise," she finished, and pasted the smile back into place. "Why, Mr. St. James, how lovely." She stepped forward, hand extended. "I'm Mrs. McPike."

"How do you do?"

"It's so nice to meet you at last. I hope you had a pleasant trip."

"An…interesting one, all in all."

"Even better than pleasant." She patted his hand before releasing it, approving his level gaze and well-pitched voice. "Please, come in. I believe a person should begin as they mean to go on, so I want you to begin to make yourself at home right now. I'll just fix us all some tea."

"Aunt Coco," C.C. said in a low voice.

"Yes, dear, would you like something other than tea?"

"I want an explanation, and I want it now."

Coco's heart hammered a bit, but she gave her niece an open, slightly curious smile. "Explanation? For what?"

"I want to know what the hell he's doing here."

"Catherine, really!" Coco tsk-tsked. "Your manners, one of my very few failures. Come, Mr. St. James—or may I call you Trenton?—you must be a bit frazzled after the drive. You did say you were driving? Why don't we just go in and sit in the parlor?" She was easing him along as she spoke. "Marvelous weather for a drive, isn't it?"

"Hold it." C.C. moved quickly and planted herself in their path. "Hold it. Hold it. You're not tucking him up in the parlor with tea and small talk. I want to know why you invited him here."

"C.C." Coco gave a long-suffering sigh. "Business is more pleasant and more successful on all sides when it's conducted in person, and in a relaxed atmosphere. Wouldn't you agree, Trenton?"

"Yes." He was surprised that he had to hold back a grin. "Yes, I would."

"There."

"Not another step." C.C. flung out both hands. "We haven't agreed to sell."

"Of course not," Coco said patiently. "That's why Trenton is here. So we can discuss all the options and possibilities. You really should go up and wash before tea, C.C. You've engine grease or whatever on your face."

With the heel of her hand, C.C. rubbed at it. "Why wasn't I told he was coming?"

Coco blinked and tried to leave her eyes slightly unfocused. "Told? Why, of course you were told. I would hardly have invited company without telling all of you."

Face mutinous, C.C. held her ground. "You didn't tell me."

"Now, C.C., I..." Coco pursed her lips, knowing— since she'd practiced in the mirror—that it made her look befuddled. "I didn't? Are you certain? I would have sworn I told you and the girls the minute I got Mr. St. James's acceptance."

"No," C.C. said flatly.

"Oh, my." Coco lifted her hands to her cheeks. "Oh, how awful, really. I must apologize. What a dreadful mix-up. And all my fault. C.C., I do beg your pardon. After all, this is your house, yours and your sisters'. I would never presume on your good nature and your hospitality by..."

Before Coco had trailed off again, the guilt was working away. "It's your house as much as ours, Aunt Coco. You know that. It's not as if you have to ask permission to invite anyone you like. It's simply that I think we should have—"

"No, no, it's inexcusable." Coco had blinked enough to have her eyes glistening nicely. "Really it was. I just don't know what to say. I feel terrible about the whole thing. I was only trying to help, you see, but—"

"It's nothing to worry about." C.C. reached out for her aunt's hand. "Nothing at all. It was just a little confusing at first. Look, why don't I make the tea, and you can sit with—him."

"That's so sweet of you, dear."

C.C. muttered something unintelligible as she walked down the hall.

"Congratulations," Trent murmured, sending Coco an amused glance. "That was one of the smoothest shuffles I've ever witnessed."

Coco beamed and tucked her arm through his. "Thank you. Now, why don't we go in and have that chat?" She steered him to a wing chair by the fireplace, knowing that the springs in the sofa were only a memory. "I must apologize for C.C. She has a very quick temper but a wonderful heart."

Trent inclined his head. "I'll have to take your word for it."

"Well, you're here and that's what matters." Pleased with herself, Coco sat across from him. "I know you'll find The Towers, and its history, fascinating."

He smiled, thinking he'd already found its occupants a fascination.

"My grandfather," she said, gesturing to a portrait of a dour-faced thin-lipped man above the ornate cherrywood mantel. "He built this house in 1904."

Trent glanced up at the disapproving eyes and lowered brows. "He looks...formidable," he said politely.

Coco gave a gay laugh. "Oh, indeed. And ruthless in his prime, so I'm told. I only remember Fergus Calhoun as a doddering old man who argued with shadows. They finally put him away in 1945 after he tried to shoot the butler for serving bad port. He was quite insane—Grandfather," she explained. "Not the butler."

"I...see."

"He lived another twelve years in the asylum, which put him well into his eighties. The Calhouns either have long lives or die tragically young." She crossed her long, sturdy legs. "I knew your father."

"My father?"

"Yes, indeed. Not well. We attended some of the same parties in our youth. I remember dancing with him once at a cotillion in Newport. He was dashingly handsome, fatally charming. I was quite smitten." She smiled. "You resemble him closely."

"He must have fumbled to let you slip through his fingers."

Pure feminine delight glowed in her eyes. "You're quite right," she said with a laugh. "How is Trenton?"

"He's well. I think if he had realized the connection, he wouldn't have passed this business on to me."

She lifted a brow. As a woman who followed the society and gossip pages religiously, she was well aware of the senior St. James's current messy divorce. "The last marriage didn't take?"

It was hardly a secret, but it made Trent uncomfortable just the same. "No. Should I give him your regards when I speak with him?"

"Please do." A sore point, she noted, and skimmed lightly over it. "How is it you ran into C.C.?"

Fate, he thought, and nearly said so. "I found myself in need of her services—or I should say my car needed them. I didn't immediately make the connection between C.C.'s Automovations and Catherine Calhoun."

"Who could blame you?" Coco said with a fluttering hand. "I hope she wasn't too, ah, intense."

"I'm still alive to talk about it. Obviously, your niece isn't convinced to sell."

"That's right." C.C. wheeled in a tea cart, steering it across the floor like a go-cart and stopping it with a rattle between the two chairs. "And it's going to take more than some slick operator from Boston to convince me."

"Catherine, there is no excuse for rudeness."

"That's all right." Trent merely settled back. "I'm becoming used to it. Are all your nieces so...aggressive, Mrs. McPike?"

"Coco, please," she murmured. "They're all lovely women." As she lifted the teapot, she sent C.C. a warning glance. "Don't you have work, dear?"

"It can wait."

"But you only brought out service for two."

"I don't want anything." She plopped down on the arm of the sofa and folded her arms over her chest.

"Well then. Cream or lemon, Trenton?"

"Lemon, please."

Swinging one long, booted leg, C.C. watched them sip tea and exchange small talk. Useless talk, she thought nastily. He was the kind of man who had been trained from diapers on the proper way to sit in a parlor and discuss nothing.

Squash, polo, perhaps a round of golf. He probably had hands like a baby's. Beneath that tailored suit, his body would be soft and slow. Men like him didn't work, didn't sweat, didn't feel. He sat behind his desk all day, buying and selling, never once thinking of the lives he affected. Of the dreams and hopes he created or destroyed.

He wasn't going to mess with hers. He wasn't going to cover the much-loved and much-cracked plaster walls with drywall and a coat of slick paint. He wasn't going to turn the drafty old ballroom into a nightclub. He wasn't going to touch one board foot of her wormy rafters.

She would see to it. She would see to him.

It was quite a situation, Trent decided. He parried Coco's tea talk while the Amazon Queen, as he'd begun to think of C.C., sat on a sagging sofa, swinging a scarred boot and glaring daggers at him. Normally he would have politely excused himself, headed back to Boston to turn the whole business over to agents. But he hadn't faced a true challenge in a long time. This one, he mused, might be just what he needed to put him on track.

The place itself was an amazement—a crumbling one. From the outside it looked like a combination of English manor house and Dracula's castle. Towers and turrets of dour gray stone jutted into the sky. Gargoyles—one of which had been decapitated—grinned wickedly as they clung to parapets. All of this seemed to sit atop a proper two-story house of granite with neat porches and terraces. There was a pergola built along the seawall. The quick glimpse Trent had had of it had brought a Roman bathhouse to mind for reasons he couldn't fathom. As the lawns were uneven and multileveled, granite walls had been thrown up wherever they were terraced.

It should have been ugly. In fact, Trent thought it should have been hideous. Yet it wasn't. It was, in a baffling way, charming.

The way the window glass sparkled like lake water in the sun. Banks of spring flowers spread and nodded. Ivy rustled as it inched its patient way up those granite walls. It hadn't been difficult, even for a man with a pragmatic mind, to imagine the tea and garden parties. Women floating over the lawns in picture hats and organdy dresses, harp and violin music playing.

Then there was the view, which even on the short walk from his car to the front door had struck him breathless.

He could see why his father wanted it, and was willing to invest the hundreds of thousands of dollars it would take to renovate.

"More tea, Trenton?" Coco asked.

"No, thank you." He sent her a charming smile. "I wonder if I might have a tour of the house. What I've seen so far is fascinating."

C.C. gave a snort Coco pretended not to hear. "Of course, I'd be delighted to show you through." She rose and with her back to Trent wiggled her eyebrows at her niece. "C.C., shouldn't you be getting back?"

"No." She rose and, with an abrupt change of tactics, smiled. "I'll show Mr. St. James through, Aunt Coco. It's nearly time for the children to be home from school."

Coco glanced at the mantel clock, which had stopped weeks before at ten thirty-five. "Oh, well..."

"Don't worry about a thing." C.C. walked to the doorway and with an imperious gesture of her hand waved Trent along. "Mr. St. James?"

She started down the hall in front of him then up a floating staircase. "We'll start at the top, shall we?" Without glancing back, she continued on and up, certain Trent would start wheezing and panting by the third flight.

She was disappointed.

They climbed the final circular set that led to the highest tower. C.C. put her hand on the knob and her shoulder to the thick oak door. With a grunt and a hard shove, it creaked open.

"The haunted tower," she said grandly, and stepped inside amid the dust and echoes. The circular room was empty but for a few sturdy and fortunately empty mouse traps.

"Haunted?" Trent repeated, willing to play.

"My great-grandmother had her hideaway up here." As she spoke, C.C. moved over to the curved window. "It's said she would sit here, on this window seat, looking out to sea as she pined for her lover."

"Quite a view," Trent murmured. It was a dizzying drop down to the cliffs and the water that slapped and retreated. "Very dramatic."

"Oh, we're full of drama here. Great-Grandmama apparently couldn't bear the deceit any longer and threw herself out this very window." C.C. smiled smugly. "Now, on quiet nights you can hear her pacing this floor and weeping for her lost lover."

"That should add something to the brochure."

C.C. jammed her hands into her pockets. "I wouldn't think ghosts would be good for business."

"On the contrary." His lips curved. "Shall we move on?"

Tight-lipped, C.C. strode out of the room. Using both hands, she tugged on the knob, then dug in a bit and prepared to put her back into it. When Trent's hand closed over hers, she jolted as though she'd been scalded.

It felt as though she had.

"I can do it," she muttered. Her eyes widened as she felt his body brush hers. He brought his other arm around, caging her, trapping her hands under his. C.C.'s heart bounded straight into her throat, then back-flipped.

"It looks like a two-man job." With this, Trent gave a hard tug that brought the door to and C.C. back smartly against him.

They stood there a moment, like lovers looking out at a sunset. He caught himself drawing in the scent of her hair while his hands remained cupped over hers. It passed through his mind that she was quite an armful—an amazingly sexy armful—then she jumped like a rabbit, slamming back against the wall.

"It's warped." She swallowed, hoping to smother the squeak in her voice. "Everything around here is warped or broken or about to disintegrate. I don't know why you'd even consider buying it."

Her face was pale as water, Trent noted, making her eyes that much deeper. The panicked distress in them seemed more than a warped tower door warranted. "Doors can be repaired or replaced." Curious, he took a step toward her and watched her brace as if for a blow. "What's wrong with you?"

"Nothing." She knew if he touched her again she would go off like a rocket through what was left of the roof. "Nothing," she repeated. "If you want to see anything else, we'd better go down."

C.C. let out a long, slow breath as she followed him down the circular stairs. Her body was still throbbing oddly, as if she'd brushed a hand over a live wire. Not enough to get singed, she thought, just enough to let you know there was power.

She decided that gave her two reasons to get rid of Trenton St. James quickly.

She took him through the top floor, through the servants' wing, the storage rooms, making certain to point out any cracked plaster, dry rot, rodent damage. It pleased her that the air was chill, slightly damp and definitely musty. It was even more gratifying to see that his suit was sprinkled with dust and his shoes were rapidly losing their shine.

Trent peered into one room that was crowded with furniture boxes, broken crockery. "Has anyone gone through all this stuff?"

"Oh, we'll get around to it eventually." She watched a fat spider sneak away from the dim light. "Most of these rooms haven't been opened in fifty years—since my great-grandfather went insane."

"Fergus."

"Right. The family only uses the first two floors, and we patch things up as we have to." She ran her finger along an inch-wide crack in the wall. "I guess you could say if we don't see it, we don't worry about it. And the roof hasn't crashed down on our heads. Yet."

He turned to study her. "Have you ever thought about turning in your socket wrench for a real estate license?"

She only smiled. "There's more down this way." She particularly wanted to show him the room where she had tacked up plastic to cover the broken windows.

He walked with her, gingerly across a spot where two-by-fours had been nailed over a hole in the floor. A high arched door caught his eyes, and before C.C. could stop him, he had his hand on the knob.

"Where does this lead to?"

"Oh, nowhere," she began, and swore when he pulled it open. Fresh spring air rushed in. Trent stepped out onto the narrow stone terrace and turned toward the pie-shaped granite steps.

"I don't know how safe they are."

He flicked a glance over his shoulder. "A lot safer than the floor inside."

With an oath, C.C. gave up and climbed after him.

"Fabulous," he murmured as he paused on the wide passageway between turrets. "Really fabulous."

Which was exactly why C.C. hadn't wanted him to see it. She stood back with her hands in her pockets while he rested his palms on the waist-high stone wall and looked out.

He could see the deep blue waters of the bay with the boats gliding lightly over it. The valley, misty and mysterious, spread like a fairy tale. A gull, hardly more than a white blur, banked over the bay and soared out to sea.

"Incredible." The wind ruffled his hair as he followed the passage, down another flight, up one more. From here it was the Atlantic, wild and windy and wonderful. The sound of her ceaseless war on the rocks below echoed up like thunder.

He could see that there were doors leading back in at various intervals, but he wasn't interested in the interior just now. Someone, one of the family, he imagined, had set out chairs, tables, potted plants. Trent looked out over the roof of the pergola, to the tumbling rocks below.

"Spectacular." He turned to C.C. "Do you get used to it?"

She moved her shoulders. "No. You just get territorial."

"Understandable. I'm surprised any of you spend time inside."

With her hands still tucked in her pockets, she joined him at the wall. "It's not just the view. It's the fact that your family, generations of them, stood here. Just as the house has stood here, through time and wind and fire." Her face softened as she looked down. "The children are home."

Trent looked down to see two small figures race across the lawn toward the pergola. The sound of their laughter carried lightly on the wind.

"Alex and Jenny," she explained. "My sister Suzanna's children. They've stood here, too." She turned to him. "That means something."

"How does their mother feel about the sale?"

She looked away then as worry and guilt and frustration fought for control. "I'm sure you'll ask her yourself. But if you pressure her." Her head whipped around, hair flying. "If you pressure her in any way, you'll answer to me. I won't see her manipulated again."

"I have no intention of manipulating anyone."

She gave a bark of bitter laughter. "Men like you make a career out of manipulation. If you think you've happened across four helpless women, Mr. St. James, think again. The Calhouns can take care of themselves, and take care of their own."

"Undoubtedly, particularly if your sisters are as obnoxious as you."

C.C.'s eyes narrowed, her hands fisted. She would have moved in then and there for the kill, but her name was murmured quietly behind her.

Trent saw a woman step through one of the doors. She was as tall as C.C., but willowy, with a fragile aura that kicked Trent's protective instincts into gear before he was aware of it. Her hair was a pale and lustrous blond that waved to her shoulders. Her eyes were the deep blue of a midsummer sky and seemed calm and serene until you looked closer and saw the heartbreak beneath.

Despite the difference in coloring, there was a resemblance—the shape of the face and eyes and mouth—that made Trent certain he was meeting one of C.C.'s sisters.

"Suzanna." C.C. moved between her sister and Trent, as if to shield her. Suzanna's mouth curved, a look that was both amused and impatient.

"Aunt Coco asked me to come up." She laid a hand

on C.C.'s arm, soothing her protector. "You must be Mr. St. James."

"Yes." He accepted her offered hand and was surprised to find it hard and callused and strong.

"I'm Suzanna Calhoun Dumont. You'll be staying with us for a few days?"

"Yes. Your aunt was kind enough to invite me."

"Shrewd enough," Suzanna corrected with a smile as she put an arm around her sister. "I take it C.C.'s given you a partial tour."

"A fascinating one."

"I'll be glad to continue it from here." Her fingers pressed lightly but with clear meaning into C.C.'s arm. "Aunt Coco could use some help downstairs."

"He doesn't need to see any more now," C.C. argued. "You look tired."

"Not a bit. But I will be if Aunt Coco sends me all over the house looking for the Wedgwood turkey platter."

"All right then." She sent Trent a last, fulminating glance. "We aren't finished."

"Not by a long shot," he agreed, and smiled to himself as she slammed back inside. "Your sister has quite an…outgoing personality."

"She's a fire-eater," Suzanna said. "We all are, given the right circumstances. The Calhoun curse." She glanced over at the sound of her children laughing. "This isn't an easy decision, Mr. St. James, one way or the other. Nor is it, for any of us, a business one."

"I've gathered that. For me it has to be a business one."

She knew too well that for some men business came first, and last. "Then I suppose we'd better take it one step at a time." She opened the door that C.C. had slammed shut. "Why don't I show you where you'll be staying?"

Chapter 3

"So, what's he like?" Lilah Calhoun crossed her long legs, anchoring her ankles on one arm of the couch and pillowing her head on the other. The half-dozen bracelets on her arm jingled as she gestured toward C.C. "Honey, I've told you, screwing your face up that way causes nothing but wrinkles and bad vibes."

"If you don't want me to screw my face up, don't ask me about him."

"Okay, I'll ask Suzanna." She shifted her sea-green eyes toward her older sister. "Let's have it."

"Attractive, well mannered and intelligent."

"So's a cocker spaniel," Lilah put in, and sighed. "And here I was hoping for a pit bull. How long do we get to keep him?"

"Aunt Coco's a little vague on the particulars." Suzanna sent both of her sisters an amused look. "Which means she's not saying."

"Mandy might be able to pry something out of her." Lilah wiggled her bare toes and shut her eyes. She was the kind of woman who felt there was something intrinsically wrong with anyone who stretched out on a couch and didn't nap. "Suze, have the kids been through here today?"

"Only ten or fifteen times. Why?"

"I think I'm lying on a fire engine."

"I think we ought to get rid of him." C.C. rose and, to keep her restless hands busy, began to lay a fire.

"Suzanna said you already tried to throw him off the parapet."

"No," Suzanna corrected. "I said I stopped her before she thought to throw him off the parapet." She rose to hand C.C. the fireplace matches she'd forgotten. "And while I agree it's awkward to have him here while we're all so undecided, it's done. The least we can do is give him a chance to say his piece."

"Always the peacemaker," Lilah said sleepily, and missed Suzanna's quick wince. "Well, it might be a moot point now that he's gone through the place. My guess is that he'll be making some clever excuse and zooming back to Boston."

"The sooner the better," C.C. muttered, watching the flames begin to lick at the apple wood.

"I've been dismissed," Amanda announced. She hurried into the room as she hurried everywhere. Pushing a hand through her chin-length honey-brown hair, she perched on the arm of a chair. "She's not talking, either." Amanda's busy hands tugged at the hem of her trim business suit. "But I know she's up to something, something more than real estate transactions."

"Aunt Coco's always up to something." Suzanna

moved automatically to the old Belker cabinet to pour her sister a glass of mineral water. "She's happiest when she's scheming."

"That may be true. Thanks," she added, taking the glass. "But I get nervous when I can't get past her guard." Thoughtful, she sipped, then swept her gaze over her sisters. "She's using the Limoges china."

"The Limoges?" Lilah pushed up on her elbows. "We haven't used that since Suzanna's engagement party." And could have bitten her tongue. "Sorry."

"Don't be silly." Suzanna brushed the apology away. "She hasn't entertained much in the past couple of years. I'm sure she's missed it. She's probably just excited to have company."

"He's not company," C.C. put in. "He's nothing but a pain in the—"

"Mr. St. James." Suzanna rose quickly, cutting off the finale of her sister's opinion.

"Trent, please." He smiled at her, then with some wryness at C.C.

It was quite a tableau, he thought, and had enjoyed it for perhaps a minute before Suzanna had seen him in the doorway. The Calhoun women together, and separately, made a picture any man still breathing had to appreciate. Long, lean and leggy, they sat, stood or sprawled around the room.

Suzanna stood with her back to the window, so that the last lights of the spring evening haloed around her hair. He would have said she was relaxed but for that trace of sadness in her eyes.

The one on the sofa was definitely relaxed—and all but asleep. She wore a long, flowered skirt that reached almost to her bare feet and regarded him through dreamy amused eyes as she pushed back a curling mass of waist-length red hair.

Another sat perched on the arm of a chair as if she would spring up and into action at the sound of a bell only she could hear. Sleek, slick and professional, he thought at first glance. Her eyes weren't dreamy or sad, but simply calculating.

Then there was C.C. She'd been sitting on the stone hearth, chin on her hands, brooding like some modern-day Cinderella. But she had risen quickly, defensively, he noted, to stand poker straight with the fire behind her. This wasn't a woman who would sit patiently for a prince to fit a glass slipper on her foot.

He imagined she'd kick him smartly in the shins or somewhere more painful if he attempted it.

"Ladies," he said, but his eyes were on C.C. without him even being aware of it. He couldn't resist the slight nod in her direction. "Catherine."

"Let me introduce you," Suzanna said quickly. "Trenton St. James, my sisters, Amanda and Lilah. Why don't I fix you a drink while you—"

The rest of the offer was drowned out by a war whoop and storming feet. Like twin whirlwinds, Alex and Jenny barreled into the room. It was Trent's misfortune that he happened to be standing in the line of fire. They slammed into him like two missiles and sent him tumbling to the couch on top of Lilah.

She only laughed and said she was pleased to meet him.

"I'm so sorry." Suzanna collared each child and sent Trent a sympathetic glance. "Are you all right?"

"Yes." He untangled himself and rose.

"These are my children, Disaster and Calamity." She kept a firm maternal arm around each. "Apologize."

"Sorry," they told him. Alex, a few inches taller than his sister, looked up from under a mop of dark hair.

"We didn't see you."

"Didn't," Jenny agreed, and smiled winningly.

Suzanna decided to go into the lecture about storming into rooms later and steered them both toward the door. "Go ask Aunt Coco if dinner's ready. Walk!" she added firmly but without hope.

Before anyone could pick up the threads of a conversation, there was a loud, echoing boom.

"Oh, Lord," Amanda said into her glass. "She's dragged out the gong again."

"That means dinner." If there was one thing Lilah moved quickly for, it was food. She rose, tucked her arm through Trent's and beamed up at him. "I'll show you the way. Tell me, Trent, what are your views on astral projection?"

"Ah…" He sent a glance over his shoulder and saw C.C. grinning.

Aunt Coco had outdone herself. The china gleamed. What was left of the Georgian silver that had been a wedding present to Bianca and Fergus Calhoun glittered. Under the fantasy light of the Waterford chandelier the rack of lamb glistened. Before any of her nieces could comment, she dived cleanly into polite conversation.

"We're dining formal style, Trenton. So much more cozy. I hope your room is suitable."

"It's fine, thank you." It was, he thought, big as a barn, drafty, with a hole the size of a man's fist in the ceiling. But the bed was wide and soft as a cloud. And the view… "I can see some islands from my window."

"The Porcupine Islands," Lilah put in, and passed him a silver basket of dinner rolls.

Coco watched them all like a hawk. She wanted to see some chemistry, some heat. Lilah was flirting with him, but she couldn't be too hopeful about that. Lilah flirted with men in general, and she wasn't paying any more attention to Trent than she did to the boy who bagged groceries in the market.

No, there was no spark there. On either side. One down, she thought philosophically, three to go.

"Trenton, did you know that Amanda is also in the hotel business? We're all so proud of our Mandy." She looked down the rosewood table at her niece. "She's quite a businesswoman."

"I'm assistant manager of the BayWatch, down in the village." Amanda's smile was both cool and friendly, the same she would give to any harried tourist at checkout time. "It's not on the scale of any of your hotels, but we do very well during the season. I heard you're adding an underground shopping complex to the St. James Atlanta."

Coco frowned into her wine as they discussed hotels. Not only was there not a spark, there wasn't even a weak glow. When Trent passed Amanda the mint jelly and their hands brushed, there was no breathless pause, no meeting of the eyes. Amanda had already turned to giggle with little Jenny and mop up spilled milk.

Ah, there! Coco thought triumphantly. Trent had grinned at Alex when the boy complained that brussels sprouts were disgusting. So, he had a weakness for children.

"You don't have to eat them," Suzanna told her suspicious son as he poked through his scalloped potatoes to make sure nothing green was hidden inside. "Personally, I've always thought they looked like shrunken heads."

"They do, kinda." The idea appealed to him, as his mother had known it would. He speared one, stuck it into his mouth and grinned. "I'm a cannibal. Uga bugga."

"Darling boy," Coco said faintly. "Suzanna's done such a marvelous job of mothering. She seems to have a green thumb with children as well as flowers. All the gardens are our Suzanna's work."

"Uga bugga," Alex said again as he popped another imaginary head into his mouth.

"Here you go, little creep." C.C. rolled her vegetables onto his plate. "There's a whole passel of missionaries."

"I want some, too," Jenny complained, then beamed at Trent when he passed her the bowl.

Coco put a hand to her breast. Who would have guessed it? she thought. Her Catherine. The baby of her babies. While the dinner conversation bounced around her, she sat back with a quiet sigh. She couldn't be mistaken. Why, when Trent had looked at her little girl—and she at him—there hadn't just been a spark. There had been a sizzle.

C.C. was scowling, it was true, but it was such a *passionate* scowl. And Trent had smirked, but it was such a *personal* smirk. Positively intimate, Coco decided.

Sitting there, watching them, as Alex devoured his little decapitated heads, and Lilah and Amanda argued over the possibility of life on other planets, Coco could almost hear the loving thoughts C.C. and Trent sent out to each other.

Arrogant, self-important jerk.

Rude, bad-tempered brat.

Who the hell does he think he is, sitting at the table as if he already owned it?

A pity she doesn't have a personality to match her looks.

Coco smiled fondly at them while the "Wedding March" hummed through her head. Like a general plotting strategy, she waited until after coffee and dessert to spring her next offensive.

"C.C., why don't you show Trenton the gardens?"

"What?" She looked up from her friendly fight with Alex over the last bite of her Black Forest cake.

"The gardens," Coco repeated. "There's nothing like a little fresh air after a meal. And the flowers are exquisite in the moonlight."

"Let Suzanna take him."

"Sorry." Suzanna was already gathering a heavy-eyed Jenny into her arms. "I've got to get these two washed up and ready for bed."

"I don't see why—" C.C. broke off at the arched look from her aunt. "Oh, all right." She rose. "Come on then," she said to Trent and started out without him.

"It was a lovely meal, Coco. Thank you."

"My pleasure." She beamed, imagining whispered words and soft, secret kisses. "Enjoy the gardens."

Trent walked out of the terrace doors to find C.C. standing, tapping a booted foot on the stone. It was time, he thought, that someone taught the green-eyed witch a lesson in manners.

"I don't know anything about flowers," she told him.

"Or about simple courtesy."

Her chin angled. "Now listen, buddy."

"No, you listen, buddy." His hand snaked out and snagged her arm. "Let's walk. The children might still be within earshot, and I don't think they're ready to hear any of this."

He was stronger than she'd imagined. He pulled her along, ignoring the curses she tossed out under her breath. They were off the terrace and onto one of the meandering paths that wound around the side of the house. Daffodils and hyacinths nodded along the verge.

He stopped beneath an arbor where wisteria would bloom in another month. C.C. wasn't certain if the roar in her head was the sound of the sea or her own ragged temper.

"Don't you ever do that again." She lifted a hand to rub where his fingers had dug. "You may be able to push people around in Boston, but not here. Not with me or any of my family."

He paused, hoping and failing to get a grip on his own temper. "If you knew me, or what I do, you'd know I don't make a habit of pushing anyone around."

"I know exactly what you do."

"Foreclose on widows and orphans? Grow up, C.C."

She set her teeth. "You can see the gardens on your own. I'm going in."

He merely shifted to block her path. In the moonlight, her eyes glowed like a cat's. When she lifted her hands to shove him aside, he clamped his fingers onto her wrists. In the brief tug-of-war that followed, he noted—irrelevantly he assured himself—that her skin was the color of fresh cream and almost as soft.

"We're not finished." His voice had an edge that was

no longer coated with a polite veneer. "You'll have to learn that when you're deliberately rude, and deliberately insulting, there's a price."

"You want an apology?" she all but spat at him. "Okay. I'm sorry I don't have anything to say to you that isn't rude or insulting."

He smiled, surprising both of them. "You're quite a piece of work, Catherine Colleen Calhoun. For the life of me I can't figure out why I'm trying to be reasonable with you."

"Reasonable?" She didn't spit the word this time, but growled it. "You call it reasonable to drag me around, manhandle me—"

"If you call this manhandling, you've led a very sheltered life."

Her complexion went from creamy white to bright pink. "My life is none of your concern."

"Thank God."

Her fingers flexed then balled into fists. She hated the fact, loathed it, that her pulse was hammering double time under his grip. "Will you let me go?"

"Only if you promise not to take off running." He could see himself chasing her, and the image was both embarrassing and appealing.

"I don't run from anyone."

"Spoken like a true Amazon," he murmured, and released her. Only quick reflexes had him dodging the fist she aimed at his nose. "I should have taken that into account, I suppose. Have you ever considered intelligent conversation?"

"I don't have anything to say to you." She was ashamed to have struck out at him and furious that she'd missed. "If you want to talk, go suck up to Aunt

Coco some more." In a huff, she plopped down on the small stone bench under the arbor. "Better yet, go back to Boston and flog one of your underlings."

"I can do that anytime." He shook his head and, certain he was taking his life in his hands, sat beside her.

There were azaleas and geraniums threatening to burst into bloom around them. It should, he thought, have been a peaceful place. But as he sat, smelling the tender fragrance of the earliest spring blooms mixed with the scent of the sea, listening to some night bird call its mate, he thought that no boardroom had ever been so tense or hostile.

"I wonder where you developed such a high opinion of me." And why, he added to himself, it seemed to matter.

"You come here—"

"By invitation."

"Not mine." She tossed back her head. "You come in your big car and your dignified suit, ready to sweep my home out from under me."

"I came," he corrected, "to get a firsthand look at a piece of property. No one, least of all me, can force you to sell."

But he was wrong, she thought miserably. There were people who could force them to sell. The people who collected the taxes, the utility bills, the mortgage they'd been forced to take out. All of her frustration, and her fear, over every collection agency centered on the man beside her.

"I know your type," she muttered. "Born rich and above the common man. Your only goal in life is to make more money, regardless of who is affected or trampled over. You have big parties and summer houses and mistresses named Fawn."

Wisely he swallowed the chuckle. "I've never even known a woman named Fawn."

"Oh, what does it matter?" She rose to pace the path. "Kiki, Vanessa, Ava, it's all the same."

"If you say so." She looked, he was forced to admit, magnificent, striding up and down the path with the moonlight shooting around her like white fire. The tug of attraction annoyed him more than a little, but he continued to sit. There was a deal to be done, he reminded himself. And C. C. Calhoun was the foremost stumbling block.

So he would be patient, Trent told himself, and wily and find the hook. "Just how is it you know so much about my type?"

"Because my sister was married to one of you."

"Baxter Dumont."

"You know him?" Then she shook her head and jammed her hands into her pockets. "Stupid question. You probably play golf with him every Wednesday."

"No, actually our acquaintance is only slight. I do know of him, and his family. I'm also aware that he and your sister have been divorced for a year or so."

"He made her life hell, scraped away her self-esteem, then dumped her and his children for some little French pastry. And because he's a big-shot lawyer from a big-shot family, she's left with nothing but a miserly child-support check that comes late every month."

"I'm sorry for what happened to your sister." He rose as well. His voice was no longer sharp but fatalistic. "Marriage is often the least pleasant of all business transactions. But Baxter Dumont's behavior doesn't mean that every member of every prominent Boston family is unethical or immoral."

"They all look the same from where I'm standing."

"Then maybe you should change positions. But you won't, because you're too hardheaded and opinionated."

"Just because I'm smart enough to see through you."

"You know nothing about me, and we both know that you took an uncanny dislike to me before you even knew my name."

"I didn't like your shoes."

That stopped him. "I beg your pardon?"

"You heard me." She folded her arms and realized she was starting to enjoy herself. "I didn't like your shoes." She flicked a glance down at them. "I still don't."

"That explains everything."

"I didn't like your tie, either." She poked a finger on it, missing the quick flare in his eyes. "Or your fancy gold pen." She tapped a fist lightly at his breast pocket.

He studied her jeans, worn through at the knees, her T-shirt and scuffed boots. "This from an obvious fashion expert."

"You're the one out of place here, Mr. St. James III."

He took a step closer. C.C.'s lips curved in a challenging smile. "And I suppose you dress like a man because you haven't figured out how to act like a woman."

It was a bull's-eye, but the dart point only pricked her temper. "Just because I know how to stand up for myself instead of swooning at your feet doesn't make me less of a woman."

"Is that what you call this?" He wrapped his fingers around her forearms. "Standing up for yourself?"

"That's right. I—" She broke off when he tugged her closer. Their bodies bumped. Trent watched the temper in her eyes deepen to confusion.

"What do you think you're doing?"

"Testing the theory." He looked down at her mouth. Her lips were full, just parted. Very tempting. Why hadn't he noticed that before? he wondered vaguely. That big, insulting mouth of hers was incredibly tempting.

"Don't you dare." She meant it to come out as an order, but her voice shook.

His eyes came back to hers and held. "Afraid?"

The question was just the one to stiffen her spine. "Of course not. It's just that I'd rather be kissed by a rabid skunk."

She started to pull back, then found herself tight against him, eyes and mouth lined up, warm breath mingling. He hadn't intended to kiss her—certainly not—until she'd thrown that last insult in his face.

"You never know when to quit, Catherine. It's a flaw that's going to get you in trouble, starting now."

She hadn't expected his mouth to be so hot, so hard, so hungry. She had thought the kiss would be sophisticated and bland. Easily resisted, easily forgotten. But she had been wrong. Dangerously wrong. Kissing him was like sliding into molten silver. Even as she gasped for air, he heightened the kiss, plunging his tongue deep, taunting, tormenting, teasing hers. She tried to shake her head but succeeded only in changing the angle. The hands that had reached for his shoulders in protest slid possessively around his neck.

He'd thought to teach her a lesson—about what he'd forgotten. But he learned. He learned that some women—this woman—could be strong and soft, frustrating and delightful, all at once. As the waves crashed far below, he felt himself battered by the unexpected. And the unwanted.

He thought, foolishly, that he could feel the starlight on her skin, taste the moondust on her lips. The groan he heard, vibrating low, was his own.

He lifted his head, shaking it, as if to clear the fog that had settled over his brain. He could see her eyes, staring up at his—dark, dazed.

"I beg your pardon." Stunned by his action, he released her so quickly that she stumbled back even as her hands slid away from him. "That was completely inexcusable."

She said nothing, could say nothing. Feelings, too many of them, clogged in her throat. Instead she made a helpless gesture with her hands that made him feel like a lower form of life.

"Catherine…believe me, I don't make a habit of—" He had to stop and clear his dry throat. Lord, he wanted to do it again, he realized. He wanted to kiss the breath from her as she stood there, looking lost and helpless. And beautiful. "I'm terribly sorry. It won't happen again."

"I'd like you to leave me alone." Never in her life had she been more moved. Or more devastated. He had just opened up a door to some secret world, then slammed it again in her face.

"All right." He had to stop himself from reaching out to touch her hair. He started back down the path toward the house. When he looked back, she was still standing as he had left her, staring into the shadows, with moonlight showering her.

* * *

His name is Christian. I have found myself walking along the cliffs again and again, hoping for a few words with him. I tell myself it's because of my fascination with art, not the artist. It could be true. It must be true.

I am a married woman and mother of three. And though Fergus is not the romantic husband of my girlish dreams, he is a good provider, and sometimes kind. Perhaps there is some part of me, some small defiant part that wishes I had not bent to my parents' insistence that I make a good and proper marriage. But this is foolishness, for the deed has been done for more than four years.

It's disloyal to compare Fergus with a man I hardly know. Yet here, in my private journal, I must be allowed this indulgence. While Fergus thinks only of business, the next deal or dollar, Christian speaks of dreams and images and poetry.

How my heart has yearned for just a little poetry.

While Fergus, with his cool and careless generosity, gave me the emeralds on the day of Ethan's birth, Christian once offered me a wildflower. I have kept it, pressing it here between these pages. How much lovelier I would feel wearing it than those cold and heavy gems.

We have spoken of nothing intimate, nothing that could be considered improper. Yet I know it is. The way he looks at me, smiles, speaks, is gloriously improper. The way I look for him on these bright summer afternoons while my babies nap is not the action of a proper wife. The way my heart drums in my breast when I see him is disloyalty in itself.

Today I sat upon a rock and watched him wield his brush, bringing those pink and gray rocks, that blue, blue water to life on canvas. There was a boat gliding along, so free, so solitary. For a moment I pictured the two of us there, faces to the wind. I don't understand why I have these thoughts, but while they remained with me, clear as crystal, I asked his name.

"Christian," he said. "Christian Bradford. And you are Bianca."

The way he said my name—as if it had never been said before. I will never forget it. I toyed with the wild grass that pushed itself through the cracks in the rocks. With my eyes cast down, I asked him why his wife never came to watch him work.

"I have no wife," he told me. "And art is my only mistress."

It was wrong for my heart to swell so at his words. Wrong of me to smile, yet I smiled. And he in return. If fate had dealt differently with me, if time and place could have been altered in some way, I could have loved him.

I think I would have had no choice but to love him.

As if we both knew this, we began to talk of inconsequential matters. But when I rose, knowing my time here was at an end for the day, he bent over and plucked up a tiny spike of golden heather and slipped it into my hair. For a moment, his fingers hovered over my cheek and his eyes were on mine. Then he stepped away and bid me good day.

Now I sit with the lamp low as I write, listening to Fergus's voice rumble as he instructs his valet next door. He will not come to me tonight, and I find myself grateful. I have given him three children, two sons and a daughter. By providing him with an heir, I have done my duty, and he does not often find the need to come to my bed. I am, like the children, to exist to be well dressed and well mannered, and to be presented at the proper occasions—like a good claret—for his guests.

It is not much to ask, I suppose. It is a good life, one I should be content with. Perhaps I was content, until that day I first walked along the cliffs.

So tonight, I will sleep alone in my bed, and dream of a man who is not my husband.

Chapter 4

When you couldn't sleep, the best thing to do was get up. That's what C.C. told herself as she sat at the kitchen table, watching the sunrise and drinking her second cup of coffee.

She had a lot on her mind, that was all. Bills, the dyspeptic Oldsmobile that was first on her schedule that morning, bills, an upcoming dentist appointment. More bills. Trenton St. James was far down on her list of concerns. Somewhere below a potential cavity and just ahead of a faulty exhaust system.

She certainly wasn't losing any sleep over him. And a kiss, that ridiculous—*accident* was the best term she could use to describe it—wasn't even worth a moment's thought.

Yet she had thought of little else throughout the long, sleepless night.

She was acting as though she'd never been kissed before, C.C. berated herself. And, of course, she had, starting with Denny Dinsmore, who had planted the first sloppy mouth-to-mouth on her after their eighth-grade Valentine's dance.

Naturally there had been no comparison between Denny's fumbling yet sincere attempt and the stunning expertise of Trent's. Which only proved, C.C. decided as she scowled into her coffee, that Trent had spent a large part of his life with his lips slapped up against some woman's. Lots of women's.

It had been a rotten thing to do, she thought now. Particularly in the middle of what had been becoming a very satisfactory argument. Men like Trent didn't know how to fight fair, with wit and words and good honest fury. They were taught how to dominate, by whatever manner worked.

Well, it had worked, she thought, running a fingertip over her lips. Damn him and the horse he rode in on. It had worked like a charm, because for one moment, one brief, trembling moment, she had felt something fine and lovely—something more than the exciting press of his mouth on hers, more than the possessive grip of his hands.

It had been inside her, beneath the panic and the pleasure, beyond the whirl of sensation—a glow, warm and golden, like a lamp in the window on a stormy night.

Then he had turned off that lamp, with one quick, careless flick, leaving her in the dark again.

She could have hated him for that alone, C.C. thought miserably, if she hadn't already had enough to hate him for.

"Hey, kid." Lilah breezed through the doorway, tidy in her park service khakis. Her mass of hair was in a neat braid down her back. Swinging at each ear was a trio of amber crystal balls. "You're up early."

"Me?" C.C. forgot her own mood long enough to stare. "Are you my sister or some clever imposter?"

"You be the judge."

"Must be an imposter. Lilah Maeve Calhoun's never up before eight o'clock, which is exactly twenty minutes before she has to rush out of the house to be five minutes late for work."

"God, I hate to be so predictable. My horoscope," Lilah told her as she rooted through the refrigerator. "It said that I should rise early today and contemplate the sunrise."

"So how was it?" C.C. asked as her sister brought a cold can of soda and a wicked slice of the Black Forest cake to the table.

"Pretty spectacular as sunrises go." Lilah shoveled cake into her mouth. "What's your excuse?"

"Couldn't sleep."

"Anything to do with the stranger at the end of the hall?"

C.C. wrinkled her nose and filched a cherry from Lilah's plate. "Guys like that don't bother me."

"Guys like that were created to bother women, and thank God for it. So…" Lilah stretched her legs out to rest her feet on an empty chair. The kitchen faucet was leaking again, but she liked the sound of it. "What's the story?"

"I didn't say there was a story."

"You don't have to say, it's all over your face."

"I just don't like him being here, that's all." Evading, C.C. rose to take her cup to the sink. "It's like we're already being pushed out of our own home. I know we've discussed selling, but it was all so vague and down some long, dark road." She turned back to her sister. "Lilah, what are we going to do?"

"I don't know." Lilah's eyes clouded. It was one of the few things she couldn't prevent herself from worrying about. Home and family, they were her weaknesses. "I guess we could sell some more of the crystal, and there's the silver."

"It would break Aunt Coco's heart to sell the silver."

"I know. But we may have to go piece by piece—or make the big move." She scooped up some more cake. "As much as I hate to say it, we're going to have to think hard, and practically, and seriously."

"But, Lilah, a hotel?"

Lilah merely shrugged. "I don't have any deep, moral problem with that. The house was built by crazy old Fergus to entertain platoons of guests, with all kinds of people racing around to serve meals and tidy linens. It seems to me that a hotel just about suits its original purpose." She gave a long sigh at C.C.'s expression. "You know I love the place as much as you do."

"I know."

What Lilah didn't add was that it would break her heart to have to sell it but that she was prepared to do what was best for the family.

"We'll give the gorgeous Mr. St. James a couple more days, then have a family meeting." She offered C.C. a bolstering smile. "The four of us together can't go wrong."

"I hope you're right."

"Honey, I'm always right—that's my little cross to

bear." She took a swig of the sugar-ladened soft drink. "Now, why don't you tell me what kept you up all night?"

"I just did."

"No." Head cocked, she waved her fork at C.C. "Don't forget Lilah knows all and sees all—and what she doesn't she finds out. So spill it."

"Aunt Coco made me take him out in the garden."

"Yeah." Lilah grinned. "She's a wily old devil. I figured she was plotting some romance. Moonlight, flowers, the distant lap of water on rocks. Did it work?"

"We had a fight."

Lilah nodded, giving a go-ahead signal with her hand as she sipped. "That's a good start. About the house?"

"That..." C.C. began to pluck dried leaves from a withered philodendron. "And things."

"Like?"

"Names of mistresses," C.C. muttered. "Prominent Boston families. His shoes."

"An eclectic argument. My favorite kind. And then?"

C.C. jammed her hands into her pockets. "He kissed me."

"Ah, the plot thickens." She had Coco's love of gossip and, leaning forward, cradled her chin on her hands. "So, how was it? He's got a terrific mouth—I noticed it right off."

"So kiss him yourself."

After thinking it over a moment, Lilah shook her head—not without some regret. "Nope, terrific mouth or not, he's not my type. Anyway, you've already locked lips with him, so tell me. Was he good?"

"Yeah," C.C. said grudgingly. "I guess you could say that."

"Like on a scale of one to ten?"

The chuckle escaped before C.C. realized she was laughing. "I wasn't exactly thinking about a rating system at the time."

"Better and better." Lilah licked her fork clean. "So, he kissed you and it was pretty good. Then what?"

Humor vanished as C.C. blew out a long breath. "He apologized."

Lilah stared, then slowly, deliberately set down her fork. "He what?"

"Apologized—very properly for his inexcusable behavior, and promised it wouldn't happen again. The jerk." C.C. crumbled the dead leaves in her hand. "What kind of a man thinks a woman wants an apology after she's been kissed boneless?"

Lilah only shook her head. "Well, the way I see it, there are three choices. He *is* a jerk, he's been trained to be overly polite, or he was incapable of thinking rationally."

"I vote for jerk."

"Hmm. I'm going to have to think about this." She drummed her cerise-tipped fingers on the table. "Maybe I should do his chart."

"Whatever sign his moon is in, I still vote for jerk." C.C. walked over to kiss Lilah's cheek. "Thanks. Gotta go."

"C.C." She waited until her sister turned back. "He has nice eyes. When he smiles, he has very nice eyes."

Trent wasn't smiling when he finally managed to escape from The Towers that afternoon. Coco had insisted on giving him a tour of the cellars, every damp inch, then had trapped him with photo albums for two hours.

It had been amusing to look at baby pictures of C.C., to view, through snapshots, her growing up from toddler to woman. She had been incredibly cute in pigtails and a missing tooth.

During the second hour, his alarm bells had sounded. Coco had begun to pump him none too subtly about his views on marriage, children, relationships. It was then he'd realized that behind Coco's soft, misty eyes ticked a sharp, calculating brain.

She wasn't trying to sell the house but to auction off one of her nieces. And apparently C.C. was the front-runner, with him preselected as the highest bidder. Well, the Calhoun women were in for a rude awakening, Trent determined. They were going to have to look elsewhere on the marriage market for a suitable candidate—and good luck to him.

And the St. Jameses would have the house, Trent promised himself. By damn they would, with no strings or wedding veils attached.

He started down the steep, winding drive in a controlled fury. When he caught the sound of his own voice as he muttered to himself, Trent decided that he would take a long, calming drive. Perhaps to Acadia National Park where Lilah worked as a naturalist. Divide and conquer, he thought. He would seek out each of the women in their own work space and rattle their beautiful chains.

Lilah seemed to be receptive, he thought. Any one of them would be more so than C.C. Amanda appeared to be sensible. He was certain Suzanna was a reason-able woman.

What had gone wrong with sister number four?

But he found himself heading down to the village, past Suzanna's fledgling landscape and garden busi-ness, past the BayWatch Hotel. When he drove up to C.C.'s garage, he told himself that was what he'd meant to do all along.

He would start with her, the sharpest thorn in his side. And when he was done, she would have no illu-sions about trapping him into marriage.

Hank was climbing into the tow truck as Trent climbed out of the BMW. "'Lo." Grinning, Hank pulled on the brim of his gray cap. "Boss's inside. Got us a nice fender bender over at the visitors' center."

"Congratulations."

"Ayah, we've been needing a little bodywork 'round here. Now, once the season picks up, business'll boom." Hank slammed the door then leaned his head out of the window, disposed to chat.

For some reason, Trent found himself noticing the boy—really noticing him. He was young, probably about twenty, with a round, open face, a thick down-east accent and a shock of straw-colored hair that shot out in all directions.

"Have you worked for C.C. long?"

"Since she bought the place from old Pete. That'll be, ah, three years. Ayah. Three years, nearly. She wouldn't hire me till I finished high school. Funny that way."

"Is she?"

"Once she gets a bee in her bonnet ain't no shaking it loose." He nodded toward the garage. "She's a might touchy today."

"Is that unusual?"

Hank chuckled and switched the radio on high. "Can't say she's all bark and no bite, 'cause I've seen her bite a time or two. See ya."

"Sure."

When Trent walked in, C.C. was buried to the waist under the hood of a late-model sedan. She had the radio on again, but this time it was her hips rather than her boots keeping time.

"Excuse me," Trent began, then remembered they had been through that routine before. He walked up and tapped her smartly on the shoulder.

"If you'd just..." But she turned her head only enough to see the tie. It wasn't maroon today, but navy. Still, she was certain of its owner. "What do you want?"

"I believe it was a lube job."

"Oh." She went back to replacing spark plugs. "Well, leave it outside, put the key on the bench, and I'll get to it. It should be ready by six."

"Do you always do business so casually?"

"Yeah."

"If you don't mind, I think I'll hold on to my keys until you're less distracted."

"Suit yourself." Two minutes passed in humming silence broken only by the radio's prediction of thunderstorms that evening. "Look, if you're just going to stand around, why don't you do something useful? Get in and start her up."

"Start her up?"

"Yeah, you know. Turn the key, pump the gas." She

cocked her head up and blew at her bangs. "Think you can handle it?"

"Probably." It wasn't exactly what he'd had in mind, but Trent walked around to the driver's side. He noted that there was a car seat strapped in the front, and something pink and gooey on the carpet. He slid in and turned the key. The engine turned over and purred, quite nicely, he thought. Apparently C.C. thought differently.

Taking up her timing light, she began to make adjustments.

"It sounds fine," Trent pointed out.

"No, there's a miss."

"How can you hear anything with the radio blasting?"

"How can you not hear it? Better," she murmured. "Better."

Curious, he got out to lean over her shoulder. "What are you doing?"

"My job." Her shoulders moved irritably, as if there were an itch between the blades. "Back off, will you?"

"I'm only expressing normal curiosity." Without thinking, he set a hand lightly on her back and leaned farther in. C.C. jolted, felt a flash of pain then swore like a sailor.

"Let me see." He grabbed the hand she was busy shaking.

"It's nothing. Take off, will you? If you hadn't been in my way, my hand wouldn't have slipped."

"Stop dancing around and let me see." He took a firm grip on her wrist and examined her scraped knuckles. The faint well of blood beneath the engine grease caused him a sharp and ridiculous sense of guilt. "You'll need something on this."

"It's just a scratch." God, why wouldn't he let go of her hand? "What I need to do is finish this job."

"Don't be a baby," he said mildly. "Where's the first-aid kit?"

"It's in the bathroom, and I can do it myself."

Ignoring her, he kept hold of her wrist as he walked around to shut the engine off. "Where's the bathroom?"

She jerked her head toward the hallway that separated the garage from the office. "If you'd just leave your keys—"

"You said it was my fault you hurt your hand, so I'll take the responsibility."

"I wish you'd stop pulling me around," she said as he hauled her toward the hallway.

"Then keep up." He pushed open a door into a white-tiled bathroom the size of a broom closet. Ignoring her protests, he held C.C.'s hand under a spray of cool water. The dimensions of the room had them standing hip to hip. They both did their level best to ignore that as he took the soap and, with surprising gentleness, began to clean her hand. "It isn't deep," he said, annoyed that his throat was dry.

"I told you, it's just a scratch."

"Scratches get infected."

"Yes, doctor."

With a retort on the tip of his tongue, he glanced up. She looked so cute, he thought, with grease on her nose and her mouth in a five-year-old's pout. "I'm sorry," he heard himself say, and the petulance faded from her eyes.

"It wasn't your fault." Wanting something to do, she

opened the mirrored cabinet over the sink for the first-aid kit. "I can take care of it, really."

"I like to finish what I start." He took the kit from her and found the antiseptic. "I guess I should say this is going to sting."

"I already know it stings." C.C. let out a little hiss as he swabbed the cut. Automatically she leaned over to blow on the heat, just as he did the same. Their heads bumped smartly. Rubbing hers with her free hand, C.C. gave a half laugh. "We make a lousy team."

"It certainly looks that way." With his eyes on hers, Trent blew softly on her knuckles. Something flickered in those pretty green irises, he noted. Alarm, surprise, pleasure, he couldn't be sure, but he would have wagered half his stock options that C. C. Calhoun was totally ignorant of her aunt's romantic plotting.

He brought her hand to his lips—just a test, he assured himself—and watched what was definitely confusion darken her eyes. Her hand went limp in his. Her mouth opened and stayed that way, with no sound coming out.

"A kiss is supposed to make it better," he pointed out and, for purely selfish reasons, whispered his lips over her hand again.

"I think…it would be better if…" Lord, the room was small, she thought distractedly. And getting smaller all the time. "Thanks," she managed. "I'm sure it's fine now."

"It needs to be bandaged."

"Oh, well, I don't—"

"You'll only get it dirty." Enjoying himself enormously, he took a roll of gauze and began to wrap her hand.

Thinking it would put some distance between them, C.C. turned. As if following the moves of a dance, Trent turned as well. Now they were facing, rather than side-by-side. He shifted—there was room to do little else—and her back was against the wall.

"Hurt?"

She shook her head. She wasn't hurt, C.C. decided, she was crazy. A woman had to be crazy to have her heart pounding like a jackhammer because a man was wrapping gauze around her skinned knuckles.

"C.C." He taped the gauze competently in place. "Can I ask you a personal question?"

"I…" She lifted her shoulders and swallowed.

"What exactly is a lube job?"

She caught the amusement in his eyes, and, charmed by it, smiled back. "Forty-seven-fifty."

"Oh." They were as close as they had been the night before, when they'd been arguing. This, Trent decided, was much more pleasant. "Are you going to flush my radiator?"

"Absolutely."

"Then I'm forgiven for last night?"

Her brows lifted. "I didn't say that."

"I wish you'd reconsider." With her hand held between them, he shifted slightly closer. "You see, if I'm going to be damned for it, it's harder to resist the urge to sin again."

Flustered, she pressed back against the wall. "I don't think you're the least bit sorry about what you did."

He considered her a moment, the wide eyes, the tempting mouth. "I'm afraid you're right."

As she stood, torn between delight and terror, the

phone began to shrill. "I've got to get that." Nimble as a greyhound, she streaked by him and out of the room.

He followed more slowly, surprised at himself. There was no doubt in his mind that she was as much victim of her aunt's fantasies as he. Another woman, certainly one with matrimony on her mind, would have smiled—or pouted. Would have slid her arms seductively around him—or held him sulkily away. But another woman would not have stood with her back planted against the wall as if facing a firing squad. Another woman would not have looked at him with big, helpless eyes and stammered.

Or looked so alluring while she did so.

C.C. snatched up the phone in her office, but her mind was blank. She stood, staring through the glass wall with the phone at her ear for ten silent seconds before the voice through the receiver brought her back.

"What? Oh, yes, yes, this is C.C. Sorry. Is that you, Finney?" She let out a long, pent-up breath as she listened. "Did you leave the lights on again? Are you sure? Okay, okay. It might be the starter motor." She ran a distracted hand through her hair and started to ease a hip down on the desk when she spotted Trent. She popped back up like a spring. "What? I'm sorry, could you say that again? Uh-huh. Why don't I come take a look at it on my way home? About six-thirty." Her lips curved. "Sure. I always have a taste for lobster. You bet. Bye."

"A mechanic who makes house calls," Trent commented.

"We take care of our own." Relax, she ordered herself. Relax right now. "Besides it's easy when there's the offer of an Albert Finney lob-stah dinner on the other end."

There was a tug of annoyance he tried mightily to ignore. "How's the hand?"

She wriggled her fingers. "Fine. Why don't you hang your keys on the pegboard?"

He did so. "Do you realize you've never called me by name?"

"Of course I have."

"No, you've called me names, but never by my name." He lifted a hand to gesture the thought away. "In any case, I need to talk to you."

"Listen, if it's about the house, this really isn't the time or place."

"It isn't, precisely."

"Oh." She looked at him, feeling that odd little jolt in her heart. "I'm really getting backed up. Can it wait until you pick up your car?"

He wasn't used to waiting for anything. "It won't take long. I feel I should warn you, as I believe you're as unaware as I was, of your aunt's plans."

"Aunt Coco? What plans?"

"The white-lace-and-orange-blossom type of plans."

Her expression went from baffled to stunned to suspicious. "Marriage? That's absurd. Aunt Coco's not planning to be married. She doesn't even see anyone seriously."

"I don't think she's the candidate." He walked toward her, keeping his eyes on her. "You are."

Her laugh was quick and full of fun as she sat on the edge of the desk. "Me? Married? That's rich."

"Yes, and so am I."

Her laughter dried up. Using the palms of her hands,

she levered herself off the desk. When she spoke, her voice was very cool, with licks of temper beneath. "Exactly what are you implying?"

"That your aunt, for reasons of her own, invited me here not only to look over the house, but her four very attractive nieces."

Her face went dead pale, as he now knew it did when she was desperately angry. "That's insulting."

"That's a fact."

"Get out." She gave him one hard shove toward the door. "Get out. Get your keys, your car and your ridiculous accusations and get out."

"Hold on and shut up for one minute." He took her firmly by the shoulders. "Just one minute, and when I'm done if you still think I'm being ridiculous, I'll leave."

"I know you're ridiculous. And conceited, and arrogant. If you think for one minute that I have—have designs on you—"

"Not you," he corrected with a little shake. "Your well-meaning aunt. 'Why don't you show Trenton the garden, C.C.? The flowers are exquisite in the moonlight.'"

"She was just being polite."

"In a pig's eye. Do you know how I spent my morning?"

"I couldn't be less interested."

"Looking through photo albums." He saw the anger turn to distress and pressed on. "Dozens of them. You were quite the adorable child, Catherine."

"Oh, God."

"And bright, too, according to your doting aunt. Spelling bee champ in the third grade."

With a strangled groan, she lowered to the desk again.

"Not a single cavity in your mouth."

"She didn't," C.C. managed.

"Oh, that and more. Top honors in your auto mechanics class in high school. Using the bulk of your inheritance to buy this shop from your employer. I'm told you're a very sensible woman who knows how to keep her feet on the ground. Then again, you come from excellent stock and were well-bred."

"Like a holstein," she muttered, firing up.

"As you like. Naturally, with your background, brains and beauty, you'd make the right man the most excellent of wives."

She was no longer pale, but blushing furiously. "Just because Aunt Coco's proud of me doesn't mean she's asking you to pick out a silver pattern."

"After she finished relating your virtues and showing me the pictures—quite lovely ones—of you in your prom dress."

"My—" C.C. only shut her eyes.

"She began to ask me my views on marriage and children. Dropping rather large, heavy hints that a man in my position needs a stable relationship with a stable woman. Such as yourself."

"All right, all right. Enough." She opened her eyes again. "Aunt Coco often gets ideas in her head about what's best for my sisters and me. If she goes overboard." C.C. set her teeth. "When she goes overboard, it's only because she loves us and feels responsible. I'm sorry she made you uncomfortable."

"I didn't tell you this to embarrass you or to have you apologize." Suddenly awkward, he slipped his hands into his pockets. "I thought it best if you knew the way her thoughts were headed before, well, something got out of hand."

"Got out of hand?" C.C. repeated.

"Or was misunderstood." Odd, he thought, it was usually so easy to lay the ground rules. He certainly couldn't remember fumbling before. "That is, after last night... I realize you've been sheltered to a certain degree."

The fingers of C.C.'s good hand began to drum on the knee of her coveralls.

Perhaps he should start again. "I believe in honesty, C.C., in both my business and my personal relationships. Last night, between temper and the moonlight, we—I suppose you could say we lost control for a moment." Why did that seem so pale and inadequate a description for what had happened? "I wouldn't want your lack of experience and your aunt's fantasies to result in a misunderstanding."

"Let me see if I get this. You're concerned that because you kissed me last night, and my aunt brought up the subject of marriage along with my baby pictures this morning, that I might get some wild idea in my head that I might be the next Mrs. St. James."

Thrown off, he ran a hand over his hair. "More or less. I thought it would be better, certainly more fair, if I told you straight off so that you and I could handle it reasonably. That way you wouldn't—"

"Develop any delusions of grandeur?" she suggested.

"Don't put words in my mouth."

"How can I? There's no room with your foot in there."

"Damn it." He hated the fact that she was absolutely right. "I'm simply trying to be perfectly honest with you so that there won't be any misunderstanding when I tell you I'm very attracted to you."

She only lifted a brow, too furious to see that his own words had left him speechless. "Now, I take it, I'm supposed to be flattered."

"You're not supposed to be anything. I'm merely trying to lay out the facts."

"I'll give you some facts." She shoved a hand into his chest. "You're not attracted to me, you're attracted to the image of the perfect and enviable Trenton St. James III. My aunt's fantasies, as you call them, are a result of a wonderful loving heart. Something I'm sure you can't understand. And as far as I'm concerned, I wouldn't think about spending five minutes with you much less the rest of my life. You may end up with my home, but not with me, buster." She was revving up and feeling wonderful. "If you came crawling to me on your hands and knees with a diamond as big as my fist in your teeth, I'd laugh in your face. Those are the facts. I'm sure you can find your way out."

She turned and strode down the hall. Trent winced as the door slammed.

"Well," he murmured, pressing his fingers to his eyes. "We certainly cleared that up."

Chapter 5

Insufferable. It was the perfect word to describe him, C.C. decided, and hugged it to her throughout the rest of the day.

By the time she got home, the house was quiet and settled for the night. She could hear, faintly, the soft and haunting notes of the piano from the music room. Turning away from the stairs, she followed the music.

It was Suzanna, of course, who sat at the lovely old spinet. She had been the only one who had stuck with the lessons or shown any real talent. Amanda had been too impatient, Lilah too lazy. And C.C.…. She looked down at her hands. Her fingers had been more at home smeared with motor oil than at the keys of a piano.

Still she loved to listen. There was nothing that soothed or charmed her more than music.

Suzanna, lost somewhere in her own heart, sighed a little as the last notes died.

"That was beautiful." C.C. walked over to kiss her sister's hair.

"I'm rusty."

"Not from where I'm standing."

Smiling, Suzanna reached back to pat her hand and felt the gauze. "Oh, C.C., what did you do?"

"Just scraped my knuckles."

"Did you clean it well? When was your last tetanus shot?"

"Slow down, Mommy. It's clean as a whistle and I had a tetanus shot six months ago." C.C. sat on the bench, facing out into the room. "Where is everyone?"

"The kids are fast asleep—I hope. Wiggle your fingers."

C.C. sighed and complied.

With a satisfied nod, Suzanna continued. "Lilah's out on a date. Mandy's looking over some ledger or other. Aunt Coco went up hours ago to have a bubble bath and put cucumber slices on her eyes."

"What about him?"

"In bed, I imagine. It's nearly midnight."

"Is it?" Then she smiled. "You were waiting up for me."

"I was not." Caught, Suzanna laughed. "Exactly. Did you fix Mr. Finney's truck?"

"He left his lights on again." She yawned hugely. "I think he does it on purpose just so I can come over and recharge his battery." She stretched her arms to the ceiling. "We had lobster and dandelion wine."

"If he wasn't old enough to be your grandfather, I'd say he has a crush on you."

"He does. And it's mutual. So, did I miss anything around here?"

"Aunt Coco wants to have a séance."

"Not again."

Suzanna ran her hands lightly over the keys, improvising. "Tomorrow night, right after dinner. She insists there's something Great-Grandmother Bianca wants us to know—Trent, too."

"What does he have to do with it?"

Suzanna brushed at C.C.'s bangs. "If we decide to sell him the house, he'll more or less inherit her."

"Is that what we're going to do, Suzanna?"

"It might be what we have to do."

C.C. rose to toy with the tassels of the floor lamp. "My business is doing pretty good. I could take out a loan against it."

"No."

"But—"

"No," Suzanna repeated. "You're not going to risk your future on the past."

"It's my future."

"And it's our past." She rose, as well. When that light came into Suzanna's eyes, even C.C. knew better than to argue. "I know how much the house means to you, to all of us. Coming back here after Bax— after things didn't work out," Suzanna said carefully, "helped keep me sane. Every time I watch Alex or Jenny slide down the banister, I remember doing it myself. I see Mama sitting here at the piano, hear Papa telling stories in front of the fire."

"Then how can you even think of selling?"

"Because I learned to face realities, however unpleasant." She lifted a hand to C.C.'s cheek. Only five years separated them. Sometimes Suzanna felt it was fifty. "Sometimes things happen to you, or around you, that you just can't control. When that happens, you gather up what's important in your life, and go on."

"But the house is important."

"How much longer do you really think we can hang on?"

"We could sell the lithographs, the Limoges, a few other things."

"And drag out the unhappiness." She knew entirely too much about that. "If it's time to let go, I think we should let go with some dignity."

"Then you've already made up your mind."

"No." Suzanna sighed and sat again. "Every time I think I have, I change it. Before dinner, the children and I walked along the cliffs." Eyes dreamy, she stared through the darkened window. "When I stand there, looking out over the bay, I feel something, something so incredible, it breaks my heart. I don't know what's right, C.C. I don't know what's best. But I'm afraid I know what has to be done."

"It hurts."

"I know."

C.C. sat beside her, rested her head on Suzanna's shoulder. "Maybe there'll be a miracle."

Trent watched them from the darkened hallway. He wished he hadn't heard them. He wished he didn't care. But he had heard, and for reasons he didn't choose to explore, he did care. Quietly he went back up the stairs.

"Children," Coco said with what she was certain was the last of her sanity, "why don't you read a nice book?"

"I want to play war." Alex swished an imaginary saber through the air. "Death to the last man."

And the child was only six, Coco thought. What would he be in ten years' time? "Crayons," she said hopefully, cursing rainy Saturday afternoons. "Why don't you both draw beautiful pictures? We can hang them on the refrigerator, like an art show."

"Baby stuff," Jenny said, a cynic at five. She hefted an invisible laser rifle and fired. "Z-z-zap! You're zapped, Alex, and totally disengrated."

"Disintergrated, dummy, and I am not either. I threw up my force field."

"Nuh-uh."

They eyed each other with the mutual dislike only siblings can feel after being cooped up on a Saturday. By tacit agreement, they switched to hand-to-hand combat. As they wrestled over the faded Aubusson carpet, Coco cast her gaze to the ceiling.

At least the match was taking place in Alex's room, so little harm could be done. She was tempted to go out and close the door, leaving them to finish up themselves, but she was, after all, responsible.

"Someone's going to get hurt," she began, in the age-old refrain of adult to child. "Remember what happened last week when Jenny gave you a bloody nose, Alex?"

"She did not." Masculine pride rose to the forefront as he struggled to pin his agile sister to the mat.

"Did too, did too," she chanted, hoping to do so again. She scissored her quick little legs over him.

"Excuse me," Trent said from the doorway. "I seem to be interrupting."

"Not at all." Coco fluffed her hair. "Just some youthful high spirits. Children, say hello to Mr. St. James."

"'Lo," Alex said as he struggled to get his sister into a headlock.

Trent's answering grin struck Coco with inspiration. "Trenton, might I ask you a favor?"

"Of course."

"All the girls are working today, as you know, and I have just one or two quick, little errands to run. Would you mind terribly keeping an eye on the children for a short time?"

"An eye on them?"

"Oh, they're no trouble at all." She beamed at him, then down at her grandniece and grandnephew. "Jenny, don't bite your brother. Calhouns fight fair." Unless they fight dirty, she thought. "I'll be back before you know I'm gone," she promised, easing past him.

"Coco, I'm not sure that I—"

"Oh, and don't forget about the séance tonight." She hurried down the steps and left him to fend for himself.

Jenny and Alex stopped wrestling to stare owlishly at him. They would fight tooth and nail but would unite without hesitation against an outside force.

"We don't like baby-sitters," Alex told him dangerously.

Trent rocked back on his heels. "I'm already sure I don't like being one."

Alex's arm was around his sister's shoulders now, rather than her neck. Hers slipped round his waist. "We don't like it more."

Trent nodded. If he could handle a staff of fifty, he could certainly handle two sulky children. "Okay."

"When we went back to Boston last summer for a visit, we had a sitter." Jenny eyed him with suspicion. "We made everybody's life a living hell."

Trent turned the chuckle into a cough. "Is that so?"

"Our father said we did," Alex corroborated. "And he was glad to see the back of us."

The infant profanity was no longer amusing. Trent struggled to keep the burn of anger out of his eyes and merely nodded. Baxter Dumont was obviously a prince among men. "I once locked my nanny in the closet and climbed out the window."

Alex and Jenny exchanged interested glances. "That's pretty good," Alex decided.

"She screamed for two hours," Trent improvised.

"We put a snake in our baby-sitter's bed and she ran out of the house in her nightgown." Jenny smiled smugly and waited to see if he could top it.

"Nicely done." What now? he wondered. "Have you any dolls?"

"Dolls are gross," Jenny said, loyal to her brother.

"Off with their heads!" Alex shouted, sending her into giggles. He sprang up, flourishing his imaginary sword. "I'm the evil pirate, and you're my prisoners."

"Uh-uh, I had to be prisoner last time." Jenny scrambled to her feet. "It's my turn to be the evil pirate."

"I said it first."

She gave him a hefty shove. "Cheater, cheater, cheater."

"Baby, baby, baby," he jeered, and pushed her back.

"Hold it!" Trent shouted before they could dive for each other. The unfamiliar masculine tone had them stopping in their tracks. "*I'm* the evil pirate," he told them, "and you're both about to walk the plank."

He enjoyed it. Their children's imagination might have been a bit bloody-minded, but they played fair when the rules were set. There would have been any number of people he knew socially who would have been stunned to see Trenton St. James III crawling around on the floor or firing a water pistol, but he could remember being closed in on rainy days himself.

The play went from pirates to space marauders to Indian rampage. At the end of a particularly gruesome battle, the three of them were sprawled on the floor. Alex, rubber tomahawk in hand, played dead so long he fell asleep.

"I won," Jenny said, then with her feather headdress falling over her eyes, cuddled against Trent's side. She, too, in the enviable way of children, was asleep in moments.

C.C. found them like that. The rain was patting gently at the windows. In the bath down the hall, a drip fell musically into a bucket. Otherwise there was only the sound of gentle, even breathing.

Alex was sprawled on his face, his fingers still clutched over his weapon. In addition to bodies, the floor was scattered with miniature cars, defeated action figures and a few plastic dinosaurs. Avoiding the casualties, she stepped inside.

She wasn't exactly sure what her feelings were at finding Trent sleeping on the floor with her niece and nephew. What she was certain of was that if she hadn't seen it for herself, she wouldn't have believed it.

His tie and shoes were gone, his hair mussed, and there was a streak of damp down his linen shirt.

The tug on her heart was slow and tender and very real. Why, he looked…sweet, she thought, then immediately jammed her hands into her pockets. That was absurd. A man like Trent was never sweet.

Maybe the kids had knocked him unconscious, she

mused, and leaned over him. He opened his eyes, stared up at her for a moment, then made some kind of sleepy noise deep in his throat.

"What are you doing?" she whispered.

"I'm not completely sure." He lifted his head and looked around. Jenny was tucked into the curve of his arm, and Alex was down for the count on the other side. "But I think I'm the only survivor."

"Where's Aunt Coco?"

"Running a few errands. I'm keeping my eye on the kids."

She lifted a brow. "Oh, I can see that."

"I'm afraid there was a major battle, and many lives were lost."

C.C.'s lips twitched as she went to Alex's bed for a blanket. "Who won?"

"Jenny claimed victory." Gently he slipped his arm out from under her head. "Though Alex will disagree."

"Undoubtedly."

"What should we do with them?"

"Oh, we'll keep them, I suppose."

He grinned back at her. "No, I meant should they be put in bed or something?"

"No." Expertly she flipped open the blanket and spread it over both of them where they lay. "They'll be fine." She had a ridiculous urge to slip an arm around his waist and lay her head on his shoulder. She squashed it ruthlessly. "It was nice of you to offer to look after them."

"I didn't offer precisely. I was dragooned."

"It was still nice of you."

He caught up with her at the door. "I could use a cup of coffee."

C.C. hesitated only a moment. "All right. I'll fix it. It looks like you've earned it." She flicked a glance over her shoulder as she started down the stairs. "How'd your shirt get wet?"

"Oh." He brushed a hand over it, faintly embarrassed. "A direct hit with a death ray disguised as a water pistol. So, how was your day?"

"Not nearly as adventurous as yours." She turned into the kitchen and went directly to the stove. "I only rebuilt an engine."

When the coffee was started, she moved over to light a fire in the kitchen hearth. She had rain in her hair, Trent noticed. He wasn't a lyrical man, but he found himself thinking that the droplets of water looked like a shower of diamonds against the glossy cap.

He'd always preferred women with long hair, he reminded himself. Feminine, soft, wavy. And yet…the style suited C.C., showing off her slender neck, perfectly framing that glorious white skin.

"What are you staring at?"

He blinked, shook his head. "Nothing. Sorry, I was just thinking. It's ah…there's something comforting about a fire in the kitchen."

"Hmm." He looked weird, she thought. Maybe it was the lack of a tie. "Do you want milk in your coffee?"

"No, black."

Her arm brushed his as she walked to the stove. This time it was he who stepped back. "Did Aunt Coco say where she was going?"

Maybe there was static electricity in the air, he thought. That would explain the jolt he'd felt when he'd touched her. "Not exactly. It doesn't matter, the kids were entertaining."

She studied his face as she handed him a mug. "I think you mean it."

"I do. Maybe I haven't been around children enough to become jaded. Those two are quite a pair."

"Suzanna's a terrific mother." Comfortable, she leaned back against the counter as she sipped. "She used to practice on me. So, how's the car running?"

"Better than it has in months." He toasted her with the mug. "I'm afraid I didn't notice anything was off until after you'd worked on it. I don't really know anything about engines."

"That's all right. I don't know how to plot a corporate takeover."

"I was sorry you weren't there when I came around to pick it up. Hank said you'd gone to dinner. I guess you had a good time—you didn't get in until late."

"I always have a good time with Finney." She turned around to raid the cookie jar, then offered him one as he tried to ignore the little nip of jealousy.

"An old friend?"

"I guess you could say so." C.C. took a deep breath and prepared to launch into the speech she had practiced all day. "I'd like to straighten out the business you brought up yesterday."

"It isn't necessary. I got the picture."

"I could have explained things without being so hard on you."

He tilted his head, studying her thoughtfully. "You could have?"

"I like to think so." Determined to wipe the slate clean, she set the coffee aside. "I was embarrassed, and being embarrassed makes me angry. This whole situation is difficult."

He could still hear, very clearly, the unhappiness in her voice as she had spoken with Suzanna the night before. "I think I'm beginning to understand that."

Her eyes came back to his, and she sighed. "Well, in any case, I can't help but resent the fact that you want to buy The Towers, or that we might have to let you— but that's a separate thing from Aunt Coco's maneuvers. I think I realized, after I stopped being mad, that you were just as embarrassed as I was. You were just so damned polite."

"It's a bad habit of mine."

"You're telling me." She waved half a cookie at him. "If you hadn't brought up the kiss—"

"I understand that was an error in judgment, but since I'd already apologized for it, I thought we could deal with it reasonably."

"I didn't want an apology," C.C. muttered. "Then or now."

"I see."

"No, you don't. You certainly don't. What I meant was that an apology was unnecessary. I may be inexperienced by your standards, and I may not be sophisticated like the women you're used to dealing with, but I'm not foolish enough to start weaving daydreams out of one stupid kiss." She was getting angry again and was determined not to. After one deep, cleansing breath, she tried again. "I'd simply like to put that and our conversation yesterday behind us, completely and totally. If it turns out that we will have business dealings, it would be wiser all around if we can be civilized."

"I like you this way."

"What way?"

"When you're not taking potshots at me."

She finished off her cookie and grinned. "Don't get used to it. All Calhouns have hideous tempers."

"So I've been warned. Truce?"

"I suppose. Want another cookie?"

He was staring again, she noted, and her own eyes widened when he reached out to brush his fingertips down her hair. "What are you doing?"

"Your hair's wet." He stroked it again, fascinated. "It smells like wet flowers."

"Trent—"

He smiled. "Yes?"

"I don't think this is the best way to handle things."

"Probably not." But his fingers trailed down through her hair to the nape of her neck. He felt her quick shudder. "I can't quite get you out of my mind. And I keep having these uncontrollable urges to get my hands on you. I wonder why."

"Because—" she wet her lips "—I irritate you."

"Oh, you do that, without question." He pressed those fingers at the back of her neck and had her moving forward an inch. "But not simply in the way you mean. It's not simple at all. Though it should be." His other hand skimmed over the collar of her denim work shirt, then cupped her chin. "Otherwise, why would I feel this irresistible need to touch you every time I get near you?"

"I don't know." His fingers, light as a feather, trailed down to where her pulse thudded at the base of her throat. "I wish you wouldn't."

"Wouldn't what?"

"Touch me."

He slid his hand down her sleeve to her bandaged hand, then lifted it to his lips. "Why?"

"Because you make me nervous."

Something lit in his eyes, turning them almost black. "You don't even mean to be provocative, do you?"

"I wouldn't know how." Her eyes fluttered closed on a strangled moan when he brushed his lips over her jawline.

"Honeysuckle," he murmured, drawing her closer. He'd once thought it such a common flower. "I can all but taste it on you. Wild and sweet."

Her muscles turned to water as his mouth cruised over hers. So much lighter, so much gentler than the first time. It wasn't right that he could do this to her. The part of her mind that was still rational all but shouted it. But even that was drowned out by the flood of longing.

"Catherine." He had her face framed between his hands now as he nipped seductively at her lips. "Kiss me back."

She wanted to shake her head, to pull away and walk casually, even callously out of the room. Instead she flowed into his arms, her mouth lifting to his, meeting his.

His fingers tightened before he could prevent it, then slipped down to pull her more truly against him. He could think of nothing, wanted to think of nothing—no consequences, no rules, no code of behavior. For the first time in his memory, he wanted only to feel. Those sharp and sweet sensations she had racing through him were more than enough for any man.

She was strong—had always been strong—but not enough to prevent time from standing still. It was this one moment, she realized, that she had been waiting for all of her life. As her hands slid up his back, she held the moment to her as completely as she held him.

The fire crackled in the grate. The rain pattered. There was the light, spicy scent of the potpourri Lilah set everywhere about the house. His arms were so strong and sure, yet with a gentleness she hadn't expected from him.

She would remember it all, every small detail, along with the dark excitement of his mouth and the sound of her name as he whispered it against hers.

He drew her away, slowly this time, more shaken than he cared to admit. As he watched, she ran her tongue over her lips as if to savor a last taste. That small, unconscious gesture nearly brought him to his knees.

"No apology this time," he told her, and his voice wasn't steady.

"No."

He touched his lips to hers again. "I want you. I want to make love with you."

"Yes." It was a glorious kind of release. Her lips curved against his. "Yes."

"When?" He buried his face in her hair. "Where?"

"I don't know." She shut her eyes on the wonder of it. "I can't think."

"Don't." He kissed her temple, her cheekbone, her mouth. "This isn't the time for thinking."

"It has to be perfect."

"It will be." He framed her face again. "Let me show you."

She believed him—the words and what she saw in his eyes. "I can't believe it's going to be you." Laughing, she threw her arms around him, holding him close. "That I've waited all my life to be with someone. And it's you."

His hand paused on its way to her hair. "All of your life?"

Dreamily in love, she hugged him tighter. "I thought I'd be afraid the first time, but I'm not. Not with you."

"The first time." He shut his eyes. *Her* first time. How could he have been so stupid? He'd recognized the inexperience, but he hadn't thought, hadn't believed she was completely innocent. And he'd all but seduced her in her own kitchen. "C.C."

"I'm thirsty," Alex complained from the doorway, and had them springing apart like guilty children. He eyed them suspiciously. "What are you doing that stuff for? It's disgusting." He sent Trent a pained look, man-to-man. "I don't get why anybody wants to go around kissing girls."

"It's an acquired taste," Trent told him. "Why don't we get you a drink, then I need to talk to your aunt a minute. Privately."

"More mush stuff."

"What mush stuff?" Amanda wanted to know as she breezed in.

"Nothing." C.C. reached for the coffeepot.

"Lord, did I have a day," Amanda began, and grabbed a cookie.

Suzanna walked in two seconds later, followed by

Lilah. As the kitchen filled with feminine laughter and scent, Trent knew his moment was lost.

When C.C. smiled at him across the room, he was afraid his head would be lost with it.

Chapter 6

It was Trent's first séance. He sincerely hoped it would be his last. There was simply no gracious way to decline attending. When he suggested that perhaps this was a family evening, Coco merely laughed and patted his cheek.

"My dear, we wouldn't think of excluding you. Who knows, it may be you the restless spirits choose to speak through."

The possibility did very little to cheer him up.

Once the children were tucked into bed for the evening, the rest of the family, along with the reluctant Trent, gathered around the dining room table. The stage had been set.

A dozen candles flickered atop the buffet. Dimestore holders cheek by jowl with Meissen and Baccarat. Another trio of white tapers glowed in the center of the table. Even nature seemed to have gotten into the spirit of things—so to speak.

Outside, the rain had turned into a wet fitful snow, blown about by a rising wind. As warm and cold air collided, thunder boomed and lightning flickered.

It was a dark and stormy night, Trent thought fatalistically as he took his seat.

Coco had not, as he'd secretly feared, worn a turban and a fringed shawl. As always, she was meticulously groomed. Around her neck, she did wear a large amethyst crystal, which she toyed with constantly.

"Now, children," she instructed. "Take hands and form the circle."

The wind knocked at the windows as C.C. slipped her hand into Trent's. Coco took his other. Directly across from him Amanda grinned, the amusement and sympathy obvious as she linked with her aunt and Suzanna.

"Don't worry, Trent," she told him. "The Calhoun ghosts are always well behaved around company."

"Concentration is essential," Lilah explained as she closed the gap between her eldest and youngest sister. "And very basic, really. All you have to do is clear your mind, particularly of any cynicism." She winked at Trent. "Astrologically, it's an excellent night for a séance."

C.C. gave his hand a quick, reassuring squeeze as Coco took over.

"We must all clear our minds and open our hearts." She spoke in a soothing monotone. "For some time I've felt that my grandmother, the unhappy Bianca, has wanted to contact me. This was her summer home for the last years of her young life. The place where she spent her most joyous and most tragic moments. The place where she met the man she loved, and lost."

She closed her eyes and took a deep breath. "We are here, Grandmama, waiting for you. We know your spirit is troubled."

"Does a spirit have a spirit?" Amanda wanted to know and earned a glare from her aunt. "It's a reasonable question."

"Behave," Suzanna murmured, and smothered a smile. "Go ahead, Aunt Coco."

They sat in silence, with only Coco's voice murmuring over the crackle of the fire and the moan of the wind. Trent's mind wasn't clear. It was filled with the way C.C. had fit in his arms, with the sweet and generous way her mouth had opened to his. The way she had looked at him, her eyes clouded and warm with emotions. Emotions he had recklessly stirred in her.

Guilt almost smothered him.

She wasn't like Marla or any of the women he had coolly romanced over the years. She was innocent and open and, despite a strong will and a sharp tongue, achingly vulnerable. He had taken advantage of that, inexcusably.

Not that it was entirely his fault, he reminded himself. She was, after all, a beautiful, desirable woman. And he was human. The fact that he wanted her—strictly on a physical plane—was only natural.

He glanced over just as she turned her head and smiled at him. Trent had to fight down a foolish urge to lift her hand to his lips and taste her skin.

She touched something in him, damn it. Something he was determined would remain untouched. When she smiled at him—even when she scowled at him—she made him feel more, want more, wish more, than any woman he'd ever known.

It was ridiculous. They were miles apart in every way. And yet, with her hand warm in his as it was now, he felt closer to her, more in tune with her, than he'd ever felt with anyone.

He could even see them sitting together on a sunny summer porch, watching children play on the grass. The sound of the sea was as soothing as a lullaby. The air smelled of roses climbing up the trellis. And of honeysuckle, growing wild where it chose.

He blinked, afraid his heart had stopped. The image had been so clear and so terrifying. It was the atmosphere, he assured himself. The candles flickering, the wind and lightning. It was playing games with his imagination.

He wasn't a man to sit on the porch with a woman and watch children. He had work, a business to run. The idea of him becoming involved with a bad-tempered auto mechanic was simply absurd.

Cold air seemed to slap him in the face. As he stiffened, he saw the flames of the candles lean dramatically to the left. A draft, he told himself, as the cold chilled him to the bone. The place was full of them.

He felt C.C.'s shudder. When he looked at her, her eyes were wide and dark. Her fingers curled tight around his.

"She's here!" There was both surprise and excitement in Coco's voice. "I'm sure of it."

In her delight, she nearly pulled her hands free and broke the chain. She had believed—well, had wanted to believe—but she had never actually felt a *presence* so distinctly.

She beamed down the table at Lilah, but her niece had her eyes closed and a faint smile on her lips.

"A window must have come open," Amanda said, and would have bolted up to check if Coco hadn't hissed at her.

"No such thing. Sit still, everyone. Sit still. She's here. Can't you feel it?"

C.C. did, and wasn't sure whether she should feel foolish or frightened. Something was different. She was certain that Trent sensed it, as well.

It was as though someone had gently closed a hand over her and Trent's joined ones. The cold vanished, replaced by a soothing, comforting warmth. So real was it that C.C. looked over her shoulder, certain she would see someone standing behind her.

Yet all she saw was the dance of fire and candlelight on the wall.

"She's so lost." C.C. let out a gasp when she realized it was she herself who had spoken. All eyes fixed on hers. Even Lilah's lazily opened.

"Do you see her?" Coco demanded in a whisper, squeezing C.C.'s fingers.

"No. No, of course not. It's just…" She couldn't explain. "It's so sad," she murmured, unaware that tears glistened in her eyes. "Can't you feel it?"

Trent could, and it left him speechless. Heartbreak, and a longing so deep it was immeasurable. Imagination, he told himself. The power of suggestion.

"Don't close it off." Coco searched desperately for the proper procedure. Now that something had actually happened, she hadn't a clue. A flash of lightning had her jolting. "Do you think she'll speak through you?"

At the opposite end of the table, Lilah smiled. "Just tell us what you see, honey."

"A necklace," C.C. heard herself say. "Two tiers of emeralds flanked by diamonds. Beautiful, brilliant." The gleam hurt her eyes. "She's wearing them, but I can't see her face. Oh, she's so unhappy."

"The Calhoun necklace," Coco breathed. "So, it's true."

Then, as if a sigh passed through the air, the candles flickered again, then ran straight and true. A log fell in the grate.

"Weird," Amanda said when her aunt's hand fell limply from hers. "I'll fix the fire."

"Honey." Suzanna studied C.C. with as much concern as curiosity. "Are you okay?"

"Yes." C.C. cleared her throat. "Sure." She shot Trent a quick look. "I guess the storm got to me."

Coco lifted a hand to her breast and patted her speeding heart. "I think we could all use a nice glass of brandy." She rose, more shaken than she wanted to admit, and walked to the buffet.

"Aunt Coco," C.C. began. "What's the Calhoun necklace?"

"The emeralds." She passed the snifters. "There was a legend that's been handed down through the family. You know part of it, how Bianca fell in love with another man, and died tragically. I suppose it's time I told you the rest of it."

"You kept a secret?" Amanda grinned as she swirled her drink. "Aunt Coco, you amaze me."

"I wanted to wait for the right time. It seems it's now." She took her seat again, warming the brandy between her hands. "Rumor was that Bianca's lover was an artist, one of the many who came to the island in those days. She would go to meet him when Fergus was away from the house, which was often. Theirs was not precisely an arranged marriage, but the next thing to it. She was years younger than he, and apparently quite beautiful. Since Fergus destroyed all pictures of her after her death, there's no way of knowing for sure."

"Why?" Suzanna asked. "Why would he do that?"

"Grief perhaps." Coco shrugged.

"Rage, more likely," Lilah put in.

"In any case." Coco paused to sip. "He destroyed all reminders of her, and the emeralds were lost. He had given Bianca the necklace when she gave birth to Ethan, her eldest son." She glanced at Trent. "My father. He was just a child at the time of his mother's death, so the events were never very clear in his mind. But his nanny, who had been fiercely loyal to Bianca, would tell him stories about her. And those he remembered. She didn't care for the necklace, but wore it often."

"As a kind of punishment," Lilah put in. "And a kind of talisman." She smiled at her aunt. "Oh, I've known about the necklace for years. I've seen it—just as C.C. did tonight." She lifted the brandy to her lips. "There are earrings to match. Emerald teardrops, like the stone in the center of the bottom tier."

"You're making that up," Amanda accused her, and Lilah merely moved her shoulders.

"No, I'm not." She smiled at C.C. "Am I?"

"No." Uneasy, C.C. looked to her aunt. "What does all this mean?"

"I'm not altogether sure, but I think the necklace is

still important to Bianca. It was never seen after she died. Some believed Fergus threw it into the sea."

"Not on your life," Lilah said. "The old man wouldn't have thrown a nickel into the sea, much less an emerald necklace."

"Well…" Coco didn't like to speak ill of an ancestor, but she was forced to agree. "Actually, it would have been out of character. Grandpapa counted his pennies."

"He made Silas Marner look like a philanthropist," Amanda put in. "So, what happened to it?"

"That, my dear, is the mystery. My father's nanny told him that Bianca was going to leave Fergus, that she had packed a box, what the nanny called a treasure box. Bianca had secreted away what was most valuable to her."

"But she died instead," C.C. murmured.

"Yes. The legend is that the box, with its treasure, is hidden somewhere in the house."

"Our house?" Suzanna gaped at her aunt. "Do you really think there's some kind of treasure chest hidden around here for—what—eighty years, and no one's found it?"

"It's a very big house," Coco pointed out. "For all we know she might have buried it in the roses."

"If it existed in the first place," Amanda murmured.

"It existed." Lilah sent a nod toward C.C. "And I think Bianca's decided it's time to find it."

When everyone began to talk at once, arguments and suggestions bouncing around the table, Trent raised a hand. "Ladies. Ladies," he repeated, waiting for them to subside. "I realize that this is family business, but as I was invited to participate in this…experiment, I feel obligated to add a calming note. Legends are most often exaggerated and expanded over time. If there ever was a necklace, wouldn't it be more likely that Fergus sold it after the death of his wife?"

"He couldn't sell it," Lilah pointed out, "if he couldn't find it."

"Do any of you really think your great-grandfather buried treasure in the garden or hid it behind a loose stone?" One glance around the table told him that was precisely how they were thinking. Trent shook his head. "That kind of fairy tale's more suited for Alex and Jenny than for grown women." He spread his hands. "You don't even know for certain if there was a necklace in the first place."

"But I saw it," C.C. said, though it made her feel foolish.

"You imagined it," he corrected. "Think about it. A few minutes ago six rational adults were sitting around this table holding hands and calling up ghosts. All right as an odd sort of parlor game, but for anyone to actually believe in messages from the otherworld…" He certainly wasn't going to add that for a moment, he'd felt something himself.

"There's something appealing about a cynical, practical-minded man." Lilah rose to open one of the drawers of the buffet and unearthed a pad and pencil. After coming over to kneel by C.C.'s chair, she began to sketch. "I certainly respect your opinion, but the fact is not only did the necklace exist, I'm certain it still does."

"Because of a nanny's bedtime stories?"

She smiled at him. "No, because of Bianca." She slid the pad toward C.C. "Is that what you saw tonight?"

Lilah had always been a careless and clever artist. C.C. stared at the rough sketch of the necklace, two ornate and filigreed tiers studded with square-cut emeralds, sprinkled with diamond brilliants. From the bottom tier a large gem in the shape of a teardrop dripped.

"Yes." C.C. traced a fingertip over it. "Yes, this is it."

Trent studied the drawing. If indeed such a piece did exist, and Lilah's drawing was anywhere close to scale, it would undoubtedly be worth a fortune.

"Oh, my," Coco murmured as the pad was passed to her. "Oh, my."

"I think Trent has a point." Amanda gave the sketch a hard look before handing it to Suzanna. "We can hardly take the house apart stone by stone, even if we wanted to. Despite any sort of paranormal experience, the first order of business is to make certain—absolutely certain," she added when Lilah sighed, "that the necklace is a fact. Even eighty years ago, something like this had to cost an incredible amount of money. There has to be a record. If Lilah's famous vibes are wrong and it was sold again, there would be a record of that as well."

"Spoken like a true stick-in-the-mud," Lilah complained. "I guess this means we spend our Sunday pushing through a paper mountain."

C.C. didn't even try to sleep. She wrapped herself in her flannel robe and, with the house creaking around her, left her room for Trent's. She could hear the murmur of the late news from Amanda's room. Then the hum of sitars from Lilah's. It didn't occur to her to feel awkward or to hesitate. She simply knocked on Trent's door and waited for him to answer.

When he did, with his shirt open and his eyes a little sleepy, she felt her first frisson of nerves.

"C.C.?"

"I need to talk to you." She glanced toward the bed, then away. "Can I come in?"

How was a man to deal fairly when even flannel had become erotic? "Maybe it would be better if we waited until morning."

"I'm not sure I can."

The knots in his stomach tightened. "Okay. Sure." The sooner he explained himself to her, the better. He hoped. Trent let her in and closed the door. "Do you want to sit down?"

"Too much nervous energy." Hugging herself, she walked to the window. "It stopped snowing. I'm glad. I know Suzanna was worried about some of her flowers. Spring's so unpredictable on the island." She dragged a hand through her hair as she turned. "I'm making small talk, and I hate that." A deep breath settled her. "Trent, I need to know what you think about tonight. Really think about it."

"Tonight?" he said carefully.

"The séance." She rubbed her hands over her face. "Lord, I feel like an imbecile even saying it, but, Trent, something happened." Now she thrust those restless hands toward him, waiting for him to clasp them in his. "I'm very grounded, very literal minded. Lilah's the one who believes in all this stuff. But now…Trent, I need to know. Did you feel anything?"

"I don't know what you mean. I certainly felt foolish several times."

"Please." She gave his hands an impatient shake. "Be honest with me. It's important."

Wasn't that what he'd promised himself he would do? "All right, C.C. Tell me what you felt."

"The air got very cold. Then it was as if something—someone—was standing behind us. Behind and between the two of us. It wasn't something that frightened me. I was surprised, but not afraid. We were holding hands, like this. And then..."

She was waiting for him to say it, to admit it. Those big green eyes demanded it. When he did so, it was with great reluctance. "It felt as though someone put a hand over ours."

"Yes." Eyes closed, she brought his hands to her curved lips. "Yes, exactly."

"Shared hallucination," he began, but she cut him off with a laugh.

"I don't want to hear that. No rational explanations." She pressed his hand to her cheek. "I'm not a fanciful person, but I know it meant something, something important. I *know*."

"The necklace?"

"Only a part of it—and not this part. All the rest— the necklace, the legend, we'll figure it out sooner or later. I think we'll have to because it's meant. But this, this was like a blessing."

"C.C.—"

"I love you." Eyes dark and brilliant, she touched his cheek. "I love you, and nothing in my life has ever felt so right."

He was speechless. Part of him wanted to step back, smile kindly and tell her she was letting the moment run away with her. Love didn't happen in a matter of days. If it happened at all, which was rare, it took years.

Another part, buried deep, wanted to hold her close so that the moment would never end.

"Catherine—"

But she was already moving into his arms. They seemed to be waiting for her. As if he had no control over them, they wrapped around her. The warmth, her warmth, seeped into him like a drug.

"I think I knew the first time you kissed me." She pressed her cheek to his. "I didn't want it, didn't ask for it, but it's never been like that for me before. I don't think I ever expected it to be. There you were, so suddenly, so completely in my life. Kiss me again, Trent. Kiss me now."

He was helpless to do otherwise. His lips were already burning for hers. When they met, the fire only sparked hotter. She was molten in his arms, sending white licks of flame shooting through his system. When he couldn't prevent his demand from increasing, she didn't hesitate, but strained against him, offering everything.

She slid her hands under his shirt, delighted to feel his quick, involuntary tremor. His muscles bunched under her fingers with the kind of strength she wanted, needed.

The wind sighed outside the windows as she sighed in his arms.

He couldn't get enough. He found himself wanting to devour her as his lips raced crazily over her face, down her throat where his teeth scraped lightly over her skin. The scent of honeysuckle wheeled in his head. She arched back, her low whimpers of pleasure pounding in his blood.

He had to touch her. He would go mad if he didn't.

Mad if he did. When he parted her robe, he groaned, discovering she was naked for him beneath. Desperate, he filled his hand with her.

Now she knew what it was to have the blood swim. She could all but feel it racing under her skin, beating hot wherever he touched. There was a weakness here, a glorious one, mixed with a kind of manic strength. She wanted to give him both somehow and found the way when his mouth came frantically back to hers.

She trembled even as she answered. She surrendered even as she heated. As her head fell back and her fingers dug hard into his shoulders, he felt something move through him that was more than desire, deeper than passion.

Happiness. Hope. Love. As he recognized the feelings, terror joined them.

Breath heaving, he pulled away.

Her robe had fallen off one shoulder, baring it. Already his mouth had supped there. Her eyes were as brilliant as the emeralds she had imagined. Smiling, she lifted a trembling hand to his cheek.

"Do you want me to stay tonight?"

"Yes—no." Holding her at arm's length was the hardest thing he'd ever done. "Catherine…" He did want her to stay, he realized. Not just tonight, and not simply because of that glorious body of hers. The fact that he did made it all the more important to set things right. "I don't—I haven't been fair with you, and this has gotten out of hand so quickly." A long, unsteady breath escaped him. "Lord, you're beautiful. No," he said quickly when she smiled and started to step forward. "We need to talk. Just talk."

"I thought we had."

If she continued to look at him that way, he'd stop giving a damn about fairness. Or his own survival. "I haven't made myself clear," he began slowly. "If I had known—if I had realized how completely innocent you are, I wouldn't—well, I hope I would have been more careful. Now I can only try to make up for it."

"I don't understand."

"No, that's the problem." Needing some distance, he walked away. "I said I was attracted to you, very attracted. And that's obviously true. But I would never have taken advantage of you if I had known."

Suddenly cold, she drew the robe around her. "You're upset because I haven't been with a man before?"

"Not upset." Frustrated, he turned back. "'Upset' isn't the word. I can't seem to find one. There are rules, you see." But she only continued to stare at him. "Catherine, a woman like you expects—deserves—more than I can give you."

She lowered her gaze to her hands as she carefully fastened the belt to her robe. "What is that?"

"Commitment. A future."

"Marriage."

"Yes."

Her knuckles were turning white. "I suppose you think this—what I said—is part of Aunt Coco's plans."

"No." He would have gone to her then if he'd dared. "No, of course I don't."

"Well." She struggled to make her fingers relax. "That's something, I suppose."

"I know your feelings are honest—exaggerated perhaps—but honest. And it's completely my fault. If this hadn't happened so quickly, I would have explained to you from the first that I have no intention of marrying, ever. I don't believe that two people can be loyal to each other, much less happy together for a lifetime."

"Why?"

"Why?" He stared at her. "Because it simply doesn't work. I've watched my father go from marriage to divorce to marriage. It's like watching a tennis match. The last time I heard from my mother, she was on her third marriage. It simply isn't practical to make vows knowing they'll only be broken."

"Practical," she repeated with a slow nod. "You won't let yourself feel anything for me because it would be impractical."

"The problem is I do feel something for you."

"Not enough." Only enough to cut out her heart. "Well, I'm glad we got that sorted out." Blindly she turned for the door. "Good night."

"C.C." He laid a hand on her shoulder before she could find the knob.

"Don't apologize," she said, praying her control would hold a few more minutes. "It isn't necessary. You've explained it all perfectly."

"Damn it, why don't you yell at me? Call me a few of the names I'm sure I deserve." He'd have preferred that to the quiet desolation he'd seen in her eyes.

"Yell at you?" She made herself turn and face him. "For being fair and honest? Call you names? How can I call you names, Trent, when I feel so terribly sorry for you?"

His hand slipped away from her. She held her head up. Under the hurt, just under it, was pride.

"You're throwing away something—no, not throwing," she corrected. "You're politely handing back something you'll never have again. What you've turned out of your life, Trent, would have been the best part of it."

She left him alone with the uneasy feeling that she was absolutely right.

There was a party tonight. I thought it would be good for me to fill the house with people and lights and flowers. I know that Fergus was pleased that I supervised all the details so carefully. I had wondered if he had noticed my distraction, or how often I walked along the cliffs these afternoons, or how many hours I have begun to spend in the tower, dreaming my dreams. But it does not seem so.

The Greenbaums were here, and the McAllisters and the Prentisses. Everyone who summers on the island, that Fergus feels we should take note of, attended. The ballroom was banked with gardenias and red roses. Fergus had hired an orchestra from New York, and the music was both lovely and lively. I believe Sarah McAllister drank too much champagne, for her laugh began to grate on my nerves long before supper was served.

My new gold dress suited very well, I think, for it gathered many compliments. Yet when I danced with Ira Greenbaum, his eyes were on my emeralds. They hung like a shackle around my neck.

How unfair I am! They are beautiful, and mine only because Ethan is mine.

During the evening, I slipped up to the nursery to check on the children, though I know how doting Nanny is to all of them. Ethan woke and sleepily asked if I had brought him any cake.

He looks like an angel as he sleeps, he and my other sweet babies. My love for them is so rich, so deep, that I wonder why it is my heart cannot transfer any of that sweet feeling to the man who fathered them.

Perhaps the fault is in me. Surely that must be so. When I kissed them good-night and stepped out into the hall again, I wished so desperately that rather than go back to the ballroom to laugh and dance, I could run to the cliffs. To stand at the cliffs with the wind in my hair and the sound and smells of the sea everywhere.

Would he come to me then, if I dared such a thing? Would he come so that we would stand there together in the shadows, reaching out for something we have no business wanting, much less taking?

I did not go to the cliffs. My duty is my husband, and it was to him I went. Dancing with him, my heart felt as cold as the jewels around my neck. Yet I smiled when he complimented me on my skill as a hostess. His hand at my waist was so aloof, but so possessive. As we moved to the music, his eyes scanned the room, approving what was his, studying his guests to be certain they were impressed.

How well I know what status and opinion mean to the man I married. And how little it seems they have come to mean to me.

I wanted to shout at him, "Fergus, for God's sake, look at me. Look at me and see. Make me love you, for fear and respect cannot be enough for either of us. Make me love you so that I will never again turn my steps toward the cliffs and what waits for me there."

But I did not shout. When he told me impatiently that it was necessary for me to dance with Cecil Barkley, I murmured my assent.

Now the music is done and the lamps are snuffed out. I wonder when I will see Christian again. I wonder what will become of me.

Chapter 7

C.C. sat cross-legged in the center of an ocean of papers. Her assignment—whether or not she'd chosen to accept it—had been to go through all of the notes and receipts and scraps that had been stuffed into three cardboard boxes marked *miscellaneous*.

Nearby Amanda sat at a card table, with several more bulging boxes at her feet. With her hair clipped back and reading glasses sliding down her nose, she meticulously studied each paper before laying it on one of the various stacks she had started.

"This should have been done decades ago," she commented.

"You mean it should have been burned decades ago."

"No." Amanda shoved the glasses back into place. "Some of it's fascinating, and certainly deserves to be preserved. Stuffing papers into cardboard boxes is not my idea of preserving family history."

"Does a recipe for gooseberry jam rate as family history?"

"For Aunt Coco it does. That goes under kitchen, subheading menus."

C.C. shifted then waved away a cloud of dust. "How about a bill for six pairs of white kid gloves and a blue silk parasol?"

"Clothing, by the date. Hmm, this is interesting. Aunt Coco's progress report from her fourth-grade teacher. And I quote, 'Cordelia is a delightfully gregarious child. However, she tends to daydream and has trouble finishing assigned projects.'"

"That's a news flash." Stiff, C.C. arched her back and rotated her head. Beside her, the sun was streaming through the smudges on the storeroom window. With a little sigh, she rested her elbows on her knees and studied it.

"Where the devil is Lilah?" Impatient as always, Amanda tapped her foot as she grumbled. "Suzanna had dispensation because she took the kids to the matinee, but Lilah's supposed to be on duty."

"She'll show up," C.C. murmured.

"Sure. When it's done." Digging into a new pile, Amanda sneezed twice. "This is some of the dirtiest stuff I've ever seen."

C.C. shrugged. "Everything gets dirty if it sits around long enough."

"No, I mean really dirty. It's a limerick written by Great-Uncle Sean. 'There was a young lady from Maine, whose large breasts drove the natives insane. They...' Never mind," Amanda decided. "We'll start a file on attempted pornography." When C.C. made no comment, she glanced over to see her sister still staring at a sunbeam. "You okay, sweetie?"

"Hmm? Oh, yeah. I'm fine."

"You don't look like you slept very well."

C.C. shrugged then busied herself with papers again. "I guess the séance threw me off."

"Not surprising." Her lips pursed as she sorted through more receipts. "I never put any stock in that business. Bianca's tower was one thing. I guess we've all felt something—well, something up there. But I always thought that it was because we knew Bianca had tossed herself out of the window. Then last night…" When the shiver caught her, she rubbed her chilled arms. "I know that you really saw something, really experienced something."

"I know the necklace is real," C.C. said.

"I'll agree it *was* real—especially when I have a receipt in my hand."

"Was and is. I don't think I would have seen it if it had been pawned or tossed into the sea. It might sound loony, but I know Bianca wants us to find it."

"It does sound loony." With a sigh, Amanda leaned back in the creaking chair. "And what's loonier is that I think so, too. I just hope nobody at the hotel finds out I'm spending my free time looking for a buried treasure because my long-dead ancestor told us to. Oh!"

"Did you find it?" C.C. was already scrambling up.

"No, no, it's an old date book. 1912. The ink's a bit faded, but the handwriting's lovely—definitely feminine. It must be Bianca's. Look. 'Send invitations.' And here's the guest list. Wow, some party. The Prentises." Amanda took off her glasses to gnaw on the earpiece.

"I bet they were Prentise Hall—one of the cottages that burned in '47."

"'Speak to gardener about roses,'" C.C. read over her sister's shoulder. "'Final fitting on gold ball gown. Meet Christian, 3:00 p.m.' Christian?" She laid a tensed hand on Amanda's shoulder. "Could that have been her artist?"

"Your guess is as good as mine." Quickly Amanda pushed her glasses back on. "But look here. 'Have clasp on emeralds strengthened.' Those could be the ones."

"They have to be."

"We still haven't found any receipts."

C.C. gave a tired look at the papers littering the room. "What are our chances?"

Even Amanda's organizational skills quaked. "Well, they improve every time we eliminate a box."

"Mandy." C.C. sat on the floor beside her. "We're running out of time, aren't we?"

"We've only been at it for a few hours."

"That's not what I mean." She rested her cheek on Amanda's thigh. "You know it's not. Even if we find the receipt, we still have to find the necklace. It could take years. We don't have years. We're going to have to sell, aren't we?"

"We'll talk about it tomorrow night, at the family meeting." Troubled, she stroked C.C.'s hair. "Look, why don't you go take a nap? You really do look beat."

"No." She rose, pacing over the papers to the windows and back. "I'm better off keeping my mind and my hands busy. Otherwise, I might strangle someone."

"Trent, for instance?"

"An excellent place to start. No." With a sigh, she

stuck her hands into her pockets. "No, this mess isn't really his fault."

"Are we still talking about the house?"

"I don't know." Miserable, she sat on the floor again. At least she could be grateful she'd cried herself dry the night before. "I've decided that all men are stupid, selfish and totally unnecessary."

"You're in love with him."

A wry smile curved her lips. "Bingo. And to answer your next question, no, he doesn't love me back. He's not interested in me, a future, a family, and he's very sorry he didn't make that clear to me before I made the mistake of falling for him."

"I'm sorry, C.C." After taking off her glasses, Amanda got up to cross the room and sit on the floor beside her sister. "I know how it must hurt, but you've only known him for a few days. Infatuation—"

"It's not infatuation." Idly she folded the recipe for jam into a paper airplane. "I've found out that falling in love doesn't have anything to do with time. It can take a year or an instant. It happens when it's ready to happen."

Amanda put an arm around C.C.'s shoulders and squeezed. "Well, I don't know anything about that. Fortunately, I've never had to worry about it." The fact made her frown, but only for a moment. "I do know this. If he hurt you, we'll make him sorry he ever crossed a Calhoun."

C.C. laughed then sent the gooseberry plane flying. "It's tempting, but I think it's more a matter of me hurting myself." She gave herself a little shake. "Come on, let's get back to work."

They'd barely gotten started again when Trent came

in. He looked at C.C., met a solid wall of ice. When he turned to Amanda, he fared little better.

"I thought you might be able to use some help," he told them.

Amanda glanced at C.C., noted her sister was employing the silent treatment. A very effective weapon, in Amanda's estimation. "That's nice of you, Trent." Amanda gave him a smile that would have frosted molten lava. "But this is really a family problem."

"Let him help." C.C. didn't even bother to look up. "I imagine he's just terrific at pushing papers."

"All right then." With a shrug, Amanda indicated another folding chair. "You can use that if you like. I'm organizing according to content and year."

"Fine." He took the chair and sat across from her. They worked in frigid silence, with the crinkle of papers and the tap of Amanda's shoe.

"Here's a repair bill," he said—and was ignored. "For repairing a clasp."

"Let me see." Amanda had already snatched it out of his hand before C.C. made the dash across the room. "It doesn't say what kind of necklace," she muttered.

"But the dates are right." C.C. stabbed a finger on it. "July 16, 1912."

"Have I missed something?" Trent asked them.

Amanda waited a beat, saw that C.C. wasn't going to answer and glanced up herself. "We came across a date book of Bianca's. She had a note to take the emeralds to have the clasp repaired."

"This might be what you need." His eyes were on C.C., but it was Amanda who answered.

"It may be enough to satisfy all of us that the Calhoun necklace existed in 1912, but it's a long way from helping us find it." She set the receipt aside. "Let's see what else we can turn up."

In silence, C.C. went back to her papers.

A few moments later, Lilah called from the base of the stairs. "Amanda! Phone!"

"Tell them I'll call back."

"It's the hotel. They said it's important."

"Damn." She set down the glasses before sending Trent a narrowed look. "I'll be back in a few minutes."

He waited until the sound of her rapid footsteps had finished echoing. "She's very protective."

"We stick together," C.C. commented, and set a paper on a pile without a clue to its contents.

"I've noticed. Catherine…"

Braced, C.C. flicked him her coolest glance. "Yes?"

"I wanted to make certain you were all right."

"All right. In what way?"

She had dust on her cheek. He wanted, badly, to smile and tell her. To hear her laugh as she brushed it off. "After last night—I know how upset you were when you left my room."

"Yes, I was upset." She turned over another piece of paper. "I guess I made quite a scene."

"No, that's not what I meant."

"I did." She forced her lips to curve. "I guess I'm the one who should apologize this time. The séance, all that happened during it, went to my head." Not my head, she thought, but my heart. "I must have sounded like an idiot when I came to your room."

"No, of course not." She was so cool, he thought. So composed. And she baffled him. "You said you loved me."

"I know what I said." Her voice dropped another ten

degrees, but her smile stayed in place. "Why don't we both chalk it up to the mood of the moment?"

That was reasonable, he realized. So why did he feel so lost? "Then you didn't mean it?"

"Trent, we've only known each other for a few days." Did he want to make her suffer? she wondered.

"But you looked so—devastated when you left."

She arched a brow. "Do I look devastated now?"

"No," he said slowly. "No, you don't."

"Well, then. Let's forget it." As she spoke, the sun lost itself behind the clouds. "That would be best for both of us, wouldn't it?"

"Yes." It was just what he'd wanted. Yet he felt empty when he stood up again. "I do want what's best for you, C.C."

"Fine." She studied the paper in her hand. "If you're going down, ask Lilah to bring up some coffee when she comes."

"All right."

She waited until she was sure he was gone before she covered her face with her hands. She'd been wrong, C.C. discovered. She hadn't nearly cried herself dry.

Trent went back to his room. His briefcase was there, stacked with work he had intended to do while away from his office. Taking a seat at the scarred knee-hole desk, he opened a file.

Ten minutes later, he was staring out the window without having glanced at the first word.

He shook himself, picked up his pen and ordered himself to concentrate. He succeeded in reading the first word, even the first paragraph. Three times. Disgusted, he tossed the pen aside and rose to pace.

It was ridiculous, he thought. He had worked in hotel suites all over the world. Why should this room be any different? It had walls and windows, a ceiling—so to speak. The desk was more than adequate. He could even, if he chose, light a fire to add some cheer. And some warmth. God knew he could use some warmth after the thirty icy minutes he'd spent in the storeroom. There was no reason why he shouldn't be able to sit down and take care of some business for an hour or two.

Except that he kept remembering—how lovely C.C. had looked when she'd come into the room in her gray flannel robe and bare feet. He could still see the way her eyes had glowed when she had stood almost where he was standing now, smiling at him. Frowning, he rubbed at a dull pain around his heart. He wasn't accustomed to aches there. Headaches certainly. Never heartaches.

But the memory of the way she'd slipped into his arms haunted him. And her taste—why was it that it still hovered just a breath from his own lips?

It was guilt, that was all, he assured himself. He had hurt her, the way he was certain he'd never hurt another woman. No matter how cool she had been today, no matter how composed, that was a guilt he would live with for a long time.

Maybe if he went up and talked to her again. His hand was on the knob before he stopped himself. That would only make things worse, if possible. Just because he wanted to assuage some guilt was no excuse to put her in an uncomfortable position again.

She was handling it, better than he by all accounts.

She was strong, obviously resilient. Proud. Soft, his mind wandered. Warm. Incredibly beautiful.

On an oath he began to pace again. It would be wiser for him to concentrate on the house rather than any of its occupants. The few days he'd spent in it might have caused a personal upheaval, but it had given him time and opportunity to formulate plans. From the inside. It had given him a taste of the mood and tone and the history. And if he could settle down for a few moments, he could put some of those thoughts on paper.

But it was hopeless. The minute he took his pen in hand, his mind went blank. He was feeling closed in, Trent told himself. He just needed some air. Snatching up a jacket, he did something he hadn't given himself time to do in months.

He took a walk.

Following instinct, he headed toward the cliffs. Down the uneven lawn, around a crumbling stone wall. Toward the sea. The air had a bite. It seemed that spring had decided to pick up her pretty skirts and retreat. The sky was gray and moody, with a few hopeful patches of blue. Wildflowers that had been brave enough to shove their way through rock and soil blew fitfully in the wind.

Trent walked with his hands in his pockets, and his head down. Depression wasn't a familiar sensation, and he was determined to walk it off. When he glanced back, he could just see the peaks of towers above and behind. He turned away and faced the sea—unknowingly mirroring the stance of a man who had painted there decades before.

Breathtaking. It was the only word that came to his mind. Rocks tumbled dizzily down, pink and gray where the wind buffeted them, black where the water struck and funneled. Bad-tempered whitecaps churned, slicing at the darker water. Smoky fog rolled and shredded, and the air held a fresh threat of rain.

It should have been gloomy. It was simply spectacular.

He wished she was with him. That she would be here, now, beside him before time passed or the wind changed. She would smile, he thought. Laugh, as she planted those long, gorgeous legs and lifted her face to the blow. If she had been there, the beauty of it wouldn't make him feel so lonely. So damned lonely.

The tingle at the base of his neck had him turning, nearly reaching out. He'd been so certain that he would look and see her walking toward him. There was nothing but the slope of rock, and the wind. Yet the feeling of another presence remained, very real, so that he almost called out.

He was a sensible man, Trent assured himself. He knew he was alone. Yet it seemed as though someone was there with him, waiting. Watching. For a moment, he was certain he caught the light, drifting scent of honeysuckle.

Imagination, he decided, but his hand wasn't quite steady as he lifted it to push the blowing hair out his eyes.

Then there was weeping. Trent froze as he listened to the sad, quiet sound that sobbed just under the wind. It ebbed and flowed, like the sea itself. Something clenched inside his stomach as he strained to hear—though common sense told him there could be nothing to hear.

A nervous breakdown? he wondered. But the sound

was real, damn it. Not a hallucination. Slowly, ears pricked, he climbed down a jumble of rocks.

"Who's there?" he shouted as the sound sighed and drifted on the wind. Chasing it, he hurried down, driven by an urgency that drummed through his blood. A shower of loose stones rattled into space, bringing him sharply back to reality.

What in God's name was he doing? Scrambling down a cliff wall after a ghost? He lifted his hands and saw that despite the brisk wind his palms were sweating. All he could hear now was the frantic pounding of his own heart. After forcing himself to stand still and take a few calming breaths, he looked around for the easiest form of ascent.

He had just started back when the sound came again. Weeping. No, he realized. Whimpering. It was quite clear now and nearly under his feet. Crouching, Trent searched behind an outcrop of rock.

It was a poor, pitiful sight, he thought. The little black puppy was hardly more than a ball of fur-covered bones. Relief poured through him, making him laugh out loud. He wasn't going crazy after all. As Trent studied it, the terrified pup tried to inch back, but there was nowhere to go. Its little frightened eyes fixed on Trent as it trembled.

"Had a rough time, have you?" Cautiously Trent reached out, ready to snatch his hand back if the pup snapped. Instead it simply cowered and whined. "It's okay, fella. Relax. I won't hurt you." Gently he stroked the puppy between the ears with his fingertips. Still shivering, the pup licked Trent's hand. "Guess you're feeling pretty lonely." He sighed as he calmed the dog. "Me, too. Why don't we go back to the house?"

He gathered the dog up, zipping it inside his jacket for the climb. When he was halfway to the top, Trent stopped then turned blindly around. It was at least fifty yards from where he had stood looking out to sea to where he had discovered the stray. His palms grew damp again when he realized it would have been impossible for him to have heard the puppy's whines from the ridge above. The distance and the wind would have smothered the whimpers. Yet he had heard…something. And, hearing it, had climbed down to find the lost dog.

"What the devil was it?" Trent murmured, and cuddling the pup closer, headed for home. He was just beginning to feel foolish when he crossed the lawn. What was he supposed to say to his hostesses? *Look what followed me home?* How about… *Guess what? I decided to take my life in my hands and climb back down the cliff. Look what I found.* Neither opening seemed quite suitable.

The sensible thing would be to get in the car and drive the dog down to the village. There was bound to be an animal shelter or vet. He could hardly march into the parlor and dump his find on the rug.

But he couldn't, Trent discovered. He simply couldn't turn the shivering ball of fur over to strangers. The little guy trusted him and was even now curling softly under his heart. As he stood hesitating, C.C. came out of the house.

Trent shifted and tried to look natural. "Hi."

"Hi." She paused to button her denim jacket. "We're out of milk. Do you need anything from the village?"

A can of dog food, he thought, and cleared his

throat. "No, thanks. I, ah…" The pup wriggled against his shirt. "Did you find anything?"

"Lots of things, but nothing that tells us where to look for the necklace." Her misery turned to curiosity as she watched the ripples run along his jacket. "Is everything all right?"

"Fine. Just fine. "Trent cleared his throat, folded his arms. "I took a walk."

"Okay." It was awful, she thought, just awful. He could hardly meet her eyes. "Aunt Coco's making a light lunch if you're hungry."

"Oh—thanks."

She started to move by him when a high-pitched yip stopped her in her tracks. "What?"

"Nothing." He smothered an involuntary chuckle as the puppy wiggled along his ribs.

"Are you all right?"

"Yes, yes, I'm fine." He gave her a sheepish smile as the dog poked his nose above the zipper of the jacket.

"What have you got?" C.C. forgot her vow to keep her distance and stepped closer to tug the zipper down. "Oh! Trent, it's a puppy."

"I found him down in the rocks," he began quickly. "I wasn't sure just what to—"

"Oh, you poor little thing." She was already cooing as she gathered the puppy to her. "Are you lost?" She rubbed her cheek over its fur, nuzzled nose to nose. "There now, it's all right." The puppy wagged his tail so fast and hard he nearly fell out of her grip.

"Cute, isn't he?" Grinning, Trent moved closer to stroke. "Looks like he's been on his own for a while."

"He's just a baby." She crooned and cuddled. "Where did you say you found him?"

"Down on the rocks. I was walking." *And thinking of you.* Before he could stop himself, Trent reached out to touch her hair. "I couldn't just leave him there."

"Of course not." She looked up and saw that she was all but in his arms. His hand was in her hair, his eyes on hers.

"Catherine—"

The pup yipped again and had her jolting back. "I'll take him in. He must be cold, and hungry."

"All right." The only place left for his hands was his pockets. "Why don't I run down and get the milk?"

"Okay." Her smile was strained as she backed toward the steps. She turned and, murmuring to the puppy, dashed inside.

By the time Trent returned, the stray had a place of honor by the kitchen hearth and the undivided attention of four beautiful women.

"Wait until Suze and the kids get back," Amanda was saying. "They'll flip. He sure goes for your liver pâté, Aunt Coco."

"Obviously a gourmet among dogs." Lilah, already on her hands and knees, leaned her nose against his. "Aren't you, cutie?"

"I'm sure he should have something more bland." Coco was also on the floor, charmed. "With the proper care, he'll be very handsome."

The pup, amazed at his good fortune, raced in circles. Spotting Trent, he gamboled over, tripping over his own feet. The women scrambled up, all asking him questions at the same time.

"Hold on." Trent set the grocery bag on the table, then crouched down to scratch the pup's belly. "I don't know where he came from. I found him when I was walking along the cliffs. He was hiding out. Weren't you, boy?"

"I suppose we should ask around, to see if anyone's lost him," Coco began, then held up a hand as her nieces voiced unanimous dissent. "It's only right. But it is up to Trent, since he found him."

"I think you should do what you think's best." He rose to pull the milk out of the bag. "He could probably use some of this."

Amanda already had a saucer and was arguing with Lilah on the proper amount to give their new guest.

"What else did you get?" C.C. poked at the bag.

"A few things." He moved his shoulders, then gave up. "I thought he should have a collar." Trent pulled out a bright red collar with silver studs.

C.C. couldn't hold back the grin. "Very fashionable."

"And a leash." Trent set that on the table, as well. "Puppy food."

"Uh-huh." C.C. began to go through the bag herself. "And puppy treats, rawhide bones."

"He'll want to gnaw," Trent told her.

"Sure, he will. A ball and a squeaky mouse." Laughing, she squeezed the rubber toy.

"He should have something to play with." He didn't want to add that he'd searched for a dog bed and cushion but hadn't come across them.

"I didn't know you were a softie."

He glanced down at the happily lapping puppy. "Neither did I."

"What's his name?" Lilah wanted to know.

"Well, I..."

"You found him, you get to name him."

"Do it quick," Amanda advised him. "Before Lilah sticks him with something like Griswold."

"Fred," Trent said on impulse. "He looks like a Fred to me."

Unimpressed with his christening, Fred plopped down with one ear in the saucer of milk and went to sleep.

"Well, that's settled." Amanda gave the pup one last pat before she rose. "Come on, Lilah, it's your turn to take a shift."

"I'll give you a hand." Instincts humming, Coco hustled her two nieces out of the room and left C.C. alone with Trent.

"I'd better go, too." C.C. started for the door. Trent laid a hand on her arm to stop her.

"Wait."

"What for?"

"Just...wait."

She stood, battling back hurt. "I'm waiting."

"I— How's your hand?"

"It's fine."

"Good." He felt like an idiot. "That's good."

"If that's all..."

"No. I wanted to tell you...I noticed a rattle in the car when I drove down to the village."

"A rattle?" She pursed her lips. "What kind of rattle?"

An imaginary one, he thought, but shrugged. "Just a rattle. I was hoping you could take a look at it."

"All right. Bring it in tomorrow."

"Tomorrow?"

"My tools are at the shop. Is there anything else?"

"When I was walking, I kept wishing you were with me."

She looked away until she was sure she had rebuilt the chink he'd just knocked in her defensive wall. "We want different things, Trent. Let's just leave it at that." She turned toward the door. "Try to get your car in early," she added without looking around. "I've got an exhaust system to replace tomorrow."

Chapter 8

C.C. fired up her torch, flipped down her faceplate and prepared to cut off the tail pipe on the rusted exhaust of a '62 Plymouth.

The day was not going well.

She wasn't able to get the scheduled family meeting off her mind. No other paperwork on the necklace had shown up, though they had gone through reams and reams of receipts and old ledgers. She knew, because of Amanda's refusal to talk, that the news wasn't good.

Added to that had been another restless night. She heard Fred's whimpering and had gone to check on him only to hear Trent's low murmuring soothing the puppy behind his bedroom door.

She'd stood there for a long time, listening.

The fact that he'd taken the stray into his room, cared enough to comfort and nurture, only made C.C.

love him more. And the more she loved, the more she hurt.

She knew she was hollow-eyed this morning, because she'd made the mistake of looking at a mirror. That she could handle. Her looks had never been a major concern. The bills she had found in the morning mail were.

She'd been telling the truth when she'd told Suzanna the business was doing well. But there were still rough spots. Not all of her customers paid promptly, and her cash flow was too often merely a trickle. Six months, she thought as she cut through the old metal. She only needed six months. But that was too long, much too long to help keep The Towers.

Her life was changing, changing fast, and none of it seemed to be for the better.

Trent stood watching her. She had some battered hulk of a car up on the lift and stood under it, wielding a torch. While he watched, she shifted aside as a pipe clattered to the floor. She was wearing coveralls again, thick safety gloves and a helmet. The music she never seemed to be without jingled from the radio on the workbench.

Surely a man was over the edge when he thought how delightful it would be to make love on a concrete floor with a woman who was dressed like a welder.

C.C. changed positions, then saw him. Very carefully she shut off the torch before she lifted the shield of her helmet.

"I couldn't find anything wrong with your car. Keys are in the office. No charge." She flipped down the shield again.

"C.C."

"What?"

"How about dinner?"

She pushed back the shield and eyed him warily. "How about it?"

"I mean…" With a leery glance overhead, he stepped under the car with her. "I'd like you to have dinner with me tonight."

She shifted her weight. "I've had dinner with you every night for several nights." She flipped the shield down. Trent flipped it up again.

"No, I mean I want to take you out to dinner."

"Why?"

"Why not?"

She lifted a brow. "Well, that's very nice, but I'm a little pressed tonight. We're having a family meeting." She pulled down the shield again and prepared to relight the torch.

"Tomorrow then." Annoyed, Trent pushed the shield back up. "Do you mind? I like to see you when I talk to you."

"Yes, I mind because I've got work. And no, I won't have dinner with you tomorrow."

"Why?"

She blew out a long breath that ruffled her bangs. "Because I don't want to."

"You're still angry with me."

Her eyes, which had begun to heat, went flat. "We settled all that, so there's no reason to go out on a date."

"Just dinner," he said, finding he couldn't let go. "No one's calling it a date. One simple meal, as friends, before I go back to Boston."

"You're going back?" She felt her heart drop to her knees and turned away to rattle through some tools.

"Yes, I have meetings scheduled for the middle of the week. I'm expected in the office Wednesday afternoon."

Just like that, she thought as she picked up a pipe wrench and set it down again. I've got meetings scheduled, see you later. Sorry I broke your heart. "Well, then, have a nice trip."

"C.C." He laid a hand on her arm before she could hide behind the shield again. "I'd like to spend a little time with you. I'd feel a lot better about everything if I was sure we parted on good terms."

"You want to feel better about things," she muttered, then made herself relax her jaw. "Sure, why not? Dinner tomorrow night is fine. You deserve a send-off."

"I appreciate it. Really." He touched her cheek, started to lean toward her. C.C. pulled the shield down with a snap.

"Better stand back from the torch, Trent," she said sweetly. "You might get burned."

Family meetings with the Calhouns were traditionally noisy, argumentative and drenched with tears and laughter. This one was abnormally subdued. Amanda, in her capacity as adviser on finances, sat at the head of the table.

The room was silent.

Suzanna had already put the children to bed. It had been a little easier than usual as both of them had exhausted themselves with Fred—and vice versa.

Trent had excused himself discreetly, directly after dinner. It hardly mattered, C.C. thought. He would know the outcome soon enough.

She was afraid everyone knew it already.

"I guess we all know why we're here," Amanda began. "Trent's going back to Boston on Wednesday, and it would be best all around if we gave him our decision about the house before he left."

"It would be better if we concentrated on finding the necklace." Lilah's stubborn look was offset by the nervous way she twisted the obsidian crystals around her neck.

"We're all still looking for the papers." Suzanna laid a hand on Lilah's arm. "But I think we have to face the reality that finding the necklace could take a long time. Longer than we have."

"Thirty days is longer than we have." All eyes turned to Amanda. "I got a notice from the lawyer last week."

"Last week!" Coco put in. "Stridley contacted you and you didn't mention it?"

"I was hoping I could get an extension without worrying everyone." Amanda laid her hand on the file she set on the table. "No deal. We've been chipping away at the back taxes, but the hard fact is that we haven't been making enough headway. The insurance premiums are due. We can make them all right, and the mortgage— for the time being. The utility bills over the winter were higher than usual, and the new furnace and repairs to the roof ate up a lot of our principal."

C.C. held up a hand. "How bad is it?"

"As bad as it gets." Amanda rubbed at an ache in her temple. "We could sell off a few more pieces, and keep our head above water. Just. But taxes are due again in a couple months, and we'll be back where we started."

"I can sell my pearls," Coco began, and Lilah cut her off.

"No. Absolutely not. We agreed a long time ago that there were some things that couldn't be sold. If we're going to face facts," she said grimly, "then let's face them."

"The plumbing's shot," Amanda continued, and had to clear her tightening throat. "If we don't get the re-wiring done, we could end up burning the place down around our ears. Suzanna's lawyer's fees—"

"That's my problem," Suzanna interrupted.

"That's *our* problem," Amanda corrected, and got a unanimous note of assent. "We're a family," she continued. "We've been through the very worst together, and we handled it. Six or seven years ago, it looked as if everything was going to be fine. But…taxes have gone up, along with the insurance, the repairs, everything. It's not as though we're paupers, but the house eats up every cent of spare cash, and then some. If I thought we could weather this, hang in for another year or two, I'd say sell the Limoges, or a few antiques. But it's like trying to plug a hole in a dam and watching others spring out while your fingers are slipping."

"What are you saying, Mandy?" C.C. asked her.

"I'm saying." Amanda pressed her lips together. "I'm saying the only realistic choice I see is for us to sell the house. With the offer from St. James, we can pay off the debts, keep most of what's important to all of us and buy another. If we don't sell, it's going to be taken away from us in any case within a few months." A tear trickled down her cheek. "I'm sorry. I just can't find a way out."

"It's not your fault." Suzanna reached out for her hand. "We all knew it was coming."

Amanda sniffled and shook her head. "What buffer we had, we lost in the stock market crash. We just haven't been able to recover. I know I made the investments—"

"*We* made the investments." Lilah leaned over to join hands, as well. "On the recommendation of a very reputable broker. If the bottom hadn't fallen through, if I'd won the lottery, if Bax hadn't been such a greedy bastard, maybe things would be different now. But they're not."

"We'll still be together." Coco added her hand. "That's what matters."

"That's what matters," C.C. agreed, and laid her hand on top. And that, if nothing else, felt right. "What do we do now?"

Struggling for composure, Amanda sat back. "I guess we ask Trent to come down and make sure the offer still stands."

"I'll get him." C.C. pushed away from the table to walk blindly from the room.

She couldn't believe it. Even as she walked through the huddle of rooms, into the hallway, up the steps with her hand trailing along the banister, she couldn't believe it. None of it would be hers much longer.

There would come a time very soon when she wouldn't be able to step from her room onto the high stone terrace and look out at the sea. She wouldn't be able to climb the steps to Bianca's tower and find Lilah curled on the window seat, dreaming out through the dusty glass. Or Suzanna working in the garden with the children racing on the lawn nearby. Amanda wouldn't come bolting down the stairs in a hurry to get somewhere, do something. Aunt Coco would no longer fuss over the stove in the kitchen.

In a matter of moments, the life she'd known was over. The one to come had yet to begin. She was somewhere in a kind of limbo, too stunned from the loss to ache.

Trent crouched beside the fire where Fred snored on the bright red cushion in his new wicker dog bed. He was going to miss the little devil, Trent realized. Even if he had the time or inclination for a pet back in Boston, he didn't have the heart to take Fred away from the children, or from the women, if it came to that.

He'd seen C.C. tossing the ball for the pup in the side yard that afternoon when she'd come home from work. It had been so good to hear her laugh, to see her wrestle with the dog and Suzanna's children.

Oddly it reminded him of the image he'd had—daydream, he corrected. The daydream he'd had when his mind had wandered the night of the séance. Of him and C.C. sitting on a sunny porch, watching children play in the yard.

It was foolishness, of course, but something had tugged at him that afternoon when he'd stood at the door and looked at her tossing a ball to Fred. A good something, he remembered, until she'd turned and had seen him. Her laughter had died, and her eyes had gone cool.

He straightened, studying the flames in the fire. It was crazy, but he wished with his whole heart that she would flare up, just once more. Throw another punch at him. Call him names. The worst kind of punishment was her steady, passionless politeness.

The sound of the knock on the door had Fred yipping quietly in his sleep. When Trent answered, finding C.C. on the other side of the threshold, twin twinges of delight and distress danced through his system. He wouldn't be able to turn her away this time. It wouldn't be possible to tell her, or himself, that it couldn't be. He had to... Then he looked into her eyes.

"What's wrong? What's happened?" He reached out to comfort, but she stepped stiffly away.

"We'd like you to come downstairs, if you don't mind."

"Catherine—" But she was already walking away, her stride lengthening in her hurry for distance.

He found them all gathered around the dining-room table, their faces composed. He was astute enough to understand that he was facing one combined will.

The Calhouns had closed ranks.

"Ladies?"

"Trent, sit down, please." Coco gestured to the chair beside her. "I hope we didn't disturb you?"

"Not at all." He looked at C.C., but she was staring fixedly at the wall above his head. "Are we having another séance?"

"Not this time." Lilah nodded toward Amanda. "Mandy?"

"All right." She took a deep breath and was relieved when Suzanna's hand gripped hers under the table. "Trent, we've discussed your offer for The Towers, and have decided to accept it."

He gave her a blank look. "Accept it?"

"Yes." Amanda pressed her free hand to her quivering stomach. "That is, if your offer still stands."

"Yes, of course it does." He scanned the room, his gaze lingering on C.C. "You're certain you want to sell?"

"Isn't that what you wanted?" C.C.'s voice was clipped. "Isn't that what you came for?"

"Yes." But he'd gotten a great deal more than he'd bargained for. "My firm will be delighted to purchase the property. But…I want to be certain that you're all agreed. That this is what you want. All of you."

"We're all agreed." C.C. went back to staring at the wall.

"The lawyers will handle the details," Amanda began again. "But before we hand things over to them, I'd like to review the terms."

"Of course." He named the purchase price again. Hearing it had tears burning in C.C.'s eyes. "There's no reason why we can't be flexible on the timing," he went on. "I realize you'll want to do some kind of inventory before you—relocate."

It was what they wanted, he reminded himself. It was business. It shouldn't make him feel as if he'd just crawled out from under a rock.

"I think we'd like to make the move quickly." Suzanna glanced around the table for confirmation. "As soon as we can find another house."

"If there's anything I can do to help you—"

"You've done enough," C.C. interrupted coolly. "We can take care of ourselves."

"I'd like to add a condition." Lilah leaned forward. "You're purchasing the house, and the land. Not the contents."

"No. Naturally the furniture, heirlooms, personal possessions remain yours."

"Including the necklace." She inclined her head. "Whether it's found before we leave, or after, the Calhoun necklace belongs to the Calhouns. I want that in writing, Trent. If anytime during your renovations, the necklace is recovered, it belongs to us."

"All right." The little clause would drive the lawyers crazy, he thought. But that was their problem. "I'll see that it's put in the contract."

"Bianca's tower." She spoke slowly, afraid her voice would break. "Be careful what you do with it."

"How about some wine?" Coco rose, hands fluttering. "We should have some wine."

"Excuse me." C.C. made herself stand slowly, fighting the impulse to race from the room. "If we're all through, I think I'll go up. I'm tired."

Trent started after her, but Suzanna stopped him. "I don't think she'd be receptive right now. I'll go."

C.C. went to the terrace to lean out over the wall and let the cold wind dry the tears. There should be a storm, she thought. She wished there was a storm, something as angry and as passionate as her own heart.

Pounding a fist on the wall, she cursed the day she'd ever met Trent. He wouldn't take her love, but he would take her home. Of course, if he had accepted the first and returned it, he could never have taken the house.

"C.C." Suzanna stepped out to slip an arm around her shoulders. "It's cold. Why don't we go inside?"

"It's not right."

"No." She gathered her sister closer. "It's not."

"He doesn't even know what it means." She dashed the angry tears away. "He can't understand. He wouldn't want to."

"Maybe he doesn't. Maybe no one can but us. But it's not his fault, C.C. We can't blame him because we couldn't hang on." She looked away from the gardens she loved, toward the cliffs that always drew her. "I left here once before—it seems like a lifetime ago, but it was only seven years. Nearly eight now." She sighed. "I thought it was the happiest day of my life, leaving the island for my new home in Boston."

"You don't have to talk about that. I know it hurts you."

"Not as much as it once did. I was in love, C.C., a new bride with the future in the palm of my hand. And when I turned around and saw The Towers disappearing behind me, I cried like a baby. I thought it would be easier this time." As tears threatened, she closed her eyes. "I wish it were. What is it about this place that pulls us so?" she wondered.

"I know we can find another house." C.C. linked fingers with her sister. "I know we'll be all right, even happy. But it hurts. And you're right, it's not Trent's fault. But…"

"You have to blame someone." Suzanna smiled.

"He hurt me. I really hate to admit that, but he hurt me. I want to be able to say that he made me fall in love with him. Even that he let me fall in love with him. But I did it all by myself."

"And Trent?"

"He isn't interested."

"From the way he looks at you, I'd say you're wrong."

"Oh, he's interested," C.C. said grimly. "But love has nothing to do with it. He very politely refused to take advantage of my—my lack of experience, as he called it."

"Oh." Suzanna looked out toward the cliffs again. Rejection, she knew, was the sharpest blade of all. "It doesn't help much, but it might have been more difficult for you if he hadn't been—sensible."

"He's sensible, all right," C.C. said through her teeth. "And being a sensible and a civilized man, he'd like us to be friends. He's even taking me to dinner tomorrow so he can be certain I'm not pining away for him, and he can go back to Boston guilt free."

"What are you going to do?"

"Oh, I'll go to dinner with him. I can be just as damned civilized as he can." She set her chin. "And when I'm finished, he's going to be sorry he ever set eyes on Catherine Calhoun." She whirled toward her sister. "Do you still have that red dress? The beaded one that's cut down to sin?"

Suzanna's grin spread. "You bet I do."

"Let's go take a look at it."

Well, well, well, C.C. thought. What a difference a day and a tight silk dress could make. Lips pursed, she turned in front of the cracked cheval glass in the corner of her room. The dress was just a smidgen too small for her—even with the frantic alterations Suzanna had made. It only made more of a statement.

Don't you wish you had me, it said quite clearly. C.C. ran her hands over her hips. And he could wish until his head exploded.

The dress was a form-fitting glitter of flame that licked down from its plunging neckline to the abbreviated hem. Suzanna had ruthlessly slashed it off so that it hit C.C. midthigh. The long sleeves ended in points over her wrists. And she'd added Coco's rhinestone ear clips, with their wicked sparkle.

The thirty minutes she'd spent on makeup seemed

to have paid off. Her lips were as red as the dress, thanks to Amanda's contribution. Her eyes were shadowed with copper and emerald, thanks to Lilah. Her hair was as glossy as a raven's wing and slicked back a bit at the temples.

All in all, C.C. thought as she turned, Trenton St. James III was in for a surprise.

"Suzanna said you needed some shoes." Lilah walked in and stopped in midyawn. The shoes dangled from her fingertips as she stared. "I must have passed through a parallel universe."

C.C. grinned and spun a circle. "What do you think?"

"I think Trent's going to need oxygen." Approving, she passed C.C. a pair of spiked snakeskin heels. "Kiddo, you look dangerous."

"Good." She pulled on the shoes. "Now if I can just walk in these without falling on my face."

"Practice. I've got to get Mandy."

A few moments later, all three sisters supervised C.C.'s walk. "You'll be having dinner," Amanda put in, wincing at each wobble. "So you'll be sitting down most of the time."

"I'm getting it," C.C. muttered. "I'm just not used to heels. How do you work in these things all day?"

"Talent."

"Walk slower," Lilah suggested. "More deliberately. As if you have all the time in the world."

"Take if from her," Amanda agreed. "She's an expert at slow."

"In this case—" Lilah gave Amanda an arched look "—slow is sexy. See?"

Taking her sister's advice, C.C. walked with a cau-

tious deliberation that came off as slinky. Amanda held
out her hands. "I stand corrected. What coat are you
wearing?"

"I haven't thought of it."

"You can wear my black silk cape," Amanda decided. "You'll freeze but you'll look great doing it. Perfume. Aunt Coco's got some of that smoldering French
stuff left from Christmas."

"No." Suzanna shook her head. "She should stick
with her usual scent." Tilting her head, she studied her
sister and smiled. "The contrast will drive him crazy."

Unaware of what was in store for him, Trent sat in
the parlor with Coco. His bags were packed. His calls
were made. He wished he could come up with a reasonable excuse to stay another few days.

"We've enjoyed having you," Coco told him when
he'd expressed his appreciation for her hospitality. "I'm
sure we'll be seeing each other again soon."

Her crystal ball didn't lie, she reminded herself. It
still linked Trent up with one of her nieces, and she
wasn't ready to wave surrender.

"I certainly hope so. I have to say, Coco, how much
I admire you for raising four such lovely women."

"Sometimes I think we raised each other." She
smiled mistily around the room. "I'm going to miss
this place. To be honest I didn't think it mattered to
me until...well, until now. I didn't grow up here as the
girls did. We traveled quite a bit, you see, and my father only came back sporadically. I always thought it
was the fact that his mother had died here that put him
off. Then, of course, I spent my married life and the
first few years of my widowhood in Philadelphia. Then
when Judson and Deliah were killed, I came here for

the girls." She sent him a sad, apologetic smile. "I'm sorry to get sentimental on you, Trenton."

"Don't apologize." He sipped thoughtfully at his aperitif. "My family has never been close, and as a result, there was never a home like this in my life. I think that's why I've begun to understand what it could mean."

"You should settle down," she said, cagily, she thought. "Find a nice girl, make a home and family of your own. Why, I can't think of anything lonelier than not having anyone to go home to."

Wanting to avoid that line of thought, he reached down to throw the ball for Fred. They both watched as the dog bounded after it, tripped himself up and went sprawling.

"Not particularly graceful," Trent mused. He rose and went over to retrieve the ball himself. Scratching the dog's belly, he glanced over. The first thing he saw was a pair of very slim black heels. Slowly his gaze traveled up a long, shapely pair of legs. With the breath backing up in his lungs, he sat back on his heels.

There was a sparkle of scarlet, snug and sleek over a curvy feminine form.

"Lose something?" C.C. asked as his eyes fixed on her face.

Her lips were curved and red and slick. Trent ran his tongue over his teeth to be certain he hadn't swallowed it. On unsteady legs, he rose.

"C.C.?"

"We were having dinner tonight, weren't we?"

"We…yes. You look wonderful."

"Do you like it?" She turned a circle so that he could see the back of the dress dipped even lower than the front. "I think red's a cheerful color." And powerful, she thought, still smiling.

"It suits you. I've never seen you in a dress before."

"Impractical when it comes to changing fuel pumps. Are you ready to go?"

"Go where?"

Oh, she was going to enjoy this. "To dinner."

"Right. Yes."

She inclined her head the way Suzanna had showed her and handed him her cape. It was a service he'd performed hundreds of times for dozens of women. But his hands fumbled.

"Don't wait up, Aunt Coco."

"No, dear." Behind their retreating backs, she grinned and raised her fists in the air. The moment the front door shut, the three remaining Calhouns exchanged high fives.

Chapter 9

"I'm glad you talked me into going out tonight." C.C. reached for the door handle before she remembered to let Trent open the car for her.

"I wasn't sure you'd still be willing to go." He closed his hand over hers.

"Because of the house?" As casually as possible, C.C. slid her hand from under his and lowered herself into the car. "That's done. I'd rather not talk about it tonight."

"All right." He closed the door, rounded the hood. "Amanda recommended the restaurant." He had his hands on the keys but continued to stare at her.

"Something wrong?"

"No." Unless you counted his nervous system. After starting the car, he tried again. "I thought you might like dining near the water."

"Sounds fine." His radio was on a classical station. Not her usual style, she thought. But it wasn't a usual night. C.C. settled back and prepared to enjoy the ride. "Have you heard that rattle again?"

"What rattle?"

"The one you asked me to fix yesterday."

"Oh, that rattle." He smiled to himself. "No. It must have been my imagination." When she crossed her legs, his fingers tightened on the wheel. "You never told me why you decided to be a mechanic."

"Because I'm good at it." She shifted in her seat to face him. He caught a drift of honeysuckle and nearly groaned. "When I was six, I took apart our lawn mower's engine, to see how it worked. I was hooked. Why did you go into hotels?"

"It was expected of me." He stopped, surprised that that had been the first answer out of his mouth. "And I suppose I got good at it."

"Do you like it?"

Had anyone ever asked him that before? he wondered. Had he ever asked himself? "Yes, I guess I do."

"Guess?" Her brows lifted into her bangs. "I thought you were sure of everything."

He glanced at her again and nearly ran off the road. "Apparently not."

When they arrived at the waterfront restaurant, he was used to the transformation. Or thought he was. Then he went around to open the car door for her. She slid out, rose up. They were eye to eye, barely a whisper apart. C.C. held her ground, wondering if he could hear the way her heart was pounding against her ribs.

"Are you sure nothing's wrong?"

"No, I'm not sure." No one, he was certain, this impossibly sexy was meant to be resisted. He cupped a hand at the back of her neck. "Let me check."

She eased away the instant before his lips brushed hers. "This isn't a date, remember? Just a friendly dinner."

"I'd like to change the rules."

"Too late." She smiled and offered a hand. "I'm hungry."

"You're not the only one," he murmured, and took her inside.

He wasn't sure how to handle her. The smooth moves he'd always taken for granted seemed rusty. The setting was perfect, the little table beside the window with water lapping just outside. As the sun set away in the west, it deepened and tinted the bay. He ordered wine as she picked up her menu and smiled at him.

Under the table, C.C. gently eased out of her shoes. "I haven't been here before," she told him. "It's very nice."

"I can't guarantee the food will be as exceptional as your aunt's."

"No one cooks like Aunt Coco. She'll be sorry to see you go. She likes cooking for a man."

"Will you?"

"Will I what?"

"Be sorry to see me go."

C.C. looked down at the menu, trying to concentrate on her choices. The hard fact was, she had none. "Since you're still here, we'll have to see. I imagine you have a lot to catch up on in Boston."

"Yes, I do. I've been thinking that after I do, I may take a vacation. A real one. Bar Harbor might be a good choice."

She looked up, then away. "Thousands think so," she murmured, relieved when the waiter served the wine.

"If you could go anywhere you liked, where would it be?"

"That's a tough question, since I haven't been any-where." She sipped, found the wine as smooth as chilled silk on her tongue. "Somewhere where I could see the sun set on the water, I think. Someplace warm." She shrugged. "I suppose I should have said Paris or London."

"No." He laid a hand on hers. "Catherine—"

"Are you ready to order?"

C.C. glanced quickly at the waiter who hovered be-side them. "Yes." She slid her hand from Trent's and picked arbitrarily from the menu. Cautious, she kept one hand in her lap as she lifted her wine. The moment they were alone again, she started to speak. "Have you ever seen a whale?"

"I... No."

"You'll be coming back occasionally while you're—while you're having The Towers converted. You should take a day and go out on one of the whale-watch boats. The last time I managed it, I saw three humpbacks. You need to dress warmly though. Even in high summer it's cold once you get out on the Atlantic. It can be a rough ride, but it's worth it. You might even think about offering some sort of package yourself. You know, a weekend rate with a whale-watch tour included. A lot of the hotels—"

"Catherine." He stopped her by closing a hand over her wrist before she could lift her glass again. He could feel the rapid, unsteady beat of her pulse. Not passion this time, he thought. But heartache. "The papers haven't been signed yet," he said quietly. "There's still time to look for other options."

"There aren't any other options." He cared, she realized as she studied his face. It was in his eyes as they looked into hers. Concern, apology. It made it worse somehow, knowing he cared. "We sell to you now, or The Towers is sold later for taxes. The end result is the same, and there's a little more dignity doing it this way."

"I might be able to help. A loan."

She retreated instantly. "We can't take your money."

"If I buy the house from you, you're taking my money."

"That's different. That's business. Trent," she said before he could argue, "I appreciate the fact that you'd offer, especially since I know the only reason you're here is to buy The Towers."

It was, he thought. Or it had been. "The thing is, C.C., I feel like I'm foreclosing on those widows and orphans."

She managed a smile. "We're five strong, self-sufficient women. We don't blame you—or maybe I do, a little, but at least I know I'm being unfair when I do. My feelings for you don't make it easy to be fair."

"What are your feelings?"

She let out a little sigh as the waiter served the appetizers and lit the candle between them. "You're taking the house, you might as well take it all. I'm in love with you. But I'll get over it." With her head tilted slightly, she lifted her fork. "Is there anything else you want to know?"

When he took her hand again, she didn't pull back, but waited. "I never wanted to hurt you," he said carefully. How well her hand fit into his, he thought, looking down at it. How comforting it was to link his fingers with hers. "I'm just not capable of giving you— of giving anyone—promises of love and fidelity."

"That's sad." She shook her head as his eyes came back to hers. "You see, I'm only losing a house. I can find another. You're losing the rest of your life, and you only have one." She forced her lips to curve as she drew away from him. "Unless, of course, you subscribe to Lilah's idea that we just keep coming back. This is nice wine," she commented. "What is it again?"

"Pouilly Fumé."

"I'll have to remember that." She began to talk cheerfully as she ate the meal without tasting a thing. By the time coffee was served, she was wound like a top. C.C. knew that she would rather take an engine apart with her fingernails than face another evening such as this.

To love him so desperately, yet to have to be strong enough, proud enough to pretend she was capable of living without him. To sit, greedily storing each gesture, each word, while pretending it was all so casual and easy.

She wanted to shout at him, to rage and damn him for stirring her emotions into a frenzy then calmly walking away from the storm. But she could only cling to the cold comfort of pride.

"Tell me about your home in Boston," she invited. That would be something, she thought, to be able to picture him in his own home.

He wasn't able to take his eyes off her. The way the clusters at her ears shot fire. The way the candlelight flickered dreamily in her eyes. But all through the evening, he had felt as though she had blocked off a part of herself, the most important part of herself. And he might never see the whole woman again.

"My home?"

"Yes, where you live."

"It's just a house." It occurred to him quite suddenly that it didn't mean a thing to him. An excellent investment, that was all. "It's only a few minutes from the office."

"That's convenient. Have you lived there long?"

"About five years. Actually, I bought it from my father when he and his third wife split. They decided to liquidate some assets."

"I see." And she was very much afraid that she did. "Does your mother live in Boston, too?"

"No. She travels. Being tied down to one place doesn't agree with her."

"Sounds like Great-Aunt Colleen." C.C. smiled over the rim of her cup. "That's my father's aunt, or Bianca's oldest child."

"Bianca," he mused, and thought again of that moment when he'd felt that soft and soothing warmth over his and C.C.'s joined hands.

"She lives on cruise ships. Every now and again we get a postcard from some port of call. Aruba or Madagascar. She's eighty-something, obsessively single and mean as a shark with a hangover. We all live in fear that she might decide to visit."

"I didn't realize you had any relatives living other than Coco and your sisters." His brows drew together. "She might know something about the necklace."

"Great-Aunt Colleen?" Considering it, C.C. pursed her lips. "I doubt it. She was a child when Bianca died,

and spent most of her girlhood in boarding schools."
Without thinking, she pulled off her earrings and mas-
saged the tender lobes. Desire spread like brushfire
through Trent's blood. "Anyway, if we could find her—
which isn't likely—and mentioned the whole business,
she'd probably come steaming back to hack away at
the walls. She doesn't have any love for The Towers,
but she has a great deal for money."

"She doesn't sound like a relative of yours."

"Oh, we have a number of oddities in our family
closet." After dropping the earrings into her bag, she
leaned an elbow on the table. "Great-Uncle Sean—he
was Bianca's youngest—was shot climbing out of his
married paramour's window. One of his paramours,
I should say. He survived, then took off for the West
Indies, never to be heard of again. That was sometime
during the thirties. Ethan, my grandfather, lost the bulk
of the family fortune on cards and horses. Gambling
was his weakness, and that's what killed him. He had
a wager that he could sail from Bar Harbor to Newport and back within six days. He made it to Newport,
and was heading back ahead of schedule when he ran
into a squall and was lost at sea. Which meant he lost
his last bet as well."

"They sound like an adventurous pair."

"They were Calhouns," C.C. explained, as if that
said it all.

"I'm sorry the St. Jameses don't have anything to
compare with it."

"Ah, well. I've always wondered if Bianca would
have stepped back from that tower window if she'd
known how messed up her children would become."
C.C. looked thoughtfully out to where lights played on

the dark water. "She must have loved her artist very much."

"Or was very unhappy in her marriage."

C.C. looked back. "Yes, there is that. Maybe we should head back. It's getting late." She started to rise, remembered, then slid her bare foot around the floor beneath the table.

"What is it?"

"I've lost my shoes." So much, she thought, for the sophisticated image.

Trent bent down to look himself and got an eyeful of long, slim leg. "Ah…" He cleared his throat and trained his eyes on the floor. "Here you go." He took both, then straightening, smiled at her. "Put your foot out. I'll give you a hand." He watched her as he slipped the shoes onto her feet and remembered that he'd once thought she would never stand for being a Cinderella. He trailed his finger up her instep and caught the flicker in her eyes. The flicker of desire that, no matter what common sense told him, he very much wanted.

"Have I mentioned that you have truly incredible legs?"

"No." She had one hand balled in a fist at her side and struggled to concentrate on it rather than the sensations his touch had spurting through her. "It's nice of you to notice."

"It's difficult not to. They're the only ones I've known that look sexy in coveralls."

Ignoring the thud of her own heart, she leaned toward him. "That reminds me."

He could kiss her now, he thought. He had only to shift a mere inch to have his mouth on hers, where he wanted it. "What?"

"I don't think your shocks have more than another couple thousand miles on them." With a smile, she rose. "I'd look into that when you get home." Pleased with herself, C.C. started out ahead of him.

When they settled in the car, she congratulated herself. A very successful evening all in all, she thought. Maybe he wasn't miserable, as she was, but she was damn sure she'd made him uncomfortable a time or two. He'd go back to Boston the next day.... She turned to stare out the window until she was certain she could deal with the pain. He'd go back, but he wouldn't forget her quickly or easily. His last impression of her would be one of a composed, self-contained woman in a sexy red dress. Better, C.C. decided, much better than the picture of a mechanic in coveralls with grease on her hands.

More important, she'd proven something to herself. She could love, and she could let go.

She looked up as the car started to climb. She could see the shadowy peaks of the two towers spearing into the night sky. Trent slowed the car as he looked, as well.

"The light's on in Bianca's tower."

"Lilah," C.C. murmured. "She often sits up there." She thought of her sister sitting by the window, looking out into the night. "You won't tear it down, will you?"

"No." Understanding more than she knew, he closed his hand over hers. "I promise you it won't be torn down."

The house disappeared as the road curved away, then all but filled the view. They could hear the beat and slap of the sea as they looked at it. Lights were sprinkled on throughout, glowing against the dull gray stone. A slender shadow moved in front of the tower window, stood for a moment, then slid away.

Inside, Lilah called down the stairs. "They're back."

Four women raced to the windows to peer out.

"We shouldn't spy on them," Suzanna murmured, but moved the curtain aside a bit more.

"We're not." Amanda strained her eyes. "We're just checking, that's all. Can you see anything?"

"They're still in the car," Coco complained. "How are we supposed to see what's going on if they're going to sit in the car?"

"We could use our imaginations." Lilah shook her hair back. "If that man isn't begging her to go to Boston with him, then he really is a jerk."

"To Boston?" Alarmed, Suzanna glanced over. "You don't think she'd go to Boston, do you?"

"She'd go to the Ukraine if he had the sense to ask her," Amanda commented. "Look, they're getting out."

"Maybe if we just cracked a window a little bit, we could hear—"

"Aunt Coco, that's ridiculous." Lilah clucked her tongue.

"You're right, of course." Color tinged Coco's cheek.

"Of course I'm right. They'd hear the windows creak if we tried." Grinning, she pressed her face against the glass. "We'll just have to read their lips."

"This was nice," C.C. said as she stepped out of the car. "I haven't been out to dinner in a while."

"You had dinner with Finney."

She gave him a blank look, then laughed. "Oh, Finney, sure." The breeze played with her bangs as she smiled. "You've got quite a memory."

"Some things seem to stick to it." The jealousy he

felt was, unfortunately, no memory. "Doesn't he ever take you out?"

"Finney? No, I just go to his place."

Frustrated, Trent jammed his hands into his pockets. "He should take you out."

She smothered a chuckle as the image of old Albert Finney escorting her to a restaurant ran through her mind. "I'll be sure to mention it to him." She turned to start up the steps.

"Catherine, don't go in yet." He took her hands.

At the windows four pairs of eyes narrowed.

"It's late, Trent."

"I don't know if I'll see you again before I leave."

It took all her strength to keep her eyes steady. "Then we'll say goodbye now."

"I need to see you again."

"The shop's open at eight-thirty. I'll be there."

"Damn it, C.C., you know what I mean." His hands were on her shoulders now.

"No, I don't."

"Come to Boston." He blurted it out, shocking himself while she stood calmly waiting.

"Why?"

To give himself a moment to find control again, he stepped back. "I could show you around." How much more inane could he get? Trent wondered. How much more beautiful could she look? "You said you'd never been. We could…have some time together."

Inside her wrap, she shivered, but her voice was calm and smooth. "Are you asking me to come to Boston and have an affair with you?"

"No. Yes. Oh, Lord. Just wait." He turned to pace a few steps away and breathe.

Inside, Lilah smiled. "Why, he's in love with her after all, but he's too stupid to know it."

"Shh!" Coco waved a hand. "I can almost hear what they're saying." She had an ear at the base of the water glass she pressed up to the window.

At the bottom of the steps, Trent tried again. "Nothing I begin ends the way I expect it to when I'm with you." He turned back. She was still standing with the house behind her, the dress glimmering like liquid fire in the dark. "I know I have no business asking you, and I didn't intend to. I intended to say a very civil good-bye and let you go."

"And now?"

"Now I want to make love with you more than I want to go on breathing."

"To make love," C.C. repeated steadily. "But you don't love me."

"I don't know anything about love. I care for you." He walked back to touch a hand to her face. "Maybe that could be enough."

She studied him, realizing he didn't have any idea that he was breaking an already shattered heart. "It might be, for a day or a week or a month. But you were right about me, Trent. I expect more. I deserve more." Keeping her eyes on his, she slid her hands over his shoulders. "I offered myself to you once. That won't happen again. And neither will this."

She pressed her mouth against his, pouring every scrap of her tattered emotions into it. Her arms enfolded him even as her body swayed seductively toward his. With a sigh, her lips parted, inviting him to take.

Off balance, needy, he dragged her head back and

plundered. Unsteady, his hands skimmed beneath her wrap, urgently seeking the warmth of her skin.

So many feelings, too many feelings, bombarded him. He wanted only to fill himself with the taste of her. But there was more. She wouldn't let him take only the kiss, but all the emotion that went with it. He felt he was drowning in it, but it was so strong and heady a flood, he couldn't fight.

Love me! Why can't you love me? Her mind seemed to scream it even as she was borne away on the tide of her own longings. Everything she wanted was here, inside the circle of her arms. Everything but his heart.

"Catherine." He couldn't get his breath. Dragging her closer, he pressed his mouth to her neck. "I can't get close enough."

She held him to her a moment longer, then slowly, painfully, pulled away. "Yes, you could. And that's what hurts the most." Turning, she dashed up the steps.

"Catherine."

She paused at the door. With her head high, she turned around. He was already coming after her when he saw the tears glittering in her eyes. Nothing else would have stopped him.

"Goodbye, Trent. I hope to God that keeps you up at night."

As he listened to the echo of the door slamming, he was certain it would.

It cannot go on. I can no longer pretend that I am disloyal to my husband only between the covers of this journal. My life, so calm and ordered during my twenty-four years, has become a lie this summer. One I must atone for.

As autumn approaches and we make our plans to return to New York, I thank God I will soon leave Mount Desert Island behind me. How close, how dangerously close I have come these past days to breaking my marriage vows.

And yet, I grieve.

In another week, we will be gone. I may never see Christian again. That is how it should be. How it must be. But in my heart I know that I would give my soul for one night, even one hour, in his arms. Imagining how it could be obsesses me. With him there would finally be passion, and love, even laughter. With him it would not simply be a duty, cold and silent and soon over.

I pray to be forgiven for the adultery I have committed in my heart.

My conscience has urged me to keep away from the cliffs. And I have tried. It has demanded that I be a more patient, loving and understanding wife to Fergus. I have done so. Whatever he has asked of me, I have done. At his request, I gave a tea for several of the ladies. We have gone to the theater, to countless dinner parties. I have listened until my head was throbbing to talk of business and fashion and the possibility of war. My smile never falters, for Fergus prefers that I look content at all times. Because it pleases him, I wear the emeralds when we go out in the evenings.

They are my penance now, a reminder that a sin is not always in the action, but in the heart.

I sit here in my tower now as I write. The cliffs are below, the cliffs where Christian paints. Where I go when I sneak from the house like a randy housemaid. It shames me. It sustains me. Even now I look down and see him. He faces the sea, and waits for me.

We have never touched, not once, though the ache is in both of us. I have learned how much passion there can be in silences, in long, troubled looks.

I will not go to him today, but only sit here and watch him. When I feel I have the strength, I will go to him only to say goodbye and wish him well.

While I live through the long winter that faces me, I will wonder if he will be here next summer.

Chapter 10

"Here are the papers you asked for, Mr. St. James."

Oblivious to his secretary's presence, Trent continued to stand at the window, staring out. It was a habit he'd developed since returning to work three weeks before. Through the wide tinted glass, he could watch Boston bustling by below. Steel-and-glass towers glittered beside elegant brownstones in an architectural potpourri. Thick traffic weaved and charged on the streets. In sweats and colorful running shorts, joggers paced themselves along the path beside the river. Then there was the river itself, streaming with boats, sails puffed full of warm spring breezes.

"Mr. St. James?"

"Yes?" He glanced around at his secretary.

"I've brought you the papers you requested."

"Thank you, Angela." In an old habit, he looked at

his watch. It occurred to him, painfully, that he had rarely thought of the time when he'd been with C.C. "It's after five. You should go home to your family."

Angela hesitated. She'd worked for Trenton for six years. It had only been during the past couple of weeks that he had begun calling her by her first name or inquiring about her family. The day before, he'd actually complimented her on her dress. The change in him had the entire staff baffled. As his secretary, she felt obligated to dig out the source of it.

"May I speak with you a minute?"

"All right. Would you like to sit down?"

"No, sir. I hope you won't consider this out of place, Mr. St. James, but I wanted to know if you're feeling well."

A ghost of a smile played around his mouth. "Don't I look well?"

"Oh, yes, of course. A little tired perhaps. It's just that since you returned from Bar Harbor, you seem distracted, and different somehow."

"You could say I am distracted. I am different, and to answer your original question, no, I don't think I am entirely well."

"Mr. St. James, if there's anything I can do…"

Studying her, he sat on the edge of his desk. He had hired her because she was efficient and quick. As he recalled, he had nearly passed her over because she'd had two small children. It had worried him that she wouldn't be able to balance her responsibilities, but he'd taken what he'd considered a chance. It had worked very well indeed.

"Angela, how long have you been married?"

"Married?" Thrown off, she blinked. "Ten years."

"Happily?"

"Yes, Joe and I are happy."

Joe, he mused. He hadn't even known her husband's name. Hadn't bothered to find it out. "Why?"

"Why, sir?"

"Why are you happy?"

"I...I suppose because we love each other."

He nodded, gesturing to prod her along. "And that's enough?"

"It certainly helps you get through the rough spots." She smiled a little, thinking of her Joe. "We've had some of them, but one of us always manages to pull the other through."

"You consider yourself a team then. So you have a great deal in common?"

"I don't know about that. Joe likes football and I hate it. He loves jazz, and I don't understand it." It wouldn't occur to her until later that this was the first time she'd felt completely at ease with Trent since she'd taken the job. "Sometimes I feel like wearing earplugs all weekend. Whenever I feel like shipping him out, I think about what my life would be without him. And I don't like what I see." Taking a chance, she stepped closer. "Mr. St. James, if this is about Marla Montblanc getting married last week, well, I'd just like to say that you're better off."

"Marla got married?"

Truly baffled, Angela shook her head. "Yes, sir. Last week, to that golf pro. It was in all the papers."

"I must have missed it." There had been other things in the papers that had captured his attention.

"I realize you'd been seeing her for quite a while."

Seeing her, Trent mused. Yes, that cool, passionless

phrase described their relationship perfectly. "Yes, I had been."

"You're not—upset?"

"About Marla? No." The fact was he hadn't thought of her in weeks. Since he'd walked into a garage and spotted a pair of scarred boots.

Another woman, Angela realized. And if she'd had this kind of effect on the boss, she had all of Angela's support. "Sir, if someone—something else," she corrected cautiously, "is on your mind, you may be over-analyzing the situation."

The comment surprised him enough to make him smile again. "Do I overanalyze, Angela?"

"You're very meticulous, Mr. St. James, and analyze details finitely, which works very well in business. Personal matters can't always be dealt with logically."

"I've been coming to that same conclusion myself." He stood again. "I appreciate the time."

"My pleasure, Mr. St. James." And it certainly had been. "Is there anything else I can do for you?"

"No, thank you." He turned back to the window. "Good night, Angela."

"Good night." She was grinning when she closed the door at her back.

Trent stood where he was for some time. No, he hadn't noticed the announcement of Marla's wedding. The papers had also been full of the upcoming sale of The Towers. "Bar Harbor landmark to become newest St. James Hotel," he remembered. "Rumors of lost treasures sweeten the deal."

Trent wasn't certain where the leak had come from, though he wasn't surprised by it. As he'd expected, his lawyers had grumbled over the clause Lilah had insisted on. Whispers of emeralds had sneaked down the hallways. It was only natural that they would find their way onto the street and into print.

Newspapers and tabloids had been rife with speculation on the Calhoun emeralds for more than a week. They'd been termed priceless and tragic and legendary—all the right adjectives to ensure more newsprint.

Fergus Calhoun's business exploits had been rehashed, along with his wife's suicide. An enterprising reporter had even managed to track down Colleen Calhoun aboard a cruise ship in the Ionian Sea. The grande dame's pithy reply had been printed in italics.

"Humbug."

He wondered if C.C. had seen the papers. Of course she had, he thought. Just as she'd probably been hounded by the press.

How was she taking it? Was she hurt and miserable, forced to answer questions when some nosy reporter stuck a tape recorder in her face? He smiled a little. *Forced?* He imagined she'd throw a dozen reporters out of the garage if they had the nerve to try.

God, he missed her. And missing her was eating him alive. He woke up each morning wondering what she was doing. He went to bed each night to toss restlessly as thoughts of her invaded his brain. When he slept, she was in his dreams. She was his dream.

Three weeks, he thought. He should have adjusted by now. Yet every day that he was here and she was somewhere else, it got worse.

The revised contracts for the sale of The Towers were sitting on his desk. He should have signed them days ago. Yet he couldn't make himself take that final step. The last time he had looked at them, he had only been able to focus on three words.

Catherine Colleen Calhoun.

He'd read it over and over, remembering the first time she'd told him her name, tossing it at him as though it had been a weapon. She'd had grease on her face, Trenton remembered. And fire in her eyes.

Then he would think of other times, odd moments, careless words. The way she had scowled at him from her perch on the arm of the sofa while he'd had tea with Coco. The look on her face when they'd stood on the terrace together, watching the sea. How perfectly her mouth had fit to his when he had kissed her under an arbor of wisteria not yet in bloom.

It would be blooming now, he mused. Those first fragrant flowers would be opening. Would she think of him at all when she walked there?

If she did, he was very much afraid the thoughts wouldn't be kind.

She'd cursed him when she'd seen him last. She'd leveled those deep green eyes at him and had hoped that the kiss, the last kiss they'd shared, would keep him up at night.

He doubted even she could know how completely her wish had come true.

Rubbing his tired eyes, he walked back to his desk. It was, as always, in perfect order. As his business was—as his life had been.

Things had changed, he was forced to admit. He had changed, but perhaps he hadn't changed so completely. Once again, he picked up the contracts to study them. He was still a skilled and organized businessman, one who knew how to maneuver a deal and make it work to his advantage.

He picked up his pen and tapped it lightly on the papers. A germ of an idea had rooted in his mind a few days before. Now he sat quietly and let it form, shift, realign.

It was unusual, he considered. Maybe even mildly eccentric, but…but, he thought as a smile began to curve his mouth, if he played his cards right, it could work. It was his job to make it work. Slowly he let out a long breath. It might just be the most important deal of his life.

He picked up the phone and, employing all of the St. James clout, began to turn the first wheels.

Hank finished sanding the fender on the '69 Mustang, then stood back to admire his work. "Coming along just fine," he called to C.C.

She glanced over, but her hands were full with the brake shoes she was replacing above her head. "It's going to be a beauty. I'm glad we got the shot at reconditioning it."

"You want me to start on the primer?"

She swore as brake fluid dripped onto her cheek. "No. You told me three times today that you've got a hot date tonight. Get cleaned up and take off."

"Thanks." But he'd been too well trained to leave without replacing tools and material. "You found another house yet?"

"No." She ignored the sudden ache in her stomach and concentrated on her work. "We're all going out tomorrow to look."

"Won't be the same, not having Calhouns in The

Towers. Sure is something about that necklace, though. Papers are full of stories about it."

"They'll die down." She hoped.

"Guess if you find it, you'd be millionaires. You could retire and move to Florida."

Despite her mood, she had to chuckle. "Well, we haven't found it yet." Just the receipt, she mused, which Lilah had unearthed during her one and only shift in the storeroom. "Florida'll have to wait. The brakes won't."

"Guess I'll be going. Want me to lock up the office?"

"Go ahead. Have a good time."

He went out whistling, and C.C. stopped a moment to rest her arms and neck. She wished she'd been able to keep Hank around a while longer, for company, for the distraction. Even if he rambled on about the house and the necklace, he helped keep her mind occupied.

No matter how loudly she played the radio, once she was alone, there was too much silence.

They would hear from the lawyer any day. Perhaps Aunt Coco had gotten a call from Stridley that afternoon, telling her that the contracts had been signed and a settlement date set.

Would Trent come to the settlement? she wondered. No, no, of course not. He would send a representative, and that was for the best.

Besides, she had too much to do to worry about it. House hunting, the search through old papers for a clue to the emeralds' whereabouts, the classic Mustang she intended to baby along to gleaming perfection. She barely had a moment to catch her breath much less brood about seeing Trent over the settlement table.

If only it would stop hurting, even for a few moments.

It would get better, she told herself as she returned to the brake job. It had to. After they'd found a new house and settled in. After the talk of the necklace had died away. Everything would get back to normal—or what she would have to accept as normal. If the ache never completely went away, then she would learn to live with it.

She had her family. Together, they could handle anything.

Her shoulders were stiff by the time she'd finished. Rolling them a little, she started to step out from under the car when she realized the radio had stopped playing. She glanced over. And saw Trent standing by the workbench. The wrench she was holding clattered to the floor.

"What are you doing here?"

"Waiting for you to finish." She looked fabulous, was all he could think. Absolutely fabulous. "How are you?"

"Busy." Rocked from the pain, she turned to hit a button on the wall. The lift groaned as it brought the car down. "You're here about the house, I guess."

"Yes, you could say that's a large part of it."

"We've been expecting to hear from the lawyer."

"I know."

When the car was settled, she took a rag and wiped her hands, keeping her eyes on them. "Amanda's handling the details. She's at the BayWatch if you need to discuss anything."

"What I need to discuss concerns you. Us."

She looked up, then took a quick step back when she

realized he'd moved over to stand next to her. "I really don't have anything else to say to you."

"Okay, then I'll do the talking. In just a minute."

He moved fast. Still, she was certain if she'd been expecting it, she could have evaded him. She wasn't certain she would have tried.

It felt so good, so right, to have his mouth covering hers, his hands framing her face. Her pride faltered long enough to have her reaching up to grasp his wrists, holding on as she let her needs flow into the kiss.

"I've thought about doing that for three and a half weeks," he murmured.

She squeezed her eyes tight. "Go away, Trent."

"Catherine—"

"Damn you, I said go away." She yanked free, then turned to brace her palms on the bench. "I hate you for coming here, for making a fool out of me again."

"You're not the fool. You never were."

When his hand brushed lightly over her shoulder, she snatched up a hammer and whirled. "If you touch me again, so help me, I'll break your nose."

He looked at her. The fire was in her eyes again. "Thank God. You're back." Delighted but cautious, he held up a hand. "Just listen, please. Business first."

"My business with you is settled."

"There's been a change in the plans." He plucked some change out of the can on the bench. "Can I buy you a drink?"

"No. Say what you have to say, then get out."

With a shrug, he strolled over to the soft drink machine and plugged in the change. It was then that C.C. noticed he was wearing scuffed high-tops.

"What are those?" she asked, staring at them.

"These?" Trent grinned as he popped the top on the can. "New shoes. What do you think?" When she simply gaped, he took a long drink. "I know, not quite the usual image, but things change. A number of things have changed. Would you mind putting down that hammer?"

"What? Oh. All right." She set it aside. "You said plans had changed. Does that mean you've decided not to buy The Towers?"

"Yes and no. Would you rather go into the office to discuss this?"

"Damn it, Trent, just tell me what's going on."

"All right. Here's the deal. We take one wing, the west, I think, so it doesn't involve Bianca's tower. We have it extensively remodeled. My preference is to salvage as much of the original material as possible and reconstruct, whenever possible, according with the original blueprints. It should maintain its turn-of-the-century feel. That will be part of the draw."

"The draw?" she repeated, lost.

"We can easily have ten suites without compromising the architecture. If memory serves, the billiard room would be excellent for dining, with the west tower remodeled for more intimate meals and private parties."

"Ten suites?"

"In the west wing," he agreed. "With an accent on aesthetics and intimacy. We'll have to put all the fireplaces back in working order. I think, with what we'll offer, we'll have year-round clientele rather than just seasonal."

"What are you going to do with the rest of the house?"

"That would be up to you, and your family." He set

the drink aside and came toward her. "The way I see it, you could live very easily on the first two floors and the east wing. God knows there's plenty of room."

Confused, she pressed her fingers to her temple. "We'd be, what—renting it from you?"

"That's not exactly what I had in mind. I was thinking more of a partnership." He took her hand, examining it closely. "Your knuckles have healed."

"What kind of partnership?"

"The St. James Corporation fronts the money for the renovations, advertising and so forth. Once the retreat—I like retreat better than hotel in this case—once it's in operation, we split the profits, fifty-fifty."

"I don't understand."

"It's really very simple, C.C." He lifted her hand, kissed one finger. "We compromise. We have our hotel, you have your home. Nobody loses."

Afraid to feel it, she banked down the little flicker of hope. "I don't see how it could work. Why would anyone want to pay to stay in someone else's home?"

"A landmark," he reminded her, and kissed another finger. "With a legend, a ghost and a mystery. They'll pay very well to stay here. And when they get a taste of Coco's bouillabaisse—"

"Aunt Coco?"

"I've already offered her the position of chef. She's delighted. There's still the matter of a manager, but I think Amanda will fit the slot, don't you?" His eyes smiled as he brushed a kiss over her third finger.

"Why are you doing this?"

"I'm a businessman. It makes good business sense. I've already begun the market research." He turned her hand over and pressed his lips to the palm. "That's what I've told my board of directors. I think you know differently."

"I don't know anything." She pulled her hand away to walk to the open garage doors. "All I know is that you come back here with some sort of wild scheme—"

"It's a very solid plan," he corrected. "I'm not a wild-scheme sort of person. At least I never have been." He went to her again, taking her shoulders. "I want you to keep your home, C.C."

With her lips pressed tight, she closed her eyes. "So, you're doing it for me."

"For you, your sisters, Coco, even Bianca." Hands firm, he turned her to face him. "And I'm doing it for me. You wanted to keep me up at night, and you did."

She managed a weak smile. "Guilt works miracles."

"It has nothing to do with guilt. It never did. It has to do with love. With being in love. Don't pull away," he said quietly when she jerked against his hold. "Business is closed for the day. Now it's just you and me. This is as personal as it gets."

At her sides, her hands clenched into fists. "It's all personal with me, don't you understand? You came here and changed everything in my life, then waltzed away again. Now you come back and tell me you've altered the plans."

"You weren't the only one things changed for. Nothing's been the same for me since I met you." Panic snaked through him. She wasn't going to give him another chance. "I didn't ask for this. I didn't want it."

"Oh, you made it abundantly clear what you didn't want." She shoved against him and got nowhere. "You have no right to start this up again."

"The hell with rights." He gave her a hard shake.

"I'm trying to tell you that I love you. That's a first for me, and you're not going to turn it into an argument."

"I'll turn it into whatever I want," she tossed back, furious when her voice broke. "I'm not going to let you hurt me again. I'm not going to—" Then she went still, eyes widening. "Did you say you were in love with me?"

"Just shut up and listen. I've spent three and a half weeks feeling empty and miserable without you. I went away because I thought I could. Because I thought that was right and fair and best for both of us. Logically, it was. It still is. We're nothing alike. I couldn't see any percentage in risking both our futures when you'd certainly be better off with someone else. Someone like Finney."

"Finney?" A shout of laughter escaped. "Oh, that's rich." While her emotions whirled, she knocked a fist against his chest. "Tell you what, why don't you take your percentages back to Boston and draw a graph? Now leave me alone. I've got work to do."

"I'm not finished." When she opened her mouth to swear at him, he let instinct rule and kissed her until she quieted. As breathless as she, he rested his brow against hers. "That has nothing to do with logic or percentages." Still holding on, he took a step back so that he could see her. "Catherine, every time I reminded myself that I didn't believe in love or marriage or lifetimes, I remembered the way I felt with you."

"How? How did you feel with me?"

"Alive. Happy. And I knew I was never going to feel that way again unless I came back." He let his hands slide away. "C.C., you told me once that what we had could be the best part of my life. You were right. I don't know if I can make it work, but I need to try. I need you."

He was afraid, she realized. Even more afraid than she was. With her eyes on his, she lifted a hand to his cheek. "I can give you a guarantee on a muffler, Trent. Not on this."

"I'd settle for you telling me you still love me, that you'll give me another chance."

"I still love you. But I can't give you another chance."

"Catherine—"

"Because you haven't taken the first one yet." She touched her lips to his once, then twice. "Why don't we take it together?" she asked, then laughed when he dragged her close. "Now you've done it. You'll have grease all over you."

"I'll have to get used to it." After one last spin, he drew away to study her face. Everything he needed was right there, in her eyes. "I love you, Catherine. Very much."

She brought his hand to her cheek. "I'll have to get used to it. Maybe if you said it a few hundred times."

He told her as he held her, as he traced kisses over her face, as he lingered over the taste of her mouth.

"I think it's working," she murmured. "Maybe we should close the garage doors."

"Leave them up." He stepped back again, struggling to clear his head. "I'm still St. James enough to want to do things in their proper order, but I'm running low on control."

"What order is that?" Smiling, she ran a finger up his shirt to toy with the top button.

"Wait." Churning, he put a hand over hers. "I

thought about this all the way up from Boston. It played a lot of different ways—I'd take you out again. A little wine, a lot of candlelight. Or we'd walk in the garden again at dusk."

He glanced around the garage. Honeysuckle and motor oil, he thought. Perfect.

"But this seems like the right time, the right place." He reached in his pocket for a small box, then opening it, handed it to her. "You once said if I offered you a diamond, you'd laugh in my face. I thought I might have more luck with an emerald."

Tears backed up in her throat as she stared down at the deep green stone in its simple gold setting. It gleamed up at her, full of hope and promise. "If this is a proposal, you don't need any luck at all." Wet and brilliant, her eyes came back to his. "The answer was always yes."

He slid the ring onto her finger. "Let's go home."

"Yes." Her hand linked with his. "Let's go home."

* * * * *

*Don't miss the love stories of
Catherine's sisters Amanda and Lilah in
THE CALHOUN WOMEN: AMANDA & LILAH
available next month from Silhouette!*

FRENCH KISS

Sarah Morgan

Chapter 1

'He's here. He's arrived. Damon Doukakis just strode into the building.'

Woken by the panicky voice, Polly lifted her head from her arms and was blinded by sunlight pouring through the window. 'What? Who?' The words were slurred, her brain emerging slowly from the shadows of sleep. The headache that had been part of her life for the past week still squeezed her skull. 'I must have dozed off. Why didn't anyone wake me?'

'Because you haven't slept for days and you're scary when you're tired. There's no need to panic. I'm doing that for both of us. Here—I brought sustenance.' Balancing two mugs of coffee and a large muffin, the woman kicked the door shut. 'Wake yourself up with carbs and coffee.'

Polly rubbed her eyes and squinted at the screen of her laptop. 'What time is it?'

'Eight o'clock.'

'Eight o'clock?' She flew to her feet, sending papers
and pens spinning across the floor. 'The meeting is in
fifteen minutes! Were you hoping I'd just walk in there
and talk in my sleep or something?' Polly hit 'save'
on the document she'd been working on all night, her
hand shaking from the sudden awakening. Her heart
pounded and deep in her stomach was a solid lump
of dread.

Sleeping didn't make any of it go away and reality
pressed down on her like a heavy weight.

Everything was about to change. Life as she knew
it had ended.

'Stay calm.' Debbie swooped across the office and
put the plate and the mugs on the desk. 'If you show
him you're afraid, he'll walk all over you. That's what
men like Damon Doukakis do. They sniff out weakness and they move in for the kill.'

'I'm not afraid.' The lie wedged itself in her throat.

She *was* afraid. She was afraid of the responsibility
and of the consequences of failure. And, yes, she was
afraid of Damon Doukakis.

Only a fool wouldn't be.

'You're going to be fine. I mean, we're all depending on you, *obviously,* but I don't want the fact that you
have the future of a hundred people in your hands to
make you nervous.'

'Thanks for that calming thought.' Polly allowed
herself a quick gulp of coffee and then checked her
BlackBerry. 'I've only been asleep for two hours and
I already have a hundred e-mails. Don't these people
ever sleep?' She scrolled through them quickly, scan-
ning for anything important. 'Gérard Bonnel wants us

to move our meeting tomorrow back to the evening. Can I get a later flight to Paris?'

'You're not flying. The train was cheaper. I bought you a non-flexible ticket on the seven-thirty out of St Pancreas. If he's moved the meeting then you'll have most of the day to kill.' Debbie leaned forward and stole a large chunk from the muffin. 'Go and see the Eiffel Tower. Make love to a delicious French guy on the banks of the Seine. *Ooh la la.*'

In the process of replying to an e-mail, Polly didn't look up. 'Public sex is an offence, even in France.'

'Nowhere near as big an offence as your non-existent sex-life. When did you last go on a date?'

'I have enough problems without adding a sex-life to the mix.' Polly pressed 'send'. 'Did you sort out a purchase order for that magazine promotion?'

'Yes, yes. Do you ever stop thinking about work? The fearsome Damon Doukakis just might have met his match in you.'

'The rest of these e-mails are going to have to wait.' Polly put the phone down on her desk and glanced at the clock. 'Damn—I wanted to take another look at the presentation. I need to brush my hair—I don't know what to do first—'

'Hair. You slept with your head on your arms and you look like Mohican Barbie.' Debbie whipped a pair of hair straighteners out of Polly's drawer and plugged them in. 'Hold still. This is an emergency.'

'I need to go to the bathroom and do my make-up.'

'No time. Don't worry. You look great. I *love* that look. You're so good at mixing vintage with current.' Debbie slid the irons down Polly's hair. 'The hot pink tights really work.'

Keeping her head still, Polly reached out and unplugged her laptop. 'I can't believe my dad still hasn't rung. His company is being decimated and he's nowhere in sight. I've left about a hundred messages.'

'You know he never switches his mobile on. He hates the thing. There—' Debbie unplugged the irons '—you're done.'

Polly twisted her hair and pinned it in a haphazard knot at the back of her head. 'I even called a few of the London hotels last night to see if a middle-aged gentleman and a young woman had rented a suite with them.'

'That must have been embarrassing.'

'I grew up with embarrassing.' She retrieved her boots from under the desk. 'Damon Doukakis is going to rip us apart when he realises my father isn't showing up.'

'The rest of us will make up for it. The whole company came in early. We're all busy bees. If Doukakis is looking for slackers, he's not going to find them here. We're determined to make a good impression despite your father's absence.'

'It's too late. Damon Doukakis has already made up his mind what he wants to do with us.' And she knew what that was. Panic gripped her. He'd taken control of her father's company. He could do anything he liked with the business.

It was his revenge. His way of sending a message to her father.

But it was a crude weapon. The scorching blaze of his wrath wasn't just going to burn up her father—it was going to burn up innocent staff who didn't deserve to lose their jobs.

The weight of responsibility was suffocating. As her

father's daughter she knew she had to do something, but in truth she was powerless. She had no authority.

Debbie ate a piece of muffin. 'I read somewhere that Damon Doukakis works a twenty-hour day so at least you'll have something in common.'

After three nights with virtually no sleep Polly could barely focus. Drugged by tiredness, she struggled to shake the clouds from her brain. 'I've put together the figures. Let's just hope Michael Anderson can work the laptop. You know what he's like with technology. I've backed up the entire presentation in three places because he managed to delete the thing last time. Are the rest of the board here?'

'They all arrived at the same time as him. Not that they said anything to us.' Deep lines of disapproval bracketed Debbie's mouth. 'None of them have the bottle to face us since they sold their shares to Demon Damon. I still don't understand why a rich, powerful tycoon like him would want to buy our little company. I mean, I love working here, but we're not exactly his style are we?'

Polly thought about how hard she'd worked to try and drag the company into the twenty-first century. 'No. We're not his style.'

'So did he buy us for the fun of it?' Debbie finished the muffin and licked her fingers. 'Maybe this is billionaire retail therapy. Instead of buying shoes, he blows a fortune on an ad agency. He offered the board a whole heap of money.'

Polly kept her mouth shut but the dark dread turned to an icy chill.

She knew why he'd bought the company. And it wasn't something she could share with anyone. Damon

Doukakis had sworn her to silence in a single chilling phone call that had come a few days earlier. A phone call she hadn't mentioned to anyone. She didn't want it to be public knowledge any more than he did.

Polly forced herself to breathe slowly. 'I'm not surprised the board sold. They're greedy. I'm so sick of booking their long lunches and their first-class airfares and then being told we're not profitable. They remind me of mosquitoes, sucking up our lifeblood into their fat bodies—'

Debbie recoiled. 'Pol, that's gross.'

'*They're* gross.' Polly mentally ran through everything she'd put into the presentation. Had she missed anything? 'If I were the one giving the presentation, I wouldn't be so worried.'

'You should be the one giving it.'

'Michael Anderson is too threatened by me to let me open my mouth. He's afraid I might actually tell someone who does the work around here. And anyway, I'm just my father's executive assistant, whatever that is. My job is to keep everything running behind the scenes.' And she was horribly conscious that she had no formal qualifications. She'd learned by watching, listening and trusting her instincts and she was savvy enough to know that for most employers that wouldn't be enough. Polly pressed her hands to her churning stomach, wishing she could stride into the boardroom wielding an MBA from Harvard. 'Doukakis already has a super-slick successful advertising agency in his organisation. He doesn't need another one and he doesn't need our staff. He's just going to snap his jaws around us like—'

'No!' Debbie held up her hand and shuddered. 'Don't

tell me what it will be like. No more of your blood-sucking-mosquito analogies—I just ate your breakfast.'

'I'm just saying—'

'Well, *don't* say. And if Damon Doukakis wants your father's business that badly, well—that's sort of a compliment, isn't it? And you're assuming he'll make us all redundant, but he might not. Why buy a business and then break it up?'

Because he wanted to be in control.

Instead of being a helpless passenger like her, Damon had put himself in the driving seat. While her father was living the life of a man half his age, his company was being savaged by a ruthless predator. And she was fighting that predator single-handed.

'Cheer up.' Debbie patted her shoulder. 'Damon Doukakis might not be as ruthless as they say. You've never actually met him in person.'

Oh, yes, she had.

Feeling her face turn the same colour as her tights, Polly closed her laptop.

They'd met just once, in the head's office the day she and one other girl had been permanently excluded from the exclusive girls' boarding school they attended. Unfortunately that one other girl had been his sister and Damon Doukakis had turned the full force of his anger and recrimination onto Polly, the ringleader.

Just thinking about that day was enough to make her body tremble like a leaf in the wind.

She was under no illusions about what the future held for her.

To Damon Doukakis she was a troublemaker with an attitude problem.

When he lifted his axe, she'd be the first for the chop.

Polly ran her hand over the back of her neck. Maybe she'd just offer to resign if he kept the staff on. He wanted a sacrifice for her father's behaviour, didn't he? So she'd be the sacrifice.

Debbie picked up the empty plate. 'So who *is* your dad seeing this time? Not that Spanish woman he met at salsa classes?'

'No, I—I don't know.' The lie slid easily over her lips. 'I haven't asked.' Stressed out of her mind, Polly picked up her BlackBerry and slipped it into the pocket of her dress. 'It's crazy, isn't it? I can't believe that Damon Doukakis is about to stride in here and take away everything my dad has ever worked for and he is in some hotel somewhere—'

'—having wild monkey sex with a woman who is probably half his age?'

'Don't! I don't want to think about my father having sex, especially with a woman my age.' *Especially not this woman.*

'You should be used to it by now. Do you think your dad realises that his colourful sex-life has put you off ever having a relationship?'

'I don't have time for this conversation.' Blocking out thoughts of her father, Polly wriggled her feet into her boots and zipped them up. 'Have you arranged coffee and pastries for the boardroom?'

'All done. But Damon Doukakis is probably just going to feast on the staff. He's like a great white shark.' Adding to the aura of menace, Debbie made a fin with her hands and hummed the theme from *Jaws*. 'He glides through the smooth waters of commerce, eating everything that gets in his way. He's at the top of the food chain, whereas we're right at the bottom of the ocean. We're nothing more than plankton. Let's just hope we're too small to be a tasty snack.'

Uncomfortable with the analogy, Polly glanced protectively towards the fish tank that she kept on her desk. 'Keep your voice down. Romeo and Juliet are getting nervous. They're hiding behind the pond weed.' She wished she could join the fish. Never in her life had she ever dreaded anything as much as this meeting. Over the past few days she'd sacrificed sleep trying to put together a convincing case for saving the staff. She no longer had any illusions about her own future, but these people were like her family and she was going to fight to the death to protect them.

The phone on her desk rang and she picked it up with the same degree of enthusiasm a doomed man would display on his walk to the gallows. 'Polly Prince...' She recognised the slightly slurred tones of Michael Anderson, her father's deputy and the agency's creative director. Despite the hour, he'd obviously already had a drink. As he instructed her to bring the laptop to the boardroom, Polly gripped the phone tightly. *Snake.* The man hadn't had a creative idea for at least a decade. He'd bled the agency dry and now he'd sold his shares to Damon Doukakis for an inflated price.

Anger shot through her. If they hadn't sold out, this whole situation might have been contained.

Slamming down the phone, Polly scooped up her laptop, determined to do what she could to fight for the staff.

'Good luck.' Debbie glanced at Polly's feet. 'Wow. Those boots are perfect for kicking ass. And they make you look *tall*.'

'That's the idea.' Last time she'd met Damon Doukakis he'd made her feel small in every way. Physically and emotionally, he'd towered over her. It wasn't going to happen again. This time she was determined that when he glared at her they were going to be eye to eye.

Walking towards the boardroom felt like walking the plank. It didn't help that every two seconds someone stuck their head out of an office to wish her luck, each nervous smile making her more aware of the depth of her responsibility. They were relying on her, but deep down she knew she had no influence and virtually nothing with which to defend them. It was like going into battle armed only with her hairdryer. She was just hoping that Michael Anderson would use the presentation she'd put together to fight for them.

The doors to the boardroom were closed and she paused to draw breath, irritated by how nervous she was. Not of the board—for them she felt nothing but contempt—but of Damon Doukakis. She breathed out, slow and long, telling herself that ten years was a long time. Maybe the rumours were wrong. Maybe he'd developed a human streak.

She was relying on it.

Knocking briskly, she opened the door. For a moment all she saw were smug expressions, a litter of coffee cups and dark suits hugging bodies fattened by too many lunches.

The boys' club.

Still clutching her laptop, Polly forced herself to walk forward. As the doors were closed behind her she looked around the table at the men she'd worked with since she'd left school at eighteen. Not one of them looked her in the eye.

Bad sign, she thought grimly.

A couple of the directors stared at the notes in front of them. The atmosphere was thick with tension and anticipation. They reminded her of the bloodthirsty, voyeuristic crowds that sometimes gathered round the scene of an accident. To some, there was nothing so compelling as watching another human being in deep trouble. And she was in deep trouble. Knowing that every man around the table was now a millionaire several times over, Polly felt nothing but disgust.

They reminded her of a pack of hyenas ready to benefit from someone else's kill.

They'd sold her father out without hesitation.

And they'd sold out the staff.

She was so furious with the lot of them that it took her a moment to notice the man positioned at the head of the table.

Occupying her father's chair with arrogant assurance and no evidence of conscience, Damon Doukakis presided over the meeting like a conqueror surveying his captives. He didn't speak or move, but somehow everything about his body language screamed masculine aggression.

Her heart pumping, Polly placed the laptop carefully on the polished surface of the boardroom table.

Those dangerous black eyes watched her and she wondered how he could convey authority when he hadn't even opened his mouth. Somehow he dominated the room, his economy of movement and speech intensifying the aura of power that clung to him like a protective force field.

A superbly tailored suit skimmed his wide shoulders and a snowy white shirt dazzled against his bronzed throat. The knot of his tie was perfect—everything about him was sleek and impeccably groomed. He presented a startling contrast to the rest of the men around the table. Not for this man the excess weight that came with endless business entertaining. Under the expensive suit, his body was hard and strong—honed, no doubt, by exercise and the same rigid self-discipline he applied to his business practices.

Women found him irresistible, of course. He was pure alpha male, the controlling force behind one of the fastest-growing, most successful companies in Europe. In the darkening gloom of economic depression, the Doukakis Media Group was the bright star that shone the light of recovery.

It irritated Polly extremely that the man not only had a towering intellect and an astonishing gift for business, he also looked that good. There was no justice, she thought savagely as she opened up her laptop and reminded herself not to be fooled by the sleek suit or the other outward trappings of civility. As far as she was concerned, the clothes did nothing to mask what he was—a ruthless opportunist who was willing to stop at nothing to achieve his chosen goal. But she understood why the board had sold out to him. He was the king of the beasts, she thought numbly, and the men around him were just lunch, to be consumed in one snap of his jaws. They were weak, and the weak would never challenge a man like Damon Doukakis any more than a wildebeest would turn on a lion.

Look him in the eye, Polly. Look him in the eye.

Knowing that the worst thing she could do was show him she was afraid, she looked. It was only for a second, but something passed between them. The impact of that wordless exchange slammed into her and she dragged her gaze away, shaking from head to toe. She'd expected to feel intimidated. What she hadn't expected was the flash of sexual awareness.

Shaken, Polly switched on the laptop, desperately hoping that he wasn't aware of her reaction to him.

'Gentlemen...' She paused. 'And Mr Doukakis.'

There was grim humour in the smile that played around the corners of his mouth and despite her best intentions Polly found herself staring at the sensual curve of his lips. According to rumour, sexual conquests came as easily to him as the business deals. Doukakis was as ruthless, unemotional and calculating in his relationships as he was in the other areas of his life. Maybe that was why he was so protective of his sister, she thought numbly. He knew what men were like.

But so did she. And an inconvenient flash of chemistry wasn't going to change her opinion.

As her eyes met his again, her tongue suddenly jammed against the roof of her mouth and her lips refused to form the words that had gathered in her brain. In that single moment she saw that he knew. He knew that her heart was racing and her entire body felt as though it had been turned into an electric circuit. He knew the effect he was having on her, from the sparks to the quiver in her belly. It was the same effect he had on all women.

'Miss Prince?'

That cold, sardonic voice shocked her out of her stupor.

If she had harboured any hope that he'd forgotten her contribution to his sister's educational experience, then those hopes now lay smashed in tiny pieces at her feet.

'As you know, Polly is the daughter of our chairman and chief executive.' Apparently blind to the unspoken communication, Michael Andrews finally found the courage to speak. 'Her father always made sure she had a job here.'

The implication was that she was some sort of loser who couldn't get employment without help, and Polly felt her temper rise at the injustice of that introduction. The anger was just what she needed to blast away those other feelings.

Relieved to be back in control, she tapped a key on the laptop and opened a file. 'I've prepared a presentation outlining our business strategy and looking at our forecasts for the future. You'll see that we've won six new clients already this year and those accounts are—'

'We don't need to hear this, Polly.' Michael Anderson interrupted her hastily and Polly's fingers paused on the keyboard. Yes, they did. Without her presentation the staff didn't stand a chance of being kept on.

'But you have to—'

'It's too late, Polly.' With a glance at his fellow board members, Michael Anderson cleared his throat. 'I understand that this is a very awkward situation for you, but your father no longer has control of this company. He's always been unconventional, but now he appears to have disappeared completely. Even today, with rumours of the takeover all over the news, there is no sign of him, which just confirms that the board made the right decision to sell. The Doukakis Media Group is cutting edge. These are exciting times.' He cast a fawning glance at the man who sat still and silent at the head of the table. 'There's going to be a shake-up. We'll be announcing redundancies to the staff later but I wanted to tell you personally as your father isn't here. It's tough, I know—' he rearranged his drooping features into a look of sympathy '—but this is business.'

Polly felt as though she'd stepped into a parallel universe. Her brain was fuzzy and there was a buzzing in her ears. 'Wait a minute.' Her voice sounded robotic and nothing like her own. 'You're saying you're going to make everyone redundant just like that, with no discussion? It's your job to protect them—to show Mr Doukakis why they're needed.'

'The point is, Polly, they're not needed.'

'I disagree.' Her fingers were suddenly ice-cold. Panic crept into her throat and lodged itself there as if she'd suddenly inhaled all her worst fears. 'The accounts we've won, we've won as a team. And we're a good team.'

'Just leave the laptop, Polly.' Michael Anderson tapped the end of his pen on the table. 'If one of Mr Doukakis's people wants to look at the presentation, they can.'

That was it.

They were dismissing her.

Every eye in the room was fixed on her, waiting for her to give up and walk out.

Her father's company would be dissolved. One hundred people would lose their jobs.

'It isn't over.' The words spilled from her lips and Polly stared directly at Michael Anderson, the man who had sold her father out and was now selling out her colleagues. Desperately, she tried to appeal to his conscience. 'You *have* to stand up there and give this presentation.'

'Polly—'

'You have a responsibility! These people work for you. *They put themselves out for you.* You should be defending them.' The exhaustion and stress of the past week overflowed like a river bursting its banks after heavy rainfall. 'It's because of their hard work that you've been living the high life. Why did you ask me to put together the presentation if you never intended to use it?'

'You were anxious about your father.' Michael's tone was patronising. 'I thought it would keep you busy.'

'I'm not a child, Mr Anderson. I can keep myself busy. I've had no choice about that since the key players in this company do nothing but sit on their backsides eating and drinking their way through the profits.' Dimly aware that she was burning every bridge, she stalked round the table and had the satisfaction of seeing Michael Anderson's eyes widen in consternation.

'What are you doing? Where are you—? I can see you're angry, but—'

'Angry? I'm not angry. I'm *furious*. You have one hundred employees biting their nails out there—' Beyond caring about herself, Polly flung her arm towards the door. 'One hundred people terrified of losing their jobs who right now are wondering whether they're going to be able to afford to keep a roof over their heads and *you're not even going to fight for them?* You're a disgusting coward.'

'That's enough!' His face was red and angry. 'If it weren't for the fact that you're the boss's daughter, you would have been fired long ago. You have a real attitude problem. And as for the way you dress—'

'How a person dresses doesn't affect their ability to do a job, Mr Anderson. Not that I expect you to understand that. With the exception of the board—' she cast a derisive look around the boardroom table '—this is a young, vibrant, creative agency. I don't need to wear a boring suit with an elastic waistband to accommodate a four-course business lunch paid for by your unsuspecting clients.'

Scarlet-faced, Michael Anderson looked as though he was at high risk of a stroke. 'I'm going to overlook your behaviour because I know how difficult this week has been for you. And I'm going to give you some fatherly advice as your own father seems to take his responsibilities in that area so lightly. Take your redundancy money, go on a good long holiday and rethink your future. Apart from your extremely unfortunate temper, you're a nice girl. Beautiful.' Sweat beading his brow, he dragged his eyes away from her legs. 'You're only working on client accounts because of your father. In any other company you'd be a secretary. Not that there's anything wrong with that,' he said hastily as he saw Polly's expression darken. 'All I'm saying is that a girl with your looks doesn't need to spend her nights with her head in a spreadsheet playing with business—isn't that right, gentlemen?'

A murmur of agreement spread through the watching board members. The only person not smiling was Damon Doukakis. He stayed silent, his eyes hooded as he watched the antics from the far end of the table.

Polly saw nothing through the red mist of anger that clouded her vision. 'Don't you *dare* criticize my father.

And don't you dare make those sexist, misogynistic comments when we all know who's doing the work in this company. You sold out to the highest bidder for personal gain. You're now multimillionaires and we're unemployed.' She tried and failed to keep the emotion out of her voice. 'Where was your sense of responsibility? Shame on you. Shame on all of you.'

Michael Anderson's mouth was slack with shock. 'Who do you think you are?'

'Someone who cares about the future of this company and the people who work for it. If you make one single one of them redundant before at least considering other options then I'll—' *What?* What could she do? Aware that she was utterly powerless, the anger suddenly left her and Polly turned and stalked back round the table, furious with herself for losing control. She felt spent and exhausted and utterly dispirited. She'd let everyone down. Instead of making things better, she'd made them a thousand times worse.

Damn, damn and damn. Why couldn't she stay cool and calm like these fat, overblown men in suits? Why hadn't she gone to bed last night? Being tired always lowered her burn threshold.

Deafened by the extended silence, Polly felt misery slide through her veins. Her anger had blown itself out, but not before she'd ruined everything. 'Look—I'll go, OK? I'll walk out of here right now without a fuss. Just don't make everyone redundant.' Mortified by her behaviour, she directed her words at Damon Doukakis, who still hadn't made a move. 'Please don't make anyone redundant because of me.' Horrified to feel the hot sting of tears, she closed her laptop and was about to leave the room when Damon Doukakis spoke.

'I want to see that presentation. Send it to my hand-held.' His voice hard and inflexible, his eyes locked on Polly with the deadly accuracy of a laser-guided missile. 'I want to see everything you've put together.'

Mute with shock, Polly couldn't move, and it was Michael Anderson who recovered first.

'She's just a glorified secretary, Damon. Honestly, you really shouldn't—'

Damon Doukakis ignored him. He was still looking at Polly. 'You can tell the staff they have three months to prove their worth. The only immediate job losses will be the board.' That unexpected bombshell sent ripples of consternation across the room.

As the meaning of his words sank home, Polly felt light-headed. He wasn't getting rid of the staff. They had a stay of execution.

Making a strange choking sound, Michael Anderson tried to loosen the collar of his shirt. 'You can't get rid of the board! We're the engine of this company.'

'If my car had an engine like you it would have been scrapped,' Damon said grimly. 'You revealed your commitment to the company when you sold me your shares. I don't want anyone working for me who can be bought. Nor do I want to find myself slapped with a lawsuit for sexual discrimination, which will undoubt-edly come my way if you stay with the company.'

Watching the other man crumble, Polly felt like cheering, but Damon Doukakis was still speaking, listing his demands with a complete lack of emotion.

'I'm moving the entire operation into my London offices. I have two floors empty and a team ready to facilitate the move.'

Polly's desire to cheer instantly faded. 'But the staff have been here for ever and—'

'I don't deal in "for ever", Miss Prince. In business, the best you can hope for is "for now". My second in command, Carlos, will take over the day to day running of business for the foreseeable future.'

'But Bill Henson has been in that post for—'

'For far too long,' came the smooth reply. 'He can work with Carlos for the next three months. If we're impressed, we'll take him on. I never lose good people. But I run a meritocracy, not a charity.'

Michael Anderson's face was a strange grey colour. 'Damon—' He cleared his throat. 'You need someone to show you our systems. Explain how the company is run.'

'It took me less than five minutes with your balance sheet to assess how the company is run. The word is *badly.* And I've already decided to keep someone on who has inside knowledge.'

Michael sagged and his smile was slack and desperate. 'That's a relief. For a moment there I thought—'

'Which is why Miss Prince will come and work alongside me for the next three months.'

Work alongside him? Oh, no, not that. 'I'm ready to step down, Mr Doukakis.'

'You're not stepping anywhere, Miss Prince. You and your laptop are going to be right by my side as we sort out this mess together.' His words were deliberately ambiguous and Polly wondered which mess he was referring to—the company, or her father's relationship with his sister.

'But—'

'My people will be here within the hour to organise

the move into my offices. Anyone who would rather not move is, of course, free to leave.'

'Wait a minute—' Polly felt as if she'd been flattened under a heavy object. She'd assumed she'd be the first out of the door. She was ready and willing to make that sacrifice. In fact she was desperate to put as much distance as possible between her and Damon Doukakis. 'I resign.'

His eyes locked on hers. 'Resign and I'll make the entire workforce redundant this afternoon.' The suppressed anger in him licked through the room, sizzling everyone around the table to a crisp.

'No!' Polly felt dizzy with horror. 'They haven't done anything.'

'Having glanced at your balance sheet, I find it all too easy to believe you. I'm asking myself what anyone in this company has done over the past year. It's only fair to warn you that I don't hold out much hope that these people will still be working for me in three months. I've seen more activity in a graveyard.'

Polly's limbs weakened. She thought about Doris Cooper, who had worked for her father in the post room for forty years. Recently widowed, the woman made a habit of giving the wrong post to the wrong people, but no one wanted to upset her so they quietly reorganised everything when she wasn't looking. Then there was Derek Wills who couldn't spell his name but made lovely cups of tea to keep everyone going. If she walked out they wouldn't even make three weeks, let alone three months. 'Fine,' she croaked. 'I'll work for you. But I think your behaviour is appalling.'

'Your opinion of me is unlikely to be lower than mine of you.' He came right back at her, the full power of his anger slamming into her shaking frame with the force of a hurricane.

Polly stood rigid, impossibly intimidated despite her attempts not to be. There was something terrifying about that splintering dark gaze and the raw power of the man in front of her. She didn't need to see the contempt in his eyes to know he had a low opinion of her and even the heels on her boots didn't help. He still made her feel small in every way possible. But none of that was as scary as the other feelings she was trying so desperately to ignore. *The quickening of her pulse and the strange melting sensation inside her tummy.* 'You're not being fair.'

'Life isn't fair.' His tone was hard and uncompromising. 'Like it or not, you're all now part of my company. Welcome to my world, Miss Prince.'

Chapter 2

He'd never encountered such a shambolic operation
in his life.

Infuriated at having landed himself with a company
that offered him no benefit whatsoever, and angrier
still at the wanton carelessness the Prince board had
demonstrated towards people's job security, Damon
cleared the room with a single movement of his hand.

It frustrated him to have to deal with this situation
when all he really wanted to do was track down his
sister and protect her from the fallout of her own mistakes. Even after an intense week of reflection, he was
no closer to understanding what had driven her to make
such an appalling decision. Was her choice of Peter
Prince just another ploy to prove her independence?
Challenge him? He stood for a moment, bracing himself against the crushing weight of responsibility that

had been his closest companion since he'd been forced to take charge of his sister's welfare in his teens.

As Polly Prince stalked towards the door with the board members, he intercepted her. Slamming the door shut behind the last suited man, he turned on the woman he hadn't laid eyes on for a decade.

'Wherever you are, trouble is always close behind.'

She was taller than he remembered. Other than that, she didn't seem to have changed much from the rebellious teenager who had stood sullen and defiant in the school office hearing her fate.

Damon scanned her from head to foot in a single sweeping glance, taking her choice of dress to be just another example of her careless, irresponsible attitude to life.

Everyone else had chosen to wear a dark suit to the meeting. It was typical that Polly Prince had favoured fashionable over formal, her short dress revealing incredibly long legs showcased in hot pink tights and black ankle boots. She looked fresh, young and—sexy.

The sudden explosion of primal lust was as unexpected as it was unwelcome and Damon dragged his gaze up from the heels of her cheeky black boots to focus on her face.

Accustomed to mixing with women who dressed with understated elegance, he was exasperated that the self-discipline he exerted over his own responses appeared to have deserted him. Even as he was telling himself that he had more sophistication than to feel sexual attraction for a girl with great legs, he was wrestling with a powerful urge to shrug off his jacket and cover those slender curves.

To kill those unwanted feelings stone-dead, he focused on the issue of his sister and her father. 'Where the hell is he?'

'I don't know.'

'Then tell me what you *do* know.'

Her delicate features were set and determined as she stared directly at him. 'I know you've taken over my father's company. Clearly you're a megalomaniac.' Her cool remark threw petrol onto the fire that raged inside him.

'Don't take me on, Miss Prince. I'm a tough boss but I'm a tougher enemy. Remember that.' He delivered the warning and had the satisfaction of seeing her face lose colour. 'I don't want to hear anything from that smart mouth of yours except answers to my questions. *Where* is your father?'

'I have no idea.'

That unmistakably honest admission was a solid blow to his gut. He'd been relying on her to reveal her father's whereabouts. 'You must be able to make contact. How do you get hold of him in an emergency?'

'I don't.' She sounded genuinely surprised by the question. 'My father taught me to be self-sufficient. If there's an emergency, I handle it.'

'I've taken over your father's company, Miss Prince. This is definitely an emergency and I don't see you handling anything. I can't believe that the CEO of a company can so readily abandon his responsibilities.' It was a lie, of course. He'd seen it before, hadn't he? Tasted first-hand the bitter after-effects of another man's careless disregard for obligation. The memory of it had never left him. Even now, when success was his many times over, it was always there beneath the surface. It drove him forward from one deal to the next.

It was the reason he had never relied on another man for employment.

In the midst of discovering that the past still had the power to destabilise him, Damon found his attention snagged by the wisp of pale blonde hair that had floated down from the haphazard, kooky hairstyle she wore. It seemed that even her hair was rebellious.

This girl, he mused, knew nothing about obligation and responsibility.

She selfishly pursued her own agenda with no thought to the casualties. Ten years before it had been his sister who had suffered. Thrusting aside the fleeting thought that Polly Prince couldn't be held accountable for her father's shortcomings, he subjected her to a cold appraisal which she returned with no visible display of nerves or conscience.

'You offered an inflated price for the stock and the board members sold my father out. That was outside my control. My priority now is to do everything I can to protect our loyal staff from your predatory instincts.'

'Cut the act. We both know that you have no interest whatsoever in protecting the staff. The only reason you care about the business is because it's your meal ticket. No other company would be stupid enough to take you on. You've been bleeding this company dry for years, but it's stopping right now. If you were hoping I'd give you a pay-off to leave, then you're in for a shock because I don't carry passengers. You may be the *ex*-boss's daughter, but from now on you're going to work for your money.' The anger boiled up inside him, the past somehow mixing with the present. 'You're going to take your useless, lazy self and finally do a job. And if all you're capable of doing is clean the toilets, then you'll clean the toilets.'

Those sapphire-blue eyes were locked on his and then she made a sound that might have been a laugh. 'You really don't know anything about the company you just bought, do you? Mr Media Mogul who never makes a mistake in business—Mr Big Tycoon who is all-seeing and all-knowing—is suddenly blind.' Her voice dripped contempt and Damon, who prided himself on his lack of emotion in all his dealings, found himself wrestling the temptation to throttle her.

'My only interest in your father's business is as a way of ensuring his co-operation.'

'You have no choice but to be interested in his business. You own it. A fairly heavy-handed approach to a problem, I'd say.'

'I'll do what it takes to protect my sister.' He'd been protecting her since he was sixteen years old— since that cold February night when the policeman had knocked on the door and delivered the shattering news. Losing both parents in such a brutal way had been devastating but Damon had somehow dragged himself through each day, driven by the knowledge that another person was depending on him. He was all Arianna had in the world and what had began as the most terrifying responsibility had become the driving force behind everything he did. Now, protecting Arianna was as natural as breathing. Nothing would destroy the web of protection he'd spun around her. 'If you have any idea where they are, you should tell me now because I will find out.'

'I have no idea. I am not my father's keeper.'

'Arianna is your friend.' He watched with satisfaction as that barb slid home.

'And she's your sister. She's as likely to confide in you as she is in me.'

'She tells me nothing about her life.' The words tasted bitter in his mouth. 'And now I know why. Evidently she has much to hide.'

'Or possibly you're just not an approachable person, Mr Doukakis. Arianna is twenty-four. An adult. If she wanted you to know what she was doing, she'd tell you. Perhaps you should try trusting her.'

Worry fuelled his anger. 'My sister is ridiculously naïve.'

'Had you not been so over-protective, perhaps she would have developed some street sense.'

Damon was thrown once again by the contrast between her fragile appearance and the layer of steel he sensed in her. It had been the same ten years before, when she'd stood in the office in silence, steadfastly refusing to explain her appalling disregard for school rules and general good behaviour. Because of her, his sister had been forced to leave one of the best schools in the country. Damon had subsequently banned Arianna from seeing the appalling Polly Prince. That was before he'd understood how teenage girls worked. The ban had effectively spurred his young sister into full rebellion mode and Arianna had promptly doubled the time she'd spent with the Prince family. It was a decision that had triggered numerous high-octane explosions in the Doukakis household.

'Arianna is a very rich woman. That makes her a target for all sorts of unscrupulous individuals.'

'I don't pretend to be an expert on relationships, Mr

Doukakis, but I do know that my father isn't with Arianna because of her money.'

'Really? Then perhaps you have no idea just how much trouble this company is in.' He wiped his mind of images of his young sister with an ageing playboy.

'Has it crossed your mind that he might be with her because Arianna is warm and funny and my father finds her entertaining?'

The thought of what form that 'entertainment' was likely to take sent his anger levels soaring from dangerous to critical. 'Well, she won't be entertaining him for much longer.' Control slid from his grip. 'How the hell can you be so calm? You should be completely mortified. Your father is—how old?—fifty?'

'He's fifty-four.'

'And it doesn't embarrass you to see his name linked with an endless string of young women? He is thirty years older than Arianna. He's been divorced *four times*. That's a sign of an unstable personality.'

'Or a sign of an eternal optimist, Mr Doukakis.' Her voice was husky. 'My dad continues to believe in love and the institution of marriage.'

If it hadn't been his sister they were talking about, Damon would have laughed. 'The institution of marriage doesn't require endless practice, Miss Prince.' Her defence of her father drove his opinion of her lower still. 'When I walk out of here, I'll be giving a statement to the media. Within the hour news of my takeover will be all over the internet. Once he finds out I have control of the company, your father *will* make contact. When that happens, I want to know. And I want to know immediately.'

'My father doesn't like the internet. He says it inhibits the development of personal relationships.'

At the mention of personal relationships, sweat broke out under his collar. 'Bad news has a habit of travelling fast and we both know I'm the last person he would want at the helm of his precious company.'

'I agree. He won't be pleased. He considers you to be a man whose only goal is profit. He didn't like me mixing with you when we were teenagers.'

Transfixed by that altogether unexpected revelation, Damon stared at her with genuine astonishment. 'He considered *me* a bad influence?'

'My father has a real thing about people who only judge the world in financial terms. That isn't the way he runs his life and it certainly isn't the way he runs his business. To my father a successful business is as much about the people as the profits.'

'It took me a single glance at your company accounts to work that out. Prince Advertising is afloat through good fortune and the accidental success of a few of your campaigns,' Damon snapped out, noticing that a faint frown appeared on her forehead. 'The company is in profit despite your father's approach to business, not because of it. As for the people—your headcount is severely bloated and you need to slim down. You're carrying dead wood.'

'Don't you dare describe these people as dead wood. Everyone here has an important part to play.' Her voice shook. 'Your fight is with my father, not with the innocent people working for this company. You can't make them redundant. It would be wrong.'

'Business tip number one,' Damon said softly.

'Never let your opponent know what you're thinking. It gives them an advantage.'

Those narrow shoulders straightened. 'You already have the advantage, Mr Doukakis. You've bought my father's company. And I'm not afraid to tell you what I'm thinking. I'm thinking that you're as ruthless and cold as they say you are.' Her eyes shone and he wondered if he should warn her that it was dangerous to wear her emotions so close to the surface. And then he realised how hypocritical that would be because, for once, his own were similarly exposed.

Acting on an impulse he didn't want to examine too closely, Damon reached out and caught her chin in his hand, feeling the softness of her skin under the hard pads of his fingers as he forced her to look at him. 'You're right. I am as ruthless as they say I am. You might want to remember that. And tears just irritate me, Miss Prince.'

'I'm not crying.'

But she was close to crying. He recognised the signs and he could feel the betraying tremble of her jaw. She was the same age as Arianna and yet that was where the similarity ended. For a fleeting moment he wondered what her life must have been like—an only child brought up by her father, a notorious playboy.

'I took nothing your board of directors did not readily give.'

'You made them an offer they couldn't refuse.' Her emotional accusation almost made him smile.

'I'm Greek, not Sicilian. And the people working for me would never sell me out, no matter how good the offer.'

He saw something flicker in her eyes and then she

jerked her chin away from his grasp. 'Everyone has their price, Mr Doukakis.'

And she should know, Damon thought grimly, remembering the reason she'd been excluded from school. Definitely nothing like his sister. 'I'm afraid I have to politely decline your offer. When it comes to my bed partners I'm extremely discerning.'

For a moment she stared at him blankly and then her mouth dropped. 'I was talking about business.'

Damon found himself looking at those lips. 'Of course you were.'

'You are *so* offensive. Have you finished?'

'Finished? I haven't even started.' Damon slowly lifted his gaze and stared into her eyes. The chemistry was unmistakable but it didn't worry him in the slightest. When it came to women he made his decisions based on logic, not libido. He had no time for people who were unable to exercise control over their impulses when the need arose. 'At the moment the staff have their jobs. Whether or not they keep them is up to you and your father. I'll expect you in my offices at two o'clock this afternoon. You're going to start doing some work. And don't waste time appealing to my emotions, Miss Prince. I never let emotions cloud my decision-making.'

'Really?' Those blue eyes locked on his and he saw the same fire and determination in her he'd seen that day in the school. 'That's interesting, because I'd say that your decision-making in this instance has been entirely driven by emotion. You're using this takeover as leverage against my father. If that isn't an emotional decision, I don't know what is. And now, if you'll excuse me, I need to organise the staff for the office move. If you really want all this "dead wood" transferred to your offices by this afternoon then I'd better get my useless, lazy self moving.' She stalked towards the door, all long legs and youthful attitude as her dress swung tantalisingly round the tops of her thighs and the spiked heel of her boots tapped the floor.

Hauling his gaze away from the seductive curve of her bottom, Damon slammed the lid on that part of him that wanted to flatten her to the boardroom table and indulge in raw, mindless sex. 'And do something about the way you dress. *Theé mou*, you look like a flamingo in your hot pink tights. I expect the people working for me to look professional.'

'So you don't like what I do and you don't like the way I look.' Her back to him, she stood frozen to the spot. 'Anything else?'

He wondered if she kept her back to him as a gesture of defiance or because she was close to tears.

There was something disturbing about the fragile set of her narrow shoulders, but Damon was out of sympathy. If she really cared about the staff, the business wouldn't be in the state it was in. Because of this woman and her father, Prince Advertising was in a pitiful state and a hundred people now risked losing their jobs. A hundred families risked having their lives shattered. A chill spread down his spine as he contemplated the possible fall-out from that scenario. 'I want all the system passwords handed over to my team so that we can access everything. If I'm going to unravel the mess you've created here I need to know what I'm dealing with. That's it. You can go.'

He could have told her that he considered redundancies a sign of failure. He could have told her that he understood his responsibilities as an employer better than anyone and that he ran his business according to his own rigid principles.

He could have told her all of that, but he didn't.

She'd contributed to this shameful mess.

Let her suffer.

'I'm going to kill him. I'm going to put my hands round that bronzed throat and squeeze until he can't utter another sarcastic word and then I'm going to cut holes in his perfect suit and squirt ketchup on his white shirt...' Feeling powerless, Polly lowered her head onto her hands and thumped her fist on the desk. 'What do women see in him? I cannot *imagine* voluntarily spending a single minute in his company. He's a heartless, sexist monster.' But that hadn't stopped her being hyper-aware of him all the way through their confrontation. There was a sexual energy between them that seriously unsettled her. *How* could she find him attractive?

'I don't know about him being a monster. The man is smoking hot.' Debbie put a stack of empty boxes onto the floor and started clearing the office. 'At least we still have our jobs. Let's face it, the figures are so bad he could have dumped us all and no one could really have blamed him.'

Knowing that it was true, Polly lifted her head and stared at her friend in despair. 'Trust me, that might have been the better option.'

'You don't mean that.'

'I don't know what I mean, but I know I can't work for that man.' Exhausted and stressed, she tried to blot out images of his cold, handsome face. *Cold*, she reminded herself. *Cold, with no sense of humour.* 'I'm not going to last a week. The only thing in doubt is whether I kill him before he kills me.'

'You can't walk out! The future of the staff depends on you staying!'

'How do you know that?'

'We were listening at the door.'

Polly sank down in her chair. 'Have you no shame?'

'This was a crisis. We needed to know whether to ring the job centre or not.'

'Ring them anyway. You won't want to work for him for long.' Trying to galvanise herself into action, Polly tugged open the drawer in her desk and stared down at the jumble of belongings. 'I need a different pair of tights. Hot pink clearly isn't his favourite colour. I cannot *believe* I'm about to change my clothes because a man asked me to. How low can a girl go? I should have told him where to stuff his dress code but I'd already antagonised him more than I should have done.'

'He didn't like the tights?' Debbie raised her eyebrows. 'Did you tell him you're wearing them because—?'

'*Tell him?*' Polly rummaged through the drawer. 'No one *tells* Damon Doukakis anything. They just listen while he commands. This is a dictatorship, not a democracy. How the hell does the man keep his staff?'

'He pays top rate and he looks bloody gorgeous.' Debbie stacked books into the boxes. 'Calm down. I know you're angry, but look on the bright side—he fired the board. And you were *brilliant*.'

'I lost my temper with Michael the Moron.'

'I know. You were amazing. You really let him have it. Pow. Smack.' Debbie abandoned the packing and punched the air like a boxer. 'Take that, you sexist pig. No more looking up our skirts. No more demanding cups of coffee while we're all running round like demented baboons doing the work he's too lazy to do. We were all cheering.'

'There's nothing to cheer about. Haven't you ever heard the phrase out of the frying pan into the fire? Damon Doukakis is a macho control freak with serious anger issues—' Polly silenced the internal voice that reminded her that he was protecting his sister. That was no excuse to go completely over the top.

'You can forgive a man a lot when he looks like that.'

'I'm not interested in the way he looks.'

'Well, you should be. You're young and available. I know you're anti-marriage because of your dad, but Damon Doukakis scores a full ten on the sexometer.'

'Debbie!'

'Oh, chill, will you? You've been uptight all week. It's bad for your blood pressure.'

Polly had her nose back in the drawer. 'I don't have any boring black tights.'

'Just wear leggings. Here's a box—start packing.'

She took the box and forced herself to breathe slowly. Even though she'd grown up knowing that sex and love were two different things, the sexual tension between her and Damon horrified her. 'I wouldn't touch the man with a long pole. Apart from the fact that I can't be attracted to a man who doesn't smile, I wouldn't want to have sex with a guy who is about to make a load of innocent people redundant. It doesn't show a caring personality.'

'You can't expect him to smile when he's taking

over a company as unusual as ours.' Debbie closed the box she was packing and started on another. 'Most people just don't get the way we work here. I mean, I love it, but we're not exactly conventional, are we? Nothing about your dad is conventional.'

'Don't remind me.'

'Relax. When your dad finally emerges from wherever he is this time, at least he'll still have an intact company even if it does belong to someone else. If Demon Damon was thinking of making everyone redundant immediately he wouldn't be mobilising an army of removal people to transport us from economy city to Doukakis World.' Debbie carefully lifted a plant. 'I'm excited. I've always wanted to see inside that building. Apparently there's a fountain in the foyer. The plants are going to love that. So are the fish. Running water is very soothing. He must care about his employees to give them something as lovely as a fountain.'

'It's probably there so that despairing employees can drown themselves on their way out of the building.' Polly walked across to the noticeboard she had on her wall and started taking down photographs.

'You always say that everyone has a sensitive side.'

'Well, I was wrong. Damon Doukakis is steelplated. There's more sensitivity in an armoured tank.'

'He's super-successful.'

Polly stared at a photograph of her father standing on a table at a Christmas party with a drink in one hand and a busty blonde from Accounts in the other. 'Whose side are you on?'

'Actually, Pol, I'm on the side of the person who pays my salary. Sorry if that makes me an employment slut, but that's the way it has to be when you have dependants. Principles are all very well, but you can't eat them and I have two cats to feed. Careful with those photographs.' Debbie looked over Polly's shoulder and gave a nostalgic sigh. 'That was a good night. Mr Foster had one too many. He's been nice to me ever since that party.'

'He's a lovely man but he's not a very good accountant. He won't last five minutes if Damon Doukakis decides to analyse what he does.' Overwhelmed with the responsibility, Polly carefully slid the photographs into an envelope. 'I'm sure the Doukakis financial department are killer-sharp, like the boss. They're not going to be impressed when they see Mr Foster using a pen and a calculator. It will destroy him to lose his job.'

'Maybe he won't. You've been teaching him to use a spreadsheet.'

'Yes, but it's slow going. Every morning I have to go back over what we did the day before. I was hoping we could sneak him past the inquisition without anyone actually wanting to know what he does but it isn't going to be easy. I bet Doukakis knows if his staff stop to draw breath.' The responsibility swamped her. 'Debs, we can't give him a reason to let anyone go. Everyone has to pull their weight and if they can't pull their weight then we have to cover for them.'

'So this probably isn't a good time to tell you that Kim's child-minder is sick. She's brought the baby into the office because that's what she always does, but…' Debbie's voice tailed off. 'I'm guessing Damon doesn't have a soft spot for babies.'

Swamped by the volume of work facing her, Polly tipped the contents of a drawer into the box without bothering to sort it. 'Tell Kim to quietly take the rest of the day working from home, but get her to try and find childcare for tomorrow.'

'And if she can't?'

'We'll give her an office and she can hide in there. I suppose it's a waste of time asking if my father has phoned? I'm going to fit him with an electronic tagging device. Did you phone any of those hotels I gave you?'

'All of them. Nothing.'

'I wouldn't put it past him to have bribed some blonde hotel manager to keep his booking quiet.' Polly put the photographs into a box. 'We need to get the rest of this packed up. The barbarian hordes from Doukakis Media Group are going to be descending on us any minute to help us move.'

'The takeover is headlines on the BBC. You dad must know by now.'

Polly paused to swallow two painkillers with a glass of water. 'I don't think he's exactly watching television, Debs.'

'Do you have any idea who he's with this time?'

Yes.

Her father was with Arianna, a girl young enough to be his daughter.

Humiliation crawled up her spine as she anticipated the predictable reaction from everyone around her. Polly was no more eager to share the information with the world than Damon Doukakis.

For once in his life, couldn't her father have picked someone closer to his own age?

'I try not to think about my father's love-life.' Dodging the question, she crammed the lid onto the box. 'I just don't see how we can move our entire office in the space of a few hours. I'm exhausted. All I want to do is go to bed and catch up on sleep.'

'So go to bed. You know how chilled your dad is about flexitime. He always says if the staff don't want to be there, there's no point in them being there.'

'Unfortunately Damon Doukakis is about as chilled as the Amazon jungle. And he wants me in his office at two o'clock.'

Debbie's eyes widened. 'What for?'

'He wants me to start working for my money.'

Debbie stared at her for a moment and then burst out laughing. 'Sorry, but that's *so* funny. Did you tell him the truth?'

'What's the point? He'd never believe me and he's made it his personal mission in life to make my life hell.' Polly ripped off a piece of tape and slammed her foot down on the bulging box to flatten the lid. 'So far he's succeeding beyond his wildest fantasies.'

Debbie picked up a stack of prospectuses from universities. 'What do you want me to do with these?'

Polly stared at them and felt slightly strange. 'Just shred them.' If Damon Doukakis found those on her desk, he'd laugh at her. 'Get rid of them. I should never have sent off for them in the first place.'

'But you've always said that what you want more than anything is to—'

'I said, shred them.' She resisted the impulse to grab them and stow them carefully in a box. *What was the point?* 'It was just a stupid dream.'

A really crazy dream.

Numb, she watched as her hopes and dreams were shredded alongside the paper.

* * *

Five hours later, exhausted from having supervised the packing of the entire building and seen the staff safely into the coaches laid on to transfer them to their new offices, Polly took her first step into the plush foyer of the Doukakis Tower. The centrepiece was the much talked about water feature, a bubbling monument to corporate success, blending seamlessly with acres of glass and marble. Blinded by architectural perfection, Polly could see why the building was one of London's most talked about landmarks.

Directed to the fortieth floor by the stunning blonde on the futuristic curved reception desk, she walked towards the glass-fronted express elevator. From behind her she heard the bright-voiced receptionist answer the phone. 'DMG Corporate, Freya speaking, how may I help you?'

You can't, Polly thought gloomily. *No one can help me now. I'm doomed.*

Everywhere she looked there was evidence of the Doukakis success story.

Used to staring at a crumbling factory wall from her tiny office window, she felt her jaw drop in amazement as she saw the view from the elevator.

Through the glass she could see the River Thames curving in a ribbon through London and to her right the famous circle of London Eye with the Houses of Parliament in the distance. It was essentially a huge glass viewing capsule, as stunning and contemporary as the rest of the building. Damon Doukakis might be ruthless, she thought faintly, but he had exceptional taste.

Depressed by the contrast between his achievements and their comparative failure, Polly turned away from the view and tried not to think what it would be like to work for a company as progressive as this one. Everyone employed by him probably had a business degree, she thought enviously.

No wonder he'd been less than impressed with her.

She stared at herself in one of the two mirrored panels that bordered the doors of the elevator and wondered how she could prove to him that she knew what she was doing.

She was now working for the most notoriously demanding boss in the city of London. She still wasn't really sure why he'd kept her on instead of just firing her along with the board. Presumably because he saw her as his only possible link with her father.

Or possibly just to torture her.

Once the shock of seeing the board of directors leave the building had faded, the staff had erupted into whoops of joy, relieved to still have their jobs. Surprisingly, even the thought of moving to new offices didn't seem to disturb people. Everyone seemed excited about the prospect of a move to more exciting surroundings.

The only person not celebrating was Polly.

She didn't know much about Damon Doukakis, but she knew that he didn't do anyone favours. He was keeping people on for a reason, not out of kindness. When it suited him to let them go, he'd let them go. Unless she could persuade him that the staff were worth keeping.

All morning she'd multitasked, talking to clients via her wireless headset while packing up boxes and masterminding the move. Somewhere in the middle of the chaos she'd stripped off her pink tights and replaced them with black leggings. It was her one and only concession to the strict Doukakis dress code.

Now, she wondered if she should have avoided conflict altogether and worn a suit. Trying to summon sufficient energy to get through the rest of the day, she slapped her cheeks to produce some colour and ignored the hideous squirming in her stomach.

First days, she thought grimly. *She hated first days.* It was like being back at school. Whispers behind her back. *Is that her?* The humiliation of her father driving her to school in a flashy car with his latest embarrassingly young wife installed in the front seat. Giggles heard across the length of a playground. Mysterious collisions in the corridor that sent her books flying and her self-esteem plummeting. Standing alone in the lunch queue and then finding an empty table and trying to look as though eating alone was a choice, not a sentence.

Polly glared at her reflection in the mirror. If those days had taught her anything it was how to survive. No matter what happened, she was not going to let Damon Doukakis close down the company. Not without a fight.

Somehow, she had to impress him.

Wondering how on earth you impressed a man like Damon Doukakis, she pressed the button for the executive floor and the doors of the elevator slid closed. But at the last minute a gloved male hand clamped itself around the door and they opened again.

Her hope for two minutes peace dashed, Polly squashed herself back against the far corner as a man dressed in motorbike leathers strode into the lift. She caught a glimpse of wide, powerful shoulders and realised that it was Damon Doukakis himself.

Their eyes clashed and she had a sudden urge to bolt from the lift and use the stairs.

The temperature in the tiny capsule suddenly shot up.

He didn't even have to open his mouth, she thought desperately. Even the way he stood was intimidating. Irritated by the fact that he looked as good in leather as he did in fine wool, Polly raised an eyebrow.

'I thought we were supposed to wear suits?'

'I had a meeting across town. I used the motorbike.' He wore his masculinity like a banner, overt and un-apologetic, and Polly was horrified to feel her insides liquefy.

'So you don't change into leather just to beat your staff.'

The glance he sent in her direction was both a threat and a warning. 'When I start beating my staff,' he said silkily, 'you'll be the first to know because you'll be right at the top of my list. Perhaps if you'd had some discipline at fourteen you wouldn't have turned out to be such a disaster. Evidently your father didn't ever learn to say no to you.'

Polly didn't tell him that her father had abdicated parental responsibility right from the beginning. 'He had trouble handling me.'

'Well, I won't have trouble.' His tone lethally soft, he took in her appearance in a single glance. 'I'll give you marks for being on time and for changing out of those fluorescent tights.'

For some reason she couldn't fathom, his derision brought a lump to her throat. She had blisters on her hands from carrying boxes that were too heavy, her feet ached, her back ached, and she hadn't slept in her bed for four nights. And just to add to her frustration her phone had stopped ringing. All morning clients had called her, but now, when she was desperate for a senior client to ring her for advice so that she could sound impressive and prove to Damon just how good she was at her job, it remained silent.

And there was no point in telling him, was there? He'd made up his mind about her based on that episode in her teens and the state of her father's company.

The whole situation was made a thousand times worse by the fact that a small part of her knew she was deserving of his contempt. It *was* because of her that Arianna had been excluded from school. It didn't surprise her that he had such a low opinion of her. What surprised her was how much she cared. It shouldn't matter what he thought of her. All that mattered now were the jobs of the innocent people who worked for her father.

'The headlines on the one o'clock news were pretty brutal. They're calling you the hatchet man.'

'Good. Perhaps it will bring your father out of hiding.' His sensuous mouth curved into a grim smile as he hit a button on the panel and sent the lift gliding upwards.

Transfixed by his mouth, Polly felt her stomach drop. His features were boldly masculine, from the hard lines of his bone structure to the subtle shadow that darkened his jaw. Desperate, she looked for evidence of weakness but found none. 'My father isn't hiding.'

'Miss Prince—' his voice was a soft, dangerous purr '—unless you want first-hand experience of the impact of my temper in an enclosed space, I suggest you don't force me to think about what your father might currently be doing.'

Polly instinctively retreated against the glass. 'I'm just saying he isn't hiding, that's all. My father isn't a coward.' London slowly grew smaller and smaller until it lay beneath them like a miniature toy town. By contrast, the tension in the capsule rocketed.

'He's allowed his business to decline rather than make the difficult decisions that should have been made. He needed to make serious cuts but he chose not to do it. If that isn't cowardice, I don't know what is.'

'You shouldn't make judgements on something you know nothing about.'

'I run a multinational corporation. I make difficult decisions every day of my life.' His innate superiority infuriated her almost as much as the fact that he was right. Her father *should* have made some difficult decisions. But the fact that it was Damon Doukakis who was now pointing that out somehow made it more difficult to hear.

'I'm sure it gives you a real feeling of power to fire people.'

It happened so fast she didn't see him move, but one moment she was standing with an aerial view of London and the next she was staring at wide shoulders and a pair of fiercely angry eyes. 'Never before have I had to restrain myself around a woman, but with you—' He drew in a shaky breath, clearly struggling with the intensity of his own emotions. 'You are enough to provoke a saint. Trust me when I say you do *not* want a demonstration of my power.'

Polly stared at him in appalled fascination, wondering why everyone thought he was Mr Cool. He was the most volatile man she'd met. He simmered like a pan of water kept permanently on the boil. *And he smelt incredible...* 'I was just making the point that you really work this whole I'm-the-boss-and-you're-going-to-do-it-my-way routine.' *Please let him step away from her before she gave into the temptation to bury her face in his neck and just breathe.* 'We're used to a more relaxed approach when we work. Frankly I'm not sure how well we'll do under a reign of terror.'

Outrage rippled across his shoulders and his jaw clenched. 'That *relaxed approach* has sent your company plunging towards bankruptcy. If any redundancies come from this disaster then you and your father will be responsible.'

Brain-dead with exhaustion, Polly felt a perverse sense of satisfaction at seeing him so angry. She wanted him to suffer too. Not just for giving her the most hellish week of her life, but also because she had a desperate urge to crush her mouth to his and feeling that way aggravated her in the extreme. 'You're obviously not enjoying having us as part of your business,' she said sweetly. 'Next time perhaps you should check out your prey before you swallow it. We're obviously giving you indigestion.'

He released her as suddenly as he'd trapped her, stepping back with an exclamation in Greek that she was sure wasn't complimentary.

'The press have somehow guessed that your father and my sister are together.' Lifting a hand, he yanked down the zip of his jacket as if it were strangling him. 'Unless you enjoy fuelling gossip, I suggest you don't talk to them. I've instructed my people to put out a statement on the takeover, concentrating on our corporate vision and goals. I'm trying to focus attention on the fact that your company fits logically within my current business.'

'You mean you don't want to admit publicly you're a megalomaniac who bought a company just so that you could threaten the man having a relationship with your sister.' But she was horrified by the news that the press now had the story. She knew it wouldn't be long before they were digging for reasons and she didn't even want to think about what that would mean. She'd been there before and she loathed it. Everyone wanting to know how it felt to have a stepmother the same age as her. Everyone appalled and fascinated by the ridiculous antics of her father.

'Take a tip from me, Miss Prince.' Those thick dark lashes descended until the look in his eyes was virtually obscured. 'Even in this age of sexual equality, no real man wants to spend time with a bitch or a ball breaker. Try and cultivate a softer, more feminine side and who knows? You might find yourself a boyfriend. Possibly even one who owns a company that you can play in.'

Polly was so shocked she couldn't speak. She didn't know what appalled her most. The fact that he had this entrenched image of her as a lazy waste of space, the fact that he'd clearly asked someone about her sex-life, or the fact that part of her was wondering how he kissed.

Putting it down to tiredness, she promised herself a *really* early night. 'I'd never be interested in a man who couldn't cope with a strong woman.'

'There's strong and then there's strident, which is presumably why you're still single.'

Only the knowledge that she'd be confirming his less than flattering assessment of her prevented her from launching herself at him. Instead she smarted furiously and kept her eyes fixed on the streets shrinking beneath their feet. *This is good*, she told herself. *If he keeps this up all I'm going to want to do to him is kill him and that feels better than sizzling chemistry.* 'If the doors opened to the outside, I'd push you.'

His laugh lacked humour. 'If I thought we'd be working together for long, I'd jump.'

Boiling inside, Polly was saved from thinking up a response by the muted 'ping' of the doors as they glided silently apart, revealing a cavernous, light-filled office space.

Damon propelled her forward and she stepped into an open-plan office area like nothing she'd ever seen before.

Taken aback, momentarily forgetting their heated exchange, she stopped walking and just stared.

Despite everything she'd heard and read about Damon Doukakis, nothing had prepared her for the bustling efficiency of the Doukakis corporate headquarters. 'Oh...' She looked at the bank of desks, each with a video phone, a laptop plug-in and a printer. Most were occupied and there was no questioning the industry of those working. Barely anyone looked up from what they were doing. 'Where—?' Puzzled, she turned her head and looked around her at the clean, uncluttered workspace. 'Where's their stuff? Where do they keep books, magazines, family pictures—personal things. It's all very Spartan.'

'We operate a hot desk system.'

Her mind preoccupied, Polly suddenly had an image

of everyone burning themselves when they sat down to work. 'Hot desk?'

'Employees don't have their own fixed office space. They come in and sit at whichever work station is free. Office space is our most expensive asset and most offices only use fifty percent of their capacity at any one time. We lease the lower ten floors of this building. It's a highly profitable way of maximising the space.'

'So people don't actually have their own desks? That's awful.' Genuinely appalled, Polly tried to envisage her friends and colleagues existing in such a sterile environment. 'But what if someone wants to put up a photograph of their baby or something?'

'When they're at work they should be working. They can stare at the real live baby on their own time.' Damon Doukakis urged her through the floor, occasionally pausing to exchange a word with someone.

Polly examined the faces of the people, wondering what it must be like working in such soulless surroundings. Granted, you could have sold tickets to look at the view from the windows, but nothing about the office space was cosy. 'There's nothing personal anywhere.'

'People are here to do a job. They have everything they need to do that job. People who work for me are adaptable. Technology allows for workforce mobility. Commuting is time-consuming and expensive. I'd rather my people worked an extra two hours than spent those hours sitting in traffic. Some people work flexible hours—start late, finish late. They'll be sitting down at a desk when another person is leaving it. If they're out of the country for a meeting, then the desk is used by someone else. This is the office template of the future.'

Except that Damon Doukakis had brought the future into the present.

Polly thought about the office she'd just left. Until they'd been forced to strip it bare, the walls had been covered in framed copies of their advertising campaigns, photographs and pictures of past office parties. On her desk she'd kept numerous objects that cheered her up and made her smile. And she had Romeo and Juliet.

Here, there were no walls on which to put photographs. No cosy staffroom with soft armchairs and a gurgling coffee machine. Everywhere she looked there was chrome, glass and an industrious silence.

Hoping fish weren't afraid of heights, she stared around her. 'So is this going to be our floor?'

'No. I'm showing you an example of efficiency in action. Take a good look around, Miss Prince. *This* is how a successful company looks. To you it probably feels like landing on an alien planet.' His sensuous mouth curved into a sardonic smile. 'In order to cause minimum disruption to the rest of my operation I've allocated a separate floor to your operation.' Without waiting for her response, he pushed open a door and took the stairs two at a time. Polly poked her tongue out at his back and followed more slowly, envying his athleticism.

Following him through another set of doors, she found herself on another floor, completely circled in glass.

All the boxes and equipment had already been transferred from her old offices and the staff of Prince Advertising were laughing and joking together as they unpacked.

As they waved to her, Polly felt her eyes sting. They were so optimistic and excited. They had no idea how fragile their future was.

The responsibility almost flattened her.

'This is yours.' Damon gestured across the floor with his hand. 'There are meeting rooms over there, all of which can be used for sensitive phone calls that can't be made in open plan.' As he finished speaking the lift doors opened and Polly saw Debbie and Jen stagger out of the lift carrying boxes. After a series of 'oohs' and 'ahhs' as they saw the view, they put down the boxes.

'This is the last of it. Now we can start settling in. Won't take us long to make the place home. Not that my home looks anything like this,' Debbie said cheerfully. 'Where's the kettle?'

Polly caught sight of the shock in Damon Doukakis's eyes and realised that the only way she was going to stand a chance of preserving jobs was if she kept everyone as far away from the boss as possible. She had to protect them. 'Mr Doukakis, I haven't had a chance to send that presentation through to you. I copied it onto a flash drive so you can open it up on your own computer. Debs, if you could supervise the unpacking, that would be great.'

'Sure thing. I'll have to work out which of the plants like sunlight because there's a lot of sunlight in this building.' Deb tugged off her shoes and prepared to get stuck into the work. 'This place is epic.'

'Whatever you need to do.' Deciding that the reason the staff appeared to have no internal radar warning them of danger was because they'd worked for her father for so long, Polly frantically tried to distract their new boss. 'Perhaps we should have the meeting in your office as there is going to be some disruption on this floor.'

'Disruption appears to be a comfortable working environment for you. Are those—' he did a double take as Debbie reached into another box and, together with Jen, lifted out a huge bucket '—*fish*?'

Oh, God...

'You gave us four hours' notice of an office move,' Polly muttered. 'There wasn't time to negotiate relocation. We'll have the tank set up in no time and no one is even going to know they're here.'

'*Tank?!*'

'You're the one who insisted the whole company move here. The fish are part of the company.'

'You keep fish?'

'Look at it this way. They're not going to bother anyone and you don't have to pay them. They're motivational without being costly.'

Her feeble attempt to lighten the situation fell flat. Damon Doukakis didn't smile. Instead he turned his gaze on Polly. Silence spread across the room and Polly was hideously aware that everyone was listening.

The atmosphere changed from one of carnival to one of consternation.

Pinned by that intense, dark stare Polly felt his disapproval slam into her with lethal force.

'My office,' he growled. 'Right now.'

Chapter 3

'Take my calls, Janey.' Dropping his phone onto his PA's desk, Damon strode into his office with Polly following close behind.

The moment he heard the door close, he turned, intending to launch a blistering attack on the sloppy, unprofessional attitude of her staff, but the sight of her swaying in the centre of his enormous office killed the words before they left his mouth.

He'd never seen anyone more miserable or more exhausted.

Whatever else was going on, he could see Polly Prince had had one hell of a week. It couldn't have been easy watching her cushy life slip through her fingers. A few more strands of that shiny blonde hair had escaped from the restraining clip on top of her head, there were black smudges under her violet eyes, and her cheeks were the same pristine white as his shirt.

Standing in the centre of his enormous office, she reminded him of a lone gazelle that had lost the rest of its herd.

'What?' She was watching him warily. 'Do you think you could stop frowning at everyone? It's really hard to operate in an atmosphere of terror.'

'I do *not* create an atmosphere of terror.'

'How do you know? You're not the one on the receiving end.'

'We do three-hundred-and-sixty-degree reviews here. If staff feel *afraid*, they have the opportunity to say so.'

'Unless they're too afraid to say so.' Tiredness laced itself through her voice and suddenly her shoulders drooped slightly, as if the effort of maintaining all that attitude was just too much. 'Look, I know you think I'm a complete waste of space and actually...' She paused and pushed her hair away from her face. 'Actually, I don't completely blame you for that because all the evidence points in that direction, but sometimes things aren't entirely as they seem.'

'Your company is a circus. What exactly isn't as it seems?'

'We may look chaotic to you, but we work well in a relaxed, informal atmosphere. It helps us be creative.'

'If that's your way of asking if you can keep the fish, the answer is no. I don't allow pets in my offices.'

'Romeo and Juliet aren't pets, exactly. They're an integral part of the workforce. They cheer people up and staff motivation is hugely important. I'm asking you to relax your rigid principles for five minutes. You might be surprised what a bit of work enjoyment does.'

'What I think,' Damon said slowly, 'is that the way

you do business is sloppy and unprofessional.' And the irony was, he wasn't even interested in the business. He'd taken control in a desperate attempt to flush Peter Prince out of hiding but so far it hadn't worked. There had been no contact.

The knowledge that his sister could have called him and hadn't added layers of pain and anxiety to his anger. She always accused him of being over-protective, and maybe he was, but was it really being over-protective to want to prevent someone you loved from being hurt?

The affair was doomed, and the thought of having to deal with a heartbroken Arianna sent a cold chill through his body.

Once before he'd held her as she'd sobbed and he never wanted to do that again. *Never wanted to see his sister that sad.*

Polly was frowning at him. 'Look, I know this whole thing is a mess, but give me a chance.' There was a desperate note to her voice. 'Now that you've got rid of the board, I know I can turn this company around.'

'You?' Her astonishing claim momentarily distracted him from thoughts of his sister.

'Yes, me. At least let me try.'

For the first time since he'd walked into the Prince headquarters, Damon felt like laughing. 'You're asking me to give you free rein to do more of what you've been doing?'

'I know you won't believe me but I *do* know what our business needs to make it successful.'

'It needs someone at the helm who isn't afraid to take tough decisions. The fish have to go. I'm not running an aquarium. All you need to do your job is a laptop and an internet connection. I assume you have heard of both those things?'

But he had to admit he was surprised by her vigorous and ongoing defence of the staff. She appeared to care passionately whether they lost their jobs or not.

Presumably it had finally come home to her that if the company crashed, she'd be out of a job and an inheritance.

So pale she looked as though she might pass out, she walked towards him and put a flash drive on his desk. 'The file you want is on there. Look at the numbers. Ninety percent of our expenses were attributed to one percent of the staff. You just got rid of that one percent. Those same people were on the highest salaries but made the smallest contribution to the company. You just made a massive saving on our operating costs.'

Damon found himself distracted by the tempting curve of her lower lip. 'I'm surprised you even know what an operating cost is.'

'Please open the file.'

Ruthlessly deleting thoughts of sex, Damon slid the flash drive into his computer and opened the document. 'Do I read from the beginning of this fairy story?'

'It isn't a fairy story. You'll see from this that we've pitched for six new pieces of business in the last three months. We won all six accounts. One of those was against your own advertising team. We beat them. The client said our pitch was the most creative and exciting he'd seen.' There was an energy and confidence about her that was at odds with his impression of her and Damon was genuinely surprised.

'Creative and exciting doesn't send a company bankrupt.'

'No, but high overheads can. And so can bad management. We suffered from both.'

'Your father was in charge. Who exactly are you blaming?'

'Blame is a waste of time. I'm just asking you to look at the facts and help us move forward.' She hesitated. 'I know you're good at what you do, but we're good too. Together we could be incredible. I'll be downstairs helping the staff settle in if you want to talk about this. Start by looking at these figures.' She leaned across his desk and pressed a key on his computer and a strand of that rebellious hair floated against his cheek, soft as down.

Damon lifted a hand to brush it away at the same time she did and her fingers tangled with his. Scarlet-faced, she jumped back, clearly as horrified by the contact as he was.

'You don't need my help with this—just—it's self-explanatory.' She tucked the offending strand behind her ear and Damon watched, transfixed by those delicate fingers tipped with painted nails.

'Is that—?' His attention caught, he narrowed his eyes and squinted at her nails but she quickly whipped her hands behind her back.

'Just take a look at that presentation.'

'Show me your hands.'

There was a mutinous flash in her eyes but she stuck out her hands. 'There.'

'You have a skull and crossbones painted on your nails.'

'It's called nail art. I use different stencils.'

'And you chose a skull and crossbones for today?'

She gave a tiny shrug. 'It seemed appropriate. Look,

I know you think this is all frivolous but one of our clients owns a major brand in nail colour. We did a fantastic cover mount on one of the big women's glossies last summer, and— Never mind—it's all in the figures. What are you doing?' The stream of nervous chatter died as he took her hands firmly in his.

Making a sound in her throat, she gave a little pull but Damon tightened his grip. Her hands were smooth and delicate and he was blinded by a sudden image of those slim fingers closing around a certain part of him.

Raw sexual awareness burned through his body, brutal in its intensity. He felt her hands tremble in his. The confidence and assurance melted away from her, leaving confusion in its place.

Damon wondered if the air-conditioning in his office had broken. The atmosphere had suddenly become heavy and oppressive.

Even as he was in the process of reminding himself that this girl's father was the source of his current problems, she snatched her hands away and stepped back. 'I'll leave you to read the presentation.'

Damon felt mildly disorientated.

What the hell was he doing?

'Yes. Go.' If she hadn't already been leaving of her own free will he would have ejected her from his office with supersonic speed. Not wanting to examine his own behaviour too closely, he dragged his gaze back to the document on the screen but all he saw was golden hair and long nails.

Forcing himself to focus, he concentrated on the first slide. One glance told him that it had been prepared by someone computer literate and numerate. In fact it was the first sign of professionalism he'd seen since he walked through the doors of Prince Advertising.

He stopped thinking about Arianna and analysed the data in front of him.

'Wait—' He stopped her as she reached the door. 'Who did this?' His rough demand was met by a long, pulsing silence and then she turned to face him.

'I did.'

'You mean Mr Anderson gave you the information and you collated it.'

'No, I mean I put together the information I thought you'd need to be able to make an informed decision about the future of the company.'

Damon glanced at the complexity of the data on the screen and then back at her. 'I consider it a serious offence to take credit for someone else's work.'

A wry smile tilted the corners of her mouth. 'Really? It makes a refreshing change to hear that from someone in authority. Maybe we'll work well together after all.'

Damon stared at the spreadsheet, trying to make sense of what he was seeing. 'What exactly was your official role in the company?'

'I was my father's executive assistant, which basically means I did a bit of everything.'

A bit of everything. 'So this isn't Mr Anderson's spreadsheet?'

'Mr Anderson couldn't switch the laptop on, let alone create a spreadsheet.'

Damon leaned back in his chair. 'So you're good with computers?'

'I'm good with a lot of things, Mr Doukakis. Just because I wear pink tights and have fun with my nails it doesn't make me stupid any more than wearing jeans would make you approachable.' She still had her hand on the door handle, as if she was ready to run at a moment's notice. 'I need to get back downstairs. Having your future in someone else's hands is very traumatic for everyone. It would mean a lot if next time you go down there you could maybe smile or say an encouraging word.'

'They should be grateful I've taken control. Without me your business would have been bankrupt within three months.' And in an attempt to protect his sister he'd landed himself with still more responsibility for jobs and lives. He felt like Atlas, holding the heavens on his shoulders.

'We've had problems with our cash flow, but—'

'Is there any part of the business you *haven't* had problems with?'

'The clients love us because we're very creative.' She looked him in the eye. 'All I want is your assurance that there will be no redundancies.'

'I can't make that assurance until I've unravelled the mess your father has created.'

'I *know* parts of the business have problems. I'm not going to pretend they don't. But I'm asking you to look deeper and learn about how we work before you make an irrational decision.'

'Irrational?' Brows raised with incredulity, Damon leaned forwards in his chair. 'You think I make irrational decisions?'

'Normally, no. But in this case—' she breathed slowly '—yes. I think you're so angry with my father, and you feel so helpless about your sister, you were willing to do anything that might give you back some element of control. And as for the way you feel about me—you haven't forgotten I'm the reason your sister was permanently excluded from school at four-teen. I really messed that up, I admit it, but don't use something *I* did ten years ago to punish the staff. That wouldn't be fair.'

Damon sat still, forced to acknowledge that there was at least a partial truth in her accusation. Had he been unfair to judge her on something that had hap-pened when she was still young? 'Go and settle the staff in downstairs.' His tone was rougher than he'd intended. 'I'll call you if I have any questions.'

An hour later he had more questions than he had answers. Exasperated, he hit a button on his phone and summoned his finance director. 'Ellen, can you come in here?' His eyes still fixed on his computer screen, he drummed his fingers impatiently on the desk. 'And bring the salary details for the Prince people. There's something wrong with the numbers.'

Moments later he was staring at another set of fig-ures that still didn't make sense. Trying to unravel the puzzle, he stood up abruptly. 'According to this infor-mation, all of these people took a salary cut six months ago. And his daughter has barely been paid a living wage for the past two years.'

'I know. I've been going over the figures too.' Ellen spread the summary pages over his desk. 'The com-pany is barely afloat. It's a small agency with the over-heads of a big agency.'

'But the board are primarily responsible for those overheads.' Polly Prince had been right in her assess-ment, he thought grimly. The board had been sucking the company dry. First-class flights. Elaborate lunches.

Thousand-pound bottles of vintage wine…. The list went on and on.

'They're in serious financial trouble. They've been hit by the economic downturn but made no compensatory moves. Peter Prince badly needed to trim staff. Instead they appear to have agreed to take a cut rather than allow anyone to be laid off.' Ellen adjusted her glasses. 'The business is a mess of course, but you knew that when you bought it. On the plus side they have some surprisingly good accounts and somehow they've just won a major piece of business with the French company Santenne. Their leading brand is High Kick Hosiery. That's going to be huge. Didn't our people pitch for that?'

'Yes.' The news that they'd lost out to Prince Advertising did nothing to improve Damon's mood. 'So how did Prince win it? They're the most shambolic operation I've ever encountered.'

'That's true. Financially and structurally they're a disaster. Creatively—well, I assume you've seen this?' A strange light in her eyes, his finance director handed him a folder she'd brought with her.

'I haven't seen anything.'

'But you always research companies so carefully.'

'Well this time I didn't.' His tone was irritable and Ellen looked at him calmly.

'We've worked together a long time, Damon. Do you want to talk about this?'

'No.' Damon shook his head and lifted a hand. '*Don't* ask.'

'I'm guessing this has something to do with your sister.' Her tone was sympathetic. 'She's lucky to have you looking out for her.'

'I wish she felt the same way.'

'That's because she takes your love for granted. Which is a compliment. It means she feels secure. Trust me, I know. I have teenagers. You've done a good job.'

It didn't feel that way, but the prospect of discussing it horrified him almost as much as the situation itself. 'About this company—'

'It's not all bad news.' Fortunately Ellen took the hint and changed the subject. 'There is a creative brain at work there. You just need to harness it.'

Damon opened the file and slowly flicked through the pages. Pausing, he lifted a glossy advert featuring a teenager in a nightclub. 'That's clever.'

'It's all clever. And creative. The customer profiling is spot on. Their use of social networking is astonishingly astute. My eldest has been nagging me to buy this for months, all based on the pester power generated by their campaign.'

His interest piqued, Damon flicked through the rest of the folio. 'The creative thinking is original.' He frowned down at the tagline under a famous brand of running shoes. '*"Run, breathe, live."* It's good.' Staring at the work, he remembered Polly's words.

'Clients love us. We're very creative.'

'Their sales have quadrupled since that campaign went live. They tapped into the whole lifestyle thing. There is no doubt that Prince Advertising is a mess, but there's at least one person in the company who is exceptional. I'd go as far as to say they're afloat purely because of the talents of their creative director. Who is he?'

'His name was Michael Anderson and I fired him.' Damon was staring down at the pages in front of him.

'And there's no way these ideas came from him. The man didn't have an original thought in his head.'

'Maybe it was Prince himself?'

Just thinking of Peter Prince sent Damon's tension levels shooting skyward. 'He's in his fifties and he's notorious for abandoning the company when it suits him. From what I can gather he treats it more as a hobby than a business. This stuff is young. Fresh. Visionary.'

Ellen smiled. 'And fun.'

Fun.

Damon thought of the skull and crossbones on Polly's nails. The hot pink tights. The fish on the desk. The party atmosphere that hit him every time he went near the staff. 'They certainly have an interesting work ethic.'

'So if it wasn't the creative director, who's coming up with the ideas?' Ellen gathered up the papers. 'Thanks to their creativity they have some major pieces of business. Their billing is haphazard, their cash flow is a nightmare, but we can sort that—' she shrugged '—and absorb them into our business. Just make sure we don't lose the brain behind these campaigns. We need to find out who it is and lock them into a watertight contract. Any idea who it could be?'

'No.' Mentally scrolling through the people he'd met, Damon closed the file. 'But I intend to find out immediately. And I know just the person to ask.'

By seven o'clock Polly was the only one left on her floor of the office. She'd spent the latter half of the day juggling problems and soothing frayed nerves while taking endless calls from anxious clients who had seen news of the takeover on the TV.

'Mr Peters, I think we should be reviewing the whole media mix.' Sitting cross-legged on the floor, she talked into her headset so that her hands were free to unpack the last of the boxes. 'Yes, it's true that Mr Anderson has gone.' She retrieved a packet of balloons from the bottom of the box and slid them into her desk. 'But there are other people more than qualified to advise you on the best strategy.' *Like me*, she thought, rescuing the charger for her BlackBerry and adding it to the stuff accumulating in the drawer. 'I'm going to schedule a meeting in your diary, get the team to put together some ideas and then we'll present them to you. I promise you will be blown away by our ideas… Uhuh…mmm, definitely…absolutely top priority.'

When she finally hung up, she keyed in the task to the ever-growing to-do list in her BlackBerry and carried on sorting out her desk area. The rest of the staff had gone home hours before, all apparently excited by the prospect of riding down to street level in the glass elevator.

Left alone, Polly removed her boots and settled down to an evening of hard work. Darkness spread slowly over the city as she worked her way steadily through her calls. After a few hours she glanced up at the towering panes of glass and saw that the view had changed from daytime city-slick to night-time sparkle and she paused for a moment, captivated by the wide-angled view of London at night. The moon sent a sliver of light across the River Thames and for the first time in a horrid, hideous week she felt peaceful.

Maybe, just maybe, this could turn out to be a good

thing. Damon Doukakis was probably one of the few people with the talent to turn the company round, providing he didn't fire all of them first.

Romeo and Juliet seemed happy enough in their new surroundings and Polly had discovered that there were enough workstations for everyone without having to operate the Doukakis 'hot desk' system. She wondered how his employees must feel, coming to work every day and sitting down at an empty, featureless surface, greeted by nothing more than a power point and a phone socket.

Damon Doukakis was focused on the success of his business to the exclusion of everything else.

She paused in the middle of deleting an e-mail.

Well, not *quite* everything else.

Her cheeks burned and she stared down at her hands, remembering. The attraction had been like a searing blade, driven straight through her. And she was pretty sure he'd felt it too.

He'd looked horrified, she remembered, which should have dented her ego except that she was a realist. There was no way he would sully himself with a mongrel like her. She'd seen enough pictures of him in the gossip columns to know that the women he chose were sleek and groomed. Elegant. Dignified. Controlled. Everything about his life was ruthlessly controlled, from work to women.

Polly looked down at herself. The women he dated would no more dream of sitting shoeless and cross-legged on the floor unpacking a box than they would be seen in public without perfectly blow-dried hair.

Wondering why she was wasting time thinking about what sort of women Damon Doukakis dated,

Polly finished emptying the box and put it ready for recycling.

Her desk was covered in pink sticky notes with various phone messages taken by Debbie while she'd been on the phone to other people.

Urgent. Call Vernon White about the Honey Hair campaign.

Ring the media buyer at Cool Campaigns about the media strategy for Fresh Mouth mints.

David Mills from Fox Consumer wants to talk urgently...

Urgent, urgent, urgent. It was all urgent. She felt a rush of panic as she contemplated all the work she still had to do. Everyone had heard the news of the takeover and was wondering whether Prince Advertising was going to exist in a month. And she couldn't give them an answer. She had no idea what Damon Doukakis intended to do so all she could do was sound positive and up-beat.

Knowing that if all her clients walked in the opposite direction then the staff would definitely lose their jobs, Polly peeled off the notes one by one and added the calls to the list. Then she settled back into her cross-legged position on the floor and worked out a priority for the morning.

She was wondering whether it would be any help to get a second phone, when she heard the swish of a door opening and saw Damon Doukakis striding towards her.

Her confidence melted away like chocolate held in a child's palm.

When it came to work she was more than ready to fight her corner but she had no idea how to fight these other feelings that squirmed inside her whenever she was in the same room as him.

One glance at the exquisitely cut black dinner jacket and bowtie told her that his plans for the evening were infinitely more exciting than hers and she held her breath as he approached. His startling good looks made it impossible to do anything but stare when he was in the room. It didn't help that he carried himself with that inborn confidence that seemed genetically embedded in people born into wealth. It had been years since she'd felt that awful creeping sense of inferiority but she felt it now as she stood trapped by those glittering dark eyes.

Polly's head began to spin and suddenly she was glad she was sitting down, because at least sitting down didn't require strength in one's legs. It was just the tiredness, she told herself. Nothing more. He wasn't *that* gorgeous.

As he stood looking down at her from his formidable height, she was forced to revise that opinion. OK, so maybe he was gorgeous. To look at. But it was all on the surface.

Feeling out of her depth, she made a vague attempt to defuse the crackling tension. 'Nice outfit. I didn't know you had a second job as a waiter.'

There was no answering smile and she felt a flash of relief. There was no way she could ever find a man without a sense of humour remotely attractive, even if he *did* have an incredible body that did miracles for a dinner jacket. She told herself that the flutter of nerves in her stomach was down to the ominous look in his eyes as he scanned her appearance.

'*Theé mou*, why are you sitting on the floor? Where are your boots?'

'Under the desk. I was emptying boxes and my heels kept catching in my hem—' Realising that his eyes were fixed on her legs, she felt her body heat. 'Never mind. I promise to wear shoes when I see a client, so save the lecture.'

'You have absolutely no—' He broke off in mid-sentence, his attention snagged by the dramatic transformation of his previously ordered office space. '*What* happened here?'

'You told us we could do what we wanted with the space.' Knowing that she sounded defensive, Polly scrambled up from the floor, acutely conscious of his height now that she wasn't wearing her heels. She followed his appalled gaze and saw the calendar of half-naked firemen someone had stuck to one of the steel rods that supported the ceiling. *Oops.* 'That was a project we did for one of our clients. It's a photographic masterpiece, don't you think? We put it up because it helps us to think creatively.'

A dark brow lifted in mockery. 'The more I discover about your creative process, the more fascinated I am.'

Polly shrugged awkwardly. 'I accept we're a bit more—er—informal than you, but to be honest the whole "hot desk" thing doesn't really work for us. I think we're very possibly cold desk people. Or maybe lukewarm desk. We like knowing where we're going to sit instead of playing musical chairs when we come to work every day. We like having a *home*. A little space to call our own.'

'The place looks like a Sunday market.' He picked

up the pink fluffy pen she always kept on her desk, his gaze incredulous. 'What do you do with this thing?'

'I write with it. If I'm brainstorming ideas I need to doodle on paper. It helps me think.' Exhausted, her head throbbing, Polly wished she'd hidden the pen. 'It's my happy pen. I like it. It makes me smile and I'm more creative when I'm happy.'

'Well, that's good, because obviously your happiness is my first priority.' His silky-smooth tone held a deadly edge. 'Talking of happiness, how are the fish settling in? Are they homesick? Enjoying the view? Anything I can get them to make them feel more comfortable?'

She decided to ignore the sarcasm. 'Just don't get too close. They're afraid of sharks.'

'I am *not* a shark, Miss Prince.'

'You just gobbled up my father's company in one mouthful so forgive me if I disagree with you.'

'We both know I have no interest in your father's business.'

'Which is a shame, because you're stuck with us now.' And she appreciated the irony of it. 'You're stuck with our pink, fluffy, fish-loving approach to business and we're stuck with your empty-desk-eyes-forward-don't-anybody-laugh ethos. Interesting times ahead.'

Suddenly, Polly was too tired to fight and she surreptitiously slid her pink notebook under a file in the hope that it wouldn't draw his attention. 'Can I please have my pen back? It's a lucky pen. All my best creative ideas have come while I'm holding it.'

The bold curve of his brows came together in a frown and she wondered what she'd said this time. He obviously thought she was a complete numbskull.

'Could you stop frowning? It's so unsettling. We're used to working in a positive atmosphere.'

He studied her for a long moment and then dropped the pen back on her desk. 'Have you heard from your father?'

'No.'

'Doesn't the man ever call you?'

With that single sentence he unwittingly dug a knife into the most vulnerable part of her. Afraid he might see the hurt, Polly kept her eyes down. 'We live independent lives.' And not for anything would she betray how much this latest episode was upsetting her. She wasn't going to give Damon Doukakis the satisfaction of knowing she was as miserable about the whole thing as he was. 'Was that all? Because I'm pretty busy.'

There was a brief silence and then he surprised her. 'You look exhausted. You need to stop for the day.'

The fact that he'd noticed sent a flicker of warmth through her body and that feeling frightened her more than the power he wielded. The last thing she needed was to think of him as sympathetic. 'I can't stop for the day. My boss thinks I'm a lazy slacker and I have another million phone calls to make before I go home.'

'You can't go home.' He picked up a stuffed bear she kept on her desk and studied it with an air of baffled incredulity. 'There is a mob of journalists outside just waiting for one of us to leave so that they can bombard us with questions.'

Polly snatched the bear out of his hands. 'I'm not scared of journalists.'

'I'm not talking about a few intrusive questions.' He was still looking at the bear as if he couldn't quite believe what he was seeing. 'I'm talking about a horde of people hungry for juicy scandal. You and the stuffed bear can stay in the apartment tonight.' He reached into his inside jacket pocket and withdrew a plastic card. 'Take the lift up to the top floor. This opens the door. The security is more sophisticated than the Bank of England. You'll be safe there.'

He was offering her sanctuary from the press?

The unexpected gesture destabilised her. Staying in the apartment would mean she could carry on working and clear some of the backload. 'Well, that's—if you're—thanks,' she said gruffly. 'How do you plan to avoid them?'

'My car is in the underground car park.' He glanced at his watch. 'I have to go, but tomorrow we're going to talk about that presentation of yours. I have questions.'

'Right. But I can't talk tomorrow. I'm going to Paris for a client meeting.'

'What time is your flight?'

'I'm not flying, I'm catching the train. It leaves at seven-thirty. The meeting is in the evening.' Realising how that sounded, she coloured. 'They moved the meeting after I booked my train.'

'And you thought you'd have a day in Paris.' The brief moment of harmony had been blown away and contempt was stamped on his hard, handsome face.

His continued censure was too much for her after a long and stressful day and she glared at him defensively. 'It was an economy ticket. I couldn't move it.'

'I've seen the company expense account.'

'No, you've seen the *directors'* expense account.'

'Who are you meeting in Paris?'

'Gérard Bonnel, the Vice President of Marketing for

Santenne. He was there when we pitched for the business. Now he wants to go over our ideas.'

'You cannot meet someone of Gérard's seniority on your own. I'll come with you. And for God's sake wear a suit before you come face to face with a client.'

Polly opened her mouth to argue but he was already striding across the floor towards the elevator.

Her confidence well and truly punctured, she stared after him and decided that she'd rather stab herself in the eye than sleep in his apartment. So what if a few journalists were waiting for her outside? She'd dealt with journalists before. And she was so tired and moody they'd probably take one look at her face and realise the danger of getting too close.

Exhausted and dejected, Polly worked for another hour and then pushed her feet into her boots, dropped her phone into her pocket and enjoyed the silent, panoramic downward glide in the elevator. The thought of Damon Doukakis joining her on her trip to Paris horrified her. She just wanted to get on with her work and avoid him as much as possible.

She was just wondering whether there was some way she could lose him at the train station when the lift doors opened onto the foyer.

Glancing towards the security guard who was occupied with a group of people at the desk, she stepped out onto the street and was instantly mobbed.

'*Polly, do you have a statement about Damon Doukakis taking over your father's company?*'

'*Have you heard from him?*'

'*Is there any truth in the rumour that he's with Damon's sister?*'

An elbow lanced her kidneys and Polly winced

and turned. 'Ow! Just mind where you—' Jostled and pushed, she lost her balance and her head smashed against something hard and cold. There was a blinding flash and something hot and wet trickled down her face.

Blood, she thought dizzily, and then the world went black.

Chapter 4

'She *what*? Which hospital?' Abandoning his date in the middle of dinner, Damon pocketed his phone and strode out to the limo, his security team clearing the throng of journalists who haunted his every move. 'How badly is she hurt?'

'The hospital wouldn't give details, sir.' Franco, his driver, manoeuvred skilfully through the heavy London traffic. 'Just told me it was a head injury, but they're keeping her in overnight so it must be bad.'

Undoing his bow tie with a few flicks of his fingers, Damon leaned back against the seat of the car and attempted to rein in his frustration.

Why the hell had she left the building? He'd left precise instructions that she should stay in the apartment. Instructions she'd apparently ignored.

The girl was an utter disaster.

Part of him was tempted to leave her to suffer for her own stupidity but another part was acutely aware that she was on her own in hospital and no one knew how to contact her father.

A thought suddenly occurred to him. 'Ring the press anonymously, Franco. Make sure they know she's in hospital.'

His driver glanced in the rearview mirror. 'They put her there, boss.'

'I don't mean the tabloids, I mean broadcast media. Ring the news desk. Tell them that Miss Prince has been badly injured in an accident and we don't know how long she'll be in hospital. Keep it vague and worrying. I want the story on the next news headlines. With pictures, to make sure they know which hospital.'

Surely hearing news that his only daughter was in hospital should flush Peter Prince out from hiding?

Optimistic that this latest development could be turned to his advantage, Damon forced himself to relax as they negotiated traffic but his underlying concern for his sister was growing with every hour she failed to make contact.

Arianna had been six years old when their parents had died. Landed with the towering responsibility of caring for her, Damon had grown up overnight. He'd understood that she was now his responsibility. That it was his job to prevent his little sister from being hurt. What he hadn't realised was that the biggest threat to her happiness would come from Arianna herself.

What if she did something stupid like marrying the guy?

Fifteen minutes later his limousine pulled up in the ambulance bay of the large city hospital and Damon sprang from the car and strode into the emergency department, relieved to be able to focus on something other than the dubious life choices made by his sister.

The hospital was heaving but the crowd of people at the desk took one look at him and parted like the Red Sea.

The receptionist immediately sat up straight and smoothed her hair. 'Can I help you?'

'I'm looking for a friend of mine.' Damon bestowed his most winning smile on the dazzled woman. 'Polly Prince. She was knocked out and brought in by ambulance. I expect she's on a trolley somewhere.'

'Prince—Prince—' Her expression glazed, the girl finally dragged her eyes from his face and checked the records. 'Cubicle One. But you can't—'

'Is that left or right?' Well aware of the effect he had on women, Damon wasn't afraid to use it to his advantage when it suited him. 'I'm so grateful for your help.'

'Left through the double doors,' she said breathlessly. 'The doctor is with her.'

'*Efaristo.* Thank you.' Flashing her a smile, he strode through the doors before anyone had time to challenge him and found himself in a cubicle, empty except for a doctor who looked as though she were about to explode.

Damon felt a flash of empathy. 'Don't tell me. You just had an encounter with Polly and now you need to go to anger management classes.' In one glance he took in the empty trolley and the bloodstained bandage. 'Where *is* she?'

'She just discharged herself against medical advice. We wanted to admit her for twenty-four hours observation but she says she can't possibly stay because she has things she has to do. She's certainly a strong-minded young woman.'

Damon thought back to that day at the school when Polly had stuck out her chin and resolutely refused to explain her outrageous behaviour to anyone. Strong-minded was a polite description. 'Why did she discharge herself?'

'She said she had too much to do, but what she should be doing is lying down and resting. She's had a nasty bang on the head.' Clearly annoyed, the doctor slipped her stethoscope back into her pocket. 'She mentioned a trip to Paris and a meeting with an important client. We couldn't get her to let go of her phone. It was welded to her hand right the way through my examination.' The doctor relented. 'I have to admit her dedication impressed me.'

Struggling to reconcile the word 'dedication' with Polly, Damon wondered if he and the doctor were talking about the same person. 'So you're saying that you advised her to stay in, but she walked out?'

'That's right. She'll probably be all right at home as long as she isn't on her own. Just make sure you know what to look out for and you can bring her back in if anything about her condition unsettles you.'

Damon didn't waste time correcting the doctor's assumption that he'd be spending the night with Polly. Instead he scanned the exits. 'Which way did she go?'

'She went out of the ambulance entrance. She said she had a lift home.' Puzzled, the doctor looked at him. 'I assumed that was why you were here?'

But Damon was already on his way out of the door, his phone in his hand as he instructed his driver to bring the car round. 'Have you seen Polly Prince?'

'No.'

Damon swore fluently and then looked around him. Even this late in the evening the hospital was buzzing with activity. There was no sign of Polly. 'Which is the nearest underground station?'

'I believe it's Monument, boss.'

Following a hunch, Damon slid into the car. 'Let's go. Take the most obvious pedestrian route.'

Within two minutes he saw her, walking with her head down and her shoulders hunched, looking as though she were going to collapse at any minute.

'Pull over.' Damon sprang from the car and was next to her in three strides. '*Theé mou*, do you have a death wish? First you leave the office when I warn you about the mob, and then you discharge yourself from hospital against doctor's orders. *What is wrong with you?* Why do you have this urge to do the opposite of what you're told?'

'Damon?' Bemused, she turned her head and he saw the bloody streaks in her blonde hair and the purple shadow darkening one side of her face.

'*Maledizione*. They *hit* you?'

Looking distinctly disorientated, she glanced from him to the limousine and then back again. 'What are you doing here? I thought you were on a date.'

'I was told you'd had an accident.'

'But what is that to do with you?'

'Naturally I immediately went to the hospital.'

'Why "naturally"? Why would you even care that I was in hospital? You're not my next of kin.'

Frustrated that she would question what had been a natural decision to him, Damon raked his hand through his hair. 'Your father is absent and clearly you couldn't be left to cope with something like that alone.'

'I deal with things on my own all the time. And, frankly, from the way you've been speaking to me all day I was under the distinct impression that given half a chance you'd put me in the hospital yourself. Are you telling me that you abandoned your date because you heard I was hurt?'

'I didn't "abandon" her,' Damon breathed. 'I arranged for her to be driven home.'

'But you deprived her of the pleasure of your company and the promise of bedroom athletics. Wow.' Her mouth tilted into a crooked smile. 'Poor her.'

Ignoring her flippant tone, Damon lifted a hand and touched the side of her head. 'What the hell happened?'

'They jostled me and I lost my balance and fell into a camera. It had hard edges. But I'm fine. It was kind of you to check on me, but I can get myself home.' She tried to dodge past him and he caught her arms in tight grip. Her body brushed against his and the subtle scent of her perfume wound itself around his senses.

He gritted his teeth, wondering why control was such an effort when he was with her. 'You cannot travel on the underground and you're not supposed to be sleeping alone tonight.'

'Are you volunteering to sleep with me?' She gave an awkward laugh. 'I wish you could see your face. Relax. I know you'd rather cuddle up with a bed bug than have me in your sheets.'

Damon, who had a disturbingly clear idea of what he'd do to her if she were in his sheets, ignored that comment. 'Why did you discharge yourself?'

'I have to go to Paris tomorrow and I still have some ideas to finish off.'

'*Obviously* you won't now be going to Paris in the morning.' Damon drew her towards him as a group of passers-by jostled them.

'Yes, I will.'

'If your father were here, he'd stop you going.'

She didn't look at him. 'No, he wouldn't. I make my own decisions about what I do, and I'm going to Paris.' Twisting herself out of his grip, she turned and carried on walking towards the underground station.

Never having encountered anyone quite as stubborn as Polly, Damon stood for a moment, his emotions veering between exasperation and concern. Clearly she wasn't prepared to listen to reason so what was he supposed to do? Fling her over his shoulder?

Noticing two men staring hard at her legs, Damon decided that wasn't a bad idea. In four strides he caught up with her. 'Why is it so important that you get to Paris tomorrow? Are you sleeping with the client or something?'

A choked sound came from her throat and she stopped dead. 'You really do have a high opinion of me, don't you?'

Heat crawled up the back of his neck. 'I know Gérard. Like most Frenchmen, he appreciates a beautiful woman. And you *are* arriving nine hours before your meeting.'

'Which naturally means I'm leaving plenty of time for afternoon sex before we move from bedroom to boardroom, is that it?' Ignoring the flow of people around them, she fixed those blue eyes on him. 'Make up your mind. This morning you told me I looked like a flamingo and now you think I've turned into a *femme fatale*? Or does a bruised head suddenly make you feel all protective and macho or something?'

He wasn't sure what he was feeling and Damon certainly didn't need her to question behaviour that he was already questioning himself. 'I'm just asking myself what makes this meeting so important that you'd discharge yourself from hospital against medical advice.'

'Everybody's jobs are under threat. He's a new client and I work in the service industry!' Hauling her bag more firmly onto her shoulder, she glared at a man who brushed past her. 'And before you make another insensitive remark, not *that* sort of service industry.' She turned away again but this time Damon shot out a hand and halted her escape.

'You are intentionally misunderstanding everything I say to you.'

'There is another interpretation for the phrase "you look like a flamingo"?'

'I was commenting on the inappropriateness of your dress. I never said you weren't beautiful.' The words launched themselves from some unidentified part of his brain and his own shock mirrored the confusion he saw in her eyes. He released her immediately, disconcerted by the lethal sexual charge that seemed to power every contact, no matter how small. 'Look—you can't be on your own tonight and any minute now the press waiting in the hospital will realised you've legged it out of the back door. Get in the car before you're mobbed for a second time.'

'I don't need a lift. And I have to go back to my house to get my things for the meeting tomorrow.'

'I'm *trying* to help you.'

'And I'm trying to tell you that I don't need help. I handle things myself. I always have.'

'Well, tonight I'm handling them.' Damon held out his hand. 'Give me your keys. Franco will drop us and then go on to your house to get whatever it is you need. You can make him a list in the car. I'll decide if you're well enough to go to Paris in the morning. Until then you'll stay in the penthouse. If you'd done that the first time you wouldn't be in this mess now.'

There was a stunned silence and then she gave a strangled laugh. 'Do you always take control?'

'When the situation demands it, yes.'

'So you're inviting me to stay at your place?' Her eyes glinted a beautiful sapphire blue. 'Aren't you afraid I'll throw a wild party? Sully the place with my wanton ways? You know me—I can't resist any opportunity to indulge in men and alcohol.'

He ignored her reference to the incident at school. 'Hopefully a bang on the head will quell your intrinsic desire to cause havoc. I'll take the risk.' Even as he said the words, part of him was wondering what the hell he was doing creating a situation where they'd be in close contact.

'I appreciate the gesture, but I'm fine. I'm used to looking out for myself.' She added that last observation in a gruff little voice that made him wonder exactly what role her father had played in her life.

Damon was about to probe further when he caught movement out of the corner of his eye. 'We have company. Let's move.'

With that, Damon scooped her up and deposited her in the back seat of the limo, slamming the door shut just seconds before the press pack descended. 'Drive.'

* * *

Polly had conflicting emotions as she stepped out of the car in the underground car park of the Doukakis Tower. Smarting at being literally dumped in the car, but relieved at having escaped the hungry press pack, she eyed the high security steel doors that had closed behind them. 'The place is like a fortress.'

'It can be a fortress when it needs to be.' Without looking at her, Damon strode towards the elevator, his footsteps echoing on the concrete.

Polly followed more slowly, and not just because her whole body was starting to ache from her fall.

What was the matter with him now?

It was obvious that he was angry but she had no idea why.

Having locked her safely in the car, he'd proceeded to converse in Greek with his driver, leaving her to stare out of the tinted glass and stew in her own emotions.

'Are you angry because I ruined your evening or because I don't slavishly follow orders? Because I didn't *ask* you to come to my rescue. I would have been fine.'

'Which bit would have been fine, exactly?' He strode into the elevator like a man on a mission and thumped his palm against the button. 'The bit where you were knocked unconscious or the part where you discharged yourself from hospital against medical advice?'

'I'm capable of making my own decisions.'

He looked unimpressed. 'Anyone can make a decision. The skill is making the right one at the right time.'

'That's what I do.'

'What you do, Miss Prince, is disagree with me on principle.'

'That isn't true.'

'Isn't it? You were about to be mobbed by journalists for a second time in one evening. Would you have got into the car if I hadn't forced you?'

She shifted uncomfortably, suddenly realising just how much she'd inconvenienced him. 'Yes, I would. If you'd given me time to think about it.'

'We didn't have time to debate options.' His savage tone intensified her growing guilt.

'I'm sorry! I loused up your evening and I feel bad about that. And I'm grateful to you for helping me out. I'm just not—well, I'm not used to accepting help. It feels strange.' Polly felt as small as a field mouse. Not only had he come to her rescue, he'd abandoned a hot date to come to the hospital and all she'd done was give him grief.

When had anyone ever come to her rescue before?

When had anyone given her any help?

A strange, unfamiliar feeling spread through her and she wondered whether the bang on the head had been worse than she'd thought. Suddenly she was relieved he'd forced her into the car. It felt as though a heavy metal rock group was rehearsing inside her skull and she was wondering whether discharging herself had been such a clever idea. Was it normal to feel this bad?

But she had to get to Paris, didn't she? Winning the High Kick Hosiery account was crucial to the business. And they couldn't afford to lose that business.

'P?' Polly focused her gritty, tired eyes on the glowing panel as the lift moved upwards. 'P for prison? P for punishment?'

'Penthouse.'

'Of course. Penthouse. You live above the shop.' Looking at him, she saw how tightly he held onto control and wondered what it took to make him snap. 'I really am sorry I ruined your evening.' Gingerly, she touched her fingers to her head. 'I didn't realise they'd be that eager for a story. How did you find out?'

'My head of security rang me. He was close enough to see it happen, but not close enough to stop it. Why didn't you stay at the hospital?'

'I can't stay in hospital. I have a very unsympathetic boss. He told me to take my lazy, useless self and do a proper day's work.'

'So I'm to blame for your decisions?'

'Well those were your words but no, you're not to blame. I would have done the same thing regardless of what you said. The meeting is important.' The movement of the elevator was starting to make her feel sick. 'It's tough out there. If I don't deliver, Gérard will just pick up the phone to the next agency on his list. I don't want that to happen.'

'I am *not* an unsympathetic boss.' He spoke the words through gritted teeth. 'And anyone with any sense would take time off after an injury like that. Or are you trying to impress me?'

'I'm not stupid enough to think I could ever impress you.' She wondered why being trapped in a confined space with him should make it hard to breathe. 'I'm just trying to get the job done. The meeting tomorrow is important. With everything so unstable, I can't not turn up. We worked hard to win that business and we need to show them that we can do a good job. Do you have any painkillers in your fancy apartment?'

He breathed deeply. 'Yes.' Even with his top button undone and his bow tie dangling round his neck, he looked sleek and handsome. He also looked supremely irritated.

Polly wondered about the woman he'd abandoned halfway through a date. Who was she? Someone exceptionally beautiful, obviously, who wouldn't dream of wearing hot pink tights or writing with a fluffy pink pen.

She stole a glance at his profile.

No one had ever come to her rescue before. Even the time she'd come off the trampoline at school and broken her arm she'd had to get a taxi home from the hospital because no one had been able to contact her father. Confused by her own feelings, Polly looked away quickly. She was so used to rescuing herself that it felt strange having someone else step in. Thanking someone for help was a whole new experience. 'You could go back and spend the rest of your evening with whoever she is. It isn't too late. I don't need a babysitter. I'm just going to have a bath, wash off the blood— that sort of thing. Go and finish your date.'

'Since you seem determined to launch yourself from one disaster to another, you need supervision.'

Polly laughed and then wished she hadn't because the movement amplified the pain in her head. Supervision? She hadn't been supervised since she was a toddler. Right from the moment she could walk, her father had expected her to sort her own problems out.

Find a way, Pol.

'Unless you're planning on lying down on the bed next to me, I don't see how you can supervise me.' As his eyes met hers, she wished she hadn't used those words. It was uncomfortably easy to think about sex around this man and she wasn't used to thinking about sex. 'I'm going to be fine. I just need painkillers and sleep, that's all. I don't need company for that.'

But the comfort she felt at knowing he was going to be close by shook her. Why did it matter? She'd never been a dependent sort of person. Just because the man had broad shoulders, it didn't mean she had to lean on him.

Seriously unnerved, Polly was relieved when the elevator doors finally slid open and she could put some space between them.

Like everyone, she'd heard whispers and speculation about the duplex apartment that graced the top of the building. Everyone had. When the Doukakis Tower had been under construction there had been hushed talk of the penthouse with its three-hundred-and-sixty-degree views of London, roof garden and glass enclosed heated swimming pool. None of the rumours had prepared her for reality.

'Oh—' Stunned into silence, she stared at the sparkling cityscape that stretched in every direction. The architect had created a space to maximise the view and yet had managed to merge contemporary with homely by dividing that space into distinct living areas.

Polly had never seen so much glass in one place. 'Well—no one is ever going to suffer from claustrophobia here,' she said faintly. 'It's amazing. Seriously cool.'

'I like the feeling of space. My villa in Greece is modern. I like light.'

It was the first personal thing he'd said to her and Polly stood awkwardly, realising just how useless she was at making small talk with men. 'You have a villa

in Greece? Lucky you.' *God, what a lame response.*
No wonder he thought she was a complete idiot. He
was obviously regretting playing nursemaid instead of
continuing his date with someone who was no doubt a
master at sophisticated conversation.

Chewing her lip, she decided to pretend he was a
client. She never felt tongue-tied or awkward talking
to clients, did she?

Damon gestured to the end of the room where the
space narrowed. 'You can use the guest suite at the end
of this floor. I'll show you where.'

Polly took one look at the thick white rugs covering
the polished wooden floor and automatically tugged
off her boots. Padding after him, she felt like a stray
dog that had wandered into someone's home. 'It really
is incredible.' Gazing longingly at the deep, luxurious
sofas, she followed him through the apartment. Despite the glass and the space it was surprisingly cosy
and she felt a stab of envy. This man didn't lie awake at
night worrying about how to keep his company afloat
and protect people's jobs. He was so phenomenally
successful his only worry about money would be how
to count it all.

She caught a glimpse of a futuristic-looking kitchen
and he intercepted her look.

'Are you hungry? I can ask my chef to make you
something.'

'Not unless he does pasta with painkiller sauce.
Honestly, I couldn't eat. But thanks for the thought.'
For the first time Polly noticed the spiral staircase ris-
ing from the centre of the room. Cleverly lit by tiny
spotlights, it looked like something from a fairy tale.
She'd never considered herself remotely romantic, but

suddenly she was wondering if he'd ever carried a woman up that transparent staircase the way he'd carried her to the car...

'Polly?' His rough tone cut through her daydream. Scarlet-faced, she followed him through to a large guest suite and caught her breath. Flames flickered in a sleek, contemporary fireplace and the bed was positioned to take advantage of the spectacular view. It was as if someone had twisted a million fairy lights around every building in London.

Any guest staying here would never want to leave, she thought wistfully.

'The bathroom is through that door. You have blood in your hair—' He lifted a hand and then lowered it again as if he was unsure whether to touch her or not.

The relentless pull of sexual awareness was like an invisible rope dragging them together.

With a faint frown he took a step backwards and they both started to talk at the same time.

'I don't expect—'

'Do you want help?'

No one had ever asked her if she wanted help before and it threw her—but nowhere near as much as the sudden urge to say yes. It was only the thought of stripping off in front of him that kept her from accepting his offer. 'I'll be fine now. I appreciate you bothering.' Part of her wished he hadn't. By helping her he'd tipped the balance of emotion. To feel angry with him was ungrateful, but to feel grateful was uncomfortable. It felt strange, she realised, to know that someone was looking out for her, even if only because of a sense of duty. It turned out that his advice not to leave the building had been sound and when he'd heard she'd got herself in trouble he'd come straight to help her.

Maybe he was ruthless, but he was also decent.

And horribly, terrifyingly attractive.

Damon reached forward and pressed a button by the bed. The cuff of his shirt shifted, the movement revealing a strong wrist dusted with dark hairs. A television screen appeared in the wall but Polly didn't notice. She was transfixed by the contrast between white silk and bronzed male skin.

She swallowed hard. This was worse than she'd thought.

She was in a seriously bad way if she found a man's wrist sexy.

'I'm expecting news of your accident to hit the headlines within the hour. If your father is watching, then he's going to get in touch. If he tries to contact you I want you to dial two on the phone by the bed. It goes through to the master suite.'

Her mind was so busy creating an image of what he would look like naked that it took Polly a moment to process what he was saying. News of her accident? 'There weren't any TV cameras there. They were just photographers and a couple of reporters. It's not going to be on the news.'

'Yes, it is.'

His words sank slowly through her bruised skull. 'But—you *told* them?' Images of him naked vanished in an instant. It was as if someone had pulled the power cord on her brain. Sickness rose inside her and her cheeks flamed as she acknowledged her own gullibility. 'Oh, my God—you used my accident as a publicity stunt.'

'I was not responsible for your accident. *You* made the decision to leave the building and take on a pack of gossip-hungry journalists.' His cool response was the final straw.

Reeling from the discovery that his help had been driven by a desire to flush her father out of hiding, Polly grabbed the door to the bathroom to steady herself. 'And to think that just for a moment there I thought you were a nice guy who didn't want me found dead on my own in the house.' Her light tone painted a thin veneer over the hurt. 'You should have talked to me before you went to all that trouble. I could have told you that it won't make any difference to my father. I could be in Intensive Care and he still wouldn't come.'

His dark brows were already locked in a deep frown as he digested her emotional confession. 'You're saying that your father would see the news that you're in hospital and still not get in touch?'

His appalled response drove her mood lower still. If there was one thing worse than having a parent who didn't care, it was the world knowing about it.

Why on earth had she told him that much?

It was the headache, she thought miserably. 'Look, just leave me alone. I've had enough of you to last me a lifetime. I hope your conscience doesn't keep you awake.'

He stared at her for a long moment and it was obvious he wanted to say more. Instead, his mouth tightened. 'Don't lock the door. If you collapse, I want to know.'

'Why? So that you can call the paparazzi and have them take close-ups?' Feeling worse than she'd ever felt in her life, Polly stalked into the bathroom, slammed the door and defiantly turned the key in the lock.

Damn.

Discovering that tears stung the cut next to her eye, she ground her teeth and held back the emotion, knowing that a crying fit would simply add to her throbbing headache.

'Miserable man—vile, inhuman machine—' Venting in front of the mirror, she wet the corner of a towel and gingerly touched her head. 'Oww.' She was used to looking out for herself, wasn't she? She'd always done it. She didn't *need* Damon Doukakis flying to her rescue.

So why did she feel so let down? Why did it matter that his reasons for dumping his date to come and find her had been self-serving?

Polly stared at her white face in the mirror.

Because, just for a moment, she'd been taken in by those distracting flashes of chemistry. Just for a moment she'd forgotten this was all about his sister and made the mistake of thinking he cared about her a little bit.

That was what you got for dropping your guard.

Trying to ignore the pain, she took her time in the bathroom, wanting to make sure he'd gone before she emerged.

When she finally opened the door, the room was empty.

On the bed was a suitcase, presumably packed with the clothes she'd put on the list.

Fantastic Franco obviously worked fast.

On the table next to the bed were painkillers and a jug of water.

Polly sniffed, determined not to be grateful. Delivering painkillers didn't make him thoughtful.

She swallowed them and then pulled on the lacy shorts and camisole she wore to bed, trying not to think about the serious-faced Franco packing her clothes. Digging out her BlackBerry from her bag, she checked her e-mails. Having satisfied herself that there was nothing that couldn't wait until the morning, she settled on top of the bed, pulled out her notebook and started to scribble down thoughts for the following day's meeting. Determined to show Gérard that he'd done the right thing appointing them as his agency, she sketched out a few new ideas until drowsiness got the better of her and she flopped back onto the pillows.

His hand locked around a glass of whisky, Damon watched the news report from the hospital. There were stills of Polly being lifted into an ambulance, blood visible on her face, and an interview with the doctor who refused to comment on her patient's condition. It was enough to drive the most laid-back parent to the nearest telephone.

But the phone remained ominously silent.

What would it take, he wondered, to flush Peter Prince out of his love nest? Clearly more than an injured daughter.

What sort of man saw that his daughter was in hospital and still didn't call her?

Contemplating that question, Damon drained the whisky. Responsibility towards family flowed through him, as much a part of his being as the blood that was his life force. He could no more abdicate that responsibility than he could stop breathing.

From the moment the police had broken the news about his parents he'd buried his own feelings and focused all his energies on providing for his sister.

Clearly Peter Prince felt no such sense of obligation.

Damon thought back to that day a decade earlier when he'd received the call from the school. He'd walked out of an important meeting to go to his sister and, yes, he'd given her a hard time. Children, especially teenagers, needed rules and discipline. But his abiding memory of that day wasn't anything to do with Arianna. It was of Polly Prince, standing in one corner of the office, alone and defiant as he'd torn strips off her. *Alone.* There had been no sign of her father. At the time, Damon had taken that evidence of lax parenting to be the reason his daughter had slid so far off the rails.

Now he was wondering whether 'lax' should be replaced with 'absent'.

Just what part had the man played in Polly's life?

His phone buzzed. As he answered the call Damon glanced towards the guest room but the door remained firmly closed and he wondered uneasily if he should have checked on her again. The doctor had told him she needed someone around.

Trying to block out an unsettling image of Polly stretched unconscious on the floor of the guest bathroom, he spoke to his pilot and then terminated the call and considered his options.

Of course she wasn't unconscious.

The girl was tougher than Kevlar.

But the image stayed with him as he gave a soft curse and strode through the apartment towards the guest suite. *One look*, he promised himself. As long as she was breathing, he'd leave her alone.

Pushing open the door, he saw her curled up in a ball on top of the bed, a notebook face down on the white silk cover, ink from a discarded pen spreading black blotches across the delicate fabric.

But it wasn't the ink that caught his attention. It was the exceptional pallor of her face. Remembering the doctor's comment that she should have stayed in hospital, he crossed the room swiftly, his overriding emotion one of concern. Was the wound bleeding again? He gently pushed her hair away from her face and the soft strands flowed over his hand like liquid gold, the scent of it distracting him from his purpose.

Reminding himself that he was supposed to be checking her head, he stroked her hair back and studied her face.

There were dark violet shadows under her eyes and the livid bruise on her forehead was an angry smudge. Asleep, she looked younger than ever.

How did she feel, he wondered, knowing that her father didn't care enough to call?

Staring down at her, he remembered the words she'd thrown at him in the boardroom.

'If there's an emergency, I'm expected to handle it.'

To her credit, she'd been trying to handle it all day. Whatever he might think of the way he used office space, there was no denying that she'd worked hard to help settle the staff into their new surroundings and she'd defended them with a passion that had surprised him.

Wondering how anyone so small could be so monumentally aggravating, Damon gently removed the offending pen from her limp fingers and put it on the table next to the bed.

As he leaned forward and pulled the duvet over her, the pink notebook tumbled onto the floor.

Damon retrieved it, smoothed the crumpled pages, and was about to close it when something caught his eye.

Run, breathe, live....

She'd scribbled the words over the pages of her notebook in scrawling, loopy handwriting but what caught his attention were the other combinations.

Run, live
Run right
Live to run
Feel alive

She'd obviously been playing with a million combinations in an attempt to come up with a tagline that worked for the brand.

His attention still fixed on the book, Damon sank onto the side of the bed. With no qualms about delving into her privacy, he flicked back to the beginning, reading what she'd written.

One thing stood out with startling, unsettling clarity.

He'd been completely and utterly wrong in his assessment of Polly Prince.

The creative brain behind every brilliant campaign belonged to the girl lying on the bed.

Chapter 5

Polly woke to an insistent buzzing sound. Cracking open one eye, she was dazzled by an intense beam of light and she gave a moan and stuck her head under the pillow. 'Turn that spotlight off.'

'It's the sun.'

'Well, what's the sun doing up at this time?' Irritable, she stuck her head under the pillow and then howled with pain as it brushed against her wound. 'Ow. That hurts. And that noise is—'

'You set the alarm on your phone.' A strong bronzed hand appeared in front of her face and he picked up her BlackBerry and silenced the noise. 'It's six o'clock.'

'*Nooooo.* It can't be...' Her voice was muffled by the pillow. 'Go away.'

'You are welcome to turn over and go back to sleep, but you've slept without moving all night and I wanted to know you were alive.'

'I'm not alive. No one is ever truly alive at this hour of the morning.' She gave a whimper and huddled under the covers. 'Leave me alone.'

'You feel ill?' His voice was tight. 'I will call the doctor and ask him to come.'

'I don't need a doctor. I'm always like this in the morning whether I've banged my head or not. I'm not a morning person. I have to wake up slowly in my own time. What are you doing in my room anyway? I suppose you're sitting there planning new methods to use me to flush my father out of hiding. I'm just a worm on a hook.' All the horrors of the night before rushed down on her and Polly touched her fingers to her forehead. 'Did you put your hook through my head?'

'No, but that's still on my list of possible actions.' He sounded exasperated. 'Just for the record, I'm in your room because I was worried about you.'

'How long have you been there?'

'Most of the night. I slept in the chair. I wanted to be sure you didn't develop any of the signs the doctor mentioned.'

Carefully, so that she didn't brush her wound again, Polly cautiously removed the pillow and looked at him. Some time during the night he'd changed out of his tuxedo, discarded his bloodstained shirt and showered. Casually dressed in black jeans and a polo shirt, he looked every bit as striking as he did in a suit.

'You don't look like a guy who slept in a chair.' He looked sickeningly energetic, she thought gloomily, resentful at being forced to start her day confronted by all that vibrant masculinity. 'You watched me sleeping? Isn't that a little creepy?'

'It's boring. You're not very exciting when you're

asleep.' Despite the mockery in his tone, his words jarred uncomfortably with the forbidden thoughts she'd been having.

'So why did you watch me? Were you afraid your hostage might die?'

'You are *not* my hostage.'

'You brought me here because you're hoping my father will come and find me, not because you care about me, so stop the saint act. That makes me your hostage.'

Stunned by the discovery that he'd spent the night watching over her, Polly sat up slowly and noticed the cup of coffee on the low table next to the bed. The aroma of fresh coffee seduced her brain, sliding underneath her defences. 'Oh—is that for me?'

'Yes. I'm fast learning that your preference is for pink, but I'm afraid I don't own a pink cup.'

She didn't know which irritated her more—his dry tone, or the fact that he radiated vitality while she felt like a wet rag.

'Of course you don't. You're the sort of man who has to constantly prove his masculinity by bossing everyone around. A real man isn't afraid to have pink in his life. It's a very happy colour. Real men often wear pink ties or pink shirts.'

'Real men?' His sardonic smile was the final straw and she glared at him over the rim of the mug.

'Yes. And by that I don't mean all that muscle and testosterone stuff.' Her eyes dropped to the hint of dark stubble that was already shadowing his jaw. 'Masculinity isn't just about looking as if you can split a log with one swing of an axe.' Which he did. Oh, God, how could a man look so incredibly good first thing in the morning? Particularly after he'd slept in a chair.

Stubble on most men just looked unkempt. On Damon Doukakis it simply amplified his ferocious sex appeal. It wasn't fair.

'I've split logs in my time, but I confess I've never done it wearing a pink shirt.'

Assailed by an unsettling image of those broad shoulders swinging an axe, Polly was about to put the mug down when she spotted the ink on the bedcover. 'Oh, *no*! Did I do that? I'm so sorry. I must have fallen asleep holding my pen.'

'Your pink, fluffy, happy pen. The one that is necessary for all your creative thinking.'

Something in his tone didn't sound quite right but Polly was too mortified by the damage she'd caused to work out what. She licked her finger and rubbed at the stain. When that didn't work, she looked at him apologetically. 'I'll buy you another duvet cover. I know you have a low opinion of me but damage to property isn't on my usual list of crimes. I really *am* sorry.'

'Compared to most of the disasters that appear to happen when you are around, I would say I escaped lightly. Get dressed. I want to talk to you.'

'What have I done this time?'

'That's what I intend to find out.'

Polly racked her brains to think of something he could have discovered that might have got her into trouble. Was this something about the way they'd decorated the office? 'It's not a great time to talk right now. I need to get going if I'm going to make my train to Paris.'

'A moment ago you were all but unconscious. You're not going to Paris.'

'I slept like the dead because I'm really tired, not because I banged my head. I haven't slept properly since you rang me to tell me that you were about to ruin my life. And I *have* to go to Paris. The staff are depending on me to keep that account.' Trying to wake herself up, Polly pushed her hair away from her face and winced as she encountered the bruise. 'If I hurry, I can still make it.'

'Why are you so determined to protect the staff?'

'What sort of a question is that? Because I care about them, that's why. I don't want them to lose their jobs—especially because part of the blame for the current mess lies with my father. I feel responsible. They've always been kind to me. And helpful. When I first started in the company I'd just left school—I was clueless.'

'You didn't go to university?'

Polly thought wistfully of the prospectuses they'd shredded. 'I went straight to work in my father's company when I left school. I learned on the job. You can learn a lot about something by doing it.' Knowing that someone like him was never going to agree with her, she slumped back against the pillows. 'Anything else you want to know?'

Her notebook landed on the bed next to her and she stared at it, her cheeks hot as she mentally ran through all the secrets that might have been revealed from that book.

He waited a beat. 'Well?'

'Well, what?'

'It made for extremely illuminating bedtime reading.'

'It's very bad manners to read someone else's private notes,' she said in a small voice. 'I suppose you also peep through keyholes and listen at doors.'

'Yesterday I asked you who came up with the creative ideas. Why didn't you just tell me the truth?'

'I told you it was a team effort. That's the truth.'

'The tagline and thinking behind the running shoe campaign came from you. If this notebook is to be believed, you're responsible for every decent creative idea that has come from Prince Advertising in the past three years. I've been looking through the portfolio and your company accounts—'

Polly flinched. 'More bedtime reading? You obviously like a good horror story.'

'More like a mystery. My financial director, Ellen, has unpicked the finances and those numbers make for interesting reading. Why did everyone agree to take such a drastic pay cut?'

'You have a *female* financial director?'

'Don't change the subject.'

'Why did we take a pay cut? Because no one wanted anyone to be made redundant. Close your eyes while I find something decent to wear. You're right, I can't have this sort of conversation in my pyjamas.' Sliding out of bed, Polly grabbed something from her suitcase and shot towards the bathroom. 'As I said, we're a team. We're in this together.'

'You clearly have significant creative talent. Why wasn't it recognised?'

The compliment stopped her in her tracks. Her smile faltered. 'You think I have talent?'

'Answer my question.'

Holding the clothes in front of her like a shield, she shrugged. 'You met the board.'

'When you hinted that they'd stolen your work, I assumed you were talking about the spreadsheets.'

Polly just looked at him and he sighed.

'They claimed credit for all your ideas, didn't they? When they pitched for business, you were part of the team?'

'I had to be. No one on the board was able to present the ideas. So they went along as the figurehead and I did the talking.'

'And you won High Kick Hosiery.' He shook his head in disbelief. 'We should have won that account.'

'We were better. Which just goes to show that even a hot desk doesn't always produce hot ideas. And now, if you'll excuse me, I have a train to catch.' The mere thought of battling her way through the train station made her want to lie down in a dark room, but she'd rather walk to Paris in bare feet than admit that to him.

'You're not travelling on a train. A doctor will examine you and then if he says you're fit to fly then we'll go to Paris on my jet.'

'Your jet? Er—why?'

'Because I don't travel by train.'

'No, I mean—' She licked her lips. 'Why are *you* coming? I'm assuming you're not joining me for a romantic mini-break.' She hoped that being flippant would break the tension between them.

It didn't.

He was obviously as aware of it as she was because he narrowed his eyes.

'I make you nervous. Why?'

Her stomach curled and her mouth dried. What was she supposed to say to that? *Because you have monumental sex appeal.* 'You're the boss. You can fire me.'

His eyes held hers. 'That isn't why you're nervous.'

Wondering why she was such a mess when it came

to men, Polly gave what she hoped was a dismissive
shrug. 'Look, there's a lot going on, OK? Gérard's business is important. He has one of the largest marketing
budgets in Europe. It's not just about this brand, it's
about the rest of his portfolio. If I do well in this meeting, he might give us more business.'

'That's why I'm coming with you. You shouldn't be
seeing someone of his seniority on your own.'

'You mean you don't trust me not to mess it up.'

'On the contrary. I want to watch you in action.
I want to know more about your novel creative process.' Infuriatingly calm, he glanced at his watch. 'Get
dressed. We'll finish this discussion later.'

'Well, that's something to look forward to. Yippee.'
She subsided as he shot her a warning look.

He walked towards the door and then paused. 'You
ought to know that an hour ago I had a call from the
private investigator I hired to track your father. It seems
that he's also in Paris.'

'Oh?' Was it wrong not to be pleased that he'd been
tracked down? Her mouth was dry and she wondered
whether it was the bang on the head that was making
her feel sick or whether it was the thought of weather-
ing the reality of her father's next relationship. And this
time it would be worse because the woman in question
was Arianna. Her friend. Damon's sister. 'He could be
in Paris. My father is a romantic person.'

'There is nothing romantic about a relationship between a fifty-four-year-old guy and a twenty-four-year-
old girl.'

'You don't know that. You're very judgemental.'

'When it comes to protecting my family, yes, I'm
judgemental.' His voice was suddenly hard. 'And, talk-

ing of judgemental, I hope you put 'formal business wear' on the list you gave Franco. If you're going to take on the responsibility of a high-flying business executive then you need to look like one. You may be used to flouncing into work in party clothes, but if you're meeting a vice president of marketing you need to clean up your image. The French appreciate chic. The look you should be going for is high-class and elegant.'

Smug in the knowledge that there was so much more he yet had to discover about her, Polly couldn't resist a dig of her own. 'Is that how your team was dressed when they *didn't* win the pitch? You're very traditional. Maybe the client didn't want traditional. He said he was blown away by our creativity and individuality.'

'Presumably he wasn't referring to your appearance.'

Polly gave an innocent smile. 'Or maybe he just has a thing for flamingos. I'll get dressed and meet you in the living room. I need to make some calls before we leave. And for goodness' sake get changed into something more rigid and formal. I'm not taking you to Paris wearing those jeans.' Without giving him the chance to reply, she escaped into the bathroom and bolted the door.

'This is the wrong hotel. I booked myself somewhere cheap and miserable.' Prepared for something seedy, Polly blinked at the glamour and elegance of the luxurious hotel foyer. After seeing the inside of Damon's private jet she'd thought that nothing could ever impress her again. Evidently she'd been wrong. 'Unless the place has had a major upgrade in the past twenty-four hours, this definitely isn't the place I chose.' Light shafted off gold, marble and glass and every person who glided through the revolving doors looked like a multi-millionaire. A sense of inferiority nibbled the edges of her confidence and she stood up a little straighter and tried to look as if she belonged.

No matter how many times she told herself that she deserved to be here she still felt like a fake. It depressed her that she could still feel that way.

The moment Damon set foot in the exclusive hotel there was a subtle shift in the atmosphere. Heads turned, staff straightened uniforms and descended on him with just the right degree of discretion and deference. Smiles were plentiful. Nothing was too much trouble.

Accustomed to staying in cheap hotels, checking in with grumpy, overworked staff and hauling her ancient suitcase up endless stairs only to find herself in an airless room with a window overlooking a grim car park, Polly was fascinated by the contrast.

The staff were attentive to the point of smothering. Damon's presence had an electrifying effect on those around him. He barely acknowledged them, accepting the fawning attention with the same arrogant assurance he displayed in every other part of his life.

This was his normal.

'I can't afford to stay here.' Seriously worried, Polly was mentally running through the budget. 'I could never charge this to the client.'

'I think we both know that finances aren't your strong point. From now on you can leave that side of the business to me. You just concentrate on the creative side, which apparently is your forte.' Leaving his security team to sort out the details with the hotel staff, Damon strode through the foyer. 'I've booked out a floor for us.'

A floor? 'Could you slow down? Just wait a minute.' Worried that her 'creative side' might have gone on vacation, Polly jogged to keep up with him as he strode towards a bank of elevators. 'I can't ignore the finances. I have to think about it.'

'You're the one who mentioned teamwork. This is teamwork. We each do the bit we do best. For you, that's scribbling in your pink notebook. Leave the money to me.'

'Yes, but—' Her phone buzzed and she paused outside the elevator. 'Wait a minute. I need to answer this... *Bonjour,* Gérard, *ça va? Oui...d'accord...*' When she finally finished her call, Damon was standing inside the elevator, watching her through those thick, dusky lashes that tipped his looks from handsome to spectacular.

Her heart skittered and bumped as she joined him. 'Sorry about that, but I couldn't exactly put a VP of marketing on hold.'

'I didn't expect you to put him on hold. I also didn't expect you to speak French.'

'There's a lot you don't know about me. I have hidden talents.'

'So I'm discovering.' That disturbingly acute gaze didn't shift from her face. 'You haven't stopped e-mailing and talking to people since you woke up. When did you learn to speak French?'

'We had a seriously hot French master at school. It was the only lesson we were all awake in—' Remembering too late that mentioning school probably wasn't a good idea, Polly flushed. 'Just kidding. I promised myself that if a gorgeous Frenchman ever whispered sweet nothings in my ear I wanted to be able to understand him.'

'If he's whispering nothing it would probably be better not to understand him,' Damon said dryly and his words made her laugh.

Then she realised she was laughing and stopped instantly. But the connection remained. A connection she didn't want or need and yet still it sucked her in, driving her heartbeat faster. The sudden darkening of his beautiful eyes told her he felt it too and rejected the unwanted chemistry as completely as she did. Perversely, that rejection didn't hurt as much as aggravate. Her emotions spun and suddenly she wanted to press her mouth to his and kiss away the sarcasm and cynicism that flowed from him.

The impulse was so alien to her that if she'd been in possession of a thermometer she would have taken her own temperature. *Was she ill?*

Alarmed by her own thoughts, Polly was relieved when they reached the palatial suite.

'*C'est magnifique.*' Grateful for the size of it, she walked the length of the spacious living room and out thought the open glass doors to the roof terrace. The fresh air brushed away the claustrophobic cloud that had smothered her in the confines of the lift. That crazy impulse to kiss him faded and she breathed a sigh of relief as she stared over the rooftops of Paris. Enjoying the moment of relative calm, she tensed as she heard his footsteps behind her.

'Where would your father stay?'

'He'd stay somewhere no one would think to look

for him. That's the sort of guy he is.' Thinking wistfully that it would be nice to enjoy the luxury of the hotel and the romance of Paris without having to think about work or her father, Polly turned from her contemplation of the city. 'This isn't just about my father, you know. It's also about your sister. She hasn't been on the phone to you, has she? That sort of implies that she doesn't want to be found.'

'She's very impulsive and easily led.'

Polly clenched her jaw. 'If you're still going on about that episode at school, can I remind you that I was fourteen? That was ten years ago. She's an adult now.'

'She doesn't behave like an adult. She doesn't always make good decisions.'

'Isn't that part of growing up? You have to make some bad decisions in order to discover they're bad.' Polly attributed the sudden warm flush on her skin to the hot French sun shining down on the terrace. 'Didn't you ever make a bad decision? Or were you born doing the right thing? I suppose life just fell into place for you.'

The fruits of that success were all around him. Not just in this hotel and the private jet that had transported them to Paris in such luxury, but in his lifestyle. He owned an island in Greece, didn't he? A penthouse in New York and a ski chalet in Switzerland. People fell over themselves to befriend Damon Doukakis and his sister. They walked through life without hindrance, doors swinging open to welcome them.

'You think I was born into this? You think I had it handed to me?' His voice held a raw, rough edge that increased her tension. 'My father worked for an engineering company. A badly managed engineering company. When he was made redundant, he was so ashamed that he'd let his family down that every morning he kissed my mother goodbye and left to go to work. Only instead of going to work he used to sit in the library and hunt for jobs. But there weren't any.'

Shocked into silence by that unexpected revelation, Polly simply stared at him. When she finally managed to say something it came out as a croak. 'D-did he get another job?'

'No. My father was Greek. Proud. Not being able to provide for his family was the ultimate failure. Overwhelmed with the responsibility of it, he drove his car off a bridge.' The words were emotionless and matter of fact. 'I was waiting for them to come home when the police knocked on the door.'

Polly couldn't breathe. 'Them?'

'My mother was in the car, too. No one understood why he did it. Whether he lost all hope and decided to take her with him—whether she even knew what he intended—' His eyes were blank as he stared over the city. 'Do you know the worst thing? The redundancies weren't necessary. I found that out a few years later when I'd learned a few sharp lessons about business. It was all down to bad decisions and I decided right then that I was never going to work for anyone else. I was never going to let someone else control my destiny.'

It explained so much. His ruthless approach. The rigid control with which he managed his business.

Polly realised that her impression of him was as false as his was of her.

It was as if the pieces of a jigsaw had been thrown in the air and, on landing, had created a different picture.

'You were left to raise your sister.'

'She was six.' He gave a wry smile. 'I was sixteen years old and the only skill I had was with computers. I was always in trouble at school for hacking, so I decided there had to be a way of turning that to my advantage. I developed a way of analysing data that every company wanted.' He shrugged. 'Right place, right time. I was lucky.'

'But your business isn't computers now—'

'Something else I learned—diversify. That way if one part of the business is in trouble, another part may be performing well.'

He'd thought it all through. Done everything he could to provide security for his sister.

Feeling a strange ache behind her ribcage, Polly turned away. She shouldn't envy someone who had suffered such a tragic loss, but she did. Even without parents, they'd been a family. Everything he'd done, everything he'd achieved, had been driven by his love for Arianna. Protecting her had been his priority from the moment she'd been left in his care.

'It must have been very hard losing both your parents like that.'

'Life can be hard. It happens.' He glanced towards her, his expression unreadable. 'What happened to your mother? Presumably she was divorce number one?'

The ache behind her ribs didn't fade. 'She walked out when I was a toddler. Being a mother didn't suit her. Or maybe I was just hard work. Whichever—my dad hated being on his own. Whenever a relationship fell apart, he moved onto the next woman.'

Even now, at twenty-four, she found her father's behaviour still had the power to embarrass her and she hated that. She hated the mixed-up feelings that came with every new relationship he started.

'The women are always younger?'

Hearing the judgement in his voice, Polly felt her face heat and wanted to fall through the floor. 'Mostly.'

'Is that embarrassing?'

'Hideous.' In the face of his startling honesty about his own background there didn't seem any point in lying about her feelings.

He let out a long breath. 'So you don't approve of his relationship with Arianna?'

'You didn't ask me if I approved. You asked me if I found it embarrassing. The answer to that is yes. As for whether or not I approve—' She broke off, wondering why on earth she was sharing her deepest thoughts with this man whose opinion of her was so low. He couldn't possibly understand, could he? 'He's my dad and I love him. I just want him to be happy. Isn't that what you want for Arianna?'

'Yes, which is why I don't approve of this relationship.'

'I think all relationships are complicated and I'm not sure age makes any difference to that.'

'When you see a twenty-four-year-old girl with a fifty-four-year-old man, don't you ask yourself why they're together?'

Polly chewed her lip, wondering whether to confess that the entire relationship merry-go-round terrified her. The whole thing seemed designed to wreck lives. 'This is the twenty-first century. Age of same-sex marriages, the toyboy and the cougar. Relationships don't always conform to rigid tradition any more. Why does it bother you? You're too big and tough to care what people think.' But Damon Doukakis was rigidly traditional. Greek. If she'd learned anything about him over the past twenty-four hours it was that family was the most important thing to him.

'I don't care what people think. I do care that my sister will be hurt. Let's face it, your father doesn't have a great track record when it comes to commitment.'

Polly made a weak attempt to defend him. 'You're not exactly famed for long-term commitment.'

'That's different.'

'You move from one woman to the next. Apart from the obvious—prenuptial agreements, huge payouts to lawyers, etc—what's the difference?'

'Marriage is a responsibility and I have more than enough responsibilities.' He took a deep breath as if the mere thought of it was enough to unsettle him. 'In my relationships there are no broken promises. No one gets hurt.'

'For a woman not to care when a relationship ends, the man in question has either got to be incredibly boring or a real bastard. What I'm saying is that I'm pretty sure plenty of women get hurt when you dump them. They probably just don't show it. Pride and all that. And I don't really see the difference between your serial relationships and my father's. Not every relationship has to be about marriage.' But the fact that he felt so strongly about responsibility and commitment made her feel strange inside. It was so different from her father's approach.

'If you're about to say my sister's relationship with your father is about sex then don't,' he advised in a thickened tone. 'I don't want to think about that.'

'That makes two of us. He's my dad and no one

wants to think about their parents having sex. Yuck.'
Polly gave a dramatic shudder. 'But you have to admit
that Arianna is an adult. My father hasn't kidnapped
her against her will. They enjoy each other's company.'

His brow lifted in a cynical arch. 'Are you about to
use the word "love"?

She didn't tell him that she didn't believe in love.
She'd seen what happened to people who believed in
love and she'd made it her golden rule never to allow
herself to be sucked into that particular delusion. 'They
get on well together,' she said lamely. 'They laugh all
the time. They talk. There's chemistry between them.
Maybe they know it's crazy but find it impossible to
resist.'

'Chemistry?' There was an ominous pause and she
could see the thought appalled him. His eyes locked
on hers and suddenly thoughts of her father and his
sister faded into the background. In the distance she
heard the insistent cacophony of car horns, the shriek
of tyres as Parisians drove their city like a racetrack,
but the loudest sound was the insistent thrumming of
her pulse.

Suddenly it was hard to keep a grip on the conversation. 'Chemistry,' she croaked. 'I'm just saying that
chemistry can be a powerful thing.' Or so she'd heard.
Truthfully she couldn't imagine a sexual attraction so
strong that it overpowered caution but she wasn't going
to admit that to a red-blooded male whose sexual prow-
ess was the subject of hushed rumour. 'Perhaps it was
something they couldn't walk away from. I don't know.'

There was a long silence and then his strong hands
captured her face and he lowered his mouth to hers.
Caught off guard, Polly tumbled headlong into the ad-

dictive heat of his kiss, her mouth colliding with his in a fusion of intimacy that was shocking in its intensity. The exploding heat was fierce enough to fuel a nuclear reactor, the hunger so all-consuming it devoured her preconceptions about just how a kiss could feel because this kiss was like no other. Damon kissed the way he did everything else, with the instinctive assurance of someone who knew he was the very best at everything. That clever, sensuous mouth drove everything from her mind and he controlled it all, from the angle of her head to the depth of the kiss, the skilled erotic slide of his tongue taking over her mind, her body, her soul. She didn't feel him move his hands but he must have done because suddenly she was flattened against his hard thighs, the contours of their bodies blending as fiery heat licked through her. Burning up, she slid her palms over his chest, feeling male muscle and latent strength. Her mouth still fused with his, she slid her fingers between the buttons of his shirt, desperate to touch, frantic to feel. Instantly his hand tightened on her bottom as he brought her into firm contact with the hard ridge of his erection.

Liquid with longing, Polly moved against him but the moment she did so he released his grip on her and lifted his mouth, depriving her of the satisfaction her body craved. And that sudden deprivation was so sharply felt that she gave a faint moan of protest and swayed towards him. With a soft curse he locked his hands around the tops of her arms, holding her steady, as if he sensed she would not stay standing without his support. But he kept the distance and didn't kiss her again. Slowly, the implications of that penetrated her foggy brain and she opened her eyes to find him

watching her with those eyes as black as jet and unfathomable as a deep mountain pool.

Her body was screaming for more, refusing to ad-
just to the sudden withdrawal of pleasure. The crav-
ing was so intense she almost reached out and grabbed
him just so that she could press her mouth to his again.
She wanted to know why he'd stopped doing something
that felt so perfect.

His breathing fractionally less than steady, he released his supporting grip on her arms and stepped
away from her. 'You want to know how you walk away
from chemistry? This is how it's done. It's called self-
discipline. You just say no.' The chill in his tone was
as lethal to her tender, exposed feelings as a late frost
to an early spring bud.

Confronted by cool arrogance and an insulting degree of indifference, Polly wanted to say something
flippant. Something dismissive that would indicate that
the earth hadn't moved for her. But it had. It hadn't just
moved, it had shifted—reformed her entire emotional
landscape into something terrifyingly unfamiliar. And
that shift strangled any words she might have spoken.

She wanted to slap his handsome face, but to show
that level of emotion would be to betray what that kiss
had done to her so she stood still and silent, holding
everything inside. Fortunately she'd had decades of
practice.

Insultingly cool, Damon glanced at his watch.
'We're meeting Gérard for dinner at the Eiffel Tower at
seven.' The ease with which he moved from nirvana to
normal was another blow to her savaged pride. 'Dress
is elegant.' Having delivered that lowering statement,
he turned and walked back into the apartment—back

into his world of pampered luxury and elegance where real life was filtered and sifted until it appeared in its most refined form.

Polly stood for a moment feeling displaced. Really, what had just happened? She was the same and yet she wasn't the same. Opening her mouth a fraction, she traced her lower lip with her tongue.

Her first thought was that clearly the kiss hadn't affected him as it had affected her, and yet she knew that wasn't true. She'd felt the strength of his reaction.

However easily he'd walked away, it had definitely been mutual.

He'd kissed her to prove—what? That he could walk away every time? That lust was a decision like every other? She wondered whether the intensity of the chemistry had been as much of a shock to him as it was to her.

Anger flashed through her. How dared he kiss like that and then just walk away?

No doubt he was feeling smug and superior, having successfully demonstrated the practical application of ruthless self control, whereas she—Polly breathed in and out slowly—she'd demonstrated nothing except an embarrassing degree of feminine compliance. Compelled by his breathtaking sexual expertise, she'd been ready to go the whole way. Like Icarus, she would have flown straight at that hot burning sun, the ecstasy of the flight obliterating any sense of caution.

In proving his point, he'd made a monumental fool of her.

Furious and humiliated, she turned her head and looked back towards the luxurious suite, but there was no sign of him. Presumably, having achieved his goal with such spectacular success, he'd taken himself off somewhere to focus his sought-after attentions on some aspect of his global empire before the meeting this evening. A meeting during which he was clearly expecting her to embarrass him.

Dress is elegant.

He thought she was going to mess up.

Polly's mouth tightened.

She *knew* how good she was at her job. If only she were half as good in her dealings with men he wouldn't have played that trick on her. So far he'd made nothing but false assumptions and she'd been so focused on handling the immediate crisis that she'd done nothing to challenge him on his opinions.

But tonight that was going to change.

If Damon Doukakis thought he could control everything around him then he was in for a shock.

Chapter 6

'I'll lead the meeting.' Damon sprawled in the back of the limo, grateful for a stack of e-mails that gave him a legitimate excuse to limit social contact with the woman next to him. An expanse of soft leather seat stretched between them like no man's land as they both kept a wary distance.

Why on earth had he revealed so much about himself?

'Why would you lead the meeting when you weren't the one who won the pitch?' Her tone was cool and when he risked a glance at her he saw that she was also on her BlackBerry, her slim fingers flying over the keys with enviable dexterity as she responded to an e-mail. Not once did she look at him and Damon frowned, unaccustomed to such a lack of interest from a woman, especially a woman he'd kissed.

'It makes sense that I lead the discussion. I've known Gérard for fifteen years.'

'Oh, I see. It's the boys' club approach. No worries. You just carry on and beat your chests and do all that masculine stuff, and when you've finished I'll present my ideas.'

Damon didn't know which infuriated him more—her words, or the fact that she didn't bother looking up as she spoke them.

'The way I conduct a business meeting has nothing to do with the "boys' club".' He chose to ignore the anatomical reference.

'There's no need to be defensive. You don't have to apologise for feeling the need to be the dominant male in every situation. I'm sure that basic flaw has proved fundamental to your success in business.'

'Are you calling masculinity a *flaw*?'

'Gosh, no. Not masculinity.' Her fingers flew over the keys swiftly. 'Just dominant controlling tendencies that prevent you from ever thinking another person with a different approach could be saying something worth hearing.'

Damon's jaw ached from clenching his teeth. 'I am always very receptive to fresh ideas.'

'Providing they're coming from someone dressed in a dark suit. Be honest—you took one look at me and dismissed me on the basis of my dress and my pink tights.'

'That is *not* true.'

'It is true. And once we're in the restaurant the first thing you'll discuss is the success of each other's businesses, your various achievements and how many financial goals you've scored. He'll acknowledge you as

King of the Jungle, you'll order an eye-wateringly expensive bottle of wine to prove your impeccable taste and his importance as a client, and once we've got all that alpha male posturing out of the way I can have my turn.'

Damon breathed deeply. 'You're being intentionally confrontational. You're upset because I kissed you.'

That got her attention.

She glanced up. Her brows rose. 'Why would that upset me? You're a good kisser. No woman is going to object to being kissed by a man who knows what he's doing. Although you might want to work on the ending—it was a bit abrupt. But better that than slobbery.' Having delivered what she clearly considered to be useful feedback, she returned to her phone. 'So—back to this meeting of ours. I just need to make sure I understand the ground rules. You need to have control of everything you do, and that's fine. I don't have a problem with that. I'll take a back seat until you've finished with the whole ego-massaging thing.'

Still grappling with her matter-of-fact response to the kiss, Damon found himself unable to respond.

He wondered whether her choice of long coat had anything to do with her rejection of what had happened earlier. It covered everything from her neck to her ankles, leaving no part of her uncovered. There was nothing sexual about her appearance. Nothing provocative. Which made the fact that he wanted to haul her across that void all the more unfathomable and aggravating. His fingers burned to reach out and grab her, rip open those buttons and feast on the flavours he'd sampled earlier.

Acutely aware that he was entirely to blame for his

current condition, Damon employed the last of his will-power and transferred his gaze from her face to the window. It was a mistake. Paris in darkness sparkled and glittered like a film set and lovers walked hand in hand along the banks of the Seine, creating memories that would be stored for a lifetime. Everything about the night suggested intimacy.

Exasperated by the direction of his thoughts, Damon turned his attention back to his phone, forced to admit that in an attempt to prove his self-control he'd found himself severely tested. Yes, he'd won. He always made sure he won whatever battle he fought. But it had required a strength of will he'd never before needed to apply to that type of situation.

When his driver pulled up close to the Eiffel Tower, Damon made a swift, smooth exit, relieved to be released from the claustrophobic confines of the car.

Polly emerged slowly and stood a safe distance away from him. 'This seems an odd venue for a dinner meeting. I hope you didn't misunderstand.' She stared at the long queue of people waiting for the opportunity to go up to the top of the tower.

'Gérard is trying to impress you.' Damon noticed that this time the silky soft blonde hair had been twisted into a formal up do—severe rather than sexy. The sheen on her lips suggested a faint gloss but nothing too provocative. In fact, her entire appearance was understated. And her shoes were flat—perfect for cobbled Paris streets.

Clearly she'd paid attention to his instruction for 'elegant'.

He waited to relax—for the strange tightness to leave his body.

It didn't happen.

'I've dined here before. The restaurant is up there.'

She followed his gaze and tilted her head, looking up at the iconic landmark, its metal latticework turned to gold by hundreds of tiny lights, the famous structure standing proud again the spectacular Paris sunset. 'Gérard certainly knows how to impress a girl. Or was this your idea? Maybe this is all part of your God complex—you just have to be looking down on everyone else.'

Ignoring that remark, Damon urged her forward towards the private elevator reserved for those dining in the restaurant. Bringing a personal note to their relationship had been a mistake, he thought grimly. Thank goodness the evening would be about business. He and Gérard would discuss the transition of Prince Advertising into DMG and Polly could fill in any blanks on the previous management of the account and expand on her creative ideas for the brand.

As the elevator rose through the iconic building Damon kept his eyes forward. He was aware of Polly fidgeting beside him but he didn't turn his head, determined this time to keep his focus.

As they emerged into the restaurant they were met by the *maître d'* and by Gérard himself, who had evidently arrived just moments before them.

Long-time acquaintances and sparring partners, Damon and the Frenchman greeted each other warmly while the front of house staff took Polly's coat. Deep in conversation about the strength of the euro, it took Damon a few moments to realise that he had lost his audience. Gérard's thoughts on currency fluctuations had clearly been sublimated by some higher priority

that could only be female. Amused and exasperated
in equal degrees, Damon turned his head to see who
could have caused that degree of distraction.

His attention arrested by the woman behind him, it
took him a moment to realise that it was Polly, minus
the coat that she'd handed to the hovering staff. In the
few seconds he'd had his back to her she'd gone from
understated to unbelievable.

Transfixed by the dramatic transformation, Damon
suddenly understood why she'd chosen to cover herself from head to foot. Had he seen her outfit he would
have locked her in their hotel suite and thrown away
the key. Abiding by his instruction to dress elegantly,
she'd chosen to wear a black suit, but all hint of compliance ended with the colour. The tailored jacket was
fastened by a single shapely button. A hint of black lace
camisole was peeping naughtily from under the V of
the lapels. The skirt was short, her legs showcased in a
pair of exotic black stockings that shimmered and glistened in the candlelight. Mesmerised by those incredible legs, Damon saw that the shimmer was created by
a pattern of tiny hearts embroidered in glittering silver
thread and spiralling up from ankle to thigh.

They were cheeky and sexy and perfect for a hot
date. Which made them completely unsuitable for a
client meeting in his opinion.

'Mademoiselle est ravissant.' Apparently disagree-
ing with him, Gérard took her hand in a typically Gal-
lic gesture and lifted it to his lips. 'Once again I am
impressed. Your decision to showcase the jewel in our
new product range in this high-profile venue is yet
more proof that I was right to hire you. I love these.

They are my favourite and I consider myself a con-
noisseur.'

Both of them looked down at her legs and Damon
felt his core temperature rocket to dangerous levels.
He was about to snap something when he realised they
were talking about the tights, not her legs.

'I love them.' Polly beamed up at Gérard, paying
Damon no attention whatsoever. 'They're special, sexy
and so affordable. They can transform a plain boring
black suit with no originality whatsoever—' her eyes
flickered briefly to Damon '—into an outfit that makes
any woman feel like a princess. They're the perfect
day-to-night accessory and what's more they're within
the budget of every discerning woman. I adore them.
All the girls in the office are crazy for them. They're
so very *now*.' The corners of her mouth dimpled as she
smiled up at the captivated Frenchman. 'We're going
to make sure they're the next big thing.'

'And you have ideas for me about how to turn that
adoration into a worldwide campaign that will propel
High Kick Hosiery into the must-have fashion statement of the decade?'

'Tons of ideas.' Reaching into her bag, Polly pulled
out her pink notebook and waved it under Gérard's
nose.

The notoriously hard-nosed businessman laughed
indulgently. 'Ah, the famous notebook and even more
famous pink pen. The deadly weapon with which Polly
successfully defeats the opposition. Had Napoleon had
you and your pink pen by his side, history would have
been changed.' Smiling, he took her arm and led her
towards the table. 'I want to hear your ideas. Given

your love of pink, I'm surprised you didn't opt for our hot pink tights this evening.'

'Mr Doukakis isn't a lover of hot pink.' Balancing on impossibly high heels that explained the fidgeting in the lift, Polly was almost as tall as the Frenchman. 'Apparently it makes him think of flamingos.'

Absorbing the fact that the hot pink tights had been another product in the High Kick Hosiery line, Damon wondered at what point his own agenda had obliterated his usual ability to think clearly. She'd chosen to showcase the sparkling tights at one of the most high-profile venues in Paris. Not only that, she'd worn the long black coat simply because she'd known he would have disapproved.

The fact that she could easily have told him she was wearing her client's products was something he'd raise with her later.

Poised to offer reassurance to Gérard on what the takeover would mean to his business, Damon found himself taking a back seat as Polly presented ideas for a global campaign—a campaign that left Damon speechless with its scope and creativity.

It slowly dawned on him that her contribution to the company was far greater than even his glimpse into her notebook had suggested.

Intercepting his stunned look, Gérard lifted his champagne glass. 'Incredible, isn't she?' There was a speculative look in his eyes as he looked at Polly. 'Much as it pains me to compliment a man whose ego is already robust, I salute Damon for his astute business sense in locking you into his company. Talented people are rare. With you, it is like finding a precious uncut diamond in a bucket of gravel. I admit that when my colleagues recommended that we invite Prince Advertising to pitch, I refused. But then the word spread about the girl with the pink pen and the creative brain. Only Damon Doukakis would be bold enough to take over an ailing company in order to secure one member of staff.'

Damon didn't correct him. 'She has some truly original ideas,' he agreed smoothly, 'and fortunately within the group we have the muscle to turn those big ideas into reality. We'll put our top team onto your account.'

'I don't care who is in the team.' Gérard dug his fork into marinated scallops. 'I just want Polly. You're a crafty dog, Doukakis. I was about to recruit her myself.'

Reflecting on the news that Gérard had intended to offer Polly a job, Damon frowned, but Polly had abandoned her meal and was scribbling over her pad, absorbed by the ideas she was creating.

'We've plenty of time to agree tactics, but the overall strategy should establish the brand image. Then the emphasis needs to be on social media. It isn't just about getting across a message and selling, it's about relationship-building—engaging with our customer…I've got this brilliant idea for using YouTube—' Her suggestions were clever and intelligent and she charmed her client so completely that by the end of the meal he'd agreed to triple the budget and hear her ideas for two other major brands.

Damon watched her in action, unable to think of anything other than how her mouth had felt under his. His view of her as his baby sister's disruptive friend had somehow morphed into something dramatically different. He remembered the way she'd stood up to the

board and challenged them. At the time he'd assumed
her defence was driven by self-interest, but now he understood that her behaviour stemmed from the fact that
she had a deep commitment to the people who worked
for the company. Guilt stabbed him hard. It was gradually dawning on him that, far from being lazy, she
worked every bit as hard as he did. She cared about the
employees as much as he did. Even now, she was ignoring the throb in her head to honour a meeting with
this important client when ninety nine percent of staff
would have stayed in bed and called in sick.

Unaccustomed to being wrong about people, Damon
was forced to admit that he'd allowed his anger with
her father and his past experience of her to colour his
judgement.

Brooding on how that could have happened, it took
him a few moments to notice that Gérard was increas-
ingly attentive to Polly. Recognising sexual interest
when he saw it, Damon felt a flare of outrage. When
Gérard suggested ending the evening with a trip up to
the viewing platform, Damon immediately vetoed that
idea, appalled at the thought of the notorious French
playboy accompanying Polly to a destination favoured
by those seeking romance.

Shaken by the depth of that primal response, a
devotee of rational, logical decision-making, Damon
shocked himself by launching himself out of his seat
and demanded their coats. It wasn't rational or logical,
but he wanted her covered up as fast as possible. He
wanted that coat back on, buttoned to the neck, con-
cealing those amazing legs. The thought of the whole
of Paris following the spiralling upward path of those

tiny sparkling hearts made him sweat like a man running a marathon in a desert.

'We'll send you a full proposal in the next few days, Gérard.' Taking control, he ended the evening and then guided Polly back down to the waiting limo.

As his driver opened the door for them she stopped and shook her head. 'I want to go for a walk. It's been a horrible week and it's so beautiful here. It would be nice to get some air.' Behind her the Eiffel Tower was illuminated against the dark sky and he saw her glance wistfully towards the tourist attraction. 'You go. I can find my own way back to the hotel.' Balancing on one leg like a stork, she removed her stilettos and replaced them with her flats.

Knowing that if he left her alone for two minutes she would be mobbed by Frenchmen, Damon took the shoes from her, handed them to his driver and held out his arm.

Her gaze lifted from his arm to his face and he acknowledged her astonishment with a faint smile.

'Truce. I'm protecting my asset. Clearly I should have your pink pen insured for an astronomical amount.'

Her sudden smile knocked the breath from his body.

'I know I ought to do it all electronically, and I do once I know what I'm doing, but I just can't be creative on a screen—I need to draw. I was the same at school. The only way I remembered anything was by drawing spider diagrams and mind maps.'

She hesitated just briefly and then slid her arm through his. Dismissing his driver with a discreet movement of his head, Damon led her away from the crowds hovering at the foot of the iconic tower and across the road to the river. Strains of music and laughter drifted up from the *Bateaux mouches* as they floated under the bridge and Polly snuggled deeper inside her coat and stared down at the reflection of light on the water.

'I always wanted to stand on a bridge in Paris in the sunset.' There was a wistful note in her voice that drew his attention.

'But with a lover, not your enemy.'

'This may surprise you, but I don't dream of lovers, Mr Doukakis.' There was a brief pause and then she turned her head, the lights from the boat turning her hair to a gleaming shimmer of gold. 'And I don't see you as the enemy.'

Awareness throbbed between them and Damon inhaled deeply, feeling as though he were sinking in quicksand.

'You wanted to walk. Let's walk.' He carefully withdrew his arm and instead pushed his hands into the pocket of his coat to prevent himself from touching her. He'd always known that self-discipline began in the mind, but he was fast discovering his mind wasn't as strong as he'd previously thought. Maybe, he thought, he'd never been truly tested. He'd always avoided commitment of any sort, shying away from still more responsibility. He'd always made a point of keeping his relationships superficial and that was the way he wanted it to stay.

'You've been to Paris before?'

'No. This is the first time. When we pitched we went to their London offices.' She strolled next to him, her eyes back on the river. Light flickered on the rippling surface, a kaleidoscope of colour and texture reflected from the illuminated buildings that stretched along the banks of the Seine.

'It would have saved some misunderstanding had you revealed your level of input into the company right from the first moment. Clearly you were a key member of the team.'

'If I'd walked into the boardroom yesterday and told you that all the good ideas in the company were mine, would you have believed me?'

Damon breathed deeply. 'Possibly not. At least not initially. But you could have given me evidence.'

'I'd put together a presentation. No one would listen.'

'At the time I was handling the board, but when we were alone in the room afterwards you could have said something.'

'When, exactly? Before or after you told me to get my lazy self to work?' There was humour in her tone. 'I don't think you were exactly receptive.'

'*Theé mou*, stop turning me into the bad guy!'

'I'm just pointing out that you didn't exactly start out with a good opinion of me.' Her shoulders lifted in a tiny shrug. 'And I suppose I don't blame you for that. Because of me, your sister was excluded from school. And now she's run off with my dad. Which isn't exactly my fault, but I can see why it makes you angry to be near me.'

'I'm not angry. At least, not with you. I *am* frustrated that you didn't just tell me the truth about the company.'

'At the time I thought you were just going to walk in and close us down to punish my dad.'

'Despite what you may have heard I would *never*

be that careless with people's jobs.' Forced to confront
the depth of his own misjudgement, Damon felt a stab
of guilt. 'I admit that my anger towards your father
blinded business sense. I wasn't thinking clearly. I misjudged you, but you must admit that I had reason.'

'Because I was excluded from school?'

'Because nothing about Prince Advertising is professional.'

'Actually, you're wrong about that. We don't do
things your way, but that isn't the same as being unprofessional.'

She paused to watch as a boat passed under the
bridge, lights twinkling and music playing. On the
deck, a couple were locked in a passionate embrace and
suddenly Damon wished he hadn't agreed to a walk.

Everything made him think about that kiss in the
hotel suite.

To distract himself, he kept the conversation focused on work.

'I can see that you have original ideas, but original
ideas are no good if they're not supported by sound
business practice. Money was leaking from your company. Do you have any idea how close you were to
bankruptcy?'

She was still watching the couple kissing. 'Yes.'

'Is that why you all took a pay cut?'

'The board wanted redundancies. None of us wanted
that. We're a team. We're happy working together. And
we're good. I've known some of these people since I
was a child and used to come to the office after school
to help. The problems we face aren't anything to do
with lack of talent. You're a clever man and you've
looked at the numbers. You know that the money leak-

ing from the company was pouring straight into the pockets of the board.'

'I understand that. It's the reason I fired them although at the time I didn't know just how bad they were. What I don't understand is why your father allowed it to happen. He should have had tighter control on what was going on.'

Even though it wasn't cold, she drew the coat more tightly around her. 'My father has always treated the company more as a hobby than a business. Sometimes he's interested and sometimes he isn't.' Her voice was deceptively light. 'He didn't keep a rein on the board and without him there they took more and more liberties. He stopped showing interest in the company altogether about six months ago—about the same time he started seeing your sister. He's been behaving like a teenager in love ever since. The board wanted cost savings.'

Damon kept his anger on a tight leash. 'And the obvious solution, apart from slashing their own spending, was redundancy.'

'My dad set up the company twenty-five years ago and some of the people who worked for him are still there. They're loyal, lovely people.' Her gaze flickered briefly to his. 'And before you say it, yes, I know that business can't run successfully on loyal, lovely people alone. We all figured that as long as we were still employed it could turn around so we agreed to the pay cut. I suppose we were all hoping for a miracle.' With a wry smile, she stroked a strand of blonde hair away from her face. 'And then my father and your sister went missing. And you showed up.'

Damon paused, unused to confiding in anyone but

surprised to find that he wanted to. 'We had a row. Just over two weeks ago. Arianna told me she was in love with someone and that I was going to lose it when she told me who.' He pressed his fingers to the bridge of his nose, regretting that encounter. 'She was right. I did lose it.'

'I can imagine. We were never exactly your favourite family.'

His hand dropped slowly. 'You were right when you accused me of acting emotionally—I did. But it was like watching a train crash in slow motion—you can see disaster and you want to take charge and stop it happening.'

'Why do you feel you have to stop things happening?'

'That night we were told about our parents—I thought she was too young to understand. She wasn't.' The cold feeling spread through him and he had an urgent need to shake it off, to outrun it. 'She crawled onto my lap and sobbed and sobbed. Wouldn't let go. I have never felt more helpless and inadequate than I did that night. I promised myself I was never going to let her be hurt like that again.'

Polly matched her stride to his as they crossed the bridge and started to walk along the embankment towards the hotel. 'She was a child then. She's an adult now.'

'I'm more parent than brother and I don't think a parent ever stops feeling responsible.' It was typical, he thought, that a woman would want to unpeel that statement and look beneath the surface. He wondered what had possessed him to make such an unguarded comment when normally he kept his feelings tightly locked away. 'Let's get back to the hotel.'

'In other words you don't want to talk about it. Sorry. Shouldn't have asked.' She was light on her feet, sure-footed as she negotiated paving stones and cobbles. 'So what happens now? You took over the company thinking that you'd be able to influence my father. But my father doesn't care about the company at the moment. He's obsessed with your sister.' Her face was pale in the twinkling evening light and Damon watched her, realising that he'd given virtually no thought to how she felt about it all.

'It must have been hard for you, seeing him involved with women your age.'

Her tongue moistened her lower lip. 'School was hard. My father used to drive a soft-top sports car and the blonde in the front was as much of an accessory as the CD player. If anything is designed to make you a target, it's having a parent who behaves like that.'

'Was that why you rebelled?'

She gave a funny crooked smile. 'I didn't rebel. I had a problem and I sorted it. It's what I've always done.'

'You had three boys in your bedroom—the bedroom you shared with my sister. How was that sorting a problem?'

'It happened ten years ago! I refuse to be continually judged on something I did ten years ago. Get over it.' She walked surprisingly quickly for someone quite petite and he cursed softly and followed, deciding that she was infinitely more complicated than he'd first thought.

He was getting the sense that he'd misjudged her yet again, and yet her misdemeanour had been witnessed by several members of staff so he knew that this time there was no mistake. What was there to misjudge? At fourteen years old she'd been caught in her underwear in her bedroom with three boys—an offence dealt with by exclusion.

They'd reached the hotel and she smiled at the doorman and greeted him in French.

Amazed that she managed to be chatty even in a foreign language, Damon extracted her from what promised to be a lengthy conversation and urged her forwards. 'So why is your title executive assistant when clearly you should be on the creative team? It's not a fair reflection of your responsibilities or your contribution.'

'Life isn't always fair, Mr Doukakis.' She walked into the apartment ahead of him, exchanging a cheerful greeting with his security team who Damon dismissed with a faint movement of his head.

'I think we should probably drop the formality, don't you?'

As the door closed behind the last security man she turned her head and something flickered in her eyes.

'Fine. Let's drop the formality.' There was a moment's hesitation and she drew in a long, slow breath, as if she were plucking up courage. Then, without shifting her gaze from his face, she lifted her chin and slowly, provocatively, undid the buttons of her coat and allowed it to slide to the floor. The jacket of her suit followed and his eyes slid to the thin black straps of her camisole. All evening he'd had tantalising glimpses of sexy lace and now he saw that the whole thing was lace, the elaborate pattern exposing a suggestion of creamy skin.

His mouth dried. '*Theé mou*, what are you doing?'

'I'm dropping the formality. And my clothes, now that you mention it.' A slight smile tugging at the corners of her mouth, she walked towards him. 'What's the matter, Damon? Worried about that self-control of yours? Worried you won't be able to walk away from chemistry?' Her hand locked into the front of his shirt and she pulled him towards her, her thick lashes a tempting veil over eyes that glittered like jewels. Her lips parted and Damon felt his brain shut down.

He ought to push her away right now.

He ought to—

Her fingers locked behind his head and drew his head down and his mouth melded with warm, honeyed temptation. She tasted exquisite, the subtle stroke of her tongue against his bottom lip a hot, erotic fantasy, and he felt lust slam into him with shocking force. Resisting, he lifted his hands to push her away but instead found himself cupping her face, his fingers exploring the softness of her skin and the delicate lines of her jaw. If the kiss they'd shared earlier had been a full-on demonstration of the power of sexual attraction this was softer, more subtle. But it was no less devastating in its effect. Her sweet mouth seduced his with a slow, sure gentleness that ripped away his defences and sent fire tearing through every part of him.

Balancing on the dangerous knife-edge of a new addiction, he felt his power to control his emotions and actions drain at a frightening rate. The part of his brain warning him to stop this madness right now was eclipsed by the part that reached out greedily for the fulfilment of pleasure. A whisper of silk brushed his hand and he removed the clip in her hair and dropped it on the floor, allowing the river of softness to slide over her shoulders. With a husky groan he slid his fingers into that soft sheet of hair and deepened the kiss. The intense flame of sexual chemistry scorched both of them and this time when he gently stroked her face he discovered that his hand was shaking. Devoured by emotions he'd never felt before, he smoothed his palms over her shoulders, feeling nothing but a desperate urge to explore the rest of her. The thin spaghetti straps of her camisole surrendered to the pressure of his fingers and slid away, leaving no barrier between her flesh and his mouth. As he pressed his lips to her throat he heard her gasp, felt the rapid thrum of her pulse under his mouth.

And then she stepped away.

Disorientated, unbalanced by her unexpected withdrawal, it took Damon a moment to absorb the fact that she'd retreated. He stretched out a hand to haul her back but she was already out of reach, those beautiful eyes unreadable as she slowly and deliberately slid the straps of her top back up to her shoulders.

His mind in lockdown, he struggled to speak. 'What are you doing?'

'I'm resisting chemistry. It's called self-discipline.' In a husky voice, she threw his words right back at him. 'You just have to say no. Isn't that right, Damon? Just because you're insanely good at kissing, that doesn't give you the right to make a fool of me. Don't *ever* do that again.' In a single graceful movement she retrieved her clothes and turned to walk towards the second bedroom. 'Sleep well.'

Chapter 7

Polly leaned over her private section of balcony, sucking in air and trying to lower her blood pressure. Her entire body screamed with frustration, and she didn't know whether to plunge under a cold shower or pull on her running shoes and pound the streets of Paris.

She dug her hands into her hair but that just reminded her of the moment he'd done the same thing so she folded her arms instead and paced backwards and forwards, breathing deeply.

Of all the stupid things to do.

What on earth had possessed her? She'd been running on adrenaline, on such a high after the success of her meeting with Gérard that she'd virtually danced along the streets of Paris. And, yes, it had felt *good* to witness the moment Damon had finally realised just what an enormous contribution she made to the company. But that didn't explain why she'd suddenly performed the equivalent of a pole dance in the middle of his hotel suite.

Wondering how on earth she was going to face him again, she covered her face with her hands. Perhaps it had been seeing all those lovers holding hands and kissing. Paris was a city for lovers. Romance. Or maybe it was just about pride.

All evening she'd been simmering, really angry that he'd made such a fool of her.

Her hands dropped and she swallowed hard.

In walking away from her earlier, he'd proved that he was firmly in control. She'd wanted to hit back— to snap that control.

And she had.

But now she was the one paying the price.

Yes, she'd proved her point and walked away, but her body was on fire and the way she was feeling was driving her crazy. If this was how chemistry felt then no wonder people behaved stupidly.

'Polly—'

Hearing his rough voice, she whirled round and saw him standing there. His shirt gaped where she'd ripped at his buttons and his eyes were an intense, unfathomable black in a face taut with tension.

'Get out of here.' The words stuck to her dry mouth and she licked her lips, trying not to think about the way it felt to kiss him. Her own self-control was non-existent and she hated him for that. 'We're even.'

'Kissing me was your idea of punishment?'

'You kissed me to prove a point. I was doing the same thing.' Except that it had backfired. Disturbed by the look in his eyes, she took a step backwards, terrified and fascinated in equal measure. 'You're the one who started this.'

'I know. I accept full responsibility—and you're right to be angry. It was a selfish, careless thing to do—' he slid his hand into her hair and cupped the back of her head, drawing her towards him '—and I apologise.' His soft words threw her because she hadn't thought him capable of apology any more than she'd thought him capable of gentleness. And that gentleness was all the more seductive because it came from a man for whom strength and self-assurance was the norm.

The intimacy of the moment wrapped itself around her like a thousand invisible strands drawing them together. It was a connection she didn't understand and therefore couldn't fight.

The whole of Paris was spread beneath them like a glittering magic carpet, the air scented by the flowers that tumbled from the pots that turned the terrace into an exotic rooftop garden. As a setting, it couldn't have been more romantic.

And she didn't want romantic.

She'd seen what 'romantic' did to people and suddenly she was terrified. Why the hell had she kissed him? After that first time she should have known that it was dangerous—stupid. He'd made her feel something she'd never felt and didn't want to feel.

'OK, you've said sorry and that's great—fine—now you can leave. Preferably right now because I can't breathe properly when you're standing this close.' She lifted her hand to his chest and encountered hard muscle and a man who clearly wasn't going to budge. 'Seriously, Damon, let's just forget the whole thing and—oh, God—' The sudden pressure of his mouth on hers silenced the rest of her sentence and she moaned indistinctly as his tongue swept into her mouth, the erotic invasion sending her head into a crazy spin and her senses into freefall. Sexual excitement flashed through her, ignited by the skill of his kiss and the sure strength of his hands on her body.

'Damon—' She moaned his name as he cupped her breast with his hand, the rough pad of his thumb grazing over her nipple. 'Honestly, we can't—' She gasped as he drew her against him and restraint and common sense melted in a warm puddle of molten desire. 'Or maybe we can.' Her arms were round his neck, pulling him down to her as he pulled her in. 'Just tell me quickly—are you about to walk away again?'

'No chance.' His hands were sure and bold as they slid down her back. 'Neither are you.'

'Good, because if you stop this time I just might have to kill you.'

Her hands were inside his shirt, her fingers sliding slowly over warm male skin. His body was lean and muscled but that came as no surprise because she already knew he was strong. What surprised her was the complexity and depth, the emotions that flickered under the cool, controlled surface he presented to the world.

When she'd kissed him earlier, his guard had slipped. For a fleeting moment he'd lost his grip on that rigid control that characterised the way he lived his life. The fact that she was the one who'd slid under those defences intensified the excitement.

They kissed with a searing, primitive hunger that burned up logic and caution, their mouths greedy, seeking, hot as they feasted, lost in the burning fire of the moment. The world centred on the two of them. She was no longer aware of the city that stretched beneath her, or the warm whisper of the night breeze. All she was aware of was him—this man who kissed her as if he understood everything about who she was and what she needed.

She'd never understood how sex could drive people to make foolish decisions. Until now.

When he lifted her in an easy movement and carried her from her small terrace through to the master bedroom suite, she simply tightened her arms around his neck and kept on kissing him. Paris sparkled through the windows but neither of them spared the city a single glance.

As he lowered her gently to the centre of the enormous bed, she pushed his shirt off his shoulders and he shrugged it away. The swell of muscle in his shoulders bunched as he supported his weight and came down on top of her, the movement so innately masculine that her breath caught.

Even though part of her hated to admit it, the physical power of him was part of the attraction. Dark and handsome, he was unequivocally male, every touch and kiss assured and confident as he dragged her into a whole new world of dangerous desire.

As his warm, clever mouth trailed down her body Polly writhed against the silk sheets, her body gripped by such intense excitement that she couldn't keep still. The need to move her hips was almost painful and she writhed and shifted until she felt his strong hands grasp her, holding her captive. Deprived of the only means of easing the burning ache between her thighs, she gave a murmur of protest—a murmur that turned to a gasp as he spread her thighs and used his mouth on her, the skilled flick of his tongue driving her into a frenzy of desperation. It was impossibly intimate but she didn't even care, and she surrendered to the feeling, mindless to everything except the pleasure he created and controlled. The excitement built and spread until it exploded in a bright burst of light, her climax so extraordinarily intense that she couldn't breathe.

As consciousness gradually seeped back into her spinning head she opened her eyes, but she had no time to recover before he moved up her body and kissed her. Sensation after sensation slammed into her and she wondered dimly how it was possible to want someone this much. It was a devouring hunger, a greed she'd never before imagined, and this time she took control as she pushed at his chest and rolled. She was aware that he was far too strong to be pushed anywhere he didn't want to go but it was clear he was willing to play her game and he rolled onto his back, his eyes glittering dark as he watched her from under those thick black lashes.

As she kissed her way down his body she heard him groan and then mutter something in Greek, something she didn't understand but which told her he was as carried away by the moment as she was. Relishing her own power, she slid her mouth over the velvet length of him, using her tongue and her lips to drive him wild until he groaned and lifted her towards him.

'I want you. Now.'

In the grip of the same desperation, Polly moved up his body and straddled him. His need to be in control seemed to have left him and she positioned herself over him, her nerve-endings sizzling with awareness as she felt his swollen hardness brush against her. His eyes narrowed to two dangerous slits, he closed his hands around her hips and thrust upwards. Sure and confident, he drove into her and she gave a soft gasp at the feel of him as he surged deep. Just for a moment she thought *He's too big*, but then he paused, his fingers biting into her flesh as he held her where he wanted her.

'You're incredibly tight. Relax, *agape mou*—'

She couldn't relax. Her body was on fire, the power of his invasion momentarily shocking her out of the sexual trance that had held her in its grip.

His gaze sharpened and the beginnings of a frown touched his brow. '*Theé mou*, have you ever—?'

Polly cut his sentence off with her mouth, nibbling at his lips, stroking with her tongue, until the unspoken question turned into a kiss that blew away the unexpected tension. Shivering with longing, she lifted her mouth from his so that she could look at him, her breathing rapid as she rocked her hips, taking him deep. This time as he surged into her he watched her, and that depth of connection increased the chemistry until she knew on some deep, subliminal level that this was so much more than just physical pleasure. It was the most erotic, intimate experience of her life. Sensation built and clawed at her until he drove them both over the edge and the explosion of ecstasy ripped through them both simultaneously. Wave after wave of it slammed into her until she collapsed against him, the only sound in the room the breath tearing at her throat.

She felt the pounding of his heart and then his arms tightened around her, his hand gently stroking the length of her spine. He didn't speak, but she knew he was as shocked as she was.

Lying there in the circle of his arms, Polly felt a surge of raw terror.

Oh, God, what had she done?

Not the sex—although she'd shocked herself and very probably she'd shocked Damon, too. No, what really terrified her was the intensity of emotion that had accompanied the physical. The connection, the closeness—they were the things she'd spent her life avoiding.

She lay for a minute, her head resting on the hard muscle of his chest, her thoughts private and her expression concealed.

The panic spread slowly. As deadly and insidious as smoke sneaking through a burning building, it seeped into every part of her.

She felt his hand still on her back and wondered what he was thinking.

He was bound to be regretting it, wasn't he? Damon Doukakis was a man who never lost control and he'd just lost control. And with a woman who aggravated him.

Trying to extricate herself from a hideous situation, Polly rolled away from him but a strong hand snaked out and caught her.

'Where do you think you're going?'

'To bed.'

'You're in bed.' His voice husky, he rolled her onto her back and slid his hand into her hair, forcing her to look at him. '*My* bed. What's the matter?'

She wanted to run but the weight of his body pinned her to the bed, and as his mouth lowered to hers in a possessive kiss the desire to escape evaporated and she kissed him back, driven wild by the ruthless demands of his mouth.

'*Theé mou*, you are the hottest, sexiest woman I have ever met,' he groaned, sliding his hand under her bottom and lifting her against him. 'What the hell are you doing to me?'

She felt the hunger in him, the feverish tension. Instinctively she knew he felt the same primitive chemistry that kept her trapped in the bed when she knew she should leave. The passion was raw and entirely mutual.

Wrapping her arms around his body, she looked up at him, her heart drumming against her chest in a crazy rhythm. The muscles in his shoulders were pumped up and hard and her stomach squirmed with liquid desire even as her brain rejected the image. 'Stop playing the dominant male.'

'I'm not playing at anything.' His voice thickened with lust he brought her hips into contact with the hard thrust of his arousal. 'And you want me as much as I want you.'

Oh, yes, she wanted him. She was every bit as desperate as he was. And the burning need overwhelmed the terror. 'I suppose I'll let you be the one in charge this time.' Lowering her eyelids, she teased him. 'It's only fair as I was the one in control last time.'

Teasing her right back, he gave a slow, dangerous smile and lowered his mouth to hers, murmuring words against her lips. 'I hate to break this to you, but you weren't the one in control, *agape mou*.'

'I had you on your back.'

'I was on my back, that's true—' his eyes darkened and he tightened his hand on her bottom, lifting her '—but only because that's where I chose to be. I had you exactly where I wanted you.' Shifting her position subtly, he surged into her, and Polly gave a sob as she felt him filling her, the silken force of him stretching her sensitised flesh and fusing the two of them together.

For a moment he paused, letting her feel what he did to her, and she dug her nails into the satin-smooth skin of his back as she struggled with the fire that consumed her.

With a groan he withdrew slightly and then surged into her again. 'You feel so good…' With every driving thrust he sent the excitement tighter and tighter until release came in a shattering explosion of sweet sensation, the experience so sublime, so perfect, that she felt it in every corner of her trembling frame.

Slowly, the excitement faded to pleasure and then to a soft hum of blissful contentment.

For a moment she just lay there, slightly dazed.

And then the terror returned.

Emerging from a sex-induced coma, Damon woke to find himself alone in the bed.

As the morning light poured into the bedroom, it took him a moment to orientate himself. Turning his head slowly, he eyed the tangled sheets and found himself struggling with emotions entirely foreign to him.

He'd spent a wild night with Polly Prince.

Covering his eyes with his forearm, he swore long and fluently. It didn't help to acknowledge that it had started with him trying to prove his ability to control his decisions and actions.

Control?

Where had control been during their marathon sex

session? The irony slapped him in the face. In trying to prove control, he'd disproved it. And he'd done it again and again, until she'd been limp and pliant and had finally fallen asleep on his shoulder, those incredible limbs wrapped around him.

Just thinking about it made him hard again and he gave an exclamation of frustration and sprang from the bed, trying to dispel the image of a smouldering Polly letting her coat slip to the floor.

That whole striptease had been his undoing.

Striding into the bathroom, he stepped into the shower, hoping that a blast of freezing water would cool his body and his brain.

He needed to stop feeling and *think*.

As if his life wasn't already complicated enough, he'd now complicated it still further. It wasn't just the situation between his sister and her father, or even the fact that she now worked for him and he made a point of never becoming involved with an employee. No, the real complication was that he didn't want a serious relationship. There was no way he wanted to be responsible for yet another human being's happiness. It was enough to have the burden of thousands of employees and one wayward sister. He didn't need anyone else added into the mix.

Damon turned the jets of the shower to full blast, knowing that the only way to deal with the situation was to be blunt. Honest.

The question was whether it was better to do it immediately, and risk subjecting himself to the company of an emotional female for the journey home, or whether to delay that conversation until they reached

London and he could extricate himself from the fallout with greater ease.

It was going to make it impossible to work with her, and it was clear to him that, despite his previous thoughts, she was a key player in the business. He suspected that Gérard's devotion to her was as much due to her creative imagination as her long legs.

Postponing the moment when he had to shatter Polly's romantic illusions, he shaved, dressed and dealt with his urgent calls. By the time he'd returned calls to people in London and Athens there was still no sign of her.

After the intimacies they'd shared the night before, he was surprised.

His jaw tightened and he tried to free himself of the uncomfortable suspicion that she'd been a virgin. Twenty-four-year-old virgins didn't exist, did they? Especially not virgins who seduced a man with a striptease and then proceeded to indulge in hot, steamy sex without a single blush or bat of an eyelash.

Dismissing the thought, he strode through the apartment in search of her.

Theé mou, he wasn't a man who avoided awkward situations. He just did what needed to be done, so why was he dragging his feet?

Even though he reminded himself that she'd been a more than willing partner, he still felt a sense of responsibility. He'd started it, hadn't he? By kissing her.

It was time to put an end to something he never should have started.

He found her seated on the balcony, talking to someone on the phone while she plugged numbers into a spreadsheet on her laptop.

Damon studied her face for evidence of distress but she looked animated and energised as she negotiated a price with someone on the end of the phone.

When she finally ended the call she was so absorbed in the work she was doing she didn't immediately notice him. Looking at her now, he wondered how he could ever have accused her of being lazy. It was obvious she'd been working for hours.

'Don't you ever sleep?'

She glanced up then, her cheeks dimpling into a warm smile. 'You're a fine one to talk. I hear your average working day is twenty hours.'

'I'm the boss.'

'So you're setting an example? Never mind that. I'm glad you're here because I really need to talk to you.' She hit 'save' and Damon drew in a breath, bracing himself for the inevitable conversation.

She looked so happy. Lit up inside.

It was obvious she'd succumbed to that dizzy, crazy feeling that came at the beginning of a new relationship.

No doubt she was plotting out their future as women always did. And he was about to take those plans and shatter them. *This* was why he avoided responsibilities. He never forgot that the fear of letting down the people close to him was what had driven his father over the edge of despair.

Sweat broke out on the back of his neck. 'Polly—'

'Can you take a quick look at this?' She turned the laptop so that he could see the screen. Her hair was pinned haphazardly on top of her head and she was wearing a dress in a wild shade of purple. Her pink notebook lay face-down on the table. 'I've prepared two proposals—one for a massive budget and one for a shockingly massive budget.' She gave a wicked smile. 'I'm hoping that Gérard will be so impressed by the ideas he won't look at how much they're costing. What do you think? You know him better than me—if you think I've gone over the top then just say so. I suddenly decided that we might be able to do something in Fashion Week so I've made a few calls.'

Her focus on work threw him. 'You want me to look at the budget? That's what you wanted to talk about?'

'Yes.' Her eyes were back on the screen as she reached for the glass of water she'd placed on the table. 'Ideally I'd like to e-mail this today while he's still excited about everything we discussed. I don't want him to back down on that figure he mentioned last night. If this piece of business is going to be worth that much to the company, there's no way you'll have to make the staff redundant.'

Braced for an entirely different conversation, Damon couldn't focus. 'I'll take a look at your proposal later.'

'Do you think you could do it now? When I get back to the office I want to be able to gather the team together and give them a morale-boosting talk. I thought after last night you'd find it impossible to justify doing something so mean as letting anyone go.'

'After last night?' He repeated her words, shocked by the raw emotion that rushed through him. 'You think the fact that we had sex will affect my business decisions?'

Her jaw dropped. 'I was talking about the meeting with Gérard.'

Of course. The meeting. Damon pressed his fingers to the bridge of his nose, realising that he was in serious trouble. 'We are having two different conversations here.'

'I think we must be.' She looked genuinely astonished. 'I'm having a conversation about the staff. I can't concentrate on anything or enjoy my work when I'm watching my back and worrying about job losses. I just want that sorted. What are you having a conversation about?'

His eyes dropped to her mouth and his body tightened as he remembered how she tasted. The fact that she was thinking about her staff and not the night they'd spent threw him. Normally after a night of steamy sex women wanted to know what was going to happen next. They went into full planning mode. Polly appeared to have skipped that ritual and was just making the assumption that they were already a couple.

'You're very chirpy for someone who had virtually no sleep,' he said cautiously. 'I thought you weren't a morning person.'

'I didn't think I was either.' She leaned forward and changed a figure on the spreadsheet. 'But apparently a night of crazy sex does wonders to wake me up. I wish I'd known sooner. I would have done it years ago. It's probably better for you than strong coffee.'

Digesting the implication of those words, Damon breathed deeply. 'So it *was* your first time.' Her confession intensified the suffocating feeling that had begun from the moment he'd woken up. 'Polly—'

'It's hard for me to work out how to staff this account until I know what your plans are.'

'*Theé mou*, will you *stop* talking about work?'

Startled, she looked up at him. 'Sorry, but this account is really important. It's worth loads to the company...' Her voice trailed off as she looked at his face. 'You're behaving really weirdly, if you don't mind me saying. Just a couple of days ago you were telling me to take my lazy self and do some work and now you're telling me to stop thinking about work. It's very confusing.'

She couldn't possibly be more confused than him. 'I was wrong to say that. I was wrong about *you*,' Damon breathed. 'I've already apologised, but I apologise again.'

'Well, I was pretty wrong about you, too. I thought you were a demented workaholic with an unhealthy focus on the bottom line. But right now, when I *really* need you to talk about work, you seem incapable of focusing. It's very frustrating.'

'Why were you a virgin?'

'What sort of a question is that?!' Her face turned scarlet. 'Because no man ever wanted to take me to bed before, I suppose. Thanks for pointing that out. And now can we end this conversation? I don't know much about morning-after etiquette but I'm pretty sure that embarrassing your partner isn't on the list.'

'You were excluded from school at fourteen because you had three boys in your room,' he said thickly. 'So we both know you're not some blushing innocent.' The error in his thinking blazed in front of his eyes. She might not have been blushing, but she *had* been innocent. He'd suspected it at the time but he'd been too carried away by the whole erotic experience to act on that suspicion. 'What the hell transformed you from vamp to virgin?'

'I never said I was a vamp. You made that assumption. Along with a few others.'

'I made that assumption based on the evidence.'

'Mmm. Good job you're not a lawyer.' She gave a tiny shrug and fiddled with her pen. 'So—Arianna obviously never talked to you about that episode?'

The tension was like a layer of steel in his back. 'I didn't ask for details. I decided it was safer to put the whole thing behind us.'

'Right. Probably wise.'

Exasperation rose in him. 'I remember that day very clearly and you didn't make a single excuse. You just stood there with a defiant look on your face and let them throw you out of the school. Permanently. Not *once* did you defend yourself or try and stop it happening.'

'I didn't want to stop it happening.'

Far beneath them the sound of horns blared as the impatient French negotiated the Paris traffic but Damon was oblivious. 'You *wanted* to be excluded?'

'Yes. That was the plan.'

'Plan?' He breathed slowly. 'You're telling me that you engineered the whole thing so that you'd be asked to leave the school? Why would you want that?'

'Because I was being bullied. Badly bullied.' Her tone was matter-of-fact. 'I tried other ways to sort it out but none of them worked. So I decided I had to leave the school.'

'*You* decided—?' Digesting the implications of the statement, Damon struggled to focus. 'And your father didn't have anything to say about that?'

'I didn't ask him. It was my problem. I sorted it.'

'If I have a problem, I'm expected to sort it out myself.'

'Did you talk to the teachers?'

'Yes.' She looked at him as if he were clearly stupid. 'They spoke to the bullies, who were so angry that I'd told on them they set fire to my hair. Fortunately Arianna walked into the room and we managed to put it out, which was a relief because burnt hair is *not* a good look.'

Damon gritted his teeth. 'What happened then?'

'We trimmed the ends. It was fine. It actually suited me shorter.'

'Not your hair, the bullying. Why didn't you tell your father?'

'Why would I tell my father?'

'Well, because—' Damon found himself at a loss for words. 'You were fourteen years old. It was his responsibility to come down to the school and sort it out.'

'That isn't his style. He prefers me to sort things out myself and that's fine with me. I'm grateful to him. I'm quite independent as a result of it. But I did feel guilty that Arianna got drawn into the whole episode.'

'So you didn't invite the boys to your room because you wanted to party?'

'No. I paid them to come and hang out while I danced in my underwear with a bottle of whisky in my hand. Someone tipped off the head teacher who promptly caught me. Which was as we'd planned, obviously. I thought it was an extremely creative solution. Anyway, it did the trick and the boys didn't seem to mind helping us out.'

Mind? Damon tried to obliterate the image of Polly writhing in her underwear with the express purpose of getting herself thrown out of school. 'Why did the other girls bully you?'

She wrinkled her nose. 'Mostly because of my dad, I suppose. As I said to you last night, it was social suicide having a parent turning up in a sports car with a young blonde in the front seat. I suppose if it hadn't been that it probably would have been something else. They just pick on whatever suits them—red hair, glasses, fat thighs—you know what bullies are like.'

He didn't, but she obviously did. 'What about your next school?'

'Oh, that worked out really well. I picked a nice day school close to my house.'

'*You* picked it?'

'Yes. I went to see a couple and chose one that did a lot of art and creative stuff. I thought it would suit me perfectly.'

'You—' Damon broke off, unable to believe what he was hearing. 'You're saying that you picked the school by yourself? That your father didn't go with you?'

'Why would he? I got myself kicked out of school. It was my job to find myself another one, which turned out great,' she added cheerfully. 'I don't see why you're so shocked about the whole thing.'

'Bullying is unacceptable behaviour. You should have had support. You shouldn't have had to leave.'

'Leaving was the best thing that happened to me. I hated that school and so did Arianna.'

'*Arianna* hated it?'

'Yes. The girls were vile. Honestly, I think we were just unlucky with our year group or something. She didn't really want to hang around there without me and she thought my party plan would work better if she joined in.'

The news that his sister had also hated the school was a solid blow deep in his gut. Shaken by those unexpected revelations, Damon turned the full force of his own guilt into anger. 'Why the hell didn't one of you tell me the truth?'

'Arianna did say that she might, but you were storming and ranting and looking like thunder so I think she lost her nerve. Look—just forget it. It's such a long time ago I can hardly remember.'

He didn't believe her for a moment. It had obviously left deep, permanent scars. 'Don't lie. For once, I want the truth.'

'The truth is that it doesn't matter any more. None of it. I've moved on.' She was silent for a moment, as if her own words had come as a surprise to her. Then a tiny smile touched the corners of her mouth and she sat back in her chair, as if she were surprised by something. 'Wow. I've said those words a million times and never really meant them. But this time I really mean them! I really *have* moved on.' Her smile widening, she sprang to her feet and did an impromptu twirl. Then she grabbed the front of his coat and her eyes shone into his. 'Do you have any idea how good that feels? You can deal with something, you can put it behind you, but that's not the same as actually being over it. And I'm *over* it! Honestly, truly over it.'

Observing this unrestrained display of ecstasy with growing bemusement, Damon found himself overwhelmed by a sudden urge to drag her back to bed. Staring down at the tiny dimple at the corner of her mouth, he wondered what had happened to restraint and discipline.

'I can see now what a difficult time you've had.' The words stuck in his throat. 'And then I took over your father's company and stormed and ranted and looked like thunder.' *And made things worse for her.*

And he was about to make them worse still by telling her that their relationship was over. That whatever they'd shared was just a one off, never to be repeated.

'You were worried about your sister. I get that. Don't worry.' Still smiling, she stretched her arms above her head and yawned. 'Arianna is lucky to have you. You might be misguided sometimes, but I know you care. That's the thing that matters.'

Damon dragged his eyes from her slender arms and tried to wipe the memories of her sliding those arms around his neck. 'Misguided?'

'Well, you smother her, which means she always feels the need to rebel. But don't worry about it. Plenty of parents make that mistake and you're not even her parent.' There was a flash of admiration in her gaze. 'I don't know how you did it. None of the sixteen-year-old boys I've met are capable of caring for themselves, let alone someone else. My dad, who was several decades older than you, completely freaked out when my mum walked out on him and left me with him. Not that I remember because I was only two. But I remember us both having a laugh about it one day. He told me that he sat there looking at me, and apparently I sat there looking at him. I didn't quite have to change my own nappy, but I learned pretty early on that if I wanted something done I had to do it myself. And I did things for him too.'

Damon was appalled at her parents' utterly selfish behaviour. 'How long was it until your father remarried the first time?'

'It felt like about five minutes. My dad is rubbish at being on his own. As soon as a relationship breaks down he latches onto the next person. I didn't even think much of it until I went to senior school—' She gave a matter-of-fact shrug. 'Everything is so much more complicated at senior school. Younger children are much more accepting of differences.'

Examining his own behaviour, and not liking what he saw, Damon paced to the balcony and stared down at the Paris streets, jammed with traffic. 'You are a very bright, very clever young woman. Why didn't you go to university?'

His question was met with silence and when he turned his head to look at her she gave what could only be described as a forced smile.

'I spent my childhood in and out of the company. The people were like my family. Once I started at the day school I often hung out there because it was more fun than going home to an empty house. I used to help Doris Cooper in the post room and then I'd find an empty desk somewhere and Mr Foster in Accounts used to help me with my maths homework. By the time I reached eighteen I could see the company was a mess. I could also see a way I could make a huge contribution and pay back some of their kindness to me. They were always worried that they'd lose their jobs. I didn't want that to happen.'

'My sources tell me your Mr Foster is struggling.'

'Because the board never invested in training.' She defended her colleague hotly. 'He just needs help with spreadsheets. I've been doing my best to train him because frankly he's the reason I did well at maths, but there isn't a whole lot of time in the day.'

'I imagine there isn't when you're running an entire company single-handed.' His dry tone earned him a frown.

'Don't mock me.'

'I'm not mocking you.'

'If I was responsible for the company then I didn't do a good job, did I?' she said in a gloomy voice. 'Because everyone could still be made redundant.'

'*Theé mou*, if I give you my assurance no one will be made redundant can we talk about something other than work for five minutes?!' Damon jabbed his fingers into his hair and wondered how the conversation he'd been planning had somehow been so dramatically derailed. Somehow what he had to say felt even harder in the light of what she'd just revealed. 'Polly—' with a huge effort, he controlled the tone of his voice '—we have to talk about what happens next.'

'Well, if you're serious about not making anyone redundant then I'll get straight on the phone to reassure everyone and—'

'Polly!' His tone finally snagged her attention.

'What? You're not about to tell me you were joking, are you?' Her face lost colour. 'Because that would be a really cruel thing to do.'

'I'm not joking. Everyone who previously worked for your father can keep their jobs.'

'Really?' Her expression was transformed from worry to wonderment and she flung her arms around him, dancing on the spot and hugging at the same time.

'Oh, thank you, thank you, I take back every evil thing I ever said about you.'

Easing her away from him before he found himself repeating his mistakes of the previous night, Damon realised that her cheeks were wet. 'Why are you crying?'

'I'm just so happy! You have no idea—' She covered her face with her hands and drew in a juddering breath. 'I knew what a mess everything was but I just didn't know how to sort it out.' She wiped her cheeks on her sleeve. 'Sorry. But those people have been part of my life since I was small.'

A small, lonely little girl whose father had no time for her, finding friends and comfort among the people he worked with. Shaken by a depth of emotion he hadn't felt before, Damon instinctively withdrew. 'If you could stop crying, that would be good.'

'Sorry.' She produced a tissue and blew her nose hard. 'I expect you're used to mopping up tears from all those women you make cry.'

'I do *not* make women cry.'

'Of course you do, but don't worry about it. Today you're my hero. You can do no wrong. Thank you *so* much. Can we fly straight back to London now? I want to tell everyone.' Her nose was pink and her eyes glistened with tears and *still* she'd made no reference to what had happened between them.

He wondered whether she'd already mentally moved her things into his penthouse?

'Polly, we have to talk about what happened last night.'

No longer looking at him, she pushed the tissue into her pocket. 'What is there to talk about? We both know what happened, but honestly there's nothing to talk about as far as I'm concerned.'

Damon, who recognised evasive action when he saw it, refused to be deflected. 'So that's it? We have hot sex all night and you don't intend to mention it again?'

'Basically, yes. I'd rather no one knew, obviously, because I don't want all those nudges and winks, but I'm fairly sure you don't want that either, so I'm not worried that you'll say anything. Just forget it.'

She expected him to forget it? 'Polly—'

'Last night you kissed me to prove a point. I kissed you back to prove a point. It got a bit out of control.'

'Are you saying you didn't know what you were doing?'

'Of course I knew what I was doing! I wasn't drunk or anything.' She gave a tiny shrug. 'I don't understand the post mortem. So we had sex? This is the twenty-first century. No one is involved except us. We used protection. What's the problem?'

'You'd never had sex before.'

'Well, there's a first time for everything.' Her Black-Berry buzzed and she picked it up and opened an e-mail. 'I've never visited Paris before either, so it's been a time of firsts. What time are we flying home?'

Shocked by her matter-of-fact response to the situation, Damon failed to process that question. 'So you have no intention of repeating the experience?'

'Visiting Paris?'

He ground his teeth. 'Sex.'

'Some time, probably.' Gathering up her notebook and pen, she stuffed them into her bag.

Goaded by her indifference, Damon shot out a hand

and yanked her against him. 'Are you pretending you didn't feel anything?'

'No, of course not. What is the matter with you?'

'We spent seven hours having sex last night.'

'You don't have to tell me that. I was there.'

'Generally women want to talk about it afterwards,' he said silkily, '*not* walk away.'

She was silent for a moment and then she lifted her gaze to his. 'You're telling me that after sex you like to lie there and talk about it? Sorry, but I find that incredibly hard to believe. You strike me more as the get-her-out-of-my-bed-before-she-grows-roots type.'

Damon inhaled sharply, because that assessment was startlingly close to the truth, and Polly gave a faint smile.

'See? I'm right again. And that's fine. You don't have to exhaust yourself trying to let me down tactfully. As far as I'm concerned, it's forgotten.'

The fact that she was proposing forgetting something so incredible irritated him as much as the thought of her prolonging their relationship had aggravated him just moments earlier.

The knowledge that he was behaving illogically simply fuelled his frustration. 'You want to forget it?'

'Yes, of course! You must have gathered by now that I'm rubbish at relationships. And you're obviously not exactly brilliant either. So that's fine. We're cool! I'm going to pack while you read my proposal.' With a reassuring smile, she disengaged herself, scooped up her laptop and strolled across the terrace towards the door that led to the second bedroom. 'I'm so thrilled you're not going to make people redundant. I feel really happy.'

Speechless, Damon stared after her.

She was happy because he wasn't going to make her colleagues redundant, not because they'd spent the night having mind-blowing, intimate sex.

She wanted to forget it had happened. There had been no awkward conversation, no full-scale demolition of inflated expectations. Apparently she didn't have any expectations. As far as she was concerned it had been a one-night stand.

This was his definition of a fairy tale ending and he waited to feel a rush of relief.

Nothing happened.

Chapter 8

'The budget is how much?' Debbie plopped down on the chair and fanned herself with her hand. 'That's incredible. You're a genius.'

'Gérard liked my ideas.'

'And Demon Damon can't fail to be impressed. I hope he comes crawling back with an apology.'

Careful not to look up, Polly scrolled through her 'to do' list. 'He isn't really Demon Damon. He's pretty decent, really. He just cares about his sister.' When Debbie didn't respond, Polly lifted her head. 'What?'

'Sorry, but isn't this rather an abrupt turnaround? Just two weeks ago he was the Big Bad Wolf poised to eat everyone in one gulp.'

Polly felt the fire burn in her cheeks and quickly turned back to her desk. 'He's guaranteed everyone's jobs. That wins my vote.'

'Mmm…so are you ever going to tell me what really happened in Paris? It's been two weeks and you've said virtually nothing.'

'I told you it was a very successful business meeting.'

'Obviously. But I wasn't talking about the meeting.'

'The Eiffel Tower looked pretty at night.'

'All right—let's stop messing around here and get straight to the point.' Debbie folded her arms and strolled round the desk so that she could see Polly's face. *'Did he kiss you?'*

Polly felt the breath catch in her lungs. For two weeks she'd been trying not to think about Paris. And she'd tried especially hard not to think about the way Damon kissed. 'Will you leave it alone? What is the matter with you?'

'Oh, my God, he *did* kiss you.'

'Did you feed Romeo and Juliet while I was away?'

'You think I've put them on a diet?'

'Polly, I've just managed to agree a fantastic rate for those primetime ad slots.' Kim came scurrying across the office, the baby tucked against her shoulder and her BlackBerry in her other hand. 'I've sent you an e-mail.'

Relieved to be rescued from Debbie, Polly stretched out her arms and took the baby for a cuddle. 'I gather your child-minder has let you down again? I can't believe how much he's grown in just two weeks.'

'Sorry I had to bring him in. I would have worked from home but I have to finish those magazine tie-ins for the *Run, Breathe, Live* campaign. Sam doesn't mind.'

Polly kissed Sam's downy head. 'Maybe not, but I have a feeling that the boss might. We have to introduce him to these things gradually or he'll have a heart attack. The plants and the fish almost finished him off. If he sees that you've brought Sam to work I think it might test his newfound patience.'

'He isn't going to see. Damon flew to New York two weeks ago and hasn't been seen since.'

New York?

Falling on that crumb of news like a starving bird, Polly wanted to ask how Kim knew but she could see Debbie's foot tapping impatiently as she waited to be able to continue her interrogation. It would be asking for trouble to show too much interest in Damon's whereabouts.

She wished she'd known he wasn't even in the country.

Apparently she hadn't needed to spend the past two weeks watching the door in case he walked in.

'Maybe he *was* in New York,' Debbie murmured, 'but he's not now. He just walked through the door. And you are holding a baby.'

Polly's heart pounded against her chest and she knew she was blushing. 'OK, this is *not* good. Why did he have to pick this particular moment to check on us? Kim, take Sam into one of the meeting rooms quickly. When Damon has gone, we'll come and get you. Move.' She gave the baby back to Kim and went to head Damon off.

Underneath the panic, she felt absurdly excited at the prospect of seeing him and that feeling horrified her. She was like a puppy, wagging its tail. As she walked up to him all she wanted to do was fling her arms round his neck. 'Hi there. Good trip? Did you hear back from Gérard? He called me this morning. Great news.' She tried to urge him back towards the door and away from Kim and the baby, but he stood fast, clearly happy to conduct the conversation in the middle of the office.

'He rang me five minutes ago. I gather he accepted your—how did you describe it?—"shockingly massive" budget. And he wants to talk to us about pitching for more of their brands. Congratulations. You just landed the biggest marketing fish in the pond. The only stipulation is that he wants you to lead the team.' His eyes were dark. Unfathomable. 'With that in mind I thought it was time to discuss your position in the company. I don't think we can have an executive assistant advising a vice president.'

'You'd better make me president, then. Then I can boss you around.' Not for anything was she going to reveal how pleased she was to see him again. She was about to ask him more about his call with Gérard when a faint cry came from the other side of the office. Polly froze in horror. 'So what position were you thinking of?' She raised her voice. 'Whatever you think is fine by me.'

Damon flinched. 'Why are you shouting?'

'Because I'm really, really excited. I'm excited that Gérard went with the bigger programme.' Behind her she could hear the baby's muffled yells and sweat broke out on the back of her neck. 'Could we discuss it in your office? I really think this conversation is something we should have in private.'

'You want to go somewhere more private?'

Realising that she was now trapped into the position of having to be alone with him, Polly felt her heart-rate double. But what choice did she have? She didn't want him finding out that Kim had brought her baby into the office. He'd go into meltdown. 'Absolutely. There are some things that should be confidential.' Without giving him a chance to respond, she strode towards the stairs furthest from the crying baby.

When she realised that he was following her, she sighed with relief.

As they reached his office, she smiled at his personal assistant. 'Hi, Janey, your plants are looking lovely.'

'They do cheer the place up. Thanks for the recommendations. Can I bring you coffee, Mr Doukakis?'

Damon was staring at the plants in disbelief. 'Where did those come from?'

'I ordered them and they just arrived.' Janey smiled calmly. 'I admired the ones on Polly's floor and she advised me on which to buy. The plants need to be quite tolerant.'

'I know the feeling,' Damon breathed, and Polly grinned and nudged him towards the office.

'A few little plants aren't going to destroy your mega-efficient office atmosphere. Relax.'

'Polly, that plant was at least six foot. Not by anyone's standards could it be described as "little".'

'They create a very healthy working environment.'

'Next you will be asking me to provide fish as standard office equipment.'

'No, I don't think so.' Polly wondered whether he was finding the conversation as hard as she was. They were talking about plants and fish but what she really wanted to say was *Why are you back?* and *Did you miss me?* 'Fish are very different. They need very specific care. They wouldn't be any good for people who aren't interested.'

'I was being ironic.'

'I know, but you take yourself far too seriously so I thought I'd play along. The plants aren't going to hurt you, Damon. They're not flesh-eating ones. Now, about this promotion—' Trying not to look at the width of his shoulders or the sexy curve of his mouth, she flopped down in the chair next to his desk. 'I hope I'm going to get a huge glass office and lots of fawning secretaries?'

'You'd be miserable in an office. You have to be surrounded by people and noise to function.'

The fact that he was starting to understand her so well was more than a little unsettling. 'OK, so no office and no fawning secretaries. You wanted to talk about my job?'

'I've been thinking about how best to use your skills. You seem to have been doing everything single-handed. You're undoubtedly creative, but you're also an organiser so I don't want to limit you.' He sprawled in the chair on the other side of his desk, watching her through those eyes that could make a woman's pulse rate accelerate like a racehorse at the finish line.

Remembering how he'd looked when he'd made love to her, Polly shifted in her chair and tried to concentrate. 'Whatever you think is fine by me. I'm really not that into titles and that sort of thing. I'm happy just doing the job.' She wished he'd stop looking at her as if he were contemplating pouncing from across the table.

Now that she was in front of him she couldn't stop thinking about sex, and she had a feeling he was having the same problem.

'You need to be client-facing, because you clearly have a gift for communication. So I propose to make you an account director, with full responsibility for the

High Kick Hosiery account. Any creative work can be farmed out to my in-house team, but you can join them whenever they're brainstorming for new brands. And it's time you earned a decent salary.' He named a figure that made Polly feel faint.

'Gosh. That's a lot.'

'It's slightly above market rate,' he drawled. 'I never lose anyone for money.'

'Right. Well, that's great. But you're not going to lose me.' The moment he said the words she realised how they could be interpreted. 'At work, I mean. Obviously.'

A frown touched his dark brows, as if she'd said something that hadn't occurred to him before. 'I also wanted you to take a look at this.' He pushed a file across his desk. 'I thought you might be interested.'

Puzzled, Polly opened the file cautiously. Inside were materials on an MBA course. For a moment she couldn't breathe. Her hands shaking, she flicked through the pages. 'I—I sent off for this—'

'Every year for the past four years. I know. They told me when I requested the information.'

'Y-you spoke to them?'

'I wanted to be sure they'd take you if you wanted to go.'

'You're asking if I want to do an MBA?' Delight mingled with consternation. 'You don't want me to work for you any more?'

'I just said I don't want to lose you. You'd be doing both—working and studying. This way you still work for me and take time off when you need it.'

There was a loud buzzing in her ears. 'You're saying I could study *and* carry on at DMG?'

'It would be hard work. You might want to refuse.'

'Why? Because I'm generally lazy?' She kept it light to try and stifle the lump in her throat that had come from nowhere. He knew how badly she wanted a formal business qualification. He'd taken the time to research courses for her. 'I don't have a first degree.'

'They'd take into account your experience working in the business. You might have to take a couple of exams in order to qualify.'

It felt too good to be true. 'I wouldn't be able to afford it.'

'The company would pay. We'd be the beneficiaries of all that expertise.'

The lump in her throat grew. 'Why? Why would you do this for me?'

'If you're going to be working here long term and embarking on a proper career path with DMG then it's right that you should have a career plan.'

Polly didn't know whether to laugh or sob. 'I always thought you were a traditional Greek male. A woman's place is barefoot and pregnant in the kitchen and all that.'

'I am traditional. I have no problem with a woman being pregnant and barefoot in the kitchen if that's where she wants to be. But I'm also an astute businessman. I employ the best person for the job. I want you in my company. I'm happy to have you as you are, but you've always wanted to do this and I believe that if there's something you really want to do you should do it.'

Afraid she really was going to cry, Polly stood up quickly, clutching the file like a lifebelt. 'If it's OK with you I'm going to take this away and read it.'

'Sit down. I haven't finished.'

Polly sat, still overwhelmed by what he was offering.

He was silent for a moment, his long fingers tapping a rhythm on his desk as he watched her. 'You and I are going out tonight.'

'Oh?' She tried to concentrate and behave professionally. 'We have a business dinner?'

'Not business. A date. You can leave your notebook behind.'

Date? Suddenly Polly forgot the file in her hand. 'You—you're asking me out?'

'Yes.'

Her heart pounded. 'I work for you.'

'I don't care,' he said testily. 'For once I'm going to do what I want to do just because I want to do it.'

'Oh.' If she'd thought she was happy before it was nothing to how she felt now, as her eyes met his. 'So—not for business or anything? Just for the hell of it?'

He gave a wry smile. 'Just for the sheer hell of it. You're always telling me I take myself too seriously.'

'Well—wow.'

'Does "wow" mean yes?'

She was grinning like an idiot, ridiculously pleased. 'Yes. Where are we going?'

'Somewhere special.'

'Ah, so no flamingo-pink tights.'

'You'll be dancing. I'll pick you up at ten.'

'Dancing?' Polly stood up again and this time she virtually floated towards the door, her mind already occupied by what she was going to wear.

'Oh and Polly—' his deep sexy drawl stopped her

as she reached the door '—about the baby you're hiding in the office—'

Polly froze. 'Baby?' Her voice was a squeak. 'Er—what baby?'

'I don't want to give Health and Safety a heart attack so you can tell Kim we're looking into providing crèche facilities so that she can give the boot to that unreliable child-minder of hers.'

Polly clutched the door. 'How do you know about Kim's problem with the baby?'

'He was in your offices the day I came in and fired the board.'

'You *knew* the baby was in the office? And you didn't say anything?'

'There's a limit to how much disaster a man can absorb in one session. I'm told Kim is excellent at what she does so I'm going to use her in my media department. She needs good childcare.'

Polly gaped at him. 'Are you feeling all right?'

'Never better. Why?'

'Because you're being worryingly reasonable. A couple of weeks ago you would have fired the lot of us for bringing a baby into the office.'

'Kim is extremely productive and to fire her would jeopardise the accounts you've won. On top of that, I know when I'm beaten.'

But he didn't look beaten. He looked sleek and in control. Far more in control than she was. She was fast discovering that it was possible to feel terrified, elated and panicky all at the same time.

'That's—great. Thanks. We have quite a few mothers on the team and childcare is always a nightmare.'

'So I understand. I'll fix it. And while we're at it

you can stop giving Mr Foster lessons in spreadsheets. He's going on a proper training course starting tomorrow. Now, go. And don't buy my PA any more plants. The place is turning into a bloody jungle.'

'It's hard getting ready for an evening when you don't know where you're going.' Polly kept her coat tucked round her as she slid into the back seat of his chauffeur-driven car. 'What if I'm wearing the wrong thing?' She was hyper-aware of him—of his arm stretched across the back of the seat and the proximity of his thigh to hers.

He eyed her coat with one eyebrow raised. 'Take your coat off and I'll tell you.'

'I'm wearing the coat so that you can't tell me I'm wearing the wrong thing. You have a habit of freaking out over my clothes choice so I decided it was safer not to show you until we arrive. I don't want you to dent my confidence.'

'Fine, but promise me you are wearing *something* under the coat.'

'Sort of.'

With a groan and a sexy smile, he leaned his head back against the seat. 'I have a feeling I should have made you dinner in the apartment instead of taking you out in public.' He hesitated a moment and then closed his hand over hers, his fingers warm and strong.

Suddenly her insides felt jittery. She wanted to ask what tonight was all about.

Her impression was that he was as rubbish at relationships as she was.

For two weeks she'd heard nothing from him. And she'd told herself that was a good thing.

'I'm sorry that lead on my father and Arianna being in Paris turned out to be useless. She really is so lucky to have you.' Polly curled her fingers around his. 'That day at school—I really envied her.'

'For having a brother who came and yelled at her?'

'For having a brother who cared enough to come down to the school and tell her off.'

'I had no idea she was being bullied. I didn't ask the right questions. You have no idea how much I regret that now.'

'You were always there for her. That was the most important thing.' Feeling disloyal to her father, she gave a quick smile and pulled her hand out of his. 'So, where are we going tonight?'

'It's the opening of a nightclub. Invited guests only.'

As they drew up outside, Polly looked out of the window. 'The Firebird? Oh—I read about this place. It's *seriously* cool. It has a glass dance floor, or something, and the interior looks as though there are flames going up the walls. There's a waiting list of celebrities who want to hire it. And you're invited?'

He gave her a strange look. 'Yes.'

'That's impressive. I read it's almost impossible to get on the guest list. We really wanted to pitch for their advertising just so that we could sneak in and have a look.' Smiling, Polly gave a shiver of excitement and leaned forward in her seat as she saw the crowd gathered. 'I can't wait to tell the others. They're going to be *so* jealous. I had no idea you were a nightclub sort of person. I'm discovering all sorts of things about you. Are those photographers?' She shrank slightly. 'Last time I went near a photographer I knocked myself unconscious on his stupid camera.'

'That's why I brought my security team. They can earn their keep.'

'If they're going to take pictures, I'm taking my coat off.'

Damon gave a faint smile. 'Is this going to give me a heart attack?'

'I hope not because I'm not walking through those photographers on my own.' Polly wriggled out of her coat and saw his eyes drop to her cleavage. 'Don't look at me like that. You told me I was allowed to dress up.'

'You look incredible.' His voice husky, he studied her short gold dress and then lifted his gaze to hers. 'You're not wearing Gérard's products tonight?'

'You mentioned dancing so I went for bare legs. Are you going to stare at me or are we going inside?'

It was a heady experience being out in London with Damon. The moment he stepped out of the car the flashbulbs exploded and he held her hand firmly as he walked purposefully towards the entrance of the club. The press pack, kept at bay by his security team, snapped pictures and shouted questions that Damon skilfully deflected.

'I don't see why they're so interested in who you're out with. There are major things going on in the world and all they're interested in is who's in your bed. Crazy.' Keeping her head high, Polly walked with him into the club, waving her arms and walking with a sway in her hips as she heard the seductive pulse of the music. 'I feel like dancing.'

'Good.' Damon gestured to a member of the bar staff and a moment later a bottle of champagne and two glasses appeared. 'We'll have a drink first.'

'Are you one of those men who need alcohol before they hit the dance floor?'

It turned out that he wasn't.

Watching Damon dance was a sensual feast. Every movement made her think of sex, every glance he sent in her direction was a promise of what was to come.

Enjoying herself hugely, Polly let herself go, her body flowing in time to the rhythm, her hair flying around her face as she danced on the shimmering glass floor.

The music and the atmosphere were so infectious that she was still smiling when Damon swept her off the dance floor and back to their private table.

Every few minutes people came up to shake his hand and exchange a few words and Polly wondered why he attracted so much attention wherever he went.

'There are some really famous people here and they're all coming over to talk to you.' She tapped her champagne glass against his. 'Doukakis for Prime Minister, I say.'

'How much have you drunk?'

'Nowhere near enough. This is the most delicious thing I've ever tasted. In fact the whole experience is super-cool. This place is stunning—' Out of breath, she swallowed a few mouthfuls of champagne and then noticed a couple of minor royals weaving their way towards them. 'I can't curtsey. My dress is too tight— or maybe my bottom is too big. One of the two.' She paused politely while they spoke to Damon and when they finally moved away she sidled closer to him. 'Why is everyone so determined to talk to you?'

'Because I own the place and they're sucking up.'

Calm, Damon topped up her glass. 'Do you want to dance again?'

'You own a nightclub?'

'I told you—I believe in diversification. If one part of your business is struggling, another part will be strong. Rules of commerce.'

'But—' Polly looked around her and suddenly realised why everyone had been so deferential when he'd walked in. 'So you're the boss here, too. Everywhere you go, you're the boss. Have you ever *not* been in charge?'

'I spent a crazy night in bed with a woman in Paris recently...' the words were spoken in her ear and his arm was draped across the back of her seat '...and there were definitely a few seconds when I wasn't in charge.'

Her rapid breathing had nothing to do with her exertion on the dance floor and everything to do with the way he made her feel.

'I thought we agreed to forget about that.'

'I changed my mind.'

Her eyes were on his, and then on his mouth. The desire to kiss him was so powerful she almost didn't care that they were in a public place. 'Everyone is looking at us.'

'Then it's probably time to leave.' He rose to his feet and held out his hand to her.

Polly endured the drive home in an agony of sensual anticipation and the moment they closed the door of the penthouse he hauled her against him and divested her of her dress in one slick move that had her gasping.

Equally impatient, she ripped at his shirt, sending buttons flying.

'I want you—' His voice unsteady, Damon pressed

her back against the wall and lifted her easily, encouraging her to wrap her thighs around his hips.

She was so ready, so desperate after an evening of watching him on the dance floor, that when she felt him against her she gave a low moan of encouragement and arched her hips towards him. His fingers gripping her thighs, he entered her with a slow, controlled strength that made her gasp his name. The gasp turned to a sob as she felt him deep inside her and for a moment she stilled, her hand on the sleek skin of his back, her eyes tightly closed as she absorbed the enormity of the pleasure.

'You feel fantastic.' He groaned the words against her mouth and then withdrew and surged into her again, building a rhythm so skilled, so perfect, that her senses caught fire.

Her hands were in his hair, then on his shoulders, and they kissed like savages, biting, licking, feasting as she met each hard thrust with the same frantic desperation. It was primal and out of control, sex at its most basic, a slaking of a physical need that was stronger than both of them.

She came in an exquisite rush of pleasure, her body tightening around his and sending him spinning into the same place.

For what seemed like ages, neither of them moved.

Then he lowered her gently, his forehead against hers. 'Sorry—' his voice was husky '—the bedroom was too far.'

Polly was dizzy with the intensity of it. His lack of control made her feel like a sex goddess. 'No need to apologise—'

'Better get there quickly before it happens again—'

He scooped her up again and strode through to the bedroom while Polly reflected briefly on the startling fact that she actually liked it when someone else took control.

Her last coherent thought before he brought his mouth down on hers was that she never wanted it to end.

As dawn broke, Polly sat up carefully, trying not to wake him, but a strong hand shot out and pulled her back down again.

'Where do you think you're going?'

'Back home.'

'No, you're not.' His hand slid into her hair and he kissed her with a slow thoroughness that melted her limbs. 'You're sleeping here. With me.'

She really ought to leave, she thought groggily, but he pulled her into the circle of his arms, trapping her against him.

It felt good, she thought, and the intensity of that feeling terrified her. She'd always avoided this situation, hadn't she? She'd always protected herself from that depth of emotion because she'd seen how fragile relationships were. She'd grown up watching her father's relationships crumble to dust.

But with Damon—

Bombarded with alien feelings that were as terrifying as they were exciting, she stilled in his arms and he turned his head, those dark eyes sharp and astute as he sensed the change in her.

'What's the matter?'

'Nothing.'

'Don't lie to me. I always know when you're keeping something from me. Tell me what's wrong and I'll fix it.' His voice husky and sexy and he slid his hand behind her head and drew her head towards him.

Tell me what's wrong and I'll fix it.

Polly felt a warmth flow through her. It wasn't just that he made her feel like the sexiest woman alive, he was fiercely protective and that was a whole new experience for her.

Was it wrong to enjoy the fact that someone was looking out for her?

His gaze probing, Damon lowered his head to hers, but before he could kiss her his phone buzzed.

Swearing softly, he sighed and rolled onto his back. 'Sorry. Bad timing, but I'd better take this. I'm expecting a call from Athens.' Visibly annoyed at having been disturbed, he reached out and answered it. 'Doukakis...'

Polly lay with her eyes closed, her hand resting on the hard muscle of his chest, struggling to come to terms with the way he made her feel. A night without sleep made his deep voice even huskier and she smiled to herself, thinking that when he spoke in Greek he was even sexier.

Then his voice changed from husky to harsh and he disengaged himself from her grip and launched himself from the bed.

Polly yawned. 'Where are you going?'

'Stay there, and whatever happens don't come out.'

Still lost in her own thoughts, Polly looked at him in a daze, distracted by the sight of his bare back. The swell of smooth male muscle flexed and rippled as he dressed swiftly. He reminded her of a warrior at the peak of fitness, trained and ready to go into battle.

Suddenly she wanted to put her arms round him and
drag him back to bed. He was the sexiest man she'd
ever seen and sex with him was the most breathtak-
ingly exciting experience of her life. 'Come back to
bed. Work can wait.'

He didn't look at her. 'I need to see someone. Stay
there.' Hesitating, he turned back to her, planted his
arms on the bed and leaned forward to kiss her. 'I'll
be back.'

'Mmm...' Still sleepy, Polly smiled against his
mouth. 'I'm not sure how to take that. Isn't that a line
from *Terminator*?'

He didn't laugh. Instead, he disengaged himself and
gently stroked her cheek with his fingers. '*Don't* move.
And that's an order.'

Wondering why he was suddenly so serious, she
lay still for a moment, floating on a sea of blissful
contentment.

And then she heard raised voices coming from the
living room.

Raised voices?

Why would there be raised voices?

Concerned, she slid out of bed and wriggled back
into the gold dress that lay abandoned on the floor
where Damon had thrown it the night before.

The anger in his voice intensified and her curiosity
turned to alarm as she hurried through to the living
area of the spectacular apartment.

Damon's back was towards her, his feet planted
firmly apart in a stance that was blatantly confrontational. Distracted by the display of male power and
authority, Polly didn't immediately see who was on the
receiving end of his wrath, but as she moved forward,

her bare feet making no sound on the wooden floor, the other person finally came into view.

For a moment she was so shocked she couldn't make a sound.

Neither man was aware of her presence, both trapped in their boiling cauldron of mutual animosity.

Feeling the warm threads of her newfound happiness unravel, Polly finally managed to croak out a few words.

'Dad?' Her voice cracked. 'What on earth are you doing here?'

Chapter 9

'I could ask you the same question. So the rumours are true.' Her father faced Damon, his expression twisted and ugly. 'Do you have no boundaries? No conscience? It should have been enough for you to take over my company, but no—you had to seal your revenge by seducing my daughter.' His breathing was alarmingly rapid, his hands locked in two white-knuckled fists by his sides.

Revenge?

Polly wanted to move towards her father but her body felt as if it had been encased in cement. She couldn't move. Not once, even for a moment, had it occurred to her that Damon might have seduced her because of her father's relationship with Arianna.

And in that single agonising moment she was finally able to put a name to those alien feelings.

Love.

She'd fallen in love with Damon. Her brain told her it wasn't possible in such a short time but her heart wasn't listening. And maybe it wasn't such a short time, really. He'd always been there, hadn't he? On the fringes of her life. Her friend's big brother.

Terror scraped her skin, sharp as the talons of an eagle, and she stood without speaking, aware of Damon's dangerous mood as he confronted her father.

'You *dare* to come into my home and pretend you care about your daughter? This after several weeks when you haven't bothered to get in touch with anyone?' A look of contempt on his face, Damon took a step towards the older man. 'You are a disgrace. And a coward. You hid rather than face me, but you're here now so stand up and behave like a man. Take responsibilities for your decisions instead of shifting focus onto someone else.'

Still locked in frozen silence, Polly saw her father's face redden.

'Now, you listen to me—' Clearly intimidated by Damon's cold, controlled fury, he momentarily lost some of his bluster. 'I'm no coward. I'm not afraid of you.'

'Well, you should be.' Damon's voice was silky-smooth, his soft tone a thousand times more dangerous than the older man's empty bluster. 'You abandoned your business without thought or care for the future job security of your employees and you did the same with your daughter.'

'I did not abandon her. Polly's not a kid. She's capable of looking after herself.'

'This wasn't a question of cooking herself a meal

and getting on with life. You left her to the mercy of those greedy animals you laughingly call a board, all of whom could have been dismissed for misuse of company funds, not to mention sexual harassment, but even worse than that—' the control finally snapped and Damon's voice thickened with anger '—you left her to deal with *me*. By herself. No support from anyone.' Each word thumped into her father like a rock and Polly saw him shrivel.

Torn between her love for two men, she stepped forward, forcing the words through stiff lips. 'Damon, that's enough.'

Damon ignored her. 'Was that your plan? Instead of standing up to me like a man, you left your daughter alone and unprotected in the hope that the lion wouldn't attack? Or have you just completely abdicated your responsibilities as a father?'

'Polly's good at her job. And she's good with people.' But her father's bluster was fading and he glanced warily at Polly. 'You handled him, didn't you?'

Damon exploded, first in Greek and then in English. 'She is twenty-four years old and doesn't have a ruthless bone in her body and yet you abandoned her to be eaten alive by someone of my reputation.'

'I didn't think you'd hurt her.'

Damon's laugh was layered with contempt and disgust. 'You were relying on that. You ran. And you let your defenceless daughter deal with the fall-out. You disgust me. Now, get the hell out of my home.'

'Now, wait a minute—' Her father stumbled over his words. 'Pol isn't defenceless. She's a tough thing.'

'She's had to be! When have you ever stood up for

her or helped her? When, in the whole of her life, have you ever been there for her?!'

'I gave her a home when her mother walked out.'

Damon lifted a hand, clenched it into a fist and then lowered it again. '*Don't* say another word,' he warned in a thickened tone. 'Not a word if you want to walk out of here in the same condition you walked in.'

'Stop it!' Finally dragged from her own trauma, Polly stepped between the two men. 'Stop it, both of you! That's enough.' She felt sick inside. So sick that she wanted to crawl into a corner and hide there. Although she knew that everything Damon said was the truth, it didn't stop her loving her father. Life wasn't that simple, was it? 'Dad, where's Arianna?'

'She's back at the house. It's her home now. We're married. We did in secret because we both knew *he*—' he stabbed an accusing finger towards Damon '—would go off the deep end.'

'*Married?*' Polly couldn't hide her dismay and a flash of real fear chilled her all the way through as she anticipated how Damon would react to that less than welcome news. 'Oh, Dad.'

Her father bristled. 'If I care for a woman, I don't want to just make some sort of sex trophy of her—like him.' He glared at Damon. 'He has plenty of women. He just doesn't marry any of them. What does that say about him?'

'It says that I can tell the difference between lust and love.' Damon spoke through his teeth, his effort to maintain control visible in the pumped muscle of his bare chest and shoulders. 'It says that my decision-making is ruled by my brain and not my testosterone levels.'

Sensing the extreme volatility of his mood, Polly

was terrified he was going to lose it. 'I think you'd better leave, Dad,' she said hastily, urging him towards the door.

'Not without you.' Her father dug his heels in and Damon breathed deeply.

'She's staying here. With me. She's mine now.' It was a statement of pure male possession and Polly stilled, hot tears scalding the back of her eyes, knowing that those words were spoken to aggravate her father.

What other explanation was there? Damon had already told her he didn't want a relationship—didn't want commitment or more responsibility. And she knew, as no doubt he did, that nothing would upset her father more than watching her choose Damon over him.

Damon saw their relationship as another weapon to use in the defence of his sister.

'Wait there,' she muttered. 'I'll get dressed.'

Damon turned slowly, an expression of raw incredulity stamped on his spectacularly handsome face as he looked at her. 'You're going with him?'

Polly couldn't breathe. Her mind was a mess and the pain in her chest felt as though someone had ripped her apart with burning knives. 'I don't have a choice. He's my dad.'

'Of course you have a choice.' Damon's face was unusually pale. '*Theé mou*, tell me that you don't believe any of that garbage he just spouted.'

She hadn't even questioned it.

His animosity towards her father was a living force in the room and the effort not to cry was a physical burning in the back of her throat.

She told herself that even if she were wrong it didn't

make a difference to the outcome. The two men she loved were at war with each other and there was no way to make peace. Especially not now that her father had married Arianna. Damon would never forgive him.

Polly felt sick and dizzy and a sense of crawling misery spread through her trembling frame. 'I think it's best if I leave. I—I'll be back at work on Monday, Damon.'

There was a long, agonising silence.

Damon stared at her without speaking. His eyes smouldered dark and his mouth tightened. 'You don't have to give me your work schedule,' he said coldly. 'When you're naked in my bed I'm your lover, not your boss.'

His icy response hurt more than all the words that had been flung around the room and Polly had to physically stop herself from throwing herself at him and trying to undo what had been done.

'He's upsetting you, Pol,' her father said firmly. 'We should just leave.'

It was like separating two stags, she thought numbly. There was never going to be any way of making them get along.

Devastated, she turned her back on both of them and hurried to the bedroom, trying not to remember the incredible happiness she'd felt only moments earlier. Trying to hold it together, she retrieved her shoes and bag and coat and walked back to the living room.

Bracing herself for another desperately upsetting encounter with Damon, she saw only her father.

'Where's Damon?'

'He's gone. Gave me a look and walked out.' Her

father cast a nervous look around the apartment. 'The guy's unstable. You're well rid of him, Pol. Let's get out of here.'

Arriving back at her own home, Polly felt numb with misery. She just wanted to retreat to her room but she knew there was no hope of that.

Oblivious to her agony, her father was chatting excitedly, telling her about his wedding in the Caribbean.

She felt as though she were trapped in a recurring cycle.

Another woman. Another relationship.

She should have been used to it by now, but this time it felt different and not just because Arianna was her friend.

'Are you mad with me, Pol?' Arianna hovered anxiously as Polly walked into the house with her father. 'It's going to be seriously weird being your stepmother, but once we get over that is everything going to be cool between us? I mean, I know you must be mad with Damon, but that's just the way he is. You know that, right? And we don't have to see that much of him.'

That statement depressed her more than anything else that had been said so far. 'I'm working for him,' Polly said flatly. 'I have to see him.'

'You can get another job,' her father said cheerfully, sliding his arm around Arianna and kissing her on the cheek. 'I'm thinking of setting up again. I'll employ you.'

'No, thanks.' Polly found that she couldn't look at Arianna without thinking of Damon. 'I like the job I have now. Damon is an inspirational boss.'

Her father looked affronted. 'Well, he's good with numbers, that's true, and he's certainly—'

'Dad, just—' Teetering on the edge of an emotional explosion, Polly held up her hand. 'Just don't say anything else, OK? This whole thing could have gone a completely different way. Everyone could have been made redundant and—' She broke off, too exhausted to fight with anyone. 'Never mind.'

Arianna walked over and gave her a hug. 'You've had a terrible few weeks. Believe me, no one knows better than me what it's like having Damon breathing down your neck, checking on everything you're doing. He does it because he's a complete and utter control freak.'

Polly snapped. 'Actually, he does it because he cares. He cares about *you*—' The fury shook her and she pushed her astonished friend away. 'He thinks about your welfare and he cares whether you're happy. He sees it as his role to protect you and he's made enormous personal sacrifices to care for you and make sure that you grew up with family and not a bunch of strangers. So maybe you could start seeing things from his point of view for a change. Why the hell didn't you phone him?! The guy has been worried sick!'

'Why are you defending him?' Astonished, Arianna exchanged uncertain looks with her new husband. 'Polly—'

'I'm going upstairs to do some work.' Polly turned away, seriously shaken by the intensity of her desire to defend Damon from attack. She would have thrown herself in front of a moving vehicle to protect him from harm. 'I have a job to do and I intend to keep it, no matter what shambles my personal life is in.' She knew that no matter what had happened between them there was no way that Damon would allow the personal to overtake the professional. She knew that her job was safe.

In the privacy of her bedroom, she locked the door and then flung herself on her bed, feeling something close to desperate. The emptiness inside her was a big dark hole.

It was hard to believe that it was only yesterday she'd been celebrating a promotion and the achievement of a lifetime ambition—to do a business degree—and now—

Now she felt nothing but a sense of profound loss.

All the happiness had been sucked out of her.

Polly turned her head and looked at the prospectus that lay by her bed but somehow today it didn't have the power to lift her spirits as it had the day before.

Frightened by how bad she felt, she tried to reason with herself.

She'd done everything she'd set out to do.

No one was going to be fired. Thanks to Gérard, money and business was flowing into the company. Damon was finally aware of her true role in the company.

She should feel proud. Relieved.

But suddenly none of that seemed important.

Instead of feeling as if she'd won, she felt as if she'd lost.

Everything.

The temptation to go off sick on Monday was huge.

'Don't go in,' her father urged as Polly grabbed her BlackBerry and slipped it in her bag. 'Just stay at home. Switch your phone off.'

'I have a job, Dad. Responsibilities.' She gave him a pointed look and he had the grace to colour. 'We've just won a massive account and I'm in charge of it. Excuse me. I'm going to be late.'

She travelled to work by her usual route, feeling as though she had lead weights attached to her feet.

Maybe Damon would be in meetings all day. Or perhaps he would have found a reason to travel to New York or Athens. She didn't know which would be worse—seeing him or not seeing him.

The moment she walked onto her floor she sensed something different in the atmosphere.

'Morning, Polly,' Debbie said cheerfully. 'Coffee and muffin on your desk.'

Polly decided that to confess that she wasn't hungry would simply invite questions, so she just smiled. 'Thanks. I'm going to have a team meeting at eleven to discuss the High Kick Hosiery account. Can you summon the troops?'

'Sure, but I just took a call for you—could you pop down to the tenth floor? Accounts.'

Polly put her bag down on her desk. 'Why?'

'No idea. I just follow orders. And there are enough of them flying around here.' With that enigmatic statement Debbie strolled off, leaving Polly with the distinct feeling that something was going on.

Did they all know what had happened between her and Damon?

The thought horrified her and suddenly escaping to the accounts floor seemed like a good idea.

Pushing open the doors, she walked onto the tenth floor and stopped in astonishment.

The last time she'd been down here it had been as

stark and businesslike as the rest of the Doukakis office space. Now, it had been transformed into a carbon copy of her own floor. Photographs had appeared on desks, along with small personal items. Plants clustered in a central point, bringing a soothing, relaxing quality to the huge area.

Astonished, Polly turned to the woman nearest to her. 'Er—what happened here?'

'Haven't you seen the e-mail?' Grinning, the woman tapped a few keys on her machine and brought up an e-mail. 'Here we are. It came right from the top. *"Personalising the office".'*

Polly leaned forward and read over her shoulder:

With immediate effect the hot desk system that we have operated for the past year will cease. Employees are encouraged to personalise their office space in any way that they believe will make them more productive. DD

'Isn't it great?' The woman was beaming. 'I can't tell you how tired I was of moving from one desk to another. I had to keep my books in the boot of my car. Ridiculous. I don't know who got him to change his mind but they're a genius.'

Polly managed a smile. 'Right. Great.'

What was going on?

Puzzled, she looked around, trying to absorb the magnitude of the change, but before she could ask any more questions her phone buzzed. It was Janey, Damon's PA.

Cautiously, she answered it. 'Hi, Janey.'

'The boss wants to talk to you, Polly. His office. Five minutes.'

Her hand shaking, Polly put the phone back in her pocket and the woman looked at her expectantly.

'Was there someone you wanted to see?'

Polly took a last look at the transformed office. 'No,' she croaked. 'I think I just saw it.'

But she didn't understand it.

Smoothing her dress, she stepped in the lift and felt sicker and sicker as it rose smoothly to the executive floor. As soon as she walked out Janey waved her towards the office, a huge smile on her face.

'He's waiting for you. I have orders to make sure you're not disturbed.'

'That sounds ominous.' Slowly, Polly walked forward and tapped on the door. Hearing his voice, she took a deep breath and walked into the room.

Damon sat behind his desk, talking on the phone. When he saw her he beckoned her in and gestured to the chair.

Feeling ridiculously self-conscious, she slid into the chair—and then noticed the fish tank on his desk.

Her mouth fell open.

Fish?

Wondering if she were seeing things, she blinked, but the fish remained.

Damon ended the call. 'You're wearing your flamingo-pink tights. Good. They suit you.'

Polly was still staring at the tank on his desk. 'You bought fish.'

A faint smile touched his mouth. 'Someone told me they were an excellent addition to the office environment. Relaxing. I'm feeling tense at the moment so I thought I'd give it a try.'

Her heart started to pound and she wanted to ask why he was feeling tense. 'I saw your memo.'

'Apparently I've gone up ten points in the popularity stakes,' he drawled. 'You were right. People do like personal things around them in the office. It's just one of lots of changes I'll be making.'

She licked her lips. 'Oh.'

'Now you're supposed to ask me what the others are.'

The comment was so typical of Damon that normally she would have laughed, but today she just couldn't make the sound. 'What are the others?'

'I'm making pink tights compulsory.'

Polly flushed, and he watched her for a long moment and then rose to his feet.

'The fact that you can't even raise a smile tells me that you're as miserably unhappy about this whole situation as I am. That's all I wanted to know.' He walked round his desk and hauled her to her feet in a decisive movement that left no room for protest. 'I owe you an apology. I lost my temper with your father and I shouldn't have done.'

'I don't blame you for that,' Polly muttered. 'In fact I lost it with him myself.'

'I shouldn't have put you in the position of making you choose between us.' A wry smile touched his mouth. 'I didn't think for a moment that you'd walk out on me. You have a way of cutting a guy down to size very quickly.'

'Damon, I really don't want to—'

'Talk about this. I know.' He took her face in his

hands. 'But you're going to. I know how afraid you are of relationships, Polly. Your life has been like a car park, with a constant stream of people coming and going. It's not rocket science to deduce that you're going to have commitment issues. That's why I forgive you for thinking the worst of me on Friday.'

'Forgive you?'

'Yes. Forgive you.' He bent his head and kissed her mouth gently. 'It's not very flattering when the woman you love is so ready to believe that you took her to bed out of an impulse to get revenge on her father. That hurt.'

Polly stilled, suddenly unable to breathe. 'Damon?'

'I love you.' He spoke the words softly but his eyes were full of passion and heat. 'I've spent my whole life making sure I didn't fall in love. Then I met you again and suddenly I didn't have a choice.'

The words sank slowly into her brain. 'You told me you were never going to let that happen.'

'Which means you've proved once again that I'm nowhere near as in control of things as I like to think.' He hesitated. 'You're right that I was scared of being responsible for someone else's happiness. I saw what happened when my father thought he'd let everyone down. I had Arianna, all these employees—I didn't want anyone else. Until you came back into my life. I love you more than I ever thought it possible to love someone.'

The happiness was so intense it was blinding. 'Truly?'

'I told your father that you're mine now.'

'I assumed you were trying to wind him up.'

'I was telling the truth, but I don't blame you for

questioning my motives. It's true that I'd do anything to protect Arianna, but this isn't about my sister any more. It's about us.'

'Us.' Polly whispered the word. 'I've never been an "us". I'm not sure I'll be any good at it.'

'We'll learn together. I'm already learning fast,' he assured her. 'I've turned my company upside down. From now on we're following the Polly Prince code of office management. And as for the rest of it—I know it breaks every rule, but I want us to be together.'

'But—'

'I know you're scared. I know you're thinking that your father has just married for the fifth time and that relationships can't last, but ours can and will—' He lowered his mouth to hers and kissed her, his mouth stirring up the fire inside her. 'Look at me and tell me that you don't think we'll still be together in fifty years.'

Polly looked at him, her heart aching and her eyes swimming. 'I want to be. I love you, too. Oh, God, I can't believe I'm saying that.'

'You've no idea how relieved I am to hear you say it.' The corner of his mouth tilted and he reached into his pocket and withdrew a box. 'I bought this for you. I want you to wear it always. Hopefully whenever the thought of being an "us" scares you, you can look at it and be reminded of how much I love you.' He flipped the box open and withdrew a huge, sparkling diamond ring and Polly felt as if her whole heart had been opened and exposed.

Tears fell and landed on his hand. 'It's beautiful, but I can't wear it. How can I? You say that this is just about us, but it isn't. It can't be.' It all seemed hopeless to her. The obstacles too big. 'I love my father, Damon. I know he behaves like a total idiot sometimes and, yes, he's careless, but that's just the way he is—' She wiped her tears on her sleeve. 'I'm the first to admit that he's pretty crap at a lot of things, but he was there. And now you hate him, and he's married your sister, and we can't be together with you hating him—' Hiccuping, she heard her words tumble together, and Damon gave a low curse and gathered her against him.

'*Don't* cry. I never want to see you cry. We'll work things out with your father, I promise.'

'I don't want to be in a position where I'm always having to take sides and choose.'

'You won't be,' he vowed. 'You have my word on that. I've already been to see your father. We managed to talk without killing each other so that's a good start.'

Polly sniffed. 'You've seen him?'

'This morning. After you left for work. My sister apologised to me.'

'She did?'

'Apparently you told her a few truths. She took them on board and suddenly she feels very guilty that she's caused me so much worry.' He wrapped his arms around her and held her close. 'When we were in the boardroom that day you told me I was over-protective and you were right.'

'No, I was wrong. You're brilliant and Arianna is lucky.'

'But the sense of responsibility I felt towards Arianna prevented me from letting her spread her wings. I couldn't bear the thought of anything happening to her. I'd promised myself that I was going to protect her and I never questioned that as time went on.'

'And you did an amazing job.'

'I want to stop thinking about them and think about us.' He slid his fingers gently over her cheek, wiping away her tears. 'Don't think about our families—that will be fine, I promise you. The decision about our future rests entirely on whether you can bring yourself to spend the rest of your life with me.'

'Wow. Well—' As happiness finally flowed through her, Polly's voice cracked. 'That sounds pretty tough.'

'You're *going* to marry me,' Damon breathed, 'and, unlike your father and Arianna, we're going to have a huge wedding so that we can invite all the people who have worked with you for so long, otherwise there will be a mass walk-out.'

Unable to believe that this was happening, Polly flung her arms round his neck. 'I love you *so* much. It's terrifying. Really, seriously scary.'

Damon held her close. 'Then it's a good thing that you're brave. You can meet terror head-on, the way you did that morning in the boardroom when you stalked in wearing those sexy boots, looking as if you wanted to knife me.'

'Did I ever tell you that you looked extremely hot in that suit?'

His laugh was husky as he eased her away just enough for him to see her face. 'You think I looked hot in my suit? How hot?'

Polly gave a slow smile and slid her hands down his back. 'Red-hot. Scorching.'

'In that case—I know you have a powerful work ethic, but you're about to be unexpectedly unavailable for the next hour.' Ignoring her gasp of shock, he scooped her into his arms and strode out of the office. 'Janey, hold my calls.'

Janey didn't bother hiding her smile. 'Yes, Mr Doukakis.'

Mortified, Polly hid her face in Damon's shoulder. 'This is *so* embarrassing. And I have work to do. I don't want everyone to think I'm a slacker.'

'I'm giving you permission to take the next hour off, Miss Prince.' Still holding her, he hit the lift button with his elbow and the doors closed.

Laughing, overwhelmed by happiness, Polly kissed him. 'Whatever you say,' she said happily. 'You're the boss.'

* * * * *

Don't miss the next unforgettable romance from Sarah Morgan!

Available now from Harlequin Presents:
PLAYING BY THE GREEK'S RULES

And coming next month from HQN Books:
FIRST TIME IN FOREVER

We hope you enjoyed reading
COURTING CATHERINE
by #1 *New York Times* bestselling author Nora Roberts
and FRENCH KISS
by *USA TODAY* bestselling author Sarah Morgan.

Discover the debut novel of Sarah Morgan's irresistible new **Puffin Island** series, FIRST TIME IN FOREVER.

Windswept, isolated and ruggedly beautiful, Puffin Island is a haven for day-trippers and daydreamers alike. But this charming community has a way of bringing people together in the most unexpected ways...

Available March 2015.

Turn the page to read a sneak peek now!

Be sure to connect with us at:
Harlequin.com/Newsletters
Facebook.com/HarlequinBooks
Twitter.com/HQNBooks

www.HQNBooks.com

NYTHQN0215